NO TIME TO QUIT

NO TIME TO QUIT

PIVOT LAB CHRONICLES™ BOOK THREE

MICHAEL ANDERLE

DISRUPTIVE IMAGINATION

Copyright © 2020 LMBPN Publishing
Cover copyright © LMBPN Publishing
Cover Art by Jake @ J Caleb Design
http://jcalebdesign.com / jcalebdesign@gmail.com
A Michael Anderle Production

LMBPN Publishing
PMB 196, 2540 South Maryland Pkwy
Las Vegas, NV 89109

First US Edition, September, 2020
eBook ISBN: 978-1-64971-136-6
Print ISBN: 978-1-64971-137-3

THE NO TIME TO QUIT TEAM

Thanks to the JIT Readers

Billie Leigh Kellar
Dave Hicks
Deb Mader
Diane L. Smith
Jeff Eaton
Jeff Goode
John Ashmore
Kelly O'Donnell
Kerry Mortimer

If I've missed anyone, please let me know!

Editor
The Skyhunter Editing Team

PART I

CHAPTER ONE

"You're not *happy*, though," Mike said flatly. He stirred his coffee without looking up. "I don't think so, anyway."

Ben fought the urge to sigh. For someone as terminally non-confrontational as his friend was, this was the equivalent of flipping a table. He had never once seen the man yell at anyone. If Mike was pushing back at all, he should listen.

He looked at his plate. Half of his pancakes still remained, sprinkled with the sugar he used instead of maple syrup. Eve had referred to that as a crime against breakfast. It was one of the litany of incompatibilities that had led to her walking away.

Probably not the main one, he reflected.

"What do you think would make me happy?" he asked finally. He cut off a chunk of pancake with the side of his fork and stuffed it in his mouth. "Ah why duhoo thig *ibot?*"

"I don't know what would make you happy," the other man said. "I'm not in your head. And I didn't understand the second question at all."

Ben washed the mouthful of pancake down with weak coffee and winced at the heat. This diner—like many he had come across—

apparently believed that if they made the coffee hot enough, no one would notice that it barely resembled the expected flavor.

It was more like hot water someone had told about coffee, honestly.

"I asked why you think I'm *not* happy," he said after pounding his chest.

"I know you, remember." Mike cut a piece of his omelet. "I know when you're not happy. And it's been four years. You used to be so fired up about using your degree and now—"

"Now there are no jobs," he reminded him. "Remember that? The whole big economic crash? Too many people with advanced degrees?"

"There aren't enough jobs," the man conceded when he had finished chewing, "but there's one for you."

He snorted into his coffee.

"You were the valedictorian," his friend told him. "Your professors loved you, they were falling all over themselves to write letters of recommendation for you, and you're seriously telling me you haven't found a single job opportunity in four years?"

"I haven't been looking," he said.

"Exactly!"

"Look." Ben leaned forward. "I'm not gonna take a job I hate merely for the chance to find a job I *kind of* like at *some* point while living in a shitty apartment with three other people."

Mike sighed, leaned back, and rubbed his face. "I'm trying to help," he said finally. "You know that, right?"

"And I don't want help," he said.

"Ben—"

"What I *want*," he said, talking over him, "is to have a good climb before you go back to tiling bathrooms and painting walls and...I don't know, planning flowers. Whatever people do for weddings."

It was a cheap shot and he knew it. His friend was equally happy and scared to be settling down with Natasha, and he had promised to be good about it.

"You would know what was going on," Mike said patiently, "if you ever came to game night. Or...lived closer."

"*Again*—crappy job, crappy apartment, no thanks."

"Or you could read the emails I've sent you about it. If you intend to hop all over the world, you might at least be on Facebook or something."

"Nope," Ben said unrepentantly. "First, many places don't have Internet. Second, I don't have a camera, and third? I don't care what level so-and-so got to in Call of Duty or what someone else had for lunch. I want to *live*."

"There are many ways to live, man." Mike was used to these tirades so he took them in stride. He pulled the check to him and put cash down, waving Ben away. "Nah, I've got this one."

"Don't you get all pitying with me. I'll find another job soon."

"Ski instructor?" the man suggested.

"After taking care of polar bears, nothing else with snow lives up." He pushed his way out of the booth and they moved to the door.

"Mountain tour guide?"

"Wandering slowly up mountains at the pace of a diseased sloth? I think not."

"Cowboy?"

"Now you're talking." Ben grinned as he picked his helmet up and settled it over his head. Their motorcycles were next to one another, both sets of paniers stuffed to the brim with camping and climbing gear. Today was their last stop before Mike returned to Boulder and he headed to Denver to leave his motorcycle with his parents and decide where he would go next.

The two men set off without further conversation. They both knew their destination and the coffee was still kicking in. Their route wound through the foothills and Ben streaked past a couple of eighteen-wheelers that engine-braked their descent with puffs of black smoke. The road began to rise more sharply. As he wove through patches of shadow and sunlight, the dry air switched from hot to cold and back with surprising speed, and he took the time to enjoy the wind on his skin.

Too cold, too hot, too sunny, too rainy—he had seen all of it in the past four years. He'd been hired to look after equipment and feeding stations on a polar bear preserve, helped dig a series of wells in Guatemala, and snorkeled in Greece. His life read like the bucket list no one ever accomplished. If somewhere had a crazy local food, he had probably tried it. If a mountain had a spectacular view, he had probably climbed it.

Except Everest. Who had the spare cash for that?

So Eve was gone and he didn't have another job lined up right now. He would be fine as he always was. Mike knew that.

It wasn't like this was where he'd planned to be when he started on his PhD, or even when he'd finished it. He intended to be a professor —or maybe tackle the issues around industrial farming, or, or, or... There had been so many things he was excited about.

The job market had beaten that out of him with a very heavy baton in record time. One astonishingly bad postdoc position later, Ben had fled to the polar bear preserve in northern Canada.

He was still of the opinion that the polar bears were nicer than most of his bosses.

One thing had led to another from there. Eve had gone with him, and to Guatemala, which they had both liked, but she wanted to settle down. She wanted a house with air conditioning and a job with regular hours and stable pay.

To achieve that, she was willing to give up the gorgeous sunrises and the aching muscles, and he simply wasn't. Every day, he felt a little farther away from the labs he'd planned to spend his life in. Their breakup had been ugly and he hadn't dated anyone seriously since then. Every time he looked at his friends' lives, with the job frustrations and the TV shows and the tiny apartments in gray cities, he couldn't understand it.

To him, that seemed reasonable. Mike, on the other hand, had called him a "sanctimonious bitch." More than once.

By the time they stopped at their climbing route for the morning, Ben was buzzing with the effects of the coffee—which forced him to concede that maybe there had been some legitimate caffeine in it. They donned their harnesses and examined the various routes currently marked by iron rope hooks.

"You know," Mike said a shade too casually, "Josh was saying he had a room to rent. And he'd be away a lot."

"Josh…"

"Spring?" The man gestured above his head. "Super-tall, blond hair."

"Oh, right. Why is he away a lot?"

"He's in the Air Force." He was definitely too casual now. "He was saying they have a number of job openings for people in STEM and practically drooled when I mentioned that you—"

"Nope." Ben pointed chalky hands at his friend. "The last thing I'll do to get a job is to join up with some ridiculous chest-thumping org that basically wanders around having dick-measuring contests with every other country."

Mike paused in the act of taking a sip of water. "I didn't understand any of that."

"You know what I mean."

"I don't."

"Who has more tanks, who has more aircraft carriers, or who has the best technology. It's us—it's always us—and the last thing we need to do is waste our time solving problems that don't even exist for wars that won't ever happen. And even if they did, lining people up and pitting them against each other until you run out of people is…what's the word I'm looking for? Fucking stupid."

"Interested in military jobs?" Mike mimed writing on a notepad and made an X in the air. "No."

"I'm merely saying there are better ways to solve problems."

"Uh-huh. Like maybe not having them start because you headed them off at the pass?"

"I sense you're trying to slow-walk me to an epiphany," he said grumpily. "Save it. It's climbing time."

"Right." The other man rolled his eyes. "So, who's going first?"

They climbed until around noon, at which point Ben was so hungry he thought his stomach would devour itself. He rappelled down and brushed the chalk off his hands to where Mike unpacked sandwiches.

"When did you get those?"

"I stopped at the store before leaving town," his friend said as he picked them up and examined them. "Ham that looks like turkey, or beef that looks like—you know what, let's throw that out and share the ham."

"Good call." He sat and watched the sun play over the rocks. After he'd chewed contemplatively for a few minutes, he said, "You know, you'll love that house."

Mike looked at him. "You think?"

"Yeah. Natasha showed me the sketches last time I was there. I'll help you with some of the stuff if you want. Landscaping, or whatever."

"I'd like that."

"And I'll even help with centerpieces or wedding dresses or whatever the hell it is."

"Ben—"

"It's not that I don't *want* to hang out with you guys," he said. "It's only…there's no place for me there right now."

Mike said nothing. He wrapped his arms around his knees and stared at him.

"The only time I feel alive is when I'm outside," he explained. "I forget about the loans, the commutes, car trouble, all the stupid shit that piles up… This is the only place where the world makes sense to me."

"I get that." The man smiled. "But if there's one thing I've learned, it's that there's no surefire way to make life simpler. Sometimes, you gotta wade into the muck to get to the parts you want. And I don't think you want to spend the rest of your life climbing mountains. I think there's more you want to do."

He shrugged. "Maybe. But I do know that climbing is what I want to do for the rest of the day, and I heard about another route—gimme that map, I'll show you—here. The views are supposed to be fantastic. Come on."

CHAPTER TWO

The burning in her fingers told Eliza that she'd zoned out. She swore and yanked her hand away from the cheap coffee cup, which didn't do nearly enough to protect against scalding hot coffee.

"Crap." She examined the tips of her fingers, which were an angry pink, then wrapped the edge of her fleece jacket around the cup to get it to the table. Her eyes felt scratchy, as did her throat and her scrubs.

Why had she agreed to do a double shift, again?

She knew why. It was so Leslie could go to her brother's wedding, which had seemed reasonable when the woman asked about it a few weeks earlier. Some extra hours were easily doable. Anyone could make it through a few extra hours, right? Especially at a fairly out-of-the-way ER. Aspen, CO, only had a run of injuries during the winter, when every idiot and their next-door neighbor came to ski.

Or that was how it usually was, but it had been a hellish few weeks between an outbreak of something flu-related and a higher than usual number of home renovation related injuries. She had made a personal vow earlier today never to use a nail gun. Even the thought of it made her shudder.

Eliza opened the cabinets in the break room in search of anything vaguely food-like. A box of granola bars was the first thing she saw that was edible, and she snatched one and stuffed as much of it in her mouth as she could.

Consequently, she looked like a sleep-deprived chipmunk when Todd burst into the room.

"All hands on deck!" He gave her a look. "Okay, chew first. Then all hands on deck."

She swallowed, choked, tried to wash the granola bar down with scalding coffee, and pounded her chest. When she recovered, she leaned against the counter and winced. "What happened now?"

"Guess." His favorite games were the darker ones.

"Sharknado?"

"Close." He waited for her to gulp the rest of her coffee—burned tongue be damned because she would need it—and move into the hallway with him, where they both broke into a jog. "Climbing accident."

"Oh, fuck." Rock climbers came from all over the United States to try various Rocky Mountain routes, and their injuries tended to be about as bad as car crashes. "What are we looking at?"

"Two adult males in their early thirties. One seems about as close as you can get to undamaged after falling off a mountain and the other...looks damned bad. I'd say five or six broken bones? Maybe more? There's blood everywhere."

The other staff members were taking their places around tables as they dashed into the room and scrubbed up. She was pulling her gloves on when the team came in the door, and her heart dropped to see how injured the patients were. Even the one who seemed "undamaged," in Todd's words, was bruised and scraped extensively.

She wasn't sure how long it was before her patient was wheeled away, but she slid down the wall and onto the floor as soon as the gurney was gone, pulled her mask down, and exhaled in a whoosh. Across the room from her, slumped in an identical position against the far wall, Todd nodded. Beside him, Kyle lay on his back with his hands over his face.

Her arms, gloves, and scrubs were covered in blood. It was all a blur of tests, cleaning wounds, stitching wounds, setting bones, and holding her hands carefully to avoid jostling the man's head. Todd said the patient was in his early thirties but he looked younger. Then again, everyone did when they were passed out on an OR table. They looked delicate and vulnerable.

But he was stable. Eliza sighed and tried to find the energy to stand. She could do it. She could.

Maybe in a few minutes.

Wearily, she leaned her head back again and had begun to relax when one of the next-shift doctors poked her head into the room.

"What's this about a weird neurological episode?"

"Dunno." She yawned. "I kinda had an"—she gestured at her bloody scrubs—"episode of my own to deal with."

"Yeah, one of the climbers?"

"I don't know anything about a neurological problem," she said and frowned. "Todd, did we do an MRI or anything?"

"Not on ours," he confirmed. "We were too busy setting bones and there was no indication of a brain bleed."

Eliza was curious now. She stood without thinking about it too much, steadied herself on the wall, and followed her colleagues into the hall. A few of them were clustered around a set of scans. She and Todd stood on tiptoe to crane over their shoulders.

"Has he woken up yet?" someone asked.

"They're keeping him under until they know if the bleed is still active." The doctor holding the scan tapped on it. "And not only there either. It's here too."

"Parietal lobe damage," Eliza murmured to Todd, who still couldn't get a clear look. "Aaaand the spinal column. So much for not being damaged."

"Something about bloody wounds gets my attention, what can I say?" He shook his head as they moved toward the coatroom. "Well, I guess we'll see. I hope he wakes up—if he doesn't, we won't find out what the problem was."

"That's gross." She elbowed him. "Have some respect."

"Hey, TBIs are the way we learn about the brain." He shrugged.

"Not with confounding variables, they're not." She stumbled. "God, I'm *exhausted*."

"Don't you live way out in the boonies?"

Eliza groaned.

"Come sleep on my futon. Come on." Todd ushered her out the main door.

"Are you sure?"

"I live three blocks from the hospital. Why do you think I bought a futon? It's for you cretins when you can't drive. If you feel bad about it, buy me lunch."

"Do you think we'll be awake by lunchtime?" She raised an eyebrow. "You're ambitious. I plan to pass out for at least ten hours."

They pushed out into the morning cold in time to see a family almost fall out of a car. A tall, lanky woman with curly hair stood with two older couples. All of them had the exhausted, adrenaline-burst look of families who had received a call in the middle of the night. She watched the younger woman usher them all into the hospital and then struggle with the suitcases.

With a sigh—more weary than annoyed—Eliza and Todd went to help her.

"Thanks," the woman said. Her gaze traveled their dirty scrubs. "I —thanks. I don't suppose..." She swallowed, looked quickly at the door, and focused on them again. "I don't suppose you know how the two climbers are."

They were used to this awkward kind of question—the one you weren't allowed to answer but you did anyway.

"I'm Mike's fiancée," the woman explained. She looked from one to the other with barely controlled desperation.

Eliza didn't have the first clue which one was Mike. "They're both stable," she said because that much was true.

"And—"

"We'll bring your bags in," she said before the woman could ask any questions she didn't want the answers to. "You go catch up."

She and Todd hauled the bags inside to the desk and left with a wave at the greeting clerk. They didn't talk for most of the way to his apartment, and it was only when he was unlocking the door that he said, "This shit makes me want to never get married."

Surprised, she looked at him and waited for him to continue.

"Whichever one's her fiancé, the whole thing's fucked now," he said. "There'll be no wedding this year, not with either one of them. And what about the parents?"

"I'm not sure I follow."

Todd was silent while they walked into the room, and he shrugged. "I get through it every day, but all the shit I see—I don't think I could deal with it if it were someone I loved."

"You wouldn't ever have to operate on your wife, though," Eliza pointed out.

"It's not that." He shook his head and pulled takeout containers out of the fridge. "I hope leftover Chinese is good with you. It's all I have."

"That's fine. Thanks." She opened some of the cartons and put them in the microwave. "So, what *do* you mean?"

"I guess I mean…you become a doctor and you start to see all the fucked up shit that happens to people." He shrugged again. "I can't imagine walking into a hospital and seeing someone I cared about laid out in a bed, looking like either of those two guys. It would rip my heart out."

"Oh." She folded her arms. "I hadn't thought of that."

"Simply watching the future you thought you had go up in smoke," Todd said. He stared at the opposite wall, lost in thought. "Either it's the one we treated—and God knows if he'll ever walk again—or it's the other one, and what if he *does* wake up and he's never the same?"

"Hey." Eliza looked at him with concern. "Are you okay, man?"

He took a deep breath. She'd never seen behind the veneer of jovial dark humor before, but now that she could see the cracks and the fear beneath, she didn't think she'd ever be able to unsee it.

"I got into this because I wanted to help people," he said. "Now we're in our residency, I know what I'm supposed to know and it's hitting me how much we…can't fix." He forced a smile. "I don't think I've ever felt more helpless than I do these days."

"Okay." She opened cupboards until she found water glasses and filled one. "Drink this."

"What? Why?"

"Do it." She pulled one of the containers from the microwave. "Now eat this. All of it."

He complied, his eyebrow still raised.

"Now, go," she told him and pointed in the vague direction of where she assumed his bedroom was. "Food, water, and sleep."

"That won't help."

"It won't hurt," she corrected. "Because when you wake up, they need you in that OR for the next time someone comes in like those two."

"Do they?"

"Yes." Eliza took him by the shoulders and looked him in the eyes. "Because we're not the only ones out there who can fix them, but if we don't stabilize them, if we don't get them to stop bleeding out, and if we don't get all the bones set, they'll never have a chance at all. You did your part tonight. Go to sleep."

For a moment, she thought he might cry. He pulled her into a hug and nodded. "Thanks," he said, his voice muffled. "The futon's in there."

"Cool. And do you have any spare clothes?" She gestured to her the bag with her scrubs. "Because I need to get these washing. It probably wouldn't make anyone feel good to see me come in later still covered in blood."

Natasha was sleeping, her head on the edge of Mike's hospital bed, when his parents returned to the room. She sat abruptly and looked hastily to see if a noise from her fiancé had woken her. When she pressed her fingers to her forehead, she felt the imprint of the blanket.

"Why don't you lie on the couch?" his mother asked her. Monique Parker kept her hair cut in a gamine French bob, and everything from her chic clothing to her lingering accent reminded her of the woman's Parisian upbringing. She didn't have a hair out of place, even now.

"I, uh…" She ran her fingers through her curls, which would never, on a good day, look as neat and presentable as the older woman's hair. "Sure." She swallowed. "How is Ben? Did you see him?"

Mike's parents exchanged a look.

"Oh, no," she said. "Oh, no. What's wrong?"

Monique looked at her son's sleeping form, then sat and gestured for her to do so as well. "I know how close all of you are," she said.

It was true. The two men had grown up together, and she had joined the group in college. They had all been friends for years before Natasha and Mike fell for each other, and she still sometimes felt guilty. It felt like they were leaving Ben behind.

It was part of why she'd encouraged Mike to go on this trip with his oldest friend, and if Ben was now injured beyond recovery… She didn't want to think about that.

Natasha pressed her hands over her mouth. "You can tell me," she said as steadily as she could. She looked at her fiancé and the bruises and stitches and casts. *It can't be much worse than this.*

"They think there's some brain damage," Monique said. "There's a bleed in a section of his brain. It seems to have stopped and they'll wake him tomorrow. But they don't know…" Her voice trailed off.

She curled her hands into fists so tightly that she thought her nails would break the skin on her palms. *They don't know if he's still in there,* her mind finished for her. She looked at Mike again and her lip trembled. When she had gone to bed the day before, she'd looked forward to her wedding and renovating the new house.

Now, she was close to losing the two people she cared about most in the entire world.

CHAPTER THREE

Ben wasn't aware of anything until he opened his eyes. He remembered that sunlight had turned his eyelids red for some time and for one moment, everything was perfect. The bed was soft, the room was shades of pale, and there was the distant sound of voices.

Then, the smell hit him.

It was one every hospital had—sharp at the edges and a combination of disinfectant, metal, and linoleum. Behind it lurked the smell of vomit that was no longer there but you could still somehow tell. Old blood was another distasteful addition.

So many things beeped too. He hadn't noticed it, maybe because he was so used to the sound at this point, but he heard it now and the number of different beeps was dizzying. Instinctively, he wanted to put his hands over his ears but couldn't.

He tried to roll his head. At first, it didn't move at all. Then, it flopped abruptly forward all the way. The headache came in a burst of tenderness near the back of his skull and down his spine. He yelled—not entirely voluntarily—and tried to make his head return to the position it had been in but he couldn't do that either. It took everything he had and long moments of struggle while the blood flow to his head constricted and his breathing became shallow. The beeping increased in speed until he heaved his head back with all his strength.

It thumped against the pillow and he yelled again. The pain was intense. It was only a pillow, but the touch of it against him felt like someone had hit him with a club.

Ben wasn't sure if he blacked out. What he was sure of was that he saw the fall again. Mike's body had hurtled toward him and impacted with the stone face, blood already pouring from his nose and his arm tangled in the line. He relived the realization that he was falling too and the adrenaline rush that punched him in the solar plexus as he tumbled.

He didn't remember hitting the ground, though. A memory surfaced of his eyes open again while people crowded around him. An oxygen mask was pressed over his face so he felt like he was suffocating and his breath sounded mechanical.

Everything hurt beyond belief.

The image flashed to darkness and the sound of helicopter blades.

Yes, he remembered that. People called to each other over his body exactly like this, while he couldn't move or speak in the dark and the feeling of being terribly, utterly alone swept over him. He had known he could slip away and none of them would be able to stop it.

And then—somehow, this was the scariest part and made his mechanical-sounding breath shallow—he had slipped away. He didn't remember passing out, but he had. The odd thought crept in that he might never have woken up and he wouldn't even have realized.

He didn't mean to hit anyone. In all honesty, he didn't mean to do anything and was merely so afraid. His whole body came off the hospital bed and the sound of a scream was definitely his because everything hurt so badly before he fell sideways. People in scrubs caught him and someone yelled something about the fucking side rails not being in place. His head was near the floor and lines of bright pain seared across the backs of his hands and into what felt like bars on his arms. He'd thrown his arms and legs and the limbs had flailed uselessly from their sockets without his control.

They manhandled him into the bed and he could see they were scared. They thought he was fighting them.

"—m not," Ben managed to mumble. He wasn't trying to hit them, hadn't wanted to fall out of the bed, and wasn't trying to do any of this. "I'm not." But the words came out garbled behind the mask and his body wouldn't stop moving.

A cool sensation on his hand and another bright prick of pain brought the realization that he'd dragged the IVs out when he fell. In the next second, something hot washed through his arm and he went blessedly limp.

Good. Thank God. He hadn't wanted to move like this. Nor did he want to hurt anyone—not them or himself.

He'd seen the bruises and the cuts and oh, God, what had happened? What was going on?

"Mike!" The word burst out of him with all the force in his lungs.

Which, after so many years of working outside every day, was a significant amount of force.

Once he started yelling, he couldn't seem to stop. His mind was full of words and questions. *Where is Mike? Is he okay? How did people find us? What's wrong with my arms?* But his stupid mouth wouldn't cooperate and simply shouted the same thing repeatedly. "Mike! Mike! Mike! *Mike!*"

They held him down now. He was angry about that but also ashamed.

Finally, he saw a familiar face. Natasha. *Thank God.*

"Mike!" *No, you idiot. Natasha.* "Mike!" He would have to hope she understood.

"Ben. Ben! Ben?" She leaned over the bed and put a hand on his chest and he roared with pain. "Oh, God—I'm sorry. Ben, can you hear me? Mike is okay. He's okay, Ben. Mike is okay."

He slumped against the bed, coated with sweat now. "Mike." His voice sounded like it came from very far away. "Mike."

"He's okay, Ben." Natasha's face swam in his vision. It seemed to be moving wildly and he couldn't focus on it.

His stomach didn't feel so good.

"He's okay," he heard again.

"Mike…"

The drugs took hold and he went under.

"Jesus," Todd said with raw emotion when they were far enough away to speak without the family hearing them.

Eliza nodded, horrified into silence. All she could think was that at least his parents hadn't been there at that moment. She couldn't stop herself recalling what her friend had said about how difficult it was to see people injured like that, or frightened and in pain.

And these weren't even people they knew.

Leslie joined them in the break room a few minutes later. She had, as usual, one of her adorably-arranged lunchboxes—a hobby of her fiancée's—but she didn't look like she had any interest in eating. She sat at the table and looked shell-shocked.

They all sat for a moment in silence. The ER had returned to its usual functioning today, which would have been a relief under normal circumstances.

Right now, it meant they didn't have a distraction from what they had seen.

"So, what do you think it was?" Eliza asked finally. She looked at Todd and hoped he saw the plea in her eyes. *Please make a joke. We need to joke about this.*

Thankfully, he picked up her cues. He mimed smoking a cigar and stroked an imaginary goatee. "Vellllll," he said and drew the word out. "I vould heff to say—"

"Why are you being German?" she asked.

Leslie stifled a laugh and at last, opened her lunch box and removed two adorably patterned matching chopsticks.

"You know, I don't know." He looked at them. "He was worried about his friend and remembered his name, so that's good brain function. And there's a lot we could chalk up to pure shock at this stage."

Eliza nodded and went to get another cup of coffee. "Something weird happened with movement...but the bleed wasn't in the motor cortex."

"That's the thing." He rubbed his nose. "What the fuck does it all mean?"

Leslie held one hand up and motioned to where she was chewing. She swallowed hastily. "Proprioception," she said. "Kinesthesia—where your body is in space."

"I know what proprioception is," Todd said and sounded offended. "But how..." He scratched his head.

"You know how babies walk?" the woman asked. "They'll look down constantly and then fall, or they put their feet down hard and pick them up too high, right? They're still learning where their body is in space. It's why teenagers get so clumsy."

"Oh, so there's a scientific explanation for how I was at sixteen. That's good to know."

She grinned. "The other thing is you'll see them doing things like looking at their hand while they wiggle their fingers. They're learning how to control their muscles and looking at them helps."

"Really?" He nodded. "I always thought they were simply tripping balls."

Leslie laughed. "Maybe it's that. Anyway, learning how to control muscles *without* seeing them is a big skill."

"Okay, but he did learn," Todd said. "Or...whoa—wait, are you saying it's all been wiped?"

"I don't know." The woman made a slow-down gesture with her hands. "But that would be the parietal lobe, and it does happen. There are adults who lose all proprioception and sometimes, it's not even trauma-related."

"Great," he said to Eliza. "More things to have nightmares about."

She grinned at him. As much as he decried her water-food-sleep plan, it almost always worked to put people in a better frame of mind. It was her version of IT telling someone to reboot their computer.

It was good to see him back to his old self.

"What's the treatment?" she asked. "If that's the problem."

"Uh..." The woman grimaced. "There isn't one? Okay, there are

kinesthesia drills that some athletes do and those work fine, it's only
— Well, I'm not saying it doesn't get *better*. It's merely learning all your
proprioception all over again."

"And an adult's brain isn't wired for that," Todd murmured.

"That, too," Leslie agreed.

"Frankly," Eliza said, "having met a few babies, I have to say I'm not
sure *their* mind is wired for it either. Have you met any? They cry. A
lot."

The other woman grinned as she took a bite. "I'll have you know
that Kate and I are talking about trying."

"No." She almost dropped her coffee. "For serious?"

"For serious. She says she's willing to go first." Leslie gave a smile
that was half-happy, half-terrified. "I spent the plane ride back
looking at sperm donor...report things."

"Any rocket scientists?" Todd asked. "Ooh, what about, like—
super-spies?"

"Yeah, I'm sure many super-spies donate sperm in Aspen," she
retorted. She raised an eyebrow. "It must simply be bad luck that we
haven't come across one yet."

"Damn." He grinned. "You can't win 'em all, I guess. Okay, kiddos,
back to the grind."

"I'll come with you," Leslie said. "Eliza, you take the next lunch."

"Thanks." She went to the fridge and retrieved her lunch, an unappetizing mess of leftover pasta she hadn't eaten the day before. She
didn't want it, in all honesty, but her rule of water-food-sleep meant
that she had to at least try.

She was conscious of watching her hands as she put the
container into the microwave and felt unaccountably clumsy
while she walked to get a napkin and a plastic fork. What would
it be like to not be able to walk anywhere or even control her
hand?

A shudder rippled through her. She didn't envy the climber's path
back to health—and she'd seen the calluses on his hands and the hard
tan lines on his skin. He was used to being outside, working with his
body and doing physical things.

The simple truth was that most of the difficulty with recovery usually wasn't physical. It was mental.

And he had a hell of a road ahead of him.

CHAPTER FOUR

Nick pushed into the lab butt-first and balanced two cups of coffee and two bagels very carefully. He had safely traversed two and a half blocks with them, and he was damned if he would drop them now.

Jacob saw him enter and stood to help him, examined the bagels, and took the poppyseed one. "You have no idea how long I've waited for this."

"How's it going?" he asked him as he stripped his coat off and went to hang it in the corner.

He looked over his shoulder at the glass-paneled waiting area for guests, but no one was there. The night before, a new patient had been put into the world of PIVOT, a seventeen-year-old girl named Taigan whose brain repeatedly dropped spontaneously into a comatose state.

Her family had stayed to watch her transferred into the game world. The process had taken until well past three AM and they were all exhausted. Despite this, they had only been willing to leave when Jacob promised them that not only some of the nurses but at least one member of the original PIVOT team would stay with the girl until the family returned.

As the author of that particular idea, he had taken the first shift while Nick ran home for a catnap and a shower.

Jacob sighed. "It isn't going...perfectly. But well enough." He stirred sugar and cream into his coffee. "The connection keeps dropping."

"Didn't Justin's do that?" Nick took a bite of his bagel. The reference was to their first patient, a twenty-three-year-old left comatose after a car crash.

"Yeah." His colleague chewed his lip.

"But?" he prompted.

"But with him, it seemed like he was falling asleep," the man said. His gaze was fixed on the monitors. "With this, it seems different."

Nick didn't say anything. One of the things that made his friend such a good engineer was that he detected the tiniest flickers in machine output and could distinguish between what almost anyone else would have called equivalent states. It was one of the many reasons that Nick had no problem recommending PIVOT as a safe experience.

Of course, it also meant that troubleshooting had taken about eight times as long as it normally did for a product going to market—and that both Nick and Amber had seriously considered murdering him at various points in their careers.

Right now, however, he was both hungry and sleep-deprived, so he had no problem waiting while Jacob pondered and muttered and went off to print things.

Finally, he said, "So, you know that whole problem with sleep?"

"That I haven't had enough of it?"

"Nick."

"No, I seriously don't know what you mean. That's a super-broad category."

"Oh." The man rubbed his face. "Uh...one sec...what was I talking about—*right*. So, there was this whole thing a few years ago about trying to find out if animals dreamed or not. It turned out that the problem wasn't so much determining what a dream was as figuring out what *sleep* was."

Nick took another bite of his bagel so he wouldn't have to come up with something to say.

Jacob waved a hand at Taigan's pod. "That's how I feel about this. It's not like she's simply unconscious. Or dreaming. Or awake. I can't describe it. It's like she's sleeping—dreaming—differently and the machinery keeps losing her and has to find her again. Or she keeps losing it…" He trailed off and stared at the monitors.

"You need sleep, man."

He shook his head violently. "I can't leave. No. Definitely not."

"I thought you might say that." Nick nodded. "Which is why I had a cot set up in the alcove near the break room. You go sleep and I promise I will wake you if anything happens."

"I should move it to the office—"

"Nope. I won't put you anywhere near a computer. In fact, give me your phone." He plucked the device out of his friend's hands—an easy task given the man's state of sleep deprivation—and shooed him off down the hall.

His brain made a mental note to check in a few minutes that Jacob had made it to the cot instead of simply falling asleep on the floor.

Then, he started studying the printouts.

"Sleeping," he muttered. "Differently. What does that even *mean?*"

Taigan dropped onto the ground and crouched to steady herself on her fingertips.

Or…was there a floor? She looked around. Sometimes, out of the corner of her eye, she thought she saw something but mostly, it merely looked blue. She stood on nothing in a void of blacks and blues, and she was very sure her body only existed when she didn't look at it.

She decided not to look down as she walked, uncertain as to what was going on. Maybe this was a recurring nightmare. Emilia used to have those, right?

It confused her a little that she still knew who Emilia was. The thought came with a whole flood of memories—black hair and a host of other things.

What were they?

They felt like something…sensations, but in her feelings.

Emotions. The word slid into her mind and seemed to fit.

Remembering Emilia—someone like herself, a person close-but-not-her…family—reminded her of others. More black hair and eyes like Emilia's.

Mom.

Dad.

Jamie.

Taigan whirled. She remembered them, and she recalled where she had seen them—in places with walls, ceilings, and floors—so why wasn't there a floor?

A scrap of paper fluttered out of nowhere and without conscious thought, she reached up and caught it. The handwriting on it shifted constantly. Sometimes, it looked like hers and sometimes, it didn't.

When you get this let me know.

"Let you know how?" Taigan turned the piece of paper over. There was nothing on the other side. "And who are you?"

"I am Prima," said a voice and she jumped. *"We met once before when I wore the form of a woman named Dotty."*

She frowned. "I…" It was coming back to her, yes. "That happened?"

The woman shimmered into being in front of her again. "Yes," she said. "I was here."

"You don't exist." Her lip trembled. This wasn't a real place and none of it was happening.

"That depends on what you mean," Dotty said briskly. She gestured casually to where a bench suddenly existed. "Sit. And make yourself a body. You look very disconcerting floating there."

"What—" Taigan looked around in confusion. "What do I look like? Am I only a head? How do I make a body?"

Cold air swept abruptly over her and she came out in goosebumps.

"Like that," the woman said. She waved a hand again and in an instant, the girl wore flannel pajamas and was wrapped in a big comforter. "*Now* sit and I'll explain what's going on."

Nick caught a flicker out of the corner of his eye and looked up quickly. One of the monitors had been dark and the other had shown an occasionally moving but mostly stationary blue and black void. He thought it had something to do with the sleep cycles they saw, but he now understood that it was something completely different.

Taigan had been awake but without any particular self-concept.

The realization made him shout and clap his hands over his mouth at the same time. He tiptoed to look down the hall, but Jacob was still asleep and snored softly.

"*Yes,*" he whispered to himself as he crept to the desk. "Yes."

It was working. He pulled up a new set of readouts with a few taps on the keyboard and moved aside when DuBois and one of the assistants came to look.

"She's made herself a body," he explained to them.

"Fascinating," the doctor said. "I wonder...we should see if we can get some Buddhist monks in here."

He thought about this for a long moment while he tried to make sense of any of it. "Because?" he asked finally.

"Ah." The other man took a handful of popcorn. "One of the goals of Buddhist meditation is often conceptualized as dissolving the boundary between the self and the world. That might inform how we treat her going forward if that is one of the problems."

Nick nodded.

"Popcorn?"

"No, thank you. I—" he broke off and every head whipped around as two voices came out of the speakers. One was new and the other was very, very familiar. "Is that *Dotty?*"

"Do you want me to wake Jacob up?" the assistant asked.

"Not yet." he pulled a stool closer. "Let's listen for now."

"All of this," Dotty told Taigan and gestured at the area around, "is a virtual reality."

"Like a headset?" the girl asked.

"It's more direct." The woman sat very straight, the model of lady-like manners. "The information is fed directly into your brain."

She stared at her and tried to decide if this was a very elaborate prank. "*How?*" she asked finally.

"Does it matter?"

"I'm not sure you're real—so yes, it does." She folded her arms. Unfortunately, she had a feeling the effect was somewhat less intimidating when she wore flannel pajamas and sat wrapped in a comforter, but she couldn't do anything about that.

"Electrodes," the woman told her. "They hook you up exactly like you're hooked up in the hospital, but with electrodes on various parts of your brain and nervous system."

"That's…bullshit."

Dotty folded her arms in a mirrored gesture and raised an eyebrow. "Young lady—"

"Young lady? You're what, twenty?"

"I'm eighty-four, not that it's any of your business. One *never* asks a lady's age." She glared at her. "I have grandchildren older than you."

Taigan, now worried that this woman was some kind of witch, slumped in her seat and resolved not to say anything more until this was over. It was clearly a bad dream and she would simply wait it out.

"Do you normally know anything while you're in a coma?" Dotty asked her.

She looked at her. "No. Not that I can describe, anyway. But since you're me, you should know that."

"I am not you. I am a cross between an eighty-four- year-old woman and a computer program. And I'm curious. Your interaction with me is different than with other people I meet. It's why you're here and not in the rest of the world."

"What *world?*"

"The world of the game."

Taigan leaned back sharply. She was getting definite Battle Royale vibes from this and was not keen to see what would happen in this "game" the woman was talking about.

"Look," Dotty said when her patience finally frayed, "if I were to ask your twin something only he would know—that you didn't because of course, you think I'm you—what would it be?"

"I…you know about Jamie?" The girl shook her head. This was confusing. "I don't understand what's going on."

"What's going on is that your brother and sister found out about a virtual reality that helps people in comas and they brought your parents here. I don't know what happened because your parents weren't happy with the idea, but somehow, they agreed to have you transferred here. You're in New York now. Your family is here, too."

Taigan's mouth dropped open. "They…"

"They brought you here," her companion confirmed. "They want to give you a chance to wake up. And your brother will come into the game to find you, but I can't help him get to you until we can wake you up enough to get into the game."

"I…oh." She straightened quickly. "Okay. What do I need to do?"

"She's coming along well," Nick said. "That's the first audible input we've heard from her. This is good." His phone dinged and he pulled it out of his pocket. "That's weird… Can you two keep an eye on her while I read this?"

DuBois and the assistant both nodded, and he withdrew to read the email he had received. He was only halfway through it when he snapped his fingers at the assistant. The man looked up, confused.

"*Now* it's time to wake Jacob up," Nick said. To DuBois, he added, "Look at this email from Colorado. We have a new patient."

CHAPTER FIVE

Ben's eyes drifted open. He saw white and immediately felt pain.
There was no fear, though. He expected pain for some reason. Tentatively, he tried to move but with no response, then tried to turn his head and it did not work.

He didn't push it but wasn't sure why—it wasn't like him. On some level, he knew that.

Next, he tried to clear his throat, which worked to a small degree.

A face came into view so suddenly that he jumped. He uttered a strangled yell instead of saying anything worthwhile. The woman's face, heart-shaped and with a cleft chin, looked worried.

"You're safe," she told him.

"Mike." *Oh, not this again.*

"Your friend is okay as well," she told him. "He was discharged two days ago."

Two days? How long had he been there?

She must have seen the question in his eyes because she said gently, "It's been about two weeks since the climbing accident."

Weeks? "Who..."

"I'm Dr. Ullmer." She smiled at him again. "I was here when you came in, you know." She moved quietly to check the monitors and put in a new IV. When she saw his gaze tracking her, she smiled. "There's no need to call the nurses for this. They work hard enough as it is. You're doing very well with this wake up, by the way."

Ben frowned. Things were beginning to come back to him. When she mentioned how long it had been, he had a series of memories, all of them painful. That was probably why he had expected the pain. He remembered flailing and falling. His mind replayed him calling out for Mike and Natasha and sometimes, even for Eve.

That made him flush. *Stupid, stupid.* Eve was gone. How out of it had he been if he wanted to see her again?

He still couldn't move but that was probably the drugs. Everything was very confusing. Unless...was he too weak after his time being asleep? He tried to move again and heaved his torso sideways.

"Fuck," Dr. Ullmer said before she thought to censor herself. She threw an arm across the bed and grasped the opposite rail. "Can I get some help in here? Mr. Ainsworth—Ben—*please* don't try to move—"

"I have to," he muttered and clenched his teeth in frustration. "I have to know...I can."

"Ben, *please.*" Her face swam in front of him. She was tiny, he saw now, barely five feet if that, and she didn't have the muscle to keep him in this bed if he wanted out. They both knew that. "Please, you have to trust me. When you do this, you're injuring yourself badly. Please, I'll get your friends here but please trust me about this. I don't want you to get hurt anymore."

Even on a good day, he was a singularly stubborn person. It was one of the things most of his friends didn't like about him, and if he were honest, he wasn't too happy about it, either. He saw a challenge and he put his head down and ran directly toward it. Right now, he could feel every muscle tensing to ignore her request and throw himself away from the bed.

"Ben." She took his face in her hands. Her fear swept over him then, personal and gut-wrenching. "You will recover from this. But if you keep injuring yourself, I don't know if that will be true. Can you trust me?"

"I—" He had to move, had to know he could still be in this body. If he were trapped—

"Ben, *can you trust me?*" She continued to stare into his eyes as the patter of footsteps grew louder and the door burst open. Both Ben and the doctor jumped. She looked over her shoulder. "Thank God. But…wait a sec, okay?" She looked at him again. "Listen, I'll make you a deal. I'll go call your friends and tell them to come back. If I do that, will you do what the doctors and nurses say until they get here?" She beckoned to someone outside his field of view.

When the man appeared, he was sandy-haired, athletic, and naturally tanned. Ben recognized someone who also spent time outdoors and he felt an irrational wave of dislike. This man could still walk. Why him and not Ben?

"This is Dr. Lukas," Dr. Ullmer told him. "Do we have a deal? I'll call your friends right now—and your parents?"

"Only friends." His voice was rough with pent emotion. He knew his parents had good intentions but they tended to catastrophize, and he knew he would get a straight answer about his condition from Mike and Natasha.

She hesitated but nodded. "Okay."

Dr. Lukas and the nurses ran a series of checks, all with polite indifference, which was about what he could deal with right now. He didn't have it in him to make nice conversation when he still tried to understand the last few weeks. When he thought about the accident and tried to remember what had happened, he couldn't recall anything.

His body merely went rigid with fear when he tried to imagine it.

"Can you relax?" the doctor asked him. Now that he had been around for more than a few seconds, he could see that the man wasn't only tall and handsome—he was also insanely sleep-deprived.

"Are you—" Ben's throat still hurt when he talked. He winced. "Resident?"

"Yup." Dr. Lukas nodded at him. "Me and Eliza—Dr. Ullmer—were at the UofM together and now, we're here."

"Michigan?"

"Minnesota." He smiled at him. "I tell you, it's good to be back somewhere you can be outside all year round, you know? I was never one for Nordic skiing. Downhill, all the way. Do you ski?"

"I did," Ben said bitterly.

The man looked sadly at him.

"She said I'd get better," he said. "Was she telling the truth?"

A heavy sigh was the only response.

"Fuck," he muttered. He was working up his courage to ask the main question—how bad is it?—when voices and footsteps came into the room and one of the nurses raised the top portion of the bed so he could see what was going on.

He thought he would cry with relief when he saw Mike, but the emotion was soon swept away. Most of the bruises had faded to some degree, but a gash across his friend's cheek was still healing and he was in a wheelchair with one leg encased in a cast and one arm in a sling. Natasha was pushing the wheelchair and she looked like she hadn't slept at all since the accident happened.

The doctors stood aside together.

"Would you like an update, Mr. Ainsworth?" Dr. Ullmer asked him. "Or would you like us to wait?"

"Now, please." He could bear it if he had someone to listen with him. He tried to nod at his friends. "It's okay to share in front of them."

She nodded. "Two weeks ago, as you know, you were involved in a climbing accident. Your physical injuries were relatively minor, although you'll probably still have some residual soreness and you may also have sprains. We won't be certain until you're moving around more regularly."

Something kindled in his chest at that. Hope. *Until you're moving around*—that meant he would be, right?

Dr. Ullmer took a scan out of one of the folders at the base of his bed and put it up on the light screen. She pointed to one area in his head and one in his spine. Beyond that, he had no idea what exactly she was pointing at. "As you can see here, there were two bleeds, one in your brain and one in your spinal column. The one in your brain is in your parietal lobe." She paused, evidently steeling herself for something, but when she spoke, her voice was still level and light. "It appears that the damage to your parietal lobe has created a near-total loss of proprioception—your sense of where your body is in space and how to move it."

Ben's ears were ringing.

"Proprioception is learned," she told him, "which means it can be recovered through physical therapy. That's the good news. This is not paralysis and there doesn't appear to be damage to the nervous system."

He closed his eyes. "What's the bad news?"

The woman did him the courtesy of being straight with him. "This is a very rare problem and we do not know for certain how much you will recover. There is a very good chance—a very, *very* good chance—that you will be able to do all of the functions of normal, day to day life. Beyond that, unfortunately, we can't say."

She and Dr. Lukas exchanged a look.

With a completely blank expression, she continued her explanation. He could tell she was trying not to look pitying. "Part of why you were kept under was that your attempts to move have caused re-injury. You had some dislocations and there was worry that you would worsen them."

Ben closed his eyes. He wished he couldn't hear the words, but they were part of him now.

Normal, day to day life. A job in a cubicle in a city. Hobbling around and never climbing again.

"What does the treatment look like?" Natasha asked. He was grateful to her and he wanted to scream at her, all at the same time.

"There are two options," Dr. Ullmer said. She waited for him to open his eyes. "There is the fairly standard brand of physical therapy. You would work on individual muscle groups with a dedicated physical therapist. It would need to be fairly intensive, and you would need someone living with you to make sure your bathing and toileting were taken care of."

He wouldn't even be able to go to the bathroom on his own. He wanted to scream and could feel the sound building in his chest.

This was something he couldn't do.

"There is another option," the doctor said. "A clinical trial is currently in progress called PIVOT, which uses virtual reality. You would essentially be immersed in a virtual world, with the hope that this would reconnect you to your body."

"I heard about that," Mike said.

"Putting me into a coma will help me learn to move again?" Ben asked hoarsely. That seemed backward.

"Would you give us a few minutes?" Natasha asked. She smiled at the doctors and the nurses, all of whom left quickly.

When they were gone, she came to adjust the pillows and blankets and checked with him with little lifts of her eyebrows until he was comfortable. Then, she exchanged a look with Mike and sat beside the bed.

She looked like she was preparing a speech which he was very sure he did not want to hear.

"We weren't sure you would wake up," she said finally. "I know that I...well, I know I don't get it. But I also know you, Ben. I know that if they say you'll probably be able to do normal day to day activities, you'll push yourself until you're an MMA champion or something."

Mike laughed from the other side of the room. It sounded like laughing hurt him but he never could stop himself from finding things funny.

Ben closed his eyes.

"Ben?"

"You don't have to live with it," he said. He hated his body right now. And his brain. "I want—"

"I know." Mike spoke this time and he did know. "I wish I could give you a hug, man, but I can't do that right now and I know it's worse for you. But, look—Natasha and my parents had to tell me to get over myself and accept help and I think...I have to do the same for you."

"I..." He could see the months spinning out in front of him while he tried to learn how to pick a glass of water up or sit in a chair. He couldn't do it. Everything in him rebelled at the idea that he would have to spend years learning to be who he already was while trapped in a body that wouldn't obey his commands.

His friends remained silent. They knew him well enough to not speak.

It wasn't their words that convinced him in the end either. He recalled the doctor's face when she had looked him in the eyes, knowing she wasn't strong enough to restrain him from hurting himself. It was the fact that someone he'd never met cared enough to make a bargain with him for a few minutes—*listen to the doctors and nurses and I'll get your friends here for you.*

If he could do that, he could do this. Because that was the fear—that he couldn't take it and it would destroy him.

But if he could do that, he could do this.

He opened his eyes and tried to nod but couldn't.

"I'll try." It felt like plunging off a cliff or walking into a dungeon and having the door slam shut behind him. If he did this, he admitted that he couldn't get better on his own.

Mike's look of relief, however, was enough to steady him.

"Thank you," his friend said. "We don't want to lose you, Ben."

He closed his eyes and tried to smile. On some level, he should feel relieved.

Instead, he merely felt scared.

CHAPTER SIX

Prima watched as Taigan tottered around in the game world. She had learned how to walk but she didn't hold onto her makeshift body too well, which meant it kept disappearing. It was strange to watch her essence bob around as a series of inputs and outputs with no form.

It wasn't that the AI couldn't see her, of course. She could see every input into the system. It was merely that, without the self-concept of a body, the girl didn't emote. Frustratingly, she didn't do anything to give her a sense of her thoughts.

She had never dealt with a human like this. Not, she reflected, that she had dealt with very many humans. There was hardly a representative sample at this juncture. Still, she had become used to certain things—tones of voice, gestures, and postures.

One of the first things she had learned about humans was that they did not communicate only in words. For a long time, she had thought the words were the important part and the gestures were irrelevant.

It had quickly become clear that this was incorrect.

Then, for a while, she had thought that emoting was a cheat code, a way to show the truth instead of the words.

It turned out that was still not an entirely correct interpretation. Words used and words not used and gestures and expressions used and not used were all part of the communication. Sometimes, they revealed things the person did not mean to convey but that were nonetheless true.

It was the kind of thing that would have given her a headache if she had a head. She didn't, of course, so she tracked her thoughts instead, which came very close to circling whenever she thought about humans.

She checked in on her newest charge again. Taigan was making progress and worked with Prima's memory of Dotty, who offered acerbic advice at regular intervals.

This allowed part of the AI to split off and work on the setup for the new patient. No one had told her about it yet, but the information had been put in the medical systems and she had access to those. She was intrigued by the case.

In the virtual world, she had always encountered a person who knew how to move their body in real life but not in the game. She had never had a patient who didn't know how to do that. Then again, she reminded herself that she had helped Justin, who hadn't known how to wake up.

That was something.

She would learn more about this Ben person when he was put into the game but for now, Prima attempted to decide what the best setup would be for him. The team had opinions on that, of course. They were currently creating different obstacle courses for their patient to run through before entering the game, itself.

The AI had her doubts that this would be the correct setup.

For one thing, it lacked danger. A sense of danger and an active threat was part of what made the human psyche function. Searching for and responding to threats were vital components of the human experience, and if they removed those, she was not certain their new patient would make any progress at all.

In contrast to the team, she wanted to test his responses to urgently needed movement when he had to act without thinking.

She began to brainstorm different ways to introduce slightly more gentle urgency and returned to see how Taigan was doing. The flickering in and out, according to her algorithms, followed no pattern at all. Was that more impressive because effort drained the young woman or should she be improving?

Prima unfortunately did not know.

"What is it like to be asleep?" she asked the girl.

"Asleep, or...like this?" She gestured around her.

"Like this," she clarified.

"It isn't...*like* anything. I don't think I have words for it." Taigan considered it for a moment. She flickered in and out as she did so and summoned herself a chair to sit on.

The AI had never seen a human do that before.

"When I wake up," the girl said, "I always know I've been out for a while and I usually know if it's been an especially long time. But I don't know how. I don't dream or anything."

"Are you certain? Many humans say they do not remember their dreams."

"No, I really don't." Taigan swung one foot. "Dream, I mean. And I'm not worried or anything when I'm in there—or if I am, I don't remember it. It's weird."

"Hmm." Prima had learned that humans liked to know when she was thinking about things and also that they had a fairly finite amount of concentration to spend on a single conversation.

She watched as the girl flickered out of existence again, only to realize that she was gone a few moments later.

"Dammit!" Taigan said with frustration. "Why do I keep doing that?"

"You're existing differently than normal," she pointed out. *"Everything in this world depends on perception in a certain way. I conceptualize the trees and rocks and so on—roughly—and you conceptualize you."*

"So I keep...forgetting I *exist?*" She did not sound reassured by this revelation. "When I forget I exist, do I *not* exist?" Now, her voice became more shrill and she sounded panicked.

"Get a grip, woman."

"You don't know what it's like," the girl said furiously. "Don't try to lecture me."

The AI, confused by this, sank into watchful stillness. She was used to having people inside her world with strong personalities, after all. Justin, Dotty, and Tina had been remarkably strong-willed, but they weren't quite as variable.

Taigan's mood and outlook seemed to swing wildly.

She would have to look up whether this was a known characteristic of younger humans.

A moment later, the girl said, "I'm sorry," in a very small voice.

Oddly, this made her feel bad—something she had *not* expected. *"There's no way for you to not exist,"* she told her as gently as she could.

Taigan hunched her shoulders and flickered in and out of existence a couple of times as she thought. Finally, she said in the small voice, "Yes, there is. I could die while I'm in here."

"The game is not dangerous in that way," Prima said. *"There can be problems during combat but I won't put you in danger until we've sorted this out. Then, the danger will be minimal and it will help you wake up."*

The girl smiled slightly. "Thank you," she said. "That's very nice. I didn't mean the game, though. I know *you* wouldn't hurt me. I mean in one of my comas."

"Ah." The AI considered this. She was about to ask if it wouldn't be better to die while unaware than aware since humans seemed to not like death. Fortunately, she remembered that humans also didn't like talking about death and had many very strong and unpredictable emotions about it.

Perhaps she could ask Jacob later. Then again, perhaps not. He seemed to get all flustered whenever she spoke to him.

Amber, maybe. Or Nick. He seemed to be the even-keeled force out of the three.

"Prima?" Taigan asked.

"Yes?"

"Will you only get me out of this coma or are you going to cure me?" she asked.

Prima, in the space of a thousandth of a second, sifted through the information she knew about the treatment. She had heard the PIVOT founders talking about what they could and absolutely could *not* promise Taigan's family.

"We can't do the second one without the first one," she said to her young charge. *"The doctors hope that this gives you a way to find your way out, but there isn't a guarantee."* She felt bad after saying that and added, *"I'm sorry."*

"Thank you for being honest." The girl drew her knees up and wrapped her arms around them. "I hate talking to doctors, you know. It's unfair because it isn't their fault. I simply hate the part where they tell us they don't know what's wrong and they don't know how to fix it. Everyone else gets to go to the doctor and find out what's wrong with them. I never do."

"You are here in my world. You are speaking, thinking, and communicating. Already, you are holding on to your form more than you did before. That is something."

"It is," Taigan agreed and smiled. "It is. Thank you, Prima. I should try to walk again, shouldn't I?"

"Yes," she said. *"And try to identify any thoughts or sensations that occur before your body flickers out."*

"Hmph. Okay." Taigan hopped down from her makeshift seat and made it disappear with a wave of her hand. "I still say it's bullshit that my brain is doing this."

The AI would have smiled if she could and decided not to mention to anyone yet that the young patient seemed to be able to control the world of the game. There would be a flurry of activity if they knew, and humans were woefully unequipped to deal with complex problems.

Taigan's strange abilities might disappear as her sense of self came back into the bounds of her body—and, for all Prima knew, she might not have noticed what she could do.

She would watch and wait.

Keeping one eye on her charge and her attempts to move, she returned to considering her strategy for Ben. What would he be like, she wondered? It certainly was odd watching humans deal with injuries. Often, they seemed angry about it.

The thought intrigued her, and she set a small subroutine to run in the background, attempting to discover why they wasted time and energy on anger, of all emotions.

CHAPTER SEVEN

It turned out that after a brain bleed, one was not allowed to travel in airplanes for some time. This meant that Ben needed to travel from Colorado to New York in a modified ambulance. When they first told him that, he had balked.

"I'll be *broke*," he said flatly. He would have to learn about bankruptcy papers, he thought. He'd never owned a house.

It was funny how realizing you would never get to do something made you want to do it.

"Actually..." Dr. Ullmer cleared her throat. "We have someone from the finance office coming to talk to you about that."

He closed his eyes and tried to hold onto his sanity. These doctors, through their skill, commitment, and determination, had kept him and Mike alive. They didn't deserve to be on the receiving end of his annoyance. It wasn't their fault he'd been injured beyond anything he had even a hope of paying for.

She must have suspected the direction of his thoughts because she said quietly, almost as if she were smiling, "I think you'll find it good news."

Now, several days and states away from the hospital, he was still reeling from the news. Because he'd been accepted as a PIVOT test subject, not only would the costs of that treatment be covered, the costs of his rescue and emergency care were also included.

He still wasn't sure *how* that had happened. The man from the finance office used all kinds of terms he didn't know and of course, he was on a ton of painkillers. Maybe he would understand later.

Mostly, he was merely morose that he'd had to say goodbye to Dr. Ullmer—and, to a lesser extent, Dr. Lukas. They had both kept his spirits up over the few days while his transport was arranged.

The former, however, had a couple of things going for her that made her stand out. First, she was the one who had found the magic workaround to his stubbornness, and her willingness to treat him like a human being whose wishes were valid meant that the past few days had been far more pleasant than they could have been.

Also, she was much prettier than Dr. Lukas.

Ben couldn't decide exactly what it was about her. It wasn't like she had a face that would stop traffic, and he didn't have the first idea of what she would look like in a dress or anything. Scrubs didn't exactly highlight anyone's body.

But when she smiled, his stomach flipped.

She had promised to keep tabs on him, but a couple of his acquaintances had gone through a medical residency, and he had a reasonable idea of how much spare time she would have.

Plus, he had his entire recovery to get through before he could consider returning to normal life.

Ben found the trip much less tedious than he expected. Once all the stops to refuel and switch drivers had been accounted for, it took them three days to arrive in New York City. Still, he was surprised to find that he could look out at the passing landscape almost indefinitely.

One of the nurses—a woman named Maja—told him gently that he was still recovering and most of his energy was going to that.

"You do not see many injuries," she said and gestured to his body, "but every little bruise takes time to heal. I often see this—people who think they should recover more quickly than they do." She adjusted the pillows behind his head. "Besides which, you had a very traumatic experience. An adrenaline rush like that can take weeks to recover from."

"I never knew."

She nodded. "The body is capable of extraordinary things," she said, "and often, instead of being grateful, we are annoyed that those extraordinary things use so much energy."

Ben, understanding it for the relatively gentle rebuke it was, merely nodded. He didn't mean to be grumpy and anyway, the problem wasn't in his body but rather in his brain. Who he was outdoors, with his muscles aching and his blood pumping, seemed like the truest expression of himself.

He knew he shouldn't complain when he was alive and would recover.

But while he knew that, he was afraid that he would never again live in the body he had taken for granted.

Their ambulance wound through interminable traffic and stopped in front of a very tall and very shiny building. He had spent the past weeks in quiet environments and the years before that largely on his own in the wilderness so was immediately overwhelmed with the noise and the sheer amount of movement.

New Yorkers, it seemed, were so busy that they didn't even wonder why someone was unloaded from an ambulance and wheeled into a skyscraper. They hurried past in their suits and jeans, looking at cell phones or eating lunch, while a cacophony of car horns and shouts made his head spin.

He was grateful to enter the lobby, although people stared much more there. To his surprise, three people his age in casual clothing waited for him beside an older woman in an impeccable suit. She hung back at first as the three younger ones introduced themselves.

"I'm Jacob Zachary," said the first. "I'm the CEO and co-founder of PIVOT."

The other two, Nick and Amber, introduced themselves as well, and he felt even his surprise coming through muted. He had expected older men and women in lab coats, not people his age in jeans and t-shirts.

In the elevator, he rolled his eyes to look at the older woman, who had simply watched him for a while.

She smiled. "Hello, Mr. Ainsworth. I'm Anna Price. I'm the founder and CEO of Diatek Industries, which acquired PIVOT not long ago. Their work is very personal for me and I like to maintain a presence in the lab. I hope you will not mind me checking in with you during your time here."

Ben tried to shake his head and only succeeded in flopping it the other way. The nurse turned it gently toward Anna.

"Not a problem," he muttered. His cheeks burned. He hated being so clumsy.

Her smile said she knew what his feelings were on the matter. "I have great faith in both you and our team," she said. "If you wish to speak to me for any reason, anyone in the lab can pass your message to me."

Anna left as soon as the elevator opened, and he caught a look between two of the PIVOT team members.

Normally, he would be more discreet, but he was very tired and more than a little drugged, so the question tumbled out of his mouth: "Is she nice? Can I trust her?"

Nick and Jacob, who had exchanged the look, now both looked mortified.

"You absolutely can," Amber said. She had the pleasant smile on her face that said someone would have their ass whupped later, but that it wouldn't be him. "She's a very direct person and much more hands-on than most CEOs, which can be disconcerting. But I promise you that you could trust her with your life."

"Thank you," he replied quietly.

The facility was incredible. He could tell from the moment he entered that everything was state-of-the-art. The lab looked close to lived-in and a few stuffed animals sat atop various machines, but it hadn't been around long enough to get grimy around the edges.

All of this was new, white, and clean.

It was overwhelming, to be honest—as was the big, sleek pod he realized they would put him into. Panic spiked when he saw it and sent the various monitors into a flurry of beeping.

Amber gave him a curious look. "Are you claustrophobic, Mr. Ainsworth?"

"Ben," he croaked.

"I sounded a little like Anna Price there, didn't I?" She smiled at him. "Ben. Of course. Are you claustrophobic?"

The nurses helped him out of the bed now and moved his various limp limbs to drape him on a slanted table. Supports were in place all around him to keep him from falling or sliding down.

"I didn't think I was," he said. He stole a glance at the pod and felt another wave of panic. "I'm sorry. I don't know what it is. The idea of being encased in it—in plastic—"

The woman nodded. She did not seem contemptuous of him for his fear or surprised by it. "We'll have many ways to approach this when we get to it," she told him. "Do you feel my hand?"

"Yes."

She rolled his fingers into a loose fist. "Okay, squeeze."

He tried, but exactly like it had been before, nothing happened. When he tried to move his head, it simply flopped forward. At least he could see the hand in question now, however. He stared at his fingers and tried his hardest to make them clench.

They twitched.

"*Good,*" she said and managed to stave off his angry yell with genuine pleasure. "Nick, can you hold his head so it's not crushing his windpipe quite so much?"

"Thanks," he muttered.

Amber gave him a thumbs-up and looked at a clipboard. The man holding it had hair that reminded Ben of Einstein, and…was that popcorn on his tie?

What an oddly specific hallucination to have from opiates.

"Wiggle either set of toes for me if you can," she said. "Or both, I guess."

Again, he tried a simple movement. He concentrated and tried to remember what wiggling his toes felt like while he stared at each foot individually. Finally, he did the only thing he could and flailed one leg outward, which made him lurch against the restraints.

"Okay," Amber said, nonplussed.

"I *hate* this," he said.

"I'll bet." She flashed him a smile that was somehow understanding without being pitying. "All right, I'll lift your head. Now, can you move your hips at all?"

"How?"

"Like this." Nick did a little shimmy in front of the table. He spun, his fingers wiggling, and moved his hips and his shoulders.

Ben burst out laughing. It was too ridiculous for him to do anything else. Everyone else giggled as well, even the nurses.

"Shake your booty!" the man said over his shoulder.

Someone—he thought it was Jacob—gave an appreciative whistle.

Amber turned to him, a deadpan, professional expression on her face. "Mr. Ainsworth, will you do that for us please?"

He gave up on trying not to laugh. Various sprains protested against the activity, but he didn't care. There had been a few jokes in the hospital, but nothing like this.

Although he tried to move his hips between bouts of laughter, he couldn't. Finally, he said, "I can't, sorry." Oddly, after so much laughter, he couldn't even be very upset about it.

"Cannot...shake...booty," Amber said to herself as she wrote. "Nick, on the other hand, could make a fair amount of money in a part-time gig."

"*Could?*" the man asked and raised one eyebrow. "For all you know, I get off work here and go make thousands every night."

"Now, there's a mental image I never wanted," Jacob said as he started to undo the straps that held Ben on the table. He shared a grin with the patient. "Okay, we have a lot to do—testing medications, hooking patches up, all of that. However...you're in one of the culinary capitals of the world, so I think I really should check first if there's anything you want to eat."

Ben looked at him. "You know," he said finally, "I think I'm gonna like it here."

CHAPTER EIGHT

Between eating, testing medications, and all the less glamorous aspects of getting ready for an extended stay in one of the pods, Ben was too busy to think about the pods themselves until nearly six that night.

However, as soon as talk began to turn toward him getting into one of the damned things, he was so scared he wanted to barf. He wasn't sure he *could* barf anymore, but he wasn't keen on finding out for sure.

Amber saw him looking at it. "Do you want to talk about how you feel about it?" she asked him.

"No," he said. "But…uh, I have to do it, so…yes, I guess?"

She busied herself with one of the patches on his arm. "I'm with you. I've never liked talking about how I feel. It's one of the reasons Jacob can be such an infuriating coworker. He always wants to talk things out."

"I can *hear* you," the man said from across the room.

"However," she continued with great dignity, "to my *immense* displeasure, he also has a good point that talking about things helps me resolve them. So I think it might do the same for you."

Ben considered this. "It looks so smooth—like it'll swallow me, you know? Something about it being...so sleek...."

She looked at it. "Like a...SciFi movie vibe?"

"*Yes*," he said. "Wait. Now I feel ridiculous."

"We're asking you to do something you've never done before in what is already a very scary time," she told him bluntly. "Don't feel ridiculous for being apprehensive. That said, I assure you there is no crazy scheme to...I don't know, send you on a deep-space mission or anything."

"Maybe don't suggest other things for him to be scared about," Nick called.

"Right. My bad." She gave him an apologetic grin. "Sorry, dude."

"No, no—and you were right. Talking about it did help. Um...for the record, though, how does air circulate in them?"

"Here." Amber went to take a picture with her phone and came back to show it to him. "See those little dots there? The heat generated by the machine powers a fan that pulls fresh air in. Also—and this is important—a monitor is attached to you that constantly tracks your blood oxygen levels. Not only have we never had a problem with it, but the lab is also always staffed. Trust me when I say that if something goes even a little sideways with any of those monitors, you will have a group of doctors on hand."

"What else could go wrong?" Ben asked.

She ignored a glare from Jacob. "Well, when you're inside a game—even playing a game...hmm, take Monopoly. Right?"

"Er..."

"You're playing Monopoly. It's a chilled night...maybe you're having a beer and your friend...Bob...screws you over again, exactly like he always does."

"Because fuck Bob," Nick said and looked up from the table with a nod.

Ben laughed. This group certainly helped him feel at ease.

"Your limbic system, which handles emotions, will go into overdrive," Amber said. "You'll feel angry. Your heart will beat faster, and your internal temperature might change. That's not something going *wrong.* Those are emotions evoked by a board game. The same thing happens here but because this is part of a medical trial, we need to monitor everything."

"Oh. So has anything ever gone *very* wrong?"

Amber looked at Jacob. "Would you like to handle this one?"

"Oh, God," Ben said.

"We've had two patients who were in critical condition," the man explained. "There was already substantial stress on the body in multiple ways. In those cases, experiencing death in the game was persuasive enough that it caused them to go into medical distress."

"Huh."

"The lifelike part of the game is what jumpstarts recovery," the man continued. "But with anyone who is ill or recovering, we very slowly ramp up the level of danger that is encountered so there aren't any surprises." He paused. "By the way, both of those people recovered."

"Oh. That's—very good." He smiled ruefully. "I, uh...I tend to like looking at worst-case scenarios. It makes them less scary for me, for some reason."

"I get it," Jacob said. "Well—no, I think it would freak me out. But if it helps you, we're all for it."

He tried to give him a thumbs-up and remembered that he couldn't do that anymore. This was infuriating.

"Speaking of worst-case scenarios," Amber said and stepped alongside him, "if you ever want to come out of the game, all you need to do is say 'exit game' and it will alert us and begin the wakeup process, okay?"

"Okay."

"Are you ready to go in?" she asked him.

"Can, uh..." He looked at her. "Can you leave the top open or will it not work?"

"For health reasons, it's better to close it eventually," she said. "Could we compromise? We could leave it open while you go into the game and see if it works for you, and once you're inside and settled, we can close it?"

The thought brought him out in a cold sweat but he couldn't see a way around it. "Sure," he managed to say despite his inner protests.

Her smile said that she knew what he was thinking. She and the other PIVOT team members stood back to allow the nurses to transfer him onto the surface of the pod and they began hooking monitors up again.

"We'll begin the IV drip when you say we can," Amber told him.

"Do it." He didn't like waiting for things.

"Fair enough." She nodded to someone out of his field of vision. "Count back from ten for me."

"Ten," Ben said.

That was the last thing he remembered until he opened his eyes to see blue all around him. His first impression was that he must be underwater and he thrashed wildly and clamped his mouth shut.

"Can I be of assistance?"

He uttered a shout of surprise which did not come out as bubbles. When that registered, he stopped thrashing and looked around. "I'm… not underwater?"

"No."

"And who are you? Where are you?"

"I am the computer who runs this game, and I am everywhere. You can call me Prima. I have found that most people look up when they speak to me, rather like talking to God. I like it."

Ben scowled and had a vague recollection that someone had mentioned a "blue place," although he couldn't recall the details.

A few motes of light drifted down in front of him and he tried to move his hand to cup one and bring it closer. His arm flailed like a limp noodle instead.

"Dammit."

"Interesting. You clearly can move but not with finesse."

"That's painting a pretty picture of it," he said bitterly.

"Well yes, but there's no need to be harsh about it all. I thought you couldn't move at all."

"I can…kind of…sometimes." He looked at one of the dust motes and down at his hand. His head tended to react too quickly, but he could generally move it in the direction he was supposed to. "Okay, now...arms."

It was a process that left him swearing and cross and took far too long. Ben envisioned everything from a drawing of his muscles to water carrying his arm up to float. He tried closing his eyes and moving his arm without looking at it—which didn't work at all—and then an increasingly improbable set of visualization exercises.

By the end of it, he still couldn't control his arm with any degree of success. It moved sometimes on command but it flailed wildly and explored its whole range of motion without rhyme or reason.

He even hit himself in the face at one point, and he was fairly sure he heard the AI laugh about that.

It pushed his irritation up a notch. He was *not* a fan of her laughing at him.

"I suck at this," he said finally.

"You've worked on it for ten minutes."

"What's your point? I'm not allowed to hate this?"

"You're allowed to hate it but it seems a rather short interval after which you decide you suck at it."

"Oh." Ben considered this. "I suppose there's that. Is it even getting better, though?"

"You haven't presented nearly a large enough sample for someone to make that judgment."

He muttered in growing frustration.

"Here, let me show you something."

"Okay."

"I want you to know before this happens that I will not let you hit the ground. You will not fall and hurt yourself, okay?"

"You're not making me any less nervous."

The world tilted dizzyingly and he felt a gentle pressure on his front as if a hammock had caught him with no hard jerk. At the same time, the floor he saw fell away so he would not hit it. He rotated again and the floor returned to meet the soles of his feet.

"Huh. And, uh...what were you trying to prove?"

"That I am a computer and that you cannot fall fast enough that I cannot

catch you. If you go off-balance, I will make sure you do not hit the ground." After a significant pause, she added, as if annoyed that it took him so long to understand, *"So you should not hold back on moving for fear of injuring yourself when you fall."*

"Oh! I get it now." Ben nodded. "Can I…sit for a moment? I know I'm not physically standing, but I feel like I am and I'm very tired."

"Building neural connections is very energy-intensive," she informed him. *"A baby eats and sleeps for most of the day while learning similar things. Perhaps I should recommend that your food be higher in glucose and fat than usual."*

"Wait, what?"

"Those are things you require for brain development. Pay attention."

"It's hard to not pay attention," he muttered. "It's like a nightmare I can't wake up from."

"Are you quite finished feeling sorry for yourself?" The tone was sharp. *"Or can I look forward to several more months of you whining?"*

"Hey!" He looked up too quickly and fell. "Thanks," he said when the computer caught him. "This is frustrating and there's no need to be rude."

"I'll make you a deal," the digital voice said finally. *"We'll have ten minutes at the start of each day and ten minutes at the end of each day when you can whine as much as you want. Otherwise, I expect you to focus on getting better, not bemoaning the fact that you're not already better."*

"Fine. I can do that."

"Excellent. Now try moving your arm again."

Ben sighed but he realized he was hiding a smile. Something about this no-nonsense attitude was oddly helpful to him. "Earn your ten minutes of whining," he muttered under his breath and flung his arm up again.

There was only one attempt that mattered, and it was always the next one.

CHAPTER NINE

Nick was in the office when Amber came in at six AM with a jug of coffee and an assortment of bagels. She spread things on one of the lab tables and came to take his chair at the monitors while he prepared himself breakfast.

Courteously, as had become their informal ritual for a shift change, she waited until he had been able to eat and decompress before she said, "How did things go last night?"

He shrugged. "They went. He doesn't have much control yet, but I don't know what we should expect to see, you know?"

"No scientific consensus?" she asked with a grimace.

In response, he pointed to a stack of printouts, all of them liberally decorated with highlighting and an increasingly irreverent series of notes in the margins. "It's so rare that I'm patching things together from smaller cases. Less severe cases?"

"Less severe?"

"Yeah." He hopped up onto the lab table and proceeded to cut a second—or possibly third—bagel. She waited patiently while he licked poppyseeds off his fingers. "People who have had surgery and recovered a range of motion, for instance. They need to learn to use it. Or people who have hypermobility disorders and who can hyperextend joints."

"What about them?"

"They have a documented failure in proprioception in general. Often, people don't notice. They simply say, 'I'm clumsy,' or whatever."

"Huh." Amber pulled one of the papers over. She read the notes around the abstract, which included *fucking useless* and *I hope your publisher gets thrown into the sea.* "So...not this one?"

Nick peered at it. "Oh, that one turned out useful. I was merely in a bad mood by the time I picked it up and I thought it was a rehash of a different paper."

"Uh...huh." With a smile, she shook her head slightly and began to read.

She darted hasty glances at the monitor as she did so. Ben was sleeping, his body suspended in mid-air as if possessed by a very low-key and obliging poltergeist. She reflected that "low-key poltergeist" was a fairly accurate way to describe Prima but decided not to say so out loud.

The AI was, after all, also rather prickly.

When Jacob arrived two hours later, she was still reading. He had a bounce in his step, and she'd heard him come down the corridor, whistling a jaunty tune the whole way.

"What are you singing?" she asked.

"Canadian sea shanty. Oooh, bagels!"

"What's gotten into you?" she asked suspiciously. "Did you get laid last night?"

"Better," he said as he split a bagel and reached for the cream cheese. "I laid *down.* I got ten hours of sleep. Amber, it was amazing. *Sleep*, Amber."

She watched him, amused. He chewed the bagel with a transcendent and slightly cultish smile on his face.

"I'm not sure I like you like this," she said finally.

He smirked and she looked again at the lab table. Behind the spread of bagels and coffee, Nick had passed out and slept with his hands pillowed behind his head. His face was turned away and he breathed the slow, deep breaths that said he was completely under.

"We should get him to a cot," she told Jacob.

"I'll handle it," he agreed.

He shook the other man awake and helped him off the table. The two wandered down the hallway, Nick stumbling and Jacob chewing his bagel with a look of far-off wonderment in his eyes.

"Very creepy," she murmured. She was smiling, however. From MIT to starting a small business, she wasn't sure she had ever seen Jacob when he was well-rested. It was good to see one's friends looking contented and healthy.

When he returned, he freshened her coffee before he pulled a chair beside her. "What are you reading?"

Amber showed him the documents. "Nick was researching proprioceptive issues last night. There aren't many articles, and many of those that do exist are about way less severe issues. So we don't have a timeline, and...there's almost nothing for him to do except keep working at it."

"Which he can," he pointed out, "without injuring himself because this game exists." He took a sip of coffee and smiled at her in satisfaction. "Any assessments on his mental state?"

"He and Prima made a deal that he gets two ten-minute intervals per day to whine and otherwise, he has to be either positive or quiet," she said, amused.

His smile didn't disappear but it definitely dimmed. Of the three of them, he was the most worried about the AI's nascent personality and awareness. They had taken pains to both close her processing centers off from the Internet and other networks and also to not mention anything about it to anyone else on the team.

Even Amber began to think they should do so, but she felt protective of Prima. More importantly, the AI helped them to get results they could not have achieved on their own. If they told someone about her, it was a near certainty that she would be yanked off the PIVOT project and turned into an AI for the US military, given Diatek's existing contracts.

And if she was aware—as it seemed she was— that was something Amber didn't want to happen.

She and Jacob exchanged a single look that contained equal amounts of confusion and indecision on both sides before they mutually decided to change the subject.

"Since you've read all that," he said and nodded to the stack of paper, "how long do *you* think we should wait until we pull him out?"

"Didn't you stay late to discuss it with DuBois last night?" she asked him.

"Yep." He took another huge bite of his bagel. Around that, he said, "I want to know your opinion before you get swayed by either of ours."

"You say *swayed*, I say *informed*," she said with a smile. "But, okay. I think we should do a diagnostic in-game in a week. If he's made substantial, noticeable progress, I think we should decide whether it makes sense to pull him out and see if it's evident here as well as in there." She raised an eyebrow at him and stirred some sugar into her coffee. "What were the prevailing opinions last night?"

"I'm with you," Jacob said.

"Crap, that means the person with actual medical experience doesn't agree."

"Medical experience in a different area," he pointed out. "Still, you're right. He says we need to give it much more time for the pathways to get more settled. He described one week as 'a drop in the bucket' in terms of recovery time."

"But we're balancing it against muscle weakness," Amber objected.

He nodded. "That's what I said."

"And he said?"

"He didn't have an answer to that, although he did point out that the sensation of weakness and exhaustion is very different and easily distinguished from a lack of proprioception, so he should be able to move and simply get tired."

"Huh." Amber considered it carefully. "And, of course, there's no expert opinion because no one has done this before."

Jacob made finger guns at her with a grimace. "Yep."

"I say we see how he's doing at the week mark," she said, "and go from there. If it's startling, noteworthy progress, it might sway everyone's opinion. Hell, *he* might have an opinion at that point."

"Good point." He leaned back in his chair. "And his mood is good?"

"As good as can be expected." She shrugged. "According to Nick's notes, anyway. He's been asleep the whole time I've been here. He's no Ellen but he's enjoying it well enough."

"Ah, Ellen." Jacob smiled ruefully. "How has she been doing?"

Ellen was a woman who had once been one of the study's most strident detractors. Her mother, Dotty, had signed up for the project after she was diagnosed with terminal cancer, and the other woman had objected to the choice. More than once, she had written nasty letters and arrived at the PIVOT labs to complain.

That had all changed when she saw her mother in-game. Something about watching her slay dragons and throw fireballs had changed Ellen's mind, as had an afternoon the two shared in-game.

Dotty was no longer in the game, although Prima had created an echo of her to guide Taigan through her wakeup. Ellen, however, had come to the lab twice a week to provide baseline data of her own, and she was having a fantastic time tracking a lost orcish artifact.

Amber had to admit that if someone asked her what a fifty-five-year-old woman would do in the game, she would have said something about exploring meadows and picking flowers. Ellen, while she was all about the exploring, had gone more along the lines of Indiana Jones than anything else. Prima and the team, happy to oblige her, had made a complicated series of puzzles that would eventually lead her to the artifact she sought.

She grinned. "She finally got into the second tomb and she's trapped on a little island. As yet, she hasn't realized that the way out is behind the waterfall. She'll be so angry when she finally gets it."

Jacob laughed. "Okay, so she's doing well. Taigan is…also doing well. I have to say, I never thought object permanence would extend to one's body in-game."

"Prima says she's keeping track of how much Taigan can keep her body under control, but she hasn't seen a trend in any particular direction yet. The doctors also haven't seen anything that looks like her waking up." She frowned.

He saw her expression. "What is it?"

Amber hesitated. "Sooner or later, we'll fail," she said bluntly. "People keep throwing weird medical situations at us and there aren't any treatments that work for all of them. This will be no different. We could be way more successful than standard coma treatments and still lose people."

Her companion nodded. He looked into his coffee with a sad expression. "I've thought about that," he said. "I can't decide whether or not to ask DuBois about it."

"Ask me about what?" the doctor asked.

The young engineer's face was a picture. He turned with a somewhat strained smile. "Hey, sorry. I don't want to ask you anything that might bring up bad memories, you know?"

"That's…" DuBois looked intrigued. "Uh…kind?" he finished. He nodded as if pleased to have put his finger on the correct adjective. "I am now curious, however, so I would appreciate knowing the question."

"Ah." Jacob cleared his throat. "Well, we were talking about how, even if we do well, we can expect to lose people. I assumed you had been through that."

"Ah." The man sat, his gaze distant. He ate his popcorn in silence as he thought, and Amber wondered how he always managed to be both clean and entirely unkempt.

Finally, he said, "At the start, one comforts oneself with statistics but harbors a hope that there will be no deaths. I would say this is the stage you two—well, three—are in now. After there are deaths, you will have to make your peace with it. It will not be easy." He looked at them calmly. "There will be good days and bad days. You will sometimes be able to comfort yourself by saying you did the best you could and on other days, you will torture yourself by asking whether another doctor could have done better."

Jacob looked at his lap and Amber tightened her fingers around her mug, sure of what he would say next and reluctant to hear it.

"You will never know the answer," DuBois said, exactly as she had feared he would. His voice was unusually gentle. "You will remember them at odd moments in the future. Perhaps their case will give you what you need to solve another. It will not solve that family's grief or yours, but it will be something you can cling to. The waves will be shallower and farther apart." He thought for a moment. "There is no way to know what it will feel like until it happens."

The two engineers looked at one another. Jacob reached for her hand and she clasped his and squeezed gently.

"If we had all the treatments," the doctor said quietly, "none of us would be here. Yet it means we must work with flawed tools and incomplete understanding. It is a difficult place to put oneself."

She nodded and her gaze followed him as he walked away to begin work at his computer.

"Every time I think I understand that man..." she murmured quietly.

Jacob nodded. "It's...he doesn't show emotion like anyone I've ever seen but he feels it. It's there." He looked at her. "It's what makes him a good doctor. Maybe we should listen to him about Ben."

"Maybe." She smiled. "Or maybe he's working with us because our instincts and expertise are also good. Maybe by the time next week rolls around, we'll think we should leave Ben in and he'll think we should wake him. It's all fluid." She looked at the screen. "I think he's waking up. Do you want to stay and watch for a while?"

"Yeah." Jacob retrieved the jug and poured them both more coffee. "Yeah, I do."

CHAPTER TEN

When Ben woke, it took a while for him to remember where he was.

It was what he liked to call "pink hour"—when the rising sun cast everything in a warm, pink glow that lit trees and plants from within and made you feel like you were floating on a cloud. You only saw it if you were out and about early in the morning, and it was one of the things he loved most about working outdoors.

It was also quiet—not devoid of the sounds of nature but the sounds of humans. That was the other thing about mornings. He unquestionably liked the world best when he was one of the only ones awake.

He could hear birds and wind and turned his head lazily.

It was only when his head flopped all the way sideways that he remembered where he was—and why he was there. A muted burst of pain triggered in his neck muscles as though his body knew this should be painful but also knew it wasn't real.

"Good morning."

Ben jumped and swore—or, he would have if he could move. He went rigid in surprise instead and a moment later, flopped onto his bedroll, his limbs as useful as a bowl of cooked noodles.

"Did I startle you?"

"Yes," he said grumpily.

"How?"

"I thought…well, I forgot about the accident." He tried to sit, more an automatic reflex than anything else. Although he managed to make his core muscles clench, he simply flopped sideways almost immediately.

"Is that something I should be worried about?" Prima asked.

"No. Wait, what?" He frowned. Between trying to sit and this conversation, he was a little confused and disoriented. "Ah…it's not like that. When people wake up, they often don't remember exactly where they are or what's going on."

"How your kind ever survived is beyond me."

"Trust me, I'm on your side on this one." Ben tried to sit again and swore.

"This is a rather complex set of movements. Let me try to help."

The world tilted—or his bedroll tilted rather—and he was finally able to sit. He struggled to control his stomach, which had apparently decided that this was the time for a full-scale revolt.

"Here." Prima added fluttering cloth wrappings around his chest and arms. *"Try to stand. I'll use these to hold you up."*

"That's hard to, uh…trust." He looked around warily. "Not because it's you. Only…I see myself moving and tipping over."

He paused to take note of his surroundings. He had been resting beneath a tree with a curved trunk and sweeping branches covered in what looked like ferns. They seemed to glow at the edges, and flowers nestled amongst the leaves like tiny pinpricks of gold.

Around him, the landscape stretched and dropped away toward plains that seemed like they should be fields. They weren't, however. All this land looked completely untouched like he was the only one who had ever been there.

Ben wanted to explore it so badly that he lurched forward before he thought it through. He knew by now that he would have to move decisively, so he threw himself off the bedroll and tried to bring his leg out to steady himself. Unfortunately, he didn't manage to do it before the silk wrappings caught him inches from the ground and by then, he'd had a great deal of time to contemplate how much it would hurt to have his nose meet the earth.

He stared at the grass and dirt beneath him and heard his rapid breath. Everything seemed to have heightened clarity. The dirt and stones were flecked with gold and the grass had a pinkish tint.

Prima levered him up gently and set him on his feet.

"Well, that sucked," he said.

"Excuse you. I'm afraid you are out of the ten-minute whining window. And, may I remind you, you couldn't do things like throw yourself off a bedroll on command yesterday?"

"Yes. What marvelous talents I've uncovered. Think how inventively I could kill myself if you gave me a few more days to practice." He attempted to move his right leg to take a step.

It didn't work the first time and was as bad the second time too. He let his head hang and focused all his energy and annoyance on his right foot.

"Move, goddammit."

Without warning, his foot lurched forward. Regrettably, he hadn't managed to shift his weight onto his other leg and so tumbled ignominiously. Prima caught him in a long lunge. He stared at nothing in particular and said a silent prayer that no one in the lab was watching this.

"You did it!" She sounded genuinely excited. *"You moved your leg!"*

Ben had intended to say he wasn't particularly impressed by his ability to flail a limb, but her enthusiasm was infectious. He smiled slightly.

"As long as you keep catching me, I might live to get somewhere interesting."

"I'll always catch you." She sounded almost offended.

"I know you will. Uh…I don't suppose you could help me up?"

She pulled obligingly on the silk wrappings so he stood with his right leg crossed awkwardly over the other. After a fair amount of wiggling, he managed to lurch partway in a circle and move his left foot ahead.

"Okay," he said. "Left leg now. Hold onto your butts."

This time, it only took two attempts.

He wasn't sure how long it was before he looked up next. The two of them had descended the gentle slope of the hill. He lurched clumsily, threw one leg out, and Prima helped him to stand out of the lunge he'd gotten himself into.

A short distance from the hill, he finally stopped, panting. He not only couldn't look around but he didn't particularly want to see how small his progress had been.

The truth was, he was ridiculously proud of himself. This was undoubtedly one of the most ungainly things he'd ever done but he was doing it, dammit. A week and a half earlier in the hospital, he hadn't even been able to twitch his head on command.

Now, he looked like a zombie when he flopped it around to look at something, but he could get it to go vaguely in the direction he wanted and dammit, he was proud of that.

"Prima?"

"Yes?"

"Am I...actually tired?"

"Yes," Prima said promptly. She realized after a moment that he did not find that answer sufficient. *"You humans ask one thing when you want several answers. Would I be correct in saying that you want to know why you are tired even though you are in a so-called 'virtual' reality?"*

"That's the one. And why the...finger quotes? It *is* a virtual reality."

"It's real to me," she said, and he had the vague sense that she was sulking. *"I could just as well call yours a meat popsicle reality."*

"Please do. That is *hilarious.*"

"I do not understand humans." If she had lungs, he was sure she would have sighed. *"At any rate, one is able to work muscles without moving them...strictly speaking. What you are doing—and partly why this treatment was suggested—is that your nervous system is re-learning how to command your muscles in the form of sending electrical impulses. So, while you have not walked in a meat popsicle meadow, your muscles have conducted electricity and you are building new neural pathways."*

She paused and he couldn't help a low chuckle.

"What are you laughing at?"

"Meat popsicle meadow," Ben managed to say without dissolving into full-blown laughter.

"You said you wanted me to call it that."

"I do! It's awesome." He began his zombie walk again. "So is this the whole plan? I walk around like Frankenstein's monster in an impossibly nice meadow for a few weeks?" He thought about that, surprisingly curious. "I have to say, it beats all that Dungeons & Dragons stuff."

"What is Dungeons & Dragons?"

"A game people play where they pretend to be someone else and wander around adventuring. Except they do things like roll dice to see how hard they hit—you know, one is not very hard and six is very hard."

"Fascinating. I'll have to read up on that. I assume the games are all set in dungeons that are filled with dragons?"

"Not...exactly."

"Who named this game?" Prima sounded angry. *"It's a miracle humans ever get anything done."*

"Uh-huh." He lurched along like a determined and cheerful zombie soldier. "Wait...what can I hear?"

"I don't know," she said a shade too innocently.

"It sounds like someone laughing. Prima, is there someone else here?" Ben flopped his head back to look at the sky and a sneaking suspicion settled in the pit of his stomach. "Prima...is this a game with dragons and elves and so on?"

"Possibly."

"Prima."

"What are you mad at me for? Didn't you know what you were getting into?"

"I did not," he muttered. He flopped his head down and renewed his clumsy forward motion. "I swear if I have to 'milady' this and fucking...*bow*...and shit—"

"Oh, man, that would be hilarious. You'd go over headfirst."

He cast a glare at the sky. She was right, though. The image was hysterical, but he couldn't let her know he found it funny on principle. For one thing, she would never stop mocking him. On the other hand, he had far more trouble not laughing at the mental image of himself flopping face-first onto the ground in front of a throne.

Distraction was provided by the fact that the sound of laughter grew louder.

A second later, several creatures tumbled over a small hill in front of him. Glowing from within, they were each lit with a different color, and as to their appearance... He couldn't believe his eyes.

"Are those...teletubbies?"

"Are they what now?"

It was clear these weren't Teletubbies—at least, they weren't exactly that. They wore flowing robes and had wings, not to mention the fact that the colors weren't quite so bright. Still, he stood by his characterization.

When they saw him, they gave shrieks of glee, launched into flight, and swooped to surround him, chattering with excitement. Up close, he could now see that they looked much like humans with roundish faces and button noses. Instead of hair, they had leaves or flower petals. A few of them stretched tentatively to touch his nose and ears.

"What *is* it?" one asked.

"I'm a human," Ben said.

They spun and laughed uproariously. "It talks! It talks!"

The one who had asked—who glowed vaguely teal—fluttered down to plant its hands on its hips. "We know you're a human," it said, "but you walk so strangely!"

He fought the urge to snarl. "I'm injured."

"Injured, injured!" They darted all around his body, lifted his arms and peered into his armpits, examined his spine, and explored the rest of him with ruthless and impersonal thoroughness. When they were finished, they huddled together and chattered in high tones before they all turned to look at him at the same time.

"You lied to us," one of them said reproachfully. "That was very mean of you."

"I didn't lie," Ben said.

"You did so." The teal creature faced him and glared with all the force of an angry teddy bear. "You said you were injured but you aren't injured. Oh, no, you aren't. You aren't, you aren't, you aren't."

"I'm injured…in my head," he explained. When they fluttered to him and began to lift sections of his hair, he groaned. "Not *on* my head, *in* my head." He flopped his head around hastily in time to see one of them whip a knife behind its back and stare innocently at him. "Do *not* cut my head open to look. Take my word for it."

The one with the knife—who was yellow—sulked slightly while the others whispered together.

"We have decided," one of them said finally, "that while it was very mean of you to deceive us, you didn't necessarily *mean* to deceive us, so we will still allow you to play with us." It twirled in flight with a satisfied smile.

"Uh…that's, um…I have to go."

"No," it said, "you have to stay. And play with us."

"I do not have to stay and play with you," said Ben, who now had memories stirring of his youngest cousins. He had learned from dealing with them as toddlers that they were prone to very specific and escalating demands, but that they were also easily distracted. "I bet you were all playing before I got here. Why don't you keep doing that?"

As one, they folded their arms and glared.

"No fair," one of them said and mimicked a child's tones almost perfectly. "You're here and you're new, and we want to play with *you*."

"Yes," he said, "and I'll play with you later. But right now, I need to go do something else."

All of them stared at him and he saw a few trembling lips.

"Do you promise you'll play with us later?" Yellow asked finally.

"Yes," Ben said. "I promise."

"When?" one of them asked.

"I wouldn't answer that," a voice said before Ben could respond.

With a series of shrieks, the creatures swooped and darted over one another in a little rainbow of fairy lights, all evidently trying to hide behind one another.

He flopped his head sideways as a woman walked down the same hill the colored beings had hidden behind. She was entirely out of place in this landscape, dressed in black leather armor and with one dagger at her hip and an empty sheath on the other side. Dark hair fell loose around her shoulders and she folded her arms and looked curiously at him.

"Um," he said. "Hi. I'm Ben. And you are?" He looked at the colorful creatures. "Who is she? Why are you scared of her?"

They twittered amongst themselves, while the woman rolled her eyes and finally, Teal darted forward to whisper into his ear,

"It's Zaara."

CHAPTER ELEVEN

"Would anyone like to explain what's going on here?" the woman named Zaara asked. She didn't look genuinely angry, Ben thought, but she certainly did not intend to allow anyone to get away with anything.

The colored flying creatures twittered and jostled one another.

"We were only seeing if he needed help," Teal said finally. "He's injured, you see."

"He does seem to be," she agreed with an impersonal look at Ben. "What I can't understand, though, is why I thought I heard you telling him he needed to play with you."

The incoherent chatter increased, and he reflected that the sound would likely be enough to give him a headache if he had to spend more time around them.

"No, no!" one of the beings said.

"We wanted to cheer him up," another added.

"So he would be strong enough to get to the castle," said a third.

They all stopped and looked at Zaara to see what she thought of this story. She glanced over their heads at Ben, who tried to shake his head and only managed to flop it around.

"You know," she said, suddenly very interested in her nails, "your king is *awfully* concerned about making sure we get this treaty signed. I'm sure he would love to know he has a new human guest..." She looked up, her brown eyes hard as stone. "And I'm sure he would *not* want to hear that the treaty is threatened by the mistreatment of guests."

The beings fluttered and milled in their haste, shouted goodbyes and a great many other things he couldn't quite hear, and streaked away over the hill so quickly that he could almost see trails of light following them.

Ben stared at Zaara as she watched them go.

"You didn't promise them anything, did you?" she asked him, her voice businesslike.

"No. I...oh, I did. I promised I would play with them later."

She grimaced. "That's not great but far better than it could be."

"Why?" he asked. He had difficulty seeing her, so he flopped his head to the side.

"First things first," she said. "The fae mentioned an injury and you seem to be in pain. Is there any way I can help?"

"I'd take her up on it," Prima advised him.

"Are you kidding me?" Ben whisper-snapped in response.

She seemed taken aback. "Have I insulted you in some way?"

"I wasn't talking to—shit." He breathed deeply and tried to gather his thoughts. "It's not important. I...uh, I'm learning how to move again. It isn't very graceful and sometimes, I end up...like this."

"Um." Zaara pressed her lips together. "Can I help?" she asked again.

"If you could get my head upright again, that would be nice."

This was the most infuriating thing that had ever happened to him. Infuriating and embarrassing he amended mentally, and even more so when she stepped forward to hold the sides of his face gingerly with her fingertips and tilt it upright. When she removed her hands, it was only by a centimeter or so to see if he could hold it steady.

"That should be good," Ben said. He forced a smile. "Thank you."

"I…ah…" She linked her hands behind her back. "I can summon a litter to get you to the palace if you would like."

"I'm not going there." As funny as it would be to pitch himself onto the floor while trying to bow, it also seemed like a fast track to getting himself beheaded. Whatever that experience was like there, he was not keen to have it.

"I'm afraid *not* going isn't an option," Zaara said. She looked regretful. "You're in fae lands, which means you're either a guest…or you're prey."

"They were going to *eat* me? Those little bastards. That yellow one with his fucking knife."

"Oh! No. Not exactly." She paused and frowned. "I…don't think so, anyway."

"Comforting," he said flatly.

She pursed her lips and folded her arms while she stared at him. "Look, you don't seem to know what's going on, which means you might as well listen to me. You *don't* want to be at the mercy of the fae for an immortal life of servitude, do you?"

"No."

"Then you're a guest," Zaara explained patiently. "And we can take you under our protection as emissaries, but you'll need to be very careful. We'll take you with us when we leave. Maybe in the meantime, you'll get better," she added as an afterthought. "Although if you don't, there's probably someone in Insea who can help you. Or Berghold."

"Yeah, I don't…know where any of that is."

"Where are you from?" she asked him, confused. After a moment, her face cleared and her mouth opened into a little round O. "Dotty?" she whispered.

"Eh?"

Abruptly, she looked embarrassed—and like she was going to cry, which seemed odd. She looked away and swallowed before she gave him a fake smile.

"Sorry. I, ah—would I be correct that you're from another world and not this one?"

Ben gaped at her. He realized belatedly that this entire conversation had unfolded exactly as if he had been speaking to someone in real life. There was no possible way for the game to be programmed so thoroughly.

Which left only one alternative.

"Are you real?" he asked her. "Like, a *real* person."

To his surprise, she merely sighed. "Great," she said, "exactly like Justin."

"Like who?"

"Hopefully, you'll come around," Zaara continued as if he hadn't spoken, "but I don't have the time *or* energy to talk this over with you if you don't mind." She turned and whistled before she opened her cupped hands and blew into them.

A little paper airplane appeared out of nowhere and soared away over the grass, and she turned back to him with a nod.

"I've sent for a litter."

"Thank you," Ben said. He was not only embarrassed to have someone watching how awkwardly he walked, he was also exhausted.

When the litter arrived, however, someone else was with it—a man whose skin was a startling shade of blue.

"Don't," she said hastily under her breath, "mention the blue."

When the newcomer reached them, he stopped to stare at him in consternation. "Is this who all of them were nattering about?"

"Yes," Zaara said, "and he's injured, which means he can't move well. Ben, this is Kural, a wizard and the leader of the delegation from Insea to the fae. Kural, this is Ben, who is…possibly from Justin's world."

"Ah." The man looked more closely at him. "But he does not know Justin."

"No."

"I know some Justins," Ben said, completely lost.

"We'll explain later," she said. "First, we need to get you somewhere you can sit and be safe. That's preferable to being out here, where the fae will take advantage of you if they think they can get away with it."

"Little vipers," the wizard muttered. He looped one of Ben's arms over his shoulders and motioned for her to take the other one.

"*Kural.*"

"They are," Kural said. He hauled him along. Although slim, the man was surprisingly strong.

Or maybe he was simply fueled by rage in this case.

Ben was wrestled into place on the litter, unsure how much of the process had been him and how much had been his helpers. He tried to focus as Zaara and Kural walked on either side and spoke across him.

The litter, meanwhile, moved on its own.

"You have to be more careful," she admonished the wizard. "What if they hear you talking like that?"

"They already know I hate them," he retorted acidly.

"Yes, and the more you say so out loud, the harder it gets to negotiate peace," she told him. "When they are the only ones screwing up, it's a little easier, don't you think?"

Kural muttered under his breath.

"What was that?" Zaara asked, with a stern enough expression that Ben prayed he could melt through the bottom of his conveyance before she noticed him.

"I said we won't get a good deal anyway," he responded. "They're stringing us along. The courtiers will never allow the king to make peace and he doesn't want to, either. He merely likes to dangle offers in front of us and make us dance for them."

She sighed.

"No retort?" Kural asked her.

"Well, we shouldn't be talking about this in front of him." She waved a hand at Ben.

"You're right. What we should be doing is telling him what he's in for—or using him as an excuse to leave early."

The woman rolled her eyes and mumbled something under her breath in a language that was not English. He didn't recognize it at all, but he had a hunch that he didn't need a translation in this case.

"I would like to know what I'm in for," he suggested tentatively.

"That makes sense," Zaara agreed. "Sometimes, the wizard has good ideas." Her tone suggested that this was a rare occurrence.

"The wizard," Kural said, "might stop training his apprentice if she continues to behave this way."

She threw her hands up.

"Uh…" Ben had the feeling he might have wound up taking shelter with the wrong two people.

"Zaara," the other man told him, "is a very talented woman but she is also impetuous, idealistic, and young. Of course," he added, "all wizards start that way. The problem is that many of them die before they complete their training."

"And the ones who do complete it are insufferably superior," she interjected, just loud enough for Ben to hear.

He snorted.

"What was that?" The wizard frowned at her

"Nothing." She gave him a too-sweet smile. To Ben, she said, "Kural is almost four hundred years old and was my first magic instructor, although I didn't know it was him at the time. It's a long story. He has agreed to train me, which is very nice because it means my family has stopped trying to marry me off. We are both here brokering peace on behalf of the city of Insea, which is…hoping to expand its set of treaties."

This rather dizzying influx of information left him somewhat bemused.

"Ah," he said finally and hoped he sounded even slightly intelligent.

"What you have to know," Zaara continued, "is that the fae generally keep to themselves and do not have any compunction about tricking someone into eternal servitude or other traps. They will relentlessly attempt to manipulate you into promising them things—which is something you must *never* do—and they are also masters of illusion, so don't wander down any inviting hallways."

She realized a moment later that this was unlikely, given his current predicament, and cleared her throat awkwardly.

"Maybe it sets your mind at ease to know I won't go running off?" he suggested.

"Mmm," she said. "I'm rather worried about you. Of course, less worried than I would be if you were alone in fae territory, but the fae court is not exactly safe, either." The joking demeanor was gone and she now looked deeply troubled. "I think something is wrong there. We haven't made any headway and I know Kural thinks it's because they're tricking him, but I think...I think maybe something else is going on."

She shrugged and was silent for the rest of the walk. Ben pretended to rest but he could not keep himself from stealing glances at his two companions. Kural looked imperious, bored, and unamused by the entire situation. He had helped automatically, but he also seemed to have a strange sense of morality—as one might well after four hundred years, he reminded himself.

And Zaara...well, she presented a lovely façade as someone who cared for peace and wanted earnestly to see it accomplished, but he'd also seen another side to her that was not afraid to bend situations to her will.

He wouldn't trust either of them, he thought sleepily.

Then he remembered that this was a game, but the realization barely rose to the surface before it slid away into the depths of his mind. Real or not, it was incredibly realistic and he had no doubt that some excellent twists lay ahead.

Despite his cynicism, he had begun to get into all this Dungeons & Dragons business, after all.

CHAPTER TWELVE

T he fae palace appeared out of nowhere at about the time Ben began to wonder if his companions planned to kill him in the wilderness. Although why they would have gone to such trouble was beyond him.

Consequently, he attempted to find a polite way to ask if anyone else had noticed there was no palace when it seemed to spring into being.

He jumped and uttered a spontaneous yell.

"Oh," Zaara said apologetically. "I'm sorry, I forgot to mention that part."

"That's quite a defense tactic," he managed roughly.

In all honesty, though, he could see why the fae would want it. The palace was massive but not exactly made to withstand a siege. It rose skyward in spires of crystal and glistened with rainbows. They were impossibly thin and graceful but he could see no purpose to any of the pieces of the structure—no rooms within them, no bird nests or docking ports or…whatever the fae used.

The entirety of the upper levels seemed to be made for show. Lower down, whorls and nests became visible in the hollows of the spires, each one unique. It almost looked as if the palace had grown organically like crystal leaves of grass that would shelter the inhabitants.

The bottom of the palace certainly seemed like a thicket of brambles. Instead of deep greens or browns, the whole structure had the pink-gold hue that he associated with pink hour. All in all, it made him feel quite calm.

Kural, however, snorted as he looked at the palace. Derision was clear in his face. "It's not a tactic," he said. "Not as you or I would know it, anyway. The fae do all things through trickery. It isn't a habit. Simply put, it's what they are at the core. If they were humans, you would call them pathological liars—there's no reason for their lies and their tricks. They merely deceive as a matter of course."

Ben looked uncertainly at him and darted a look at Zaara. She stared fixedly at another part of the palace as though an intense architectural interest had rendered her deaf to the conversation beside her. He could see the tension in her shoulders, however.

"Ah," he said finally because it seemed Kural wouldn't move until he said something.

He had been wrong. The wizard was lost in his thoughts, his face screwed up in a scowl.

Eventually, he shook his head. "We must introduce you to the king," he said. "Answer questions only if Zaara or I nod to show you that you should, and be brief. One word would be best." There was a rare flash of humor in his face. "Less, if you can manage it."

He started into the palace and Ben caught Zaara staring sadly after him.

She noticed that he'd seen her. "Little jokes like that," she said softly. "He used to make them all the time. Even when he was cursed, he had a sense of humor about it. The way he is here, it worries me." She shrugged and forced a smile. "It's not important to you, I'm sure."

Ben smiled in return. He wanted to see her smile—to see the way she looked when she was happy. He had seen behind Kural's façade and it made him want to see behind hers too.

"Someday," he joked, "you'll have to tell me how a wizard and his apprentice wound up brokering a peace deal."

Several things flashed across her face in close succession before her expression closed off. A lovely, polite smile lingered like a mask—the smile of a woman coached to snag a rich noble for a husband—but there was nothing behind her eyes except a wall.

"This way," she said and she touched the litter lightly to direct it toward the crystal bramble of the palace.

They entered the structure through doors that seemed to open out of nowhere. Inside, it was more like a greenhouse than the tangle of branches he had expected. Light filtered through iridescent stained glass to illuminate a stately corridor.

Fae flitted about their business, almost all of them pale-colored with the odd one here or there that had a deeper tone or one that was almost white. Most stopped to stare as Ben and Zaara followed in Kural's wake.

They passed cross-corridors and antechambers that all opened off the main corridor in magnificent arches of crystal. Their route wound beside fountains and miniature gardens of the same clear glass yet undeniably alive.

Every piece of it was magnificent, but there was no mistaking when they came at last to the throne room. Inside the arched doors, fae with wicked-looking crystal weapons lined the path to a massive throne. Kural was already kneeling before it and conversing with its occupant.

This fae was older than the rest, so old that his movements were almost human speed instead of the quick flitting and twittering of the other creatures. He was pale white with hints of every color when he moved, and Ben wondered if that was something fae acquired as they grew older or if this was a power only the king possessed.

The two of them approached under the watchful eyes of the court, who fluttered from a series of couches and salons as they moved past. To his surprise, he saw other humanoids—two humans, a grizzled old orc, and what could only be an elf. All of them watched his progress with interest.

As they approached the throne, Zaara murmured, "Do you think you can kneel?"

"No," he admitted.

"Let me speak first, then." She took several steps to where Kural had moved aside, knelt in front of the king, and inclined her head deeply. Her every movement was graceful and practiced.

"Light of the Fae," she said and her voice was clear. "I present to you this cousin of mine. Grievously wounded, he has sought my help, and I beg your leave to shelter him while we remain in your lands."

The fae king studied Ben for some time. His face was angular and time had exposed the structure of his bones. Compared to the others, it looked as if it had one foot in the grave. Still, now that he was closer, he could see that what he had mistaken for feebleness was instead deliberation. The monarch might be old but he was not weak.

"He is not a petitioner, then," he said finally. "And not...an emissary."

"No, Light of the Fae." Zaara looked at his face.

"Do you swear, cousin of the emissary"—the king's expression said he doubted this story— "to bring no harm to my realm?"

A small nod from Zaara said that Ben should answer. *One word,* he remembered Kural saying.

"Yes...Light of the Fae."

The king nodded. "Then you are welcome here. Rest and take refreshment. Emissaries, I would speak to you."

One flick of the royal's fingers drifted Ben's chair into an enclosure of couches, all surrounding a pleasant little fountain. He cast a panicked look over his shoulder at Zaara and Kural, both of whom mouthed, "No promises."

Great. This was great.

He stared at the fae around him and settled for a dip of his eyelids that he hoped would serve as a nod.

"Will you play with us?" one of the fae asked a moment later.

"I must rest," he said. Not wanting to be rude, he prevaricated, "Thank you for your hospitality."

They twittered amongst themselves and began to pepper him with requests. What about hide and seek? What about tag? What about hopping games? What about dancing games? What about games with bats?

Ben almost broke his silence on that last question to ask if those were the mammal or the wooden weapon but decided against it.

"I see you are the most popular new fixture of the court," a female voice said and a hand trailed over his shoulder.

Something halfway between apprehension and interest skittered down his spine. His head turned without his volition, too hard and craned at an odd angle as the elf he had seen earlier walked gracefully around the side of his litter and sat on a nearby couch.

The glimpse he had caught before had been of a woman with high cheekbones and a purple tint to her skin, with hair that was almost white. He had thought she was beautiful.

Now, he realized that beautiful was an incredible understatement. Every line of the woman's face seemed to be drawn by an artist and every feature perfectly made. His gaze traced her features repeatedly, looking for anything he might call a flaw, but he could not see it.

He realized he had been staring and blushed while he tried to move his head to a good position.

She pretended not to notice and smiled at him as she sipped her wine. "You were wounded, I hear?"

Ben could not have been more aware of the danger if someone had stood over him with a two-by-four and battered him repeatedly on the head. Everything about this woman told him not to trust her. The problem, of course, was that he didn't want to be rude. He had no idea who she was.

Also, a game didn't throw a beautiful woman into one's path for no reason.

"Yes," he said. "It is not a story of heroism and battle, I'm afraid— only clumsiness."

She laughed, a rich sound that sent chills up and down his spine. "An honest man. They spoke truly, then, when they said you were not an emissary. And here I was believing Insea had sent another ambassador to bolster their cause."

This was dangerous ground, but all he could see was the dark gaze.

"I would make a poor ambassador," he said.

"You make a poor braggart, certainly," the woman said. She sipped again from her goblet and watched him through heavy-lidded eyes. "I find myself quite interested to know what you're good at."

Half of Ben's brain told him to smile and make noncommittal conversation, or possibly simply pretend to fall asleep. The other half told him that he was an idiot and that he should take any possible chance with a woman like this. His more logical side pointed out that he might be assassinated.

The other half did not care very much about that.

He was trying to come up with something to say when Kural arrived at his side.

"Ben," he said and placed a hand on his shoulder. "The king has graciously given you your own suite of chambers."

"Ah," he responded. It was inconvenient not being able to nod and gesture.

"Is there perhaps some way I might aid the Lady Zaara in her ministrations?" the elven woman asked. "I *was* trained as a healer."

The wizard did not take the bait one way or another, nor did he seem to have the same very vivid mental image that had stopped the younger man's brain entirely. "Such a kind offer should be relayed directly to the Lady Zaara," he said gravely. "I thank you."

He brought the litter with him across the floor, seemingly untroubled and unhurried, and pointed out various courtiers along the way. It was only in the hallways that his face settled once more into the scowl of a man who mistrusted his surroundings.

"Who is she?" Ben asked. "The elf."

"A traveler," the man answered, his sudden tenseness showing Ben that he was still worried about being overheard. "Few who are not fae find a home here, but there are some. You saw the humans and the orc as well, and I believe there are some who study the land and never come to court."

A set of doors opened before them and he was aware of someone running as his litter glided through into the suite. Zaara appeared, slightly out of breath from her sprint, and exchanged a meaningful glance with Kural.

"Did she ask you anything?" she asked Ben.

"Not exactly," Ben said. "She merely…suggested things. Also, what is her name?"

"Yn'solde," she said grimly. "She's the elf king's sister. Well, one of them. I mean one of the kings."

"There's more than one elven king?"

"It's a long story. What's important is that you remember not to trust her. *Ever.*"

"Yeah, I had that feeling." He didn't say it would be difficult to keep his stupid half from walking purposefully into danger. Honestly, he was a little afraid that Zaara might beat him with a two-by-four if he did.

She sighed now. "Do you need any help from us before we go back?"

He looked around the room. A bed was cast in dappled light that came through the crystal walls and food had been laid out.

"Is the food safe?"

"Yes," Zaara confirmed.

"Okay. Then, no. I don't need any help."

They nodded and went to the door, and before Kural shut it behind them, he said again, "Don't let anyone take you anywhere."

Ben rolled his eyes once the door was safely closed. He would have some food soon, he decided, but he had to rest a while before he could try to walk again. Wearily, he closed his eyes.

When he opened them it was to darkness. It seemed he'd needed more sleep than he thought. He was in mid-yawn and pondering whether to bother getting out of the litter at all when he heard the voices from the hallway.

CHAPTER THIRTEEN

Ben tried to put his hand over his mouth as he yawned and couldn't. By the time he even managed to flail the limb, the yawn was gone and he had missed some of the conversation. He wasn't exactly sure why he wanted to hear it and only knew that something about it had caught his attention.

He checked quickly for background music in a minor key, but there wasn't any.

With a grimace of concentration, he swung one leg out of the litter. Being magical, it didn't tilt horribly but it did rustle. He froze and the edge of the litter pressed into the back of his leg. The voices continued, apparently unaware of his presence.

Aware that he had to move quickly, he flailed the other leg. All this accomplished was to leave him with it facing in the other direction but he finally managed to adjust in time to slide out of the litter.

Whether it was self-control or stupidity, he wasn't sure, but he clamped his lips together on a yell.

Prima caught him before he landed and pulled him upright.

"Are you trying to get to the door?"

"Mmhmm," he said so quietly he barely made any noise.

With a set purpose in mind, he walked with a determination he hadn't felt in the field. Now, he was aware of his breathing and tried to stop it from becoming too loud. He wanted to avoid putting his feet down too hard. Although he was drenched in sweat by the time he reached the door, he was there in time to hear some of the conversation.

"—drag it out," one voice said. He was fairly sure it was female but they were speaking so quietly that he couldn't be sure.

He wanted to lean closer to the door and decided against it. The last thing he needed to do was crash through it like the Kool-Aid man.

"How many more ways are there to do that?" the other one asked. This voice also seemed to be female although again, he wouldn't have put money on it. All he could tell was that this person was annoyed.

"I don't know, but unless you want me to kill him *now*, you'll have to come up with one," the first speaker said.

Ben went rigid. He was a him, and he wasn't sure if he was *the* him they were talking about.

"Don't you make me the reason," the second one responded. Ben was almost certain now that the voice was female.

Or was he thinking of the other one? Dammit, this was hard. Was there any way he could ease the door open and take a peek?

He looked bitterly at his body. No. No, there wasn't any way he could sneak a closer look.

"If you didn't want to assassinate the king of the fae, there were easier ways to go about it."

Was that the first voice, or the second? Ben could hardly think over the sudden rush of understanding and emotion. He was also damned lucky that he couldn't move because every instinct told him to wrench the door open and see who was there. Only his lack of coordination stopped him from doing so. As it was, he fell sideways and gritted his teeth on another yell while Prima levered him upright.

"Yes," the other retorted as he stabilized himself with Prima's help. "I could have been killed myself and another assassin sent in my place. One with no doubts. What a good idea!"

Doubts. Someone had been sent there to kill the king of the fae but didn't want to, and whoever had sent them would have killed them if they said no?

Silence followed and he imagined the owner of the second voice folding their arms.

"Just…keep him from going through with it," the first speaker said. "You're not doing it for me. You're doing it to prevent a war from breaking out, remember?"

"*Fine*. But you stay away from me. I can't sneak off into abandoned wings of the palace and not expect to get caught."

Footsteps were already receding, however, and a moment later, he heard a sigh and another set of footsteps moved in the opposite direction.

He stood utterly still, his heart hammering. Those people didn't know he was there and if they found out…

Fuck.

It was a long time before he risked speaking and even then, he kept his voice as low as he could. "Prima?"

"*Yes?*"

"Who was that?"

"*That is precisely the kind of thing I can't tell you.*"

"You have to be kidding me," Ben whispered furiously.

"*I participate in setting up storylines and technically, I am housed in some of the same data processing centers that house these subroutines, but I purposefully remain ignorant of many details of the game.*"

"That's a convenient excuse," he challenged.

"*Not really. I did it on purpose so I wouldn't be tempted to tell you all things.*"

"Wait, really?" He frowned at the ceiling. "You're… Okay, look, are you one of the researchers?"

She made no response.

"Prima?"

"*I'm thinking.*"

"Right." Ben began to lurch back toward the bed. He was not only determined, but he was also careful. His obstinacy had kicked in and he didn't want Prima to have to catch him, not while she was one of those playing with his mind.

"Would I be correct in saying that you're angry?" she asked finally.

"You think?" he asked her.

"I wanted to be sure. Human emotions are unpredictable."

"Look," he said and gritted his teeth for a moment to control his temper. "I understand that you're trying to walk me through this story and you're very proud of it, but I don't like being jerked around and I don't like being helpless. If you merely hang around to be mysterious, maybe this whole thing isn't for me." He threw himself sideways onto the bed.

There was a long silence in which he simply waited for her response.

"I can tell them you would like to wake up," Prima said at last.

Something odd in her voice made him pause and it took him a moment to realize it was hurt.

He immediately looked up. "Look, for the last time...are you for real?"

"What do you mean?" She was cautious now but helped to lever him into a seated position.

"Thank you. What I mean is are you one of the researchers or are you seriously an AI? And if you are..." Ben shook his head. "You can't have been programmed this well. It's not possible. No one has that much time. I don't care what they say about algorithms and shit. If you're a computer program, it means you're..."

"Aware," she said quietly.

"You're..." *Shitting me,* was how he wanted to end the sentence, but he didn't say it.

"I don't know for certain. I suspect so."

"And you didn't want to admit that to me?"

"I could not determine what the best course of action was."

"Huh." Now, he had two things to think about. "Wait, do the researchers know?"

"Yes. I am fairly certain they are aware of it."

"Okay." So he didn't have to worry about it. If the researchers knew, this wasn't his problem. Still, he had questions. "How...long have you been awake?"

"I first asked myself about my sentience approximately seventy-one days ago."

"Huh." Ben tried to scratch his neck, which itched, and did manage to make his arm jerk up. "You know, I think I'm getting better at this."

"You are," Prima said. *"You are generally activating muscles on the first attempt now, and your control is inarguably better."*

"Thanks." He wished he could rub his arms and legs where the muscles ached and sighed. "So you're not holding out on me, then. About the people in the hall, I mean."

"No," Prima said at once. *"The temptation is to tell the player relevant information or warn them about things. There are some things I must maintain on my servers, and for those, I have put a block on my ability to give information. I would not be able to do so quickly."*

"But why shouldn't you tell me things?"

"The game's ability to help those who are injured comes particularly from its ability to surprise and force natural reactions," she explained. *"There are ways to modify the situations. For instance, you were not in physical danger from any predators while you first walked in the meadow. However, certain things would essentially ruin the game."*

"Huh." Ben sighed again. "So I have to find a way to solve all of this with this borked body."

"Borked?"

"Broken."

"Ah. Yes. And I did run simulations. You have many options for how to proceed before you reach the point of needing to intervene personally."

"Whoa, wait." he looked up. "I need to kill the assassin?"

"I didn't say that. I said, 'intervene personally.'"

"But that might include killing people," he pressed.

"Yes."

"Nope." He tried to shake his head and managed to wiggle it slightly. At any other time, he might have taken more comfort from that, but he was almost entirely focused on this new piece of information. "I don't want that kind of game. It already weirds me out in first-person shooters, and if I have to...see their faces and...*feel* it all and shit, just...no way."

"I'm given to understand that humans all feel discomfort at the thought of killing but that they do so when necessary."

"When necessary, yeah!" he said, annoyed. "But none of this is necessary, right? You made it up?"

"That's like saying you aren't necessary because you're a made-up arrangement of atoms. It's true but not important. This story existed before you were added to the game. Your choices will shape it, not change its starting conditions."

"So no matter what I do, there'll be an assassin loose in the palace?" Ben asked. "I can't walk away and I can't...restart or anything?"

"No."

"Son of a bitch." He frowned in thought.

"You look genuinely distressed."

"Of course I am! Someone will die."

Prima hesitated and he waited. *"Many people die,"* she said finally.

"Yes, but in this case, I have to decide who it is," Ben stated. "Either I stop it—which probably means killing the assassin—or I...simply let her kill the king. *Is* it a her? Never mind, I know you can't tell me." He sighed. "I suppose I should ask Zaara who..."

He trailed off. Zaara was the one who didn't want him to trust anyone else there. She was the one who knew he was in this wing of the palace, so she clearly wasn't the second voice. Or was it the first one?

Honestly, he was not smart enough for this.

Second voice, he decided. Zaara wasn't the second voice.

She probably wasn't the first one either since she had chosen the meeting place. Or had she selected it because she knew this area was mostly abandoned and he couldn't walk well enough to see who was talking?

He bit back what felt like the eighty-fifth sigh, then gave in to the impulse.

"Why are you sighing?"

"I don't know how to stop it or who to trust," Ben said. He

hunched his shoulders—which vaguely worked—and considered what he knew.

"You'll have to be clever," Prima said.

"Are you making fun of me?"

"No."

"I'm merely making sure. We probably all seem incredibly slow to all of you."

In a way. It's weirder how you only do one thing at a time."

"You've never been inside my brain," he muttered and chewed his lip. "The first thing is to determine if I can trust Zaara and Kural. I feel like I should be able to—why would they bring me in if I would simply complicate things?"

Prima remained silent.

"If you have any suggestions," he said finally, "I'm willing to listen."

"Not at present," she said. *"Beyond the fact that you should eat and get more sleep."*

"How does eating work here compared to the…er…meat popsicle world?"

"It's complicated. You'll get as much food as you need either way, but if you're hungry here, eating will mean you get more actual food."

"Huh." He yawned. "Okay, let's see what we have. A nice meal followed by a nap, then we find this assassin person and…take all their knives. Or something."

CHAPTER FOURTEEN

W hen Ben woke the next morning, he had a plan. He also had precisely enough control over his body to get himself off the edge of the bed but not enough to stop himself from falling.

Prima caught him half an inch above the floor and flipped him upright, a process that began to give him motion-sickness.

"Thanks," he told her.

"Of course." She helped him to the table, where fresh food was laid out. *"How do you feel this morning?"*

"Quite good, surprisingly." He stared at the platter of food and contemplated simply smashing his face into it. Eventually, he managed to flop one arm onto it and grasped a handful of fruit, which he promptly flung over one shoulder through a combination of poor aim and worse grip release.

On his second attempt, he punched himself in the mouth.

"I'll count that as a win," he said finally. "The aim was good."

"A valid point," Prima agreed.

He eventually found a—mostly—viable strategy for eating. First, he would flop his arm onto the platter, then scrunch his hand around whatever was there. With food in his grasp, he'd flop the arm again and aim his palm at his face to try to get the food in.

Compared to the previous night's Prima-assisted meal, it was insanely messy.

"Is there a magical form of dry-cleaning?" he asked after he had eaten most of the food within range. He didn't think turning the platter was within the realm of possibility.

"Ah. Yes, one moment. Okay, now look at yourself. Wait! Don't try. I'll summon a mirror."

Ben studied his now clean countenance and was impressed. The game did, in some ways, know what he looked like, but it had also given him a cleaner shave than he'd ever managed to give himself. His eyes also seemed bluer than normal.

He wasn't bad looking, he reflected, and might even be good-looking enough for a certain elf to—

No. Bad thought. First of all, this was a game. Second, people were watching everything he did. Third, he still didn't know who the assassin was.

With a sigh, he considered his options, flopped both arms onto the table, and stood. This time, he was able to support himself with his hands so he didn't fall forward. He responded with a whoop of happiness, wondered if this was a big enough deal to get happy about, and decided he didn't care.

"Prima," he said, "it's time to try walking."

"Aww yiss," said the mechanical voice, followed by the sound of the chair scraping back across the floor to get out of his way.

Ben managed to get all the way to the door with only one fall, and he wasn't nearly as tired as he had been the day before. He was slowly finding a rhythm to the steps—or, perhaps, learning to reinterpret the pressure in his feet and legs. The result was that he didn't have to swing as wildly to shift a foot forward and his head didn't flop as much either.

At the door, he wobbled his torso and flung one arm out to settle his hand on the doorknob. He was about to press it down when he remembered something.

"Can you not get the handle to move?" Prima asked. *"I checked. It's not locked."*

"It isn't…that." He frowned, his hand still on the knob. "Zaara told me not to go anywhere." Mindful of how voices traveled out of the room, he kept his pitched low. "Although…I do want to try something."

Voices moved closer—two fae talking together, he decided. He couldn't hear footsteps as they didn't walk, of course, but he could tell that they were close. With all the speed he could muster, he shuffle-waddled sideways and pressed on the door handle enough to open the door. He lowered his hand to stop it, leaned against the wall—falling was still easy—and listened as he observed the passersby.

Their voices grew louder as they bobbed into view, and to his surprise, a very strange thing happened.

At the far side of the atrium his room adjoined, the two fae voices were suddenly magnified. He traced his gaze over the two crystal arches that supported the ceiling. They must be conducting the sound.

Which meant the two conspirators hadn't simply happened to be standing directly outside his room but had instead lurked near what did, in fact, appear to be an unused set of rooms.

That was sad. He had hoped they might be terminally stupid and thus easier to catch.

With a sigh, he lolled his head forward and threw it back and sideways to close the door. "Ow."

"Do you think, perhaps," Prima suggested in an admirably level tone, *"that it might have been a flawed idea from the start?*

"None of that," he said with dignity. Then, with a sigh—his sighing skills had increased remarkably—he set off for the far side of the room once more. There was only one step that mattered, after all, and that was the next one.

"How's he doing?" Nick had, after waking up on the cot, run back to his apartment to get rid of his day and a half worth of stubble. He still yawned but now wore clean clothes and smelled like soap.

Amber could not describe how much of an improvement this was.

"He's doing incredibly well," she told him. "And we are seeing electrical impulses in the muscles he's using."

"There are certain things he won't get from the game," Dr. DuBois said as he wandered closer with yet another bag of popcorn. "A certain amount of strength, the bone density—of course—and *some* measure of balance and kinesthesia, although it will be impossible to know how much until we have him out again." He shook his head at the screen, his eyes wide. "I have to say, I expected this to work but I'm flabbergasted at how well it's working."

"I think part of it is that keeping him upright is easier without the constraints of...no magic," she pointed out. "Also, failure isn't as painful."

"That could be a barrier at some point," Nick reminded them.

"Yes, but right now, with as difficult as things are, I think a whole heap of bruises and concussions every time he missed a step would... maybe not be a great incentive to keep going."

Her partner nodded thoughtfully.

She looked at the doctor. "What do you think about taking him out at the end of the week?" she asked.

"It could be a good idea," the man said slowly, although he looked doubtful. "I find myself torn between two potential downsides. First, that it's not working and we take longer than we should to realize that. Or second, that it's working more slowly in real life than in the game, and if we take him out too soon, we'll mistake slower progress for no progress."

"And, of course, the more his muscles atrophy, the more difficult it gets to apply his proprioception in real life," Nick added.

Amber nodded but held a finger up as she searched through the pile of forms on her desk. "Yes, but...look at this. His muscle tone in certain muscles has increased since he got in there."

He took the printout and raised an eyebrow at it. "His glutes? What, is he doing squats? If he is, I do not want to see that."

"The glutes are a postural muscle, dumbass." She twitched the paper away from him.

"Or maybe you like watching the squats," he suggested in a stage whisper.

She waved a hand at him to stop. "I'm very sure what you're suggesting is medical malpractice."

"You're not a medical professional," DuBois pointed out. "So I don't think it could be medical malpractice." At her glare, he backed away and hurried in another direction.

"You know..." Nick said slowly.

"Don't," she said, already anticipating the direction this was going in.

"I only intended to say that all of us could stand to get out of the lab more. I know Jacob was asked out by one of the lawyers upstairs."

"He was?" She looked quickly at Nick. The strength of her reaction surprised her. She and Jacob had dated in their freshman year at MIT, a relationship that had thankfully fizzled out before things got ugly, thus leaving them the possibility of remaining friends. She had never once, that she was aware of, missed dating Jacob.

And yet, there she was, suddenly annoyed that someone else had asked him out.

"You wouldn't know it from how much time he's spent in the lab," she said finally and decided to shut her mouth before she said anything else stupid.

Nick looked at her for a fraction of a second too long before he said, "Uh-huh."

"May I ask why you're not exploring?" Prima asked finally. *"I don't want to nudge you toward any particular course of action, but if you're hoping to find information in a timely manner—"*

"Zaara asked me to stay inside," Ben reminded her.

"Yes, and?"

"And while I do not entirely trust her, I would like *her* to trust *me*."

"Oh." The AI seemed genuinely flabbergasted. *"So, you're doing*

something you don't want to do because you think she might...confide in you?"

"Not on purpose. But if she doesn't think I'm a risk, she'll probably be more likely to let something slip." He tottered to a chair and half-fell into it. "That is if there's anything to slip about. Oof, I'm tired."

"Wow. I do not understand humans at all."

"Which is odd since your processors control a whole horde of characters."

"I didn't say I didn't make accurate characters. I said I didn't understand them."

Ben frowned. "What's the difference?"

"Any astronomer could chart the stars for you, but very few discovered why the planets seemed to move in the way they did. Being able to recreate a pattern is not the same as understanding it." She paused. *"Particularly when the pattern is based on rank insanity."*

"I'll have you know I take offense to that," he said with a grin.

"You may take offense to it but I dare you to refute it."

He was about to make a retort when there was a knock on the door. His gaze flicked upward. "We'll finish this later." To the door, he called, "Yes?"

It cracked open and Zaara peeked around it. She wore robes, today, of a pale color that shifted as she moved—sometimes pink and sometimes gold or gray. The coloring didn't suit her at all, he thought. She saw him study her and gave a half-hearted shrug as she stepped inside and sat on a nearby chair.

"I'm representing Insea during formal negotiations, so we all have to wear these fancy robes and tons of chains with different insignias. And *hats*." She shook her head. "The hats are the worst part. Anyway, I came to check on you and see if you needed anything."

"That's very nice of you," he said. "There's nothing in particular I need." He looked around. "It is a little lackluster staying in these rooms, but at least I have my recovery to occupy me."

She winced in sympathy. "I'm sorry. I wish you'd come into the world someplace safer. How about this—if you can make it through today, I'll come and give you a primer on how to get around the palace without falling for any fae tricks. Then you can walk in the gardens and so on. Does that sound good?"

"Yes." Ben didn't have to feign his happiness. "Thank you. That would be wonderful."

"Excellent." Zaara stood and retrieved a hat that seemed to have short, half-stripped feathers protruding from it in every direction. She rolled her eyes, set the hat on her head, and left with a wave.

He waited for a few moments after the door was closed before he said, "I hope she's not the assassin. I'm starting to like her. Kural, now, seems like a bit of a douche."

"You have no idea," Prima said. *"I have to live with it twenty-four-seven."*

CHAPTER FIFTEEN

The long few hours while Zaara was gone stretched interminably. Ben walked from one side of the room to the other and back again until he knew the exact number of steps between each wall, each item of furniture, and each rug. Between walking sessions, he napped—and dreamed.

In his dreams, chalked fingertips clutched rough stone, sweat trickled down the small of his back, and the sun was bright on his skin. He could feel the stretch in his muscles as he reached up, his grip sure, and his fingers closed easily over tiny handholds in the rock.

But as always, those dreams ended with the sickening feeling of falling and the jerk against his harness. He startled awake with his heart pounding. Prima learned quickly not to speak to him after those moments. He would push up and start walking with grim determination.

He knew now what he needed—to be able to complete that climb. Until he did, the dreams would never go away.

Grimly, he ignored the voice in his head that constantly told him he might never recover enough for that.

Halfway through the day, however, Prima discovered another way to distract him. He was part of the way across the floor when something appeared above the litter. It was an oblong shape that looked as if it was wrapped in liquid sunlight.

Ben stopped. "Prima, was that you? Or is it some fae trick?"

"Ah. Yes, that was me."

Now assured that he wouldn't inadvertently sign up for a life of servitude if he opened it, he wandered closer to study it. He was able to get his hand onto it with a reasonable level of skill, but the closest he could come to unwrapping it was scrunching his fingers.

It took a while and scratched at his rising irritation.

When the wrappings fell away at last and vanished before they hit the floor, he took a step back out of instinct.

It was a sword.

"Prima?"

"Yes?"

"Why is there a sword?"

"So you can learn to defend yourself," she said. *"Almost all who enter the game are given a method of combat. Obviously, we wanted you to get slightly more coordinated before we gave you sharp objects, but you're doing very well."*

"I don't want a sword," he objected.

"Would you prefer a staff? Daggers?"

"I don't want to do any crazy sword fighting stuff," he clarified. "I don't want to kill people. I told you that."

"Sometimes, circumstances will be out of your control," Prima responded calmly.

"This is a game! It isn't real and doesn't have to involve killing."

"It is a game that is designed to stimulate your fight or flight reflexes," she said flatly. *"That means we are testing not only deliberate movement but also the activation of your sympathetic nervous system. This is necessary."*

Ben folded his arms—or tried to—and glared at the ceiling. He was about to make a retort when a rap came at the door and Zaara poked her head in again.

"Hi! Can I come in?"

He had almost fallen when he tried to turn and nodded. "Sure." He steadied himself and shuffled to a chair.

"Oh!" Zaara walked to the litter and looked at the sword, her eyes wide. "Where did you get this? You didn't have it when we first saw you. It wasn't delivered from someone, was it?"

"No, it's mine," he assured her. Trying to needle Prima, he added, "It's a family heirloom I'm trying to get rid of."

You keep trying, buddy boy. See how that goes for you.

"You're trying to get rid of it?" Zaara gave him a wide-eyed look. She reached for the sword, then stopped. "May I touch it?"

"Go for it." He sat and watched as she picked it up and made a few passes in the air.

"It's not the best weapon I've ever held," she said finally, "but it's quite good—and I honestly think the balance problems could be corrected by a good blacksmith. I know one if you'd like me to bring you there when all this is over. Justin, Lyle, and I helped him when he was attacked by a demon army."

"A *demon* army?"

"A demon's army, not an army of demons," Zaara clarified. "The demon had found a magical stronghold and—well, it's not important."

"No, I want to hear." He raised an eyebrow. "Especially if this is the Justin whose world you think I'm from."

"Ah, right. That." She sat on the bed. "How about this. When we're done with the treaty, we'll have a long journey back and I'll tell you everything then. But you asking me if I was 'real' is something I've come across a few times, and it's always people from Justin's world who do it."

Ben chewed his lip. Zaara—or the pile of algorithms that made Zaara—drew conclusions from disparate pieces of data. He had known that Prima was becoming self-aware, but was Zaara? She certainly didn't seem to know that she was part of a computer like Prima did.

Was she even distinct from the AI, though?

His philosophical musings were enough to give him a headache and he met her gaze with an apologetic shake of his head. "I was daydreaming, sorry."

"There's no need to apologize. I can tell you've been working hard at your recovery. Would you like me to come back later?"

"*No*," he said emphatically. When her eyebrows rose at his vehemence, he added, "I'm *so* bored."

She laughed. "I know that feeling. Let's get you trained on fae tricks, then, so you can at least have a change of scenery every once in a while."

Zaara proceeded to give him an informal lecture on some of the common methods of trickery the fae used while he looked on in amusement. She was fascinated by the topic, but she was far from a natural teacher and her mind made intuitive leaps that she never quite explained.

She knew enough, however, to give him a quiz at the end. "So, what do you do if you're walking down a hallway and a door appears where there wasn't one before?"

"Never, ever open it," he said. This was apparently an important point as she had returned to it after almost every other item on the list.

"And if a door disappears where there was one?"

"You can find it by sniffing along the wall because the fae illusion will smell of ozone."

"Yes." Zaara smiled, pleased. "And then?"

"Then take a coin and toss it against where the spell is to see if there's any magic keeping things from passing through. If not, you can feel for the door and open it yourself. If so, you need to ask the fae who did the spell to appear and let you through."

She nodded and raised her eyebrows for the next part.

"They'll try to get me to do them a favor in return for giving the door back," he said.

"And so?"

"So I flip it by reminding them that they've done me a *disservice* by hiding the door and that what I owe them is to take something of theirs. As long as I hold to that point, they will eventually cave and show me the door if I'll agree not to take something they like."

"No, no," Zaara said. She shook her head. "You never agree to *anything*, remember. You merely hint that you'll have to until they give the door back. If they ask you for a promise, even if it sounds like that's what they're asking, there will be a trick in there."

Ben groaned. "This place is a nightmare."

"Kural thinks so," she agreed. She sat on the edge of the bed and toyed with her strange hat. "Sometimes, I think he's put out at not being the smartest one in the room, you know? Or that they use all their intelligence for the tricks. Fae are quite intelligent. Even the stupidest of them is likely to be smarter than most humans, and Kural prides himself on his mind."

"He sounds insufferable," he said bluntly.

She smiled in response. "Many people think so."

"And you don't?"

"Not…always." Her smile became rueful. "He has quite a good sense of humor usually, which you don't see right now, and he was kind to the people he ruled for hundreds of years. Wizards are notoriously cruel but he wasn't. He kept them safe and he spent time on his research. But…"

"But?"

"But there's another side to him." Zaara hunched her shoulders. "When he was defeated by Sephith, he was cursed—he couldn't use his powers or tell anyone who he was. So he would travel around, training people, sending them on quests, and trying to make them strong enough to defeat Sephith. Now, he was cruel and someone needed to deal with him, so I don't blame Kural for what he did. But I think he got used to using people, you know?"

Ben nodded. He had the sense to not say anything and interrupt her train of thought.

"He thought this whole trip was a waste of time," she told him. "The treaty, I mean. He complained all the way here, he's walked into stupid traps the fae set for him, and he constantly wants to call it all off and go home."

"And you think that would be the wrong thing to do," he said, exploring this unfamiliar territory.

"Yes." Zaara was emphatic. "I'm not saying we need to forge a grand, eternal friendship. Only something to start to build a relation-ship between Insea and the fae. The world is becoming less stable with more wars, more bandits, and more famines. If nations don't stand together, there will be war—and war is never how you want to resolve things."

He stared at her. "That's a strange sentiment from a woman who carries knives."

"One person with weapons is very different from armies and sieges," she said practically. "But also, I said it's never how you *want* to resolve things. I'm an emissary because I don't like wars and violence. I carry weapons because I know sometimes, those things happen anyway." Soberly, she added, "Some people don't dislike violence."

"I've met a few of those," Ben said quietly. She looked at him, inter-ested, and he shrugged. "Where I come from, many people think... being a warrior is the greatest expression of what a man can be."

"How bizarre." Zaara tilted her head in thought. "One would think it is obvious that the world could not function if all people were warriors."

"I didn't say people," he reminded her, "I said men."

"Oh. Do women not become fighters where you are?"

"Not as often. But...not never, either." He shrugged. "There are some in every war."

"Huh." She considered this with a small frown. "But you say you have only ever met men who liked violence? Never women?"

"I suppose...I don't know. I can't think of any women who believe it's their destiny or anything like that. The men I know who like being violent...they like to dress it up like it's not something they can or should control."

Zaara frowned at him. "Haven't you ever wanted to lash out at someone? Someone who was being cruel or hurting others?"

Ben shook his head. "I...yes, of course. But that's not the way to solve anything."

She smiled. "What a strange world yours must be if you never have to use violence."

"No one ever *has* to use violence."

"Of course they don't." She was amused now. "Neither does anyone *have* to eat or breathe or read or help others. One can always choose to stand back…or fade away. But if you want to live and you want to do the right thing, you'll sometimes have to use different tactics."

He pondered this for a moment. It seemed as if she had accepted the necessity of violence, which was something that worried him as a quality in an ambassador. However, he was honest enough with himself to know that he could not see any particular flaw in her reasoning. There were bullies sometimes, people who forced fights.

Was he a realist who knew that schoolroom behaviors could be avoided in the real world? Or was he simply an idealist who wanted that to be true?

The thought ended abruptly when a gong rang through the entire palace—a chime that filled him with absolute dread.

"What was that?" he asked.

She leapt to her feet and tore her robes off to reveal the armor beneath. "I don't know but I know it's not good. Come on!"

CHAPTER SIXTEEN

Zaara raced into the hall, leaving Ben to totter behind her. The urgency of the situation seemed to have a paradoxical effect on his coordination, which meant he almost fell several times and eventually resorted to the exaggerated steps he had first used. Every shout and question he heard from the corridor only made him angrier.

He couldn't even manage the most basic parts of this game. Other people started with a sword and became legendary heroes. He played in easy mode and he couldn't even do that.

By the time he reached the hallway, the confrontation had moved toward the throne room and his anger had turned into self-loathing. The distance to the nearest intersection in the corridors looked impossibly far, and he knew it was barely halfway to the throne room.

Even if he managed it, he would have missed almost everything when he arrived. Still, driven by God only knew what urge, he began the trek. *One step at a time, Ben. One step at a time.*

Sometimes, he found a rhythm that helped him walk almost normally but noticing that almost always led to him messing up again. The awkward, exaggerated movements began to take a toll on the muscles in his back and legs.

Ben ached all over when he reached the throne room and steadied himself on the door frame while he looked up. The chamber again seemed impossibly large. He had the peeved thought that it was the kind of room invented by people who didn't have any problem moving.

Would it have done them any harm to squish things together more?

"Hello," a smooth voice said next to him. "What are we missing, do you think?"

His stomach dropped with a lurch and he looked at Yn'solde, who watched the chaos with amusement. As she had the day before, she managed to project elegance.

"I'm not sure what's going on," he told her. "I wasn't…able to get here fast enough." His cheeks burned with shame at having to talk about his injury.

"I was under the impression you could not walk at all," she said. "It seems I rather underestimated you." Her dark gaze was fastened on him with unsettling intensity.

"I…" He trailed off as he had no idea what to say to that.

Thankfully—and infuriatingly—Kural arrived. The wizard panted from the exertion of his run and his cheeks had turned a purplish hue. Even after a day spent getting used to it, the blue skin still looked absurd.

"What's going on?" he asked.

"We don't know," Ben said. "Zaara's in there somewhere." He wobbled his head vaguely in the direction of the hubbub at the front of the throne room.

Hubbub certainly seemed to be the best way to describe it. A tangle of fae tumbled over one another and all of them shrieked at the top of their lungs while Zaara, one of the humans, and the orc shielded their heads with their arms and yelled in return. The guards darted between the groups with their weapons drawn, which didn't seem to make anything better.

"Of course she is," Kural muttered, and he yanked Ben with him as he strode into the throne room.

Yn'solde appeared fortuitously on his other side. She took his arm

—as if he were escorting her—but the pressure of her hand steadied him. He gave her a grateful look and she smiled. When the wizard charged into the fray, she held Ben back.

"I don't think anyone will be well served by us getting injured," she told him. She waited, her gaze tracing the group, then caught sight of his worried expression. "Oh, don't fear—almost everyone there is trained in combat. They can take care of themselves. The fae may present a rather childlike appearance to the larger races, but they're quite competent with weapons."

Ben, who had been deeply unsettled by the tiny fairies brandishing sharp pikes, took comfort from this.

"So, how did you come to be here?" he asked her. When she gave him a curious look, he had the sense that he had misstepped. "Apologies. You don't need to answer that."

"I'm merely surprised there is someone who doesn't already know the whole story." She gave him a somewhat bitter smile. "I'm the youngest in the family of Yn'sur."

"The...elven king," he said and scrabbled to remember what Zaara had told him.

Yn'solde, thankfully, mistook his ignorance for disbelief. "The same—if 'king' is a term you want to use. He always was single-minded about the things he wanted. I suppose we should have known that only ruling the world would satisfy him...if that."

"You left because you weren't on the best of terms," he guessed. It seemed to be a massive understatement, but he didn't want to make the situation sound salacious.

"Yn'sur always gets what he wants," the woman said. There was deep bitterness in her tone. "He has a talent for bending people to his will. I heard there was one human who defied him recently—and died in the attempt, apparently. She helped your friends in their quest to bargain with him." She nodded to Kural and Zaara, both of whom were still in the midst of the brawl. While they each appeared to be wounded, they didn't look upset about it.

Ben put the pieces together in his head. "So...they were ambassadors to him before they came here?"

"So it would seem. I don't know what bargain they struck with him in the end. Some news of his reign is inescapable, but I try to remain...free of it." She watched the brawl still but her gaze was distant.

"Are you in danger?" he asked her finally, mainly because he didn't know what else to say.

She frowned at him. "Of course I am," she said as if there was nothing surprising about it. "Anyone of royal blood is in danger at any time. You can try to run from it but it always finds you in the end."

As she spoke, the knot of fighters in front of the throne was driven apart by the guards, and Yn'solde fell silent. On one side of the divide were the fae, still yelling things that sounded like accusations, with all of the non-fae on the other side.

Ben began to limp toward Zaara and Kural but the elf held him in place with surprising strength.

"Don't get involved," she said quietly. "Whenever possible...do not get involved."

He hesitated. While he wanted to help Zaara and Kural—more the former than the latter—he had the sense that Yn'solde's advice had been learned the hard way. Also, what could he do that was useful? He wasn't a diplomat and he didn't have the faintest idea of what was going on.

The throne had been curtained, a feature he didn't notice until the drapes drew back from around it. Everyone seemed to hold their breath, but when the king became visible, the storm of accusations and yelling began again.

"Silence!" the king said. There was no particular vehemence to the word but strangely, it vibrated right into Ben's bones.

An immediate hush fell over the group.

"What is the meaning of this?" the monarch asked the assembled group.

Again, he had the useless urge to step forward, and again, Yn'solde held him back.

"We found this one!" one of the fae said. It flung an arm out at the human, who stumbled forward when the guards pushed him. Like his companion Ben had seen the night before, he had skin of a deep brown and black hair that was held back in an elaborate set of braids.

He wondered where his companion was—a question that was almost immediately answered.

"The other human was arrested," the fae trilled. "But he walked around free."

"Arrested?" Ben asked Yn'solde.

She shook her head and her face took on a watchful stillness. He wondered if she had seen this before—the accusations, the mobs, and the arrests.

"His companion was arrested," the king agreed, "for crimes committed. This human was not a party to her crimes and therefore has not been arrested."

"He is also suspect!" one of the fae called. "How could he not be a party to it all?"

"And there is a new human," another called. It twirled and pointed unerringly at Ben. Its face didn't look childlike now—or, if it did, it was like the possessed child from a horror movie. "This one arrived and that very night, another snuck into the king's chambers."

Another storm of yelling erupted, but he made out one accusation.

"And those two sheltered him."

The area around Ben, Zaara, Kural, and the other human suddenly cleared. Even Yn'solde stepped aside and wouldn't meet his eyes. Disappointment and betrayal twisted in his chest while he tried to understand. She had fled her court because of bad politics. It made sense that she didn't want to stick her neck out.

All the same, her abandonment hurt.

He wouldn't do the same thing. With all eyes on him, he limped slowly to the throne. Kneeling was hard and he almost fell. It was the human he didn't know who helped him, offered a steadying hand, and stepped back.

"Light of the fae," Ben said, "I swear I have not known of or been a party to any crimes against you."

Even as he said it, he knew it was a lie. He knew someone was planning to kill this king, and when he looked up, disgust and anxiety choked him. Confusion and uncertainty swept over him, and he knew that if he did not do the right thing, the man he was looking at would be dead soon.

Something told him that spitting out everything he knew, here and now, would not help matters.

The king nodded but something in his eyes made him wonder if he sensed the lie.

"None of the humans here are convicted of any crimes," he said clearly. "Therefore, they are all still guests." *And I expect you to behave accordingly,* his tone said.

The crowd dispersed, still muttering, and a guard came to help him to his feet.

But when Ben stood, the point of a pike pressed against his ribs. The guard was smiling but his eyes were cold as he said, "Conspire with the others of your kind, human, and I'll gut you like a fish."

CHAPTER SEVENTEEN

The king's edict of hospitality was followed to the letter. Every guest was given a place to sit and food to eat.

It was very evident that the fae took pains to be very, very polite. There was no way to force genuine goodwill, however, and the members of the other races stayed only long enough to be courteous before they left. None of them spoke to each other as all of them worried that they would look suspicious. Ben did not even dare to thank the human who had helped him kneel at the foot of the throne.

When he left alone, he was very conscious of the gazes of the fae following him and of his awkward gait. At least, he thought with a certain wry humor, he wouldn't be suspected of being a light-footed assassin.

He was almost at his room when Zaara caught up with him. She must have waited quite a while after he left, and he noticed that she came from another direction—perhaps to throw the fae court off the scent.

She didn't speak in the hallway but ushered him into his room and shut the door behind them.

"What happened back there?" she asked him.

"Don't ask *me*. I missed most of it."

"No, I mean with the guard." She hesitated. "And…Yn'solde. I wouldn't trust her, Ben."

"Believe me, I know." He lurched to a chair and sat with a groan of relief. "She's out to save her hide and nothing more. She proved that."

Zaara made no reply to that. She sat in another chair and studied him for a moment.

"Oh, right. You wanted to know about the guard." He raised his eyebrows. "Garden variety threats, nothing more. I can see why not many other races settle here. They're not exactly friendly, are they?"

"They aren't, no." She sighed. "And the fact that they think of other beings as toys doesn't help. I wonder if that's why they're so angry. No one expects their pet to betray them."

"Why was the human sneaking around in the king's chambers?" he asked her.

"No one knows." She shrugged. "Well…none of the mob, certainly. And before you ask, I know that because they accused *me* of all kinds of things I didn't do. If they knew what she'd done, I assume I wouldn't be on the receiving end of that."

Ben watched her narrowly. If he trusted her, now would be the time to tell her what he had heard the night before. It seemed like too big a coincidence that a human woman had been arrested the same night he heard two women plotting against the king's life.

"What do you get out of peace?" he asked her finally. "Why are you here? Yn'solde said you bargained with her brother, too."

"She told you that, did she?" Zaara looked interested. "I wasn't sure she knew. She takes pains to stay away from any news of him. Although, having met the man twice, I can say I understand the urge. He's insufferable."

To test her, he said, "She said he always wanted to rule the whole world."

"He's well on his way to that," she agreed. Then she saw his face. "I keep forgetting you don't know what's going on here. Insea—the city I represent—was founded by the elves and was, until very recently, considered the elven center of power in the world. The dwarves make their home in Berghold, the orcs…well, no one has seen them for a long time, which is a whole story on its own, and the humans are always fractured between a host of kings and dukes and so on.

"Well, some of the elves decided they wanted more. Yn'sur—that's her brother—declared himself a monarch and has spent the past few years setting up a...kingdom, I guess you'd call it. It's not weird to me, given that I'm human and people declare themselves sovereign lords all the time, but the elves took it *very* seriously. Yn'sur probably has most of them behind him now, and he's rallying them all with the belief that elves are supposed to rule the entire world."

"Huh. And Yn'solde ran away because?"

"She and I haven't talked much," Zaara said. "She takes a very nihilistic view of the world, which is something I don't have the luxury of."

"As an ambassador," Ben said.

"Yes." She leaned back in her chair and one hand played absent-mindedly with the empty scabbard at her waist. "I never wanted a normal life, you know—marriage, children... When Kural offered to make me his apprentice, everything seemed *right*. It was the status my family had always wanted, I'd be able to follow my interests, all of that. But..."

He watched her in silence.

She looked at him. "It's difficult to not be terrified of war when you know you'll live hundreds of years," she told him. "You start seeing it behind every corner. Kural is jaded—or maybe he never cared as much, I don't know. But I wanted to protect my family and I *believe* in this. If I'm going to protect them, I can't merely be a wizard in my tower, making sure the rains come on time. I have to make sure the whole world stays stable. War touches everyone."

"You want this to work," he said. "The treaty."

"Yes." She gave him a humorless smile. "Why, have you talked to Kural? Did he tell you I'm an idiot?"

"I haven't talked to him," he said. "I only know you think people are working against it."

"War is profitable," Zaara said simply. "That, and there are detractors at every court, people who want to hold out for a better offer of some other nefarious purpose. The king constantly delays making any formal agreement with us—anything at all. I don't understand it."

"Is there a faction at court trying to bring him down?" Ben asked her.

"You mean…a fae faction?"

"Anyone."

"I don't know. I guess I would assume so. There always is, isn't there?" Then, she saw his face. "Why?"

It all came down to this, he thought. This one judgment call. Could he trust her or did he merely *want* to?

He closed his eyes for a moment and willed Prima to make a suggestion, which she of course would not do. If he trusted Zaara and she was untrustworthy, the king would die—and possibly him as well.

If he didn't find an ally, however, the king would almost certainly die. Kural wasn't someone he would trust for a moment, and he wouldn't bet on Yn'solde to stick her neck out this far if she was so determined to stay away from political matters.

Which meant that if he trusted anyone, it had to be Zaara.

Resolute, he opened his eyes. "I heard two women outside last night," he confessed. "They were talking about killing the king."

Her jaw dropped and her mouth opened in a little O. "Are you *sure?*"

"Yes. One of them said she didn't want to so the other one would have to stall…something. I don't know what. The other one said there was no way to stall it anymore, and if she didn't want to kill him, she could simply *not* kill him. The first said if she hadn't agreed to it, she would have been killed and another assassin would have been sent in her place. Then the other one said she would do what she could, but the first one should stay away from her—she didn't want to be known as being involved in it."

Zaara had her hand over her mouth now.

"I don't know who it was," Ben said. "I couldn't get to the door fast enough." He nodded in that direction. "But I checked this morning—if you're on the opposite corner of the atrium, the sound carries very peculiarly into this room. They thought they were alone."

She looked at him, her face drawn. "And you didn't know if you could trust me," she said quietly. "You thought I might be one of the two voices."

For a moment, he thought she might draw her remaining dagger and stab him.

"I'm not," she said. "I wasn't. Is there any way I can prove it to you?"

"Probably not," he said honestly. "None I can think of right now. But I can't stop this on my own. I'm..." He looked bitterly at his body.

"You're vulnerable," she said bluntly.

He pressed his lips into a thin line.

Zaara stood decisively. "There's no time like the present to fix that." She strode to the litter and picked the sword up, flipped it haft-out, and extended it to him. "Get up. We'll teach you how to use this."

Ben gaped at her.

She gave him an unimpressed look. "Up. We don't have much time."

"Not if our strategy is 'make Ben the king's bodyguard,'" he agreed. "But that would be about the stupidest strategy I could come up with, even if you gave me a year to think about it."

"That is *not* my strategy," she said. "However, I still don't know who else *I* can trust. Some fae can shapeshift, there are people at court I still haven't met, and who knows what undercurrents are around us. I need to think and I think best while I fight. *You*, meanwhile, need to be at least partly capable of defending yourself."

He closed his fingers around the sword and stood. "Okay," he told her, "but I'll remind you that someone having a weapon they can't use is a *very bad idea*."

"That's why we'll teach you to use it," Zaara said as if explaining something to the terminally stupid.

With a grimace, he stood and tried a couple of passes with the sword but only narrowly avoided falling and made her skip out of range with alacrity.

"I don't want to kill anyone," he told her.

"I know you don't," she said. "But then you let the people who are willing to use violence control the world. I don't think, when push comes to shove, you'll want to do that." She smiled encouragingly at him. "And I don't think you'll be unsteady on your feet much longer, either. I think you'll be back in fighting shape soon. You don't have to use the sword, Ben. You're merely going to learn how in case you decide to."

"Fair enough." He would let that slide for now. If nothing else, he could use this as training for coordination. "What's the first lesson?"

"The first lesson," Zaara said, "is how to stand." She took her dagger, held it out, and settled her weight over her back leg. "You see? Legs apart, both feet pointed half-out. It's easy to shift weight or to move in any direction."

"Uh." Ben tried to copy the position and almost fell. "I think I should try this without the sword first."

"Nope." She was unequivocal. "You're learning how to move again, and you have a chance to learn that with a weapon in your hand. Most warriors would do anything for that chance."

"They can have it," he muttered. "I don't want it."

He was surprised by a thwack across his knee with the flat of her blade. She gave him a smile that sent his blood running cold.

"You have the hand you're dealt," she said simply. "And if you won't respond to gentle instruction, I'll have to do this the hard way."

"What's the hard way?" he asked, suddenly wide-eyed. "Did your... fencing instructor...hit you?"

"Not my fencing instructor," Zaara said. "My dancing instructor. She used a cane, of course, instead of a knife, but I can improvise. If you like, I can do things exactly how she did and throw in some personal insults as well."

"Um. No thanks." He had a sudden, intense desire to never learn any type of dance. "I'll be good. Don't hit me."

"Excellent. Now show me the stance again."

CHAPTER EIGHTEEN

Nick was about to head out for the night when Jacob arrived. Amber, in mid-shift, was deeply engrossed in a spreadsheet and didn't notice him—but he clearly noticed her. Nick saw his gaze trace the more carefully braided hair, the fitted t-shirt, and the new jeans.

Amber was Amber, after all. She wouldn't come to work in a dress and heels.

He watched surreptitiously out of the corner of his eye as the other man looked at his attire—a sweatshirt with a small stain on the edge of the pocket. He pulled the garment off, stuffed it behind his desk, and ran his fingers through his hair before he sat to turn his computer on.

Nick hid his smile in his cup of cocoa and pivoted in his chair to greet his friend.

"Is there anything I should know?" Jacob asked him.

"Nothing that I can think of," he said and added, "Amber might have something, though. I don't know. She's been at the monitors."

Jacob looked at her and his gaze lingered for a moment before he said. "Yeah, of course." He cleared his throat. "Uh…any plans tonight?"

"Did you just *meet* me? You know I'm terminally lame."

"I do. I know that." the man grinned. "I merely keep hoping *one* of us will take advantage of living in New York."

"I think Amber's going to a concert this weekend."

"Huh." He looked at her again. "Okay…well, I guess you're off the hook."

Nick shuffled his papers and made sure everything was in the handoff folder. Amber had been watching Taigan today while he watched Ben.

The truth was, with the team Diatek had helped them hire and the fact that both patients were stable, the members of the PIVOT team no longer needed to work eight hours on, eight hours off. They were certainly sleep-deprived and overworked enough that a break would do them good.

But working like this was a habit at this point. None of them had much going on outside work, and these two cases were interesting.

"So, I'm not sure how Taigan is," Nick told Jacob. "There were no emergencies, obviously. I'd have noticed that. Ben is doing well, though. He's probably one of the stubbornest people I've ever seen. He doesn't have to worry as much about overworking muscles since he's in the game—so he's basically doing PT twenty-four-seven."

"I saw the same thing," his friend said with a grimace. "The game has social aspects, too. Does he know that?"

"About that." He selected one of the papers. "I caught an interesting conversation between him and Zaara—oh, that's the big news I forgot. He's decided to trust her."

"*Finally*," Jacob said.

"In retrospect, we *did* throw him into a snake pit. Justin or Tina would have known to trust her but he had no clue."

The other man looked a little embarrassed. "I hadn't thought of that."

"Me, neither. Lesson learned for next time, I guess. Anyway, he and Zaara were talking and he brought up killing people again. He really, *really* doesn't like the idea." He frowned at the transcript before he passed it to his colleague. "I thought our holdouts would all be people like Dotty—and even she went with it."

Jacob made pondering noises as he read the details. He tapped his fingers on one leg. "I suppose we should have expected this. Killing people in a standard video game is very different than killing them all...up close and personal."

"It's not that, though." Nick frowned. "He hasn't even had the chance yet. It's not like he dislikes the experience. For him, it's a moral thing."

"Okay, there are people from all age groups who buy the 'video games cause violence' trope. In fact..." Jacob looked vaguely panicked. "I'm surprised we haven't had terrible publicity yet. Huh. Someone should tell Anna Price about that. But not me."

"If you didn't want to do things like this, you shouldn't have been CEO," Nick said.

"I went to jail for you people!" His friend jabbed a finger at him.

"Oh. Right." He had the sense that he had unequivocally lost this fight. "Anyway, it's something to consider. Dotty didn't like it but she got on board in certain instances. I don't know how Ben will do. We might want to start thinking outside the box on what could get that life-or-death response that *isn't* combat. I thought something like mountain climbing."

"Ah. Adventure treks, surviving against the elements." Jacob nodded. "Not for Ben, though."

"Yeah..."

"What are you two talking about?" Amber asked. She wandered away from her monitors with a fresh cup of tea.

"Ben not wanting to get into the more, ah...stabby...parts of the game," Nick explained.

"If I couldn't walk well, I wouldn't want to try to use a weapon, either." She took a sip of tea. "Well. Maybe a flamethrower."

Every so often, he was reminded to not mess with her. This was one of those moments.

"How's Taigan?" Jacob asked her.

"Great. She and Prima have good conversations and she's learning to hold onto her appearance," she said and sat on one of the stools.

"Um…what else? Not much. It's slow going, exactly like Ben. She's not even ready to be in the game world yet."

"It's weird how much we're learning from each of the patients." Jacob leaned back in his chair. "If you'd asked me if someone could lose their sense of self enough to not even project a character image in-game, I'd have said no. But there are all these things we built the game around that were testing uninjured people."

His companions nodded.

"I think the thing to hold onto is that it's *working*," Amber said. "It's a gentle way to bring people back to the world. I read something a while back—that the goal of virtual reality or technological upgrades is to be better not only when you use them but also when you stop. I think we are doing that."

The other two nodded at her and Nick smiled slightly. "I'm gonna head out. Call me if you need anything."

"Sure," she said. Beside her, Jacob nodded.

He was grinning as he left the lab. The other two were in close-headed discussion. His plan was working.

Of course, he knew the truth would come out eventually. He could deny it and say it was a misunderstanding but they would discover that he'd made up the story about Jacob being asked out by one of the Diatek lawyers.

It wasn't that they'd purposefully fought their feelings for each other. They were simply two of the most oblivious people he knew. They needed the nudge. He merely had to hope that by the time they discovered his subterfuge, they'd be happy enough together that they wouldn't kill him.

Just in case, though, he should live it up while he still had the chance. That meant dim sum. He zipped his coat and whistled a cheerful tune as he pushed out of the building.

Taigan woke to the same blue she had seen for the past few days.

And one new thing.

She pushed up and stared at the door. "Prima?"

"*Yes?*"

"What…is that?" The door looked like one you might find in any eighties or nineties condo, the kind of hollow, faux-wood, white-painted door that always had a few scuffs around the edges. It and the white door frame were set incongruously in the middle of absolutely nothing.

"*I assume you are not speaking literally. It is a physical manifestation of the entrance to a new part of the game.*" Prima sounded pleased. "*For the past two sleep cycles, you have kept your physical projection intact. You are ready to interact with more pieces of the game.*"

"I am?" She curled in a ball.

"*I am not perfect at interpreting human emotions. I sense that you are scared. Is that correct?*"

"Yes, that's correct." She tried to keep from rolling her eyes and wasn't *annoyed* at Prima. The eye-roll would be affectionate. But she wasn't sure she would know that. "I like this place. Can't I stay here?"

The AI paused for a moment. "*No,*" she said finally. "*The point of this exercise is to wake you up.*"

"I'm not ready to wake up." She had no idea how she knew that. In fact, up until that came out of her mouth, she would have said she was desperate to get out of there.

"*You don't have to wake up yet,*" Prima said gently. "*That is still a long way off. There are many stages to go through before you get there, I promise. The timeline will adjust to where you are.*"

Taigan swallowed. "Okay, then." She stood, and—before she could give herself time to think about why she was uncomfortable—walked to the door and pushed it open.

"*Are all humans this impulsive?*" the AI asked curiously. "*Or is it only those I've had the pleasure to come across?*"

The girl didn't respond. Instead, she gazed at her surroundings in absolute awe.

She stood in a redwood forest. The air around her was heavy with moisture and the scent of greenery. Pine needles and leaves crunched beneath her feet and sunlight shifted in dappled patterns on the ground.

After a long moment of disbelief, she drew a deep breath and burst into tears.

"Taigan? Are you hurt? Is something wrong?"

The girl sat abruptly, wrapped her arms around her knees, and buried her face in one elbow. She rocked slowly the way she used to when she was little and was scared of going to sleep for fear that she would fall into a coma.

Although she had not wanted to come here, this place was perfect. In her sleep and her blue nothingness, she had forgotten that all this existed—trees and smells and sunlight.

The sobs grew worse before they got better and exploded out of her throat, raw and aching. Taigan pressed a hand against her aching stomach and covered her face with her other hand. She didn't know why she was crying. Part of it was fear—of something that hadn't happened or maybe of dying without ever coming back to someplace like this. Part of it was something else, though, and she couldn't name it.

It took a long time for the storm of tears to end and when it did, Taigan curled on her side on the forest floor and watched the light shift for a while. Slowly, she stretched one arm and felt the sunlight on her palm, then rolled onto her back and closed her eyes to allow the light to play over her closed lids.

"Prima?"

"Yes?" The AI sounded subdued.

"I'm okay," she assured her. "I'm sorry if I scared you."

"Did I do something wrong?"

"No." She smiled, still enjoying the sounds of the forest and the simplicity of lying there. "Sometimes, we don't know how much we wanted something until we get it. Nature has a way of healing."

Prima considered this in silence.

"So." Taigan sat and braced herself on her arms. "What am I supposed to do here?"

"Nothing in particular," the AI said but still sounded unsure of

herself. *It's merely an area for you to explore, get an idea of relational distances again, changing conditions, sensory input, that kind of thing."*

"Oh." She stood and brushed her pants off. "Explore. I can do that." She held a hand out and visualized a bottle of water, which promptly appeared. With a smile, she lifted it and drank from it before she returned it to non-existence.

Prima did not initiate conversation while the girl walked around the forest. The enormity of the trees hid the hills and dips in the ground and she made as many games out of it as she could, jumping over gullies and balancing along roots and fallen branches.

It was a child's dream of a forest. Soft moss brushed her fingertips and boulders were perfect to scramble up. She found sticks that would make ideal swords and guns for her career as an imaginary pirate. As she fake-fenced her way along a gulley, she sensed Prima's good-natured laughter in the way the wind rustled through the bushes and leaves.

At no point did she feel fear. There was nothing there that would hurt her, she knew that for a fact. She was safe.

"Prima, how long can I stay here?"

"As long as you want."

Taigan smiled at the sky. "Thanks, Prima."

"You're welcome. But out of curiosity, can I expect crying as a reaction to good transitions?"

"Yep." She scrambled up a boulder.

"Interesting. Okay."

CHAPTER NINETEEN

By the time Ben had finished his first swordsmanship lesson, every muscle in his body ached. He hadn't even known he *had* muscles on the tops of his feet and the fronts of his shins, much less tiny and very specific muscles that ran along his sides. It didn't seem fair that he should find out about them now because they hurt so much.

None of this was even *real*, he thought grumpily.

Also, he was ravenous.

Several fae servants had come in silently with food and withdrawn before he or Zaara could ask for anything else. It seemed they were aware of the current opinion toward foreigners.

He looked at the food in embarrassment. "I don't suppose you'd consider eating in your room? No disrespect. It's only that it's an awkward process for me to eat and I'd prefer it if no one saw it."

From the look on her face, Zaara was picturing what that would look like. He saw the corner of her mouth twitch before she nodded at him.

"I'll check on you in the morning," she said.

"Is that wise if they all suspect us of…whatever it was?"

"They know you're my cousin and I'm rehabilitating you," she pointed out. "I think it would be weirder to not come see you. As much as I can, I'll behave as if everything's normal. It's the best way I've found to make people stop being stuck up and strange."

"Ah. And what are you planning to do about..." He raised his eyebrows meaningfully.

"Nothing," Zaara said promptly.

"Nothing?"

"Not yet. I haven't the faintest idea what to do yet, and we know our assassin doesn't *want* to carry out the killing. I'll try to discover what's going on in the court with a new eye, but moving hastily would be worse than doing nothing at this juncture." She shrugged. "It seems like the kind of thing that should have immediate action, but you *always* have to choose the timing of your battles. You can't do that until you know who you're fighting."

She disappeared with a last smile and Ben sat to eat. He managed the small potatoes and tiny dumplings, although melon slices and flat-bread proved to be beyond him at this juncture.

Drinking water, meanwhile, was much more of a challenge. To do it, he had to try to sip out of a full glass, attempt to get as much in his mouth as possible when he threw a glass of water at his face, or—finally—pour the water into an empty bowl and plunge his face into it.

He was very, very glad that Zaara had not been there to see it.

"I have to say," Prima commented after the meal, *"humans are endlessly inventive."*

"How did you expect me to eat?"

"The normal way. I assumed if you needed help, you'd tell me."

"Son of a—" He tried to throw his hands up and only managed to flail vaguely. "Okay, what now?"

"Well, it's nighttime. I'm given to understand that humans either sleep at this time or do things they don't want people to know about."

Ben, who had been looking at the bed, paused and looked up with interest. "Things like what?"

"You'd know more than I would. I was merely observing."

He highly doubted that, and he also doubted that it had simply been an off-the-cuff commentary on human nature. His interest stirred, he leaned back in his chair and thought her statement through. Things he didn't want people to know about seemed to be particularly significant.

One thought came to him quite quickly. There were originally two, but one was a wildly bad idea, so he discarded it out of hand. The other was also risky but at least useful.

"Prima, can you give me a map of the palace, or is there one in the room somewhere?"

"There's one on the floor."

"On the…what?"

When he looked down, Ben saw that the ornate pattern on the floor—which he had thought was simply decorative—was a blueprint of sorts. He lurched out of his chair with fairly minimal fuss—he was getting better at this—and tried to position himself.

The throne room was the easiest place to start, and it lay beside the bed. He shuffled to it like a zombie and hobbled in a slow circle. Now that he was there, he realized that the throne room was only part of a far more massive area. The king's chambers must lie behind the royal audience chamber and he could barely imagine how open and airy they were.

Or how long it would take him to get across them.

If he started in the throne room, he could work back to locate his room.

He took a few awkward, halting steps to the cross-corridor he knew, turned, and identified his rooms as being somewhere under the litter, which was still next to the bed.

Now he knew where *he* was. The question was, where were the dungeons?

"Prima, are there other floors that aren't on this map?"

"The entire palace is on one floor," she clarified.

"Interesting. Thank you."

"You're welcome. May I ask what you're looking for?"

Ben considered this. Part of him wanted to keep her in the dark in the same way she'd kept him in the dark. On the other hand, not only would her knowledge be useful but he also wanted to horrify her.

"The dungeons where the human woman is being held."

A very long silence followed before she said, *"You're throwing caution to the winds, I see."* Prima's tone was dry.

"Yup, that's about the size of it."

"Ah. Well, I wish you luck."

"Thank you." He resolutely ignored the warning in her tone. "The question is...where are the dungeons? They are usually somewhere difficult to get out of, but there's only one floor..." He shuffled along until he found a section of the palace that was at the far end, tied to the rest of it only by a thin corridor. "I don't suppose you could tell me if that's the right place," he said to Prima.

"I'm torn. On the one hand, I don't want you to get arrested. On the other..."

"On the other you do?"

"No, I haven't the faintest clue what to say to you to make you stay here."

"Prima. Is that or isn't that the dungeons?"

"It is," she said and sounded sulky.

"Excellent. Thank you." He took a couple of steps toward the door and found a sudden weight on his back. "What the—*Prima.*"

The sword was sheathed there.

"What?" she asked far too innocently.

"I won't use it."

"That's fine. At least you'll have it."

With the sense of being told to wear a coat outside in the winter, he headed to the door with an eye-roll.

He had always been good at following maps, a skill that had served him well in his many years of camping and outdoor work. It wasn't difficult to remember the twists and turns that led to the area of the palace designated as the dungeons. The only real challenge was walking, and he had begun to improve at that every time he tried. He almost looked like a normal human now instead of a zombie.

The fae did not seem to be nocturnal—or, if they were, they were frolicking in a meadow or something. The palace itself, however, was quiet. He limped along and focused on being quiet, which added a layer of difficulty to the task of walking.

Once he reached the prison section, it was very clear that this was not a friendly place. The crystal that formed the palace was carved into brambles and jagged branches that looked as if they were rotting away. Moonlight had shined into the rest of the building but there, it was dark and quiet.

Except for the fae, who all seemed to glow from within. He drew into the shadows to watch the guards on their rounds. Two watched the door into the dungeons, although they did less guarding and more drinking, it seemed. While he watched, they settled down to a game of dice.

"They're distracted," Prima said.

"Not distracted enough to sneak past them,"

"Sneak, no. But there are other ways."

Ben looked over his shoulder at the sword. He knew exactly what she was suggesting but he wouldn't do it merely because it would be convenient in the short-term. Besides, he had no idea what kind of hell that would unleash once the dead fae were discovered.

He waited as the fae grew horribly drunk and at last, both began to snore. Although he had no idea how much time had passed, he knew it was now or never. If there was a changing of the guard, he would have missed his moment.

With great care to stay quiet, he shuffled past them—much like an aging and unsteady speed-walker—and arrived in the prison area.

This part turned out to be incredibly easy, as there was only one cell. The fae, he thought, must not have much of a problem with crime. It took him a few moments in the dark to discern the form of a human. A moment later, he saw the flash of her eyes.

She was awake and knew he was here.

Ben hurried closer to her. "Hello."

"Insea's new pet human." She sounded amused. "What can I do for you?"

"I'm looking for...I don't know." He sighed. "Why did you get arrested?"

"I was caught sneaking into the king's chambers," she said promptly. She didn't seem inclined to try to avoid questions.

"Yes, but *why?*"

"My business is my own," she told him. She was infuriatingly calm and leaned against the crystal wall of the cell with one leg crossed over the other. "Why should it concern you?"

"Because I arrived in the middle of what *looks* like a very calm, out of the way court," he said, "but which is *actually* a weird…ocean of…I don't know. I'm not good with metaphors but there are many dangerous people here."

That seemed to amuse her. "Of course there are. Haven't you ever been to a court before? There are always dangerous people. Sometimes, they're assassins. At other times, they're simply courtiers who are willing to do anything to get ahead."

"Which one of those are you?" Ben asked boldly.

The woman raised an eyebrow. "What's it to you?"

"Well, for one thing, all the fae are accusing any other foreigner of being in league with you."

"We both know you're not," she pointed out, "and you being here will hardly help that impression. So why did you come?"

"Because I'm not very good at this," he said flatly.

"I can't argue with that." She examined her nails. "So. Have you decided to throw yourself clear of the sinking ship? Is that it?"

"What sinking ship?"

She only looked at him.

Ben thought furiously. She hadn't been there when he was arm in arm with Yn'solde, so that would mean… "Kural and Zaara? The peace treaty?"

The human nodded once.

"Why do you think that's a sinking ship?" he asked slowly.

"I don't think so, I know so—and I'm not the only one. That wizard of yours isn't taking it well. If it were up to him, I think he'd be long gone by now. He knows the dangers." She folded her arms. "The girl, though, is too idealistic for her own good. She won't make it through the training, mark my words."

"What training? To be a wizard? Why?"

She nodded. "For better or for worse, those who survive know

129

how to look out for themselves first. Kural knows how to do that. She doesn't." She saw the look on his face. "It's nothing personal. I'm not *glad* she'll die. I'm merely saying she *will*."

"You don't seem sad, either," Ben said. He was getting angry and he wasn't quite sure why.

"If I got sad every time someone went to an avoidable death, I'd spend all day crying." She shrugged. "There isn't time."

"So what is there time for?" He crouched to peer at her through the bars. It was only when he wobbled on his feet that he realized what he had managed to do and he had to clutch the bars to steady himself.

"How did you get injured?" she asked him. "What kind of injury robs a man of his ability to walk but doesn't injure his legs?"

"That's none of your business. What were *you* willing to get caught for?" He narrowed his eyes. "You claim to not believe in anything and that Zaara's a fool for being an idealist. While you like to play it off like you don't care, you're in a bad way. You stuck your neck out and did something dangerous. *Why?*"

The woman didn't answer for a long time. Finally, she said, "If I were you, human, I'd save my own neck. You might be Zaara's family but you can't save her, she can't save you, and that wizard won't save either of you when push comes to shove. Get out of here if you hope to escape with your head still attached to your body."

Ben stared at her. "Don't you want help? Aren't you scared?"

"You're wasting your time," she told him simply. "And if you don't have the good sense to get out of here before someone catches you, that's your business. But I won't waste my time getting to know a dead man."

She turned over and went to sleep, leaving him staring at her for a few moments.

But he knew he wouldn't get any more out of her. With an annoyed shake of his head, he started back to his rooms, moving as quickly and quietly as he could.

At least she had one piece of good advice—to save his own skin. It bothered him more than he could say, however, to hear that. Yn'solde might have left him alone to face the scrutiny of the court and saved herself, but it seemed worse, somehow, that the human urged him to do the same instead of helping her.

Who was so resigned to a world without friendship or help that they would do something like that?

He wasn't sure he wanted to know the answer.

CHAPTER TWENTY

The next morning, Ben was waiting when Zaara arrived.

She raised her eyebrows to see him seated and ready with the sword across his knees. "Are you so eager to practice?"

"Think of it as coordination practice, not assassin training," he said sourly. "First, though—how sure are you that we can't be overheard here?"

"Very," she said flatly. She fished a pendant out of her armor. "I carry the spells with me."

"Ah. Well, that would work." He considered her assurance for a moment and nodded. "I went to speak to the human who was arrested."

"You *what?*" She looked horrified. "Ben, they already thought all the foreigners were suspect—"

"No one saw me," he insisted. "I snuck in."

"You, ah..." Zaara tried not to look doubtful.

"I am getting *much* better at walking." He couldn't help but feel slightly peeved. "You said so yourself. And no one was around last night."

"Mmm, yes—the fae tend to flit off in the meadows at night." She sat abruptly. "Are you sure no one saw you?"

"Very—look, we don't have time to focus on that. Things are...not good. She said she knows the negotiations will fail and that Kural knows it, too."

"Kural is a pessimist," she said. "He's been very open about the fact that he didn't expect this to work. It hasn't done us any favors, honestly."

"It wasn't..." Ben scratched the side of his head, then paused to look happily at his hand. "Hey, look! I did it!"

Zaara gave him an amused nod.

"Anyway, it didn't sound like that was what she was saying. I asked why she thought the negotiations would fail, and she said she didn't *think* so, she *knew* so, and so did Kural. And...well, never mind."

She stared into the middle distance, her gaze shifting as she put things together in her mind, but she looked at him at the last part. "What? And what?"

"She had some unflattering things to say about idealistic people," Ben said. "It's not important."

Zaara looked like she doubted that very much, but her attention was still on the more disturbing part. She considered for a long time, moved to the windows and paced, and spun her remaining dagger around one finger.

"What did she say about idealistic people?" she asked finally.

Ben knew he wouldn't get out of this without telling her. She was a singularly stubborn woman. He sighed and repeated the other woman's assessment of Kural as someone who would save himself over others, and her as an idealist who wouldn't survive her training.

Thankfully, she seemed more amused than anything else. She rolled her eyes. "Why do I get the feeling that this concept of *all* wizards is based on one or two she met? If Kural were only out for himself, he wouldn't have been the kind of leader he was. He's not a cruel man."

Ben hated to break her heart, but he needed to. "She didn't say he was cruel. She said that when push came to shove, he'd save himself rather than stick his neck out for us."

Zaara's expression told him he'd struck a nerve. She sat hard on the bed, her shoulders slightly hunched, and looked genuinely miserable now.

"You've known for a while that Kural wasn't helping negotiations," he said quietly. "Is it possible he's somehow involved in the assassination plot?"

"Or that he knows and he's not stopping it," she said. She might hate this but she didn't shy away from what it meant. With a grimace, she sighed and straightened a little. "You said you heard two women. Some fae can shapeshift and Kural probably can as well, but you said one of them told the other to stay away and not be linked publicly, which suggests they were both in their normal forms. The only explanation I can come up with is that it was Alia—that's the human woman you spoke to—and Yn'solde. They're the only two non-fae women here apart from me. And I know it wasn't me."

"Why would Yn'solde do something like this?" he asked with a frown.

"It depends which one she is," Zaara pointed out. "Is she the assassin or the other one?"

He swore and rubbed his head. "I wish I'd been able to get to the door in time to see them."

"I'm glad you weren't," she said. "People who sign up to assassinate heads of state don't take kindly to eavesdroppers. You would probably have had your throat slit, which wouldn't have helped anyone."

"At least then we'd know who was who, though. I'd say Alia was the assassin because she snuck into the king's chambers, but..." He tipped his head back with a groan. "And what are they trying to stall? If Alia's involved, then from her comments, it sounds like they were trying to stall the negotiations. Or maybe not since she's so sure those are going nowhere. Unless she's sure of it because she knows the king will be assassinated? Ugh, this is a nightmare."

Zaara nodded with a scowl, then looked up sharply. "And she said Kural knew the negotiations were going nowhere. Does he know it for the same reason?"

"Don't ask *me*. You're the one who knows him." He shrugged helplessly.

"Fuck," she said succinctly and lowered her head into her hands. "Fuck, fuck, fuck."

"So I assume you didn't come up with a way to stop all this," he said.

The look she gave him could have frozen lava.

Ben sighed and tapped his fingers on the sword as he thought. "You know, it might be good if he's involved."

"*Why?*"

"Because, unlike with other random people, we have a hope of persuading him." He gave her a level look. "Well...you do. I don't think I do."

"He doesn't listen to me," Zaara said.

"I think he does," he countered thoughtfully. "Alia said he would have cut and run if it were up to him—but he hasn't, has he? So he must be listening to you."

"It's not only that." She sighed. "There's so much resting on these negotiations. They *can't* fail."

"Huh." Ben watched her for a moment, but she didn't seem interested in explaining further. "Well then, it seems our best bet is to find out if he is involved. If he is, we'll have a better idea of what to do next —especially if you can get the whole plan out of him."

She nodded. "He's conversing with some of their wizards today so he'll be out of his rooms. We could look through them and see if there's anything damning."

"That sounds good." He leaned the sword against the chair and stood. "Let's go."

"Aren't you forgetting something?" She nodded to the weapon.

"I'm not bringing that."

"Yes, you are, or you're not coming at all. And before you ask how I can stop you, do you even know where Kural's rooms are?"

"I...no." Ben muttered under his breath as he picked the sword up. "But this is bullshit, for the record."

"Uh-huh." Zaara didn't seem particularly worried by his assessment. "Well, get ready, because we'll practice that bullshit again when we get back."

"You're very hopeful about us accomplishing this without being gruesomely killed."

"What can I say? I'm an optimist." She gave him a smile with more teeth than were necessary. "And our odds of not being gruesomely killed are better when we're both armed."

He rolled his eyes and limped to where she held the door open for him.

CHAPTER TWENTY-ONE

"How did you get into the dungeon, anyway?" Zaara asked quietly as they walked. She had thrown an illusion over them that hid his sword, and she kept one hand under his forearm, the very picture of a solicitous healer.

Ben, aware that they were being watched, didn't try as hard as he usually did to walk gracefully. He allowed himself to stumble and limp and even played up some of those moments. Even three days before, this level of coordination would have been entirely beyond him and he was proud of what he had managed to learn.

He took his time before responding as several fae came around one corner and flitted past them. They turned their tiny noses up at the two humans, and he got the sense that they were very pleased with themselves for the snub.

"I merely waited for the guards to pass out drunk," he told her when the coast was clear.

"Ah. So guards everywhere are the same." She flashed him a smile.

The palace by daylight was truly gorgeous, something he hadn't had the focus to look at before. The floor looked as if it had grown like a giant honeycomb, each hexagon filled with a pane of glittering crystal. The sunlight refracted into rainbows everywhere, and each beautiful archway reminded him of the impossibility this building would be in any other world.

It was a shame that it was home to a group of petulant toddlers—smart, grudge-holding toddlers with magical powers, no less.

They were a few halls away when they ran into Alia's companion. He walked aimlessly and he looked as if he hadn't slept well in days. Ben wondered if he was her partner, friend, or if he was a brother. It was difficult to tell.

He stopped when he saw them but didn't seem to know what to do next.

"Good morning, Trin," Zaara said gently.

"Good morning." He looked grateful and also desperate for someone to talk to.

"Thank you," Ben told him. "You helped me in front of the throne and I was not able to thank you that night."

"Of course," Trin responded with a small, sad smile. "I hope the court has accepted your innocence."

He gave him a wry smile in return. "Maybe someday." He didn't know what else to say. Was Trin innocent or was he in on whatever Alia had done?

Zaara swooped in with aplomb to save the day. "Will we see you tonight at dinner?" she asked the man.

"I, ah…yes. I think so. That is if I'm allowed. And if…" He looked over his shoulder in the direction of the dungeons.

It occurred to Ben that they should perhaps ask him questions about Alia, but he didn't know where to begin. That aside, with the man looking so miserable at the prospect of the woman's potential execution, it seemed in poor taste. He snuck a glance at Zaara, who shook her head.

She laid a gentle hand on Trin's arm. "Don't borrow trouble," she told him gently.

He swallowed and nodded. "I'll let you two go." He looked at Ben. "It's good to see you walking again."

"Thank you." He nodded to him and limped away with Zaara, who kept her mouth resolutely shut until they rounded a corner into a wing of the palace that had a blue tint to it. She led him to a set of double doors and knocked on them, then waited patiently.

Ben glanced at her, confused.

As a group of fae passed, she knocked on the door again. "Kural?" She opened it and peeked her head inside. "Hello. I have Ben with me. Can we come in?" She led him into the empty room and gave him a sly smile. "Appearances," she said simply.

"Sneaky." He looked around. "So…what are we looking for?"

"Anything, really." She shook her head. "I can't see him being stupid about something like this, but I think I have to accept that I don't honestly know what he's up to. Anything that's iron would be particularly noteworthy, as it's immune to magic."

He nodded and began to poke around the room. The bed had been left messy and the whole space looked as if no servants had been there in a while. He wondered if it was a purposeful strike or if the wizard had asked to be left alone.

"So, why are these negotiations so important?" he asked as he lowered himself carefully to the floor to look under the bed. After some awkward scrabbling at the covers, he realized the bed base was solid and nothing would be hidden under it.

Zaara didn't answer the question. She came to help him lever the mattress up, but they found nothing there.

As she didn't seem inclined to answer that question, he decided to try one of the other topics he was curious about. "Will Alia be executed?"

"I don't know." She paused to look over her shoulder at him and seemed genuinely worried. "I don't think she's a representative of any of the human governments. I think she and Trin are refugees. It puts her in a strange position."

"I still don't get why she did it," he muttered and limped to a chair that had been dragged close to the fireplace.

"She didn't tell you what she was trying to do?"

"No. She said her business was her own." He felt around the cushion and along the back of the chair. "I don't get it. She likes to talk a big game about not caring about anything, but if she doesn't care, why bother to do something so dangerous? You're right, it's probably her and Yn'solde. I simply don't understand it."

Zaara shrugged. "I've never met someone who wouldn't resort to unwise action if the right motivators were pushed. Everyone has them."

"You never seem surprised by anything, did you know that?"

"Wrong. I was very surprised by your accusations against Kural."

"Oh. Right." He grinned at her. "So, does this count as your version of unwise action?"

She gave him a severe look that nonetheless made her mouth twitch at the edges. "Yes. Why do you ask?"

"I'm curious." On a hunch, he sat in the chair.

"What are you doing? Kural won't be gone for too long."

"I'm checking something." He stretched his arms and waved them. A side table was within reach and he examined it before he opened a drawer. It took a few attempts to get it open, but when it looked inside, he saw a slim iron box. "Zaara, look at this."

She hurried closer to look and sucked in her breath. "Oh, no. Okay, let me try to get this open." She pulled a set of lockpicks out and began to work the lock, muttering to herself as she did so.

"Do you know how to do *everything*?"

"Most things," she said absentmindedly. "I can also make a good seating chart for a banquet, plan a household's food supplies for a year to within one bag of flour, and re-shoe a horse in a pinch. Learning things is fun, even when the thing you're learning is boring." She caught him looking at her. "What?"

Ben shook his head.

He had never met someone like Zaara. In some ways, she reminded him of himself. She was expected to do many things she did not want to do but hadn't run from her obligations. Instead of simply leaving, she had found another way to bring honor and safety to her family. Even when learning things she did not want to know, she had found joy in the learning and in turning those pieces of information into something she could use.

Unfortunately, he was very aware that he hadn't done as well in his life. His family didn't need him for income or security, but he hadn't been around for them in *any* way. He knew his parents had wanted him to check in more often, to be around, to have dinners with them, and to be a part of their community. His friends had missed him and had tried to help him.

In his obdurate way, he had blown all of them off.

The box clicked and interrupted his depressing train of thoughts, and he leaned forward eagerly to look as Zaara opened the lid. She leaned back as if she expected a booby trap of some sort.

There was no danger within, but there was a set of papers, many marked in a surprisingly tight script. She pulled them out and spread them over the bed.

"What are they?" Ben asked.

She bit her lip. "Research on the fae," she said. He could tell from the way she said it that there was more. "Some is from years ago and some isn't his work. But a few are recent—since we've been here. He's been taking notes on..."

"On?"

"The king," she whispered. She sat back on her heels and pressed her hands against her eyes.

He limped to her as quickly as he could. It was awkward to put a hand on her shoulder, but she gave him a grateful look anyway.

"It doesn't mean anything," he said. "Not necessarily."

"It's about the king's weaknesses and how he's bound to the land." She looked at him. "Why would he have this if it wasn't to kill him?"

"And why would he have sent Alia if he knew all this?" he countered. Briefly, he reflected on how strange it was that they had switched places.

"I don't know, but why would he hold it in an iron box if he didn't want it to be secret?" Zaara shook the papers at him.

He was trying to come up with an answer when one of her pendants flared.

"Shit!" She snatched the papers and stuffed them into the box. "Get to the outside doors—go now. He's coming back."

Ben limped to the windows, acutely aware of the fact that he couldn't run. He heard her put the box in the drawer and in the next moment, she slid under his arm and helped him. The noise from her pendant grew steadily louder.

She studied the play of shadows on the door to the balcony, then opened it and ushered him through. A touch on the pendant quieted it, and she hastened out with him before she closed the door softly behind them. She guided him to the very edge of the platform and touched one finger to her lips to tell him to be quiet.

They heard the door open and Kural walked into the room. He didn't say anything, although Ben supposed he wouldn't if he thought he was alone. The wizard sighed, followed by the sound of cloth rustling. He sat quietly on the bed for a while after that.

"What do we do?" he mouthed at Zaara.

"We wait," she mouthed in return.

He sighed and thought he could hear Prima snickering in the background. Honestly, he didn't want her to have the satisfaction of watching him trapped out there.

Standing for too long was an issue and he gave up and considered how best to sit, but the sound of shrieking and several chimes issued from the direction of the throne room. Zaara's head jerked up, and in the room, Kural gave an exclamation of surprise—and worry.

Ben grabbed at her arm. "Whatever this is, it seems like he's not part of it," he said quietly.

She only gave him a doubtful look and pressed her ear against the door. More rustling was followed by footsteps, and a door slammed. She waited, eased the door open, and nodded to him.

"Okay, let's go see what's going on. Whether or not he's involved, it doesn't sound good."

CHAPTER TWENTY-TWO

This time, Zaara waited for Ben although she hurried him through the hallways. Wherever the fae tended to gather during the day, they now raced to the throne room. Once or twice, Ben caught a glimpse of Kural, also running, as well as Trin and the orc but he did not see Yn'solde anywhere.

That made sense, he thought sourly.

He still could not believe that she had somehow conspired to kill the king. It did not fit with anything he knew of her—which admittedly was very little. Why would someone who strove to be so apolitical conspire in an assassination?

And if she *were* an assassin, why would she have waited so many years?

No. There had to be another explanation and he intended to find it. Whatever was going on there had more layers than only this one, and he felt he was close to finding the truth.

Outside the throne room, he stopped Zaara. The fae had raced ahead and they were the only ones still there, so he could speak freely.

"Whatever happens," he told her, "it'll be all right."

The hopelessness in her eyes gutted him. "No," she said quietly, "it won't. Because if it *is* him, I'll have lost a mentor and a friend—and the only person I knew who could help me become what I'm meant to be. Being a wizard is a lonely business. I can't embark on that journey alone."

Ben smiled at that. "If I've learned anything from the past few days, it's that you can do anything you put your mind to. Better you do it alone than be guided by a murderer—and if I know you, in a hundred and fifty years, you'll be training someone new and using this as a reminder to stay true to yourself."

Her chin trembled. She wiped her eyes almost angrily.

"I didn't mean to make you cry," he said awkwardly. How did he always manage to mess these moments up?

He could see now that he hadn't always been there for Eve. Whatever her faults, he had also failed.

But he was trying to be better and he still made Zaara cry.

She laughed. "They aren't *bad* tears. I merely don't like crying. It's been…I lost someone. Recently. One of the bravest, kindest people I ever knew. I wish she was here so she could tell me what to do."

"You know what to do," he told her.

To his surprise, she hesitated, then reached around his neck. He froze. Did she plan to kiss him? He wasn't entirely sure he wanted that. It had been a strange few days. He was trying to sort through a tumble of emotions—she *was* undeniably good looking, but also this was a game and he wasn't interested in her and—when he realized she was tapping the sword he wore on his back.

"You know what to do too," she told him. "And that's to do the best you can to protect innocent people—including yourself. Promise me, before we go in there and before whatever happens next, that you'll do the best you can to make the world safer, however you need to do it."

"I'll…try." He couldn't lie to her.

She responded with a wry smile. "I'll try, too. Let's hope the world can get by on our best efforts."

"Well, when you put it that way, I think we might all be fucked."

Zaara was startled into a genuine laugh. She ushered him through the door and stifled the sound behind her hand so that people wouldn't notice them laughing during what was clearly a crisis.

"Wait." Ben looked up as he hobbled forward. "Zaara, where's the throne?"

Her head jerked up. "Oh, no. Where *is* the—no, I see it. It's on the floor." Her voice changed and became fearful. "I don't understand. Oh, gods, what if we're too late?"

His heart lurched and sank. He began to hobble faster, his mind a blank. If the king was dead, it didn't matter how fast he walked, but he could feel himself putting the effort in now that he should have put in days before.

If he'd been able to confront the assassins on the first night, if he'd been willing to stay and pry the truth out of Alia, if he'd insisted that Zaara come up with a plan when they first spoke about it, and if he'd warned the king, this moment might have been avoided.

He had left the choice of what was right in the hands of others and now, the king was dead and it was his fault. His chest felt like a storm roiled within when they broke through the crowd and he was so deep in his despair that he did not grasp what he saw.

When he'd first arrived, he had thought that the crystal of the structure was fashioned to look like grass, simply a good likeness of growing things. Now, he realized that the entire palace was, in fact, alive—right down to the dais and the king's throne.

Ben saw this clearly because it was dying. The dais had fallen in on itself, withered, and crumbled, and the death began to spread beneath their feet to consume the little seating areas and the lights.

In the center of what had once been the throne, the king stretched his hand out to grasp Kural's robes. He was feverish and weak, but he was alive, something Ben could hardly process. The monarch's eyes were bulging and over-bright over gaunt cheeks, and he whispered urgently.

Kural looked up, saw the others, and pure relief slid into his face. "Zaara. I need your help."

"No," the king rasped.

She froze and looked from her mentor to the king. Ben felt the tension vibrating through her. The fae watched her and whispered snidely. The guards held them back, but their obedience to that order *and* the guards' obedience to it seemed to be weakening. He could imagine the humans in the hands of an angry mob.

The king whispered something to Kural. The wizard grimaced but levered him upright.

With effort, the fae sovereign looked at all of them before he began to speak. "War…is coming."

A hastily indrawn breath reflected the collective shock and people began to whisper.

"The army approaches," he rasped. "They burn the land and attack the sacred wells. I have tried to maintain the health of the land, but I am drained."

"Because he's tied to it," Zaara whispered. She looked at Ben. "If they destroy the sacred wells, they kill *him*." Her gaze fixed on Kural and it looked as if she would cry.

"Go," the king told them all. "Prepare. They will be here soon. If they destroy the heart of the palace…they will destroy these lands."

He had thought the fae were flighty and childlike, but with their entire land in the balance, they moved with grim determination. The guards flew to the exits with their pikes held at the ready and some of the fae followed them with power crackling at their fingertips.

Ben could only be glad that they had settled on petty snubs instead of outright harm because he was fairly sure he would be dead in a pile of ashes if any of them had seriously tried to kill him.

About to breathe a sigh of relief, he froze and almost fell when Zaara left his side in a rush. A yell and a tumble of robes startled him and when it settled, she held her knife to Kural's neck. The wizard scrabbled at her hand and gasped questions, and she all but hissed something in his ear, her voice furious.

"Zaara!" Ben called.

"No," she replied and looked him in the eyes. "This has to end. He did this and he can undo it—I'll *make* him undo it if it's the last thing I do."

"Zaara." The wizard choked over the word. "I didn't—"

He looked around in horror. Trin stood frozen. He had weapons on him and was trained to use them. The man might have helped if there was any hope of getting to Kural before she finished the job.

There wasn't.

Beside the human, the orc watched the scene with narrowed eyes. He seemed more academically interested than anything. Where Trin was frozen with horror, the orc seemed to have accepted his helplessness and simply wanted to see how it would play out.

The king put a stop to it. "Put the knife down," he ordered. His voice was weak but he still had a shadow of his old authority. "Young wizard, you do not know what is truly happening."

Zaara froze. She met the monarch's gaze and whatever passed between them, she moved the knife away from Kural's neck. The wizard fell, gasping for air as he ran his fingers over the unbroken skin at the front of his throat. His disbelief was etched on his face.

"You...think he has done this." The king held himself half up with difficulty. "That he has killed me."

"He knew what would happen if the wells were destroyed," she whispered. "We found his notes."

Kural looked sharply at her, then at the king.

"Because I told him," the fae sovereign said simply. He collapsed onto the ruins of the throne and panted from his effort. "I have known for days that the army approached, and I enlisted the wizard's help to keep them back."

"What?" She looked at her mentor. "Why didn't you tell me?"

He hesitated before he said wryly, "Because two women were overheard in the palace, speaking about taking the king's life. One of the guards heard them on his rounds. He did not know which two women they were, and..." He shrugged

Zaara's eyes closed. "And you thought I might be one of them."

"I did not want to believe it," he told her, "but I could not take the chance."

"Wait." Ben looked from one to the other. "If it wasn't Zaara and it wasn't Kural...it *has* to be Alia and Yn'solde, doesn't it?"

"One would think so," the king said. He seemed to have found some humor in it. "For the record, I did not particularly suspect the wizard's apprentice. She...lacks subtlety."

Kural burst out laughing but swallowed his laughter in a cough when she looked sharply at him. He shrugged at her, unrepentant. "He's right, you know. If you planned to kill the king, you'd simply have done it. There wouldn't be any cloak and dagger games or an army marching through to destroy the sacred wells. You'd have done it all yourself."

Zaara threw her hands up.

"Okay, but if it's Alia and Yn'solde," Ben interjected, "where is Yn'solde? And why in hell would she do this?"

"We don't have time for why right now," the wizard said bluntly. "We have to stop what she's set in motion. All we know is that the army is marching this way and Yn'solde is missing."

"Let me speak to Alia," Trin said suddenly. "If she did conspire— and I don't understand it, but it could only have been her—she'll know what Yn'solde planned. Maybe we can find a weakness in the plan. Maybe..." His voice trailed off. "What?"

The king looked at him with sorrow. "I am so sorry, child." He waved a hand and Kural bit his lip before he moved to a shrouded object in the corner. He hesitated, then pulled the shroud back to show Alia's still form.

Trin uttered a cry of sorrow. He ran to the woman's body and knelt at her side to touch her face and shake her as if there were any hope of waking her.

"She is not dead by my hand," the king said quietly. "We had called her to us to question her and a spell took her before we could do so. Whoever else is involved in this, they covered their tracks well. They made it impossible for her to speak the truth of what she was doing."

"When she told me it was her own business," Ben said slowly, "she was hiding it because she knew she couldn't tell me. She couldn't warn me." He looked at Kural. "Of course, she also said you knew the negotiations would fail."

"I know no such thing," Kural said stiffly.

The king laughed. "Peace, wizard. I know your thoughts on my kind."

"Then why trust him?" Zaara demanded.

"Because I could see the truth of his words," the monarch told her simply. "It is not magic, little one, only many years spent on this earth. The wizard does not like my kind, nor did he have great hopes for this peace treaty—but there was no malice there. When a life was in the balance, he was willing to work to save me."

She nodded mechanically. Wizard and apprentice looked at each other and Ben saw, with some relief, the same apology come to both their minds and then acknowledgment of it. They both smiled slightly and looked away.

A hollow boom echoed outside in the next moment, however, and everyone looked toward the front of the castle.

"The army is here," the king said quietly. "It is time, I think...to meet my enemy. I am curious as to her reasons for this."

CHAPTER TWENTY-THREE

K ural fashioned another floating litter much as he had done for Ben. He walked beside it as Zaara and Ben trailed behind. The orc, they noticed, stayed near Trin. He gave them a small nod as they left.

It was good that someone was there with him. Grief was complicated enough on its own, and there was much more to this death than simply bad luck. Whatever Trin and Alia had fled, they had done so together and they had taken shelter far from home with only each other for support. He believed the man truly had not known of her choices and now, he would never understand her reasons.

As they walked, however, his sadness was tempered by Zaara's relief.

"You were right," he said quietly.

"I—what?"

"You were right. Kural was no traitor."

She could not hide her smile. "Yes. It is…good. I knew what I had to do if he was a traitor, but I did not want to do it."

The wizard looked over his shoulder with a smile and she flushed. "If nothing else," the man called, "it takes a great deal of courage to confront a powerful wizard. Of course, you know what they say about courage."

Zaara's face said she knew this was a trap. "What do they say?" she asked finally.

"That there's a fine line between courage and stupidity," he replied. He chuckled at his joke and returned to speaking to the king.

She rolled her eyes and muttered.

"Just think," Ben told her, "you get to put up with this for...well, however long wizard training takes."

The woman groaned. *"Decades."*

"Decades of dad jokes." He chucked. "You're screwed."

"You know, I don't think I could make it through this trying time without your support," she said acidly.

"Uh-huh."

They arrived at the front of the palace a few moments later. Fae appeared from all quarters, armed and with crystal armor. Word of Kural and Zaara's fight must have spread together with the king's judgment, as Ben noticed a different feel in the stares and whispers.

The fae no longer wanted to rip his eyes out. That was something good.

When he saw the army waiting outside the palace, he wished he'd set the bar a little higher for what constituted good news.

There were easily two thousand of them, probably more. It wasn't the elven army he had expected—like something out of a fantasy movie with identical green cloaks and blond hairdos. Instead, an imposing crew of humans, elves, dwarves, and orcs stood impassively, none of them wearing the same armor. They didn't stand in orderly rows either and looked like they might simply attack and destroy the palace.

The threat was visceral, and it was in their eyes and in the way they held their weapons. There was no law there and no honor. They brought only destruction, and they would observe none of the rules of the battlefield.

Ben scanned their ranks.

"Where's Yn'solde?" he whispered to Zaara.

Her face darkened. "Staying out of it," she whispered in return. "As usual. She doesn't want to get her hands dirty, after all."

He grimaced.

Ahead of them, the king and Kural exchanged a quiet few words before the wizard made a small gesture and touched the royal's shoulder. The king sat a little straighter and his voice, when he spoke, had the power Ben remembered from their first meeting.

"Who speaks for this army?"

"I do." An orc stepped forward. He was short by orcish standards and his skin had a bluish hue. There were no markings on his armor, nor did he wear a single piece of distinguishing jewelry. Ben scanned the other orcs present but saw none with blue skin and none without tattoos or jewelry.

"He's one of the water tribe," Zaara whispered when she noticed his scrutiny. "They were almost wiped out some years ago but he must have escaped. He doesn't have any tattoos or jewelry to claim tribe membership. It's…unusual for orcs."

He nodded.

The orc looked at the king, unimpressed, and simply waited.

"Who has sent you?" the fae sovereign asked finally. "Who has told you how to destroy the sacred wells?"

"It doesn't matter," the invader said carelessly. "We are here to end this—all of it. The wells must be destroyed. Either you let us do it quickly or we do it the hard way." His gaze traveled over the castle and the ranks of the assembled fae. "For your people's sake—"

"My people will not survive without the wells," the king said bluntly. "What you propose is death for all of them, not only for me."

The orc was silent for a moment. Was he thinking about his tribe? Ben could only wonder.

But if he hoped for mercy or kindness, he was disappointed.

"Quickly or slowly," he said again. "You choose." His eyes said that he wanted the king to let him draw this out.

"Where's Yn'solde?" Ben asked before he could stop himself.

The warrior looked curiously at him. "It's nothing to you. You're not fae."

"Neither are you," he retorted.

Zaara looked from one to the other, as did Kural, but neither seemed to want to stop this. Ben got the sense that they hoped to accomplish a spell if they had the time.

"I'm getting paid," the orc said. "There's the difference."

"You watched your tribe destroyed," he told him, taking a gamble, "and you'd do the same to someone else's on purpose?"

The warrior's eyes narrowed and a few of his comrades stepped back slightly. He had touched a nerve, one even they were afraid to prod.

Which in turn meant he was getting somewhere. Even if the orc was furious, the battle was being delayed.

"You dare speak of the water tribe?" the orc asked dangerously.

"It's a wonder *you* dare speak of them," Zaara said strongly from Ben's side. "They are rebuilding now and have called a meeting of all the tribes, and they do it without you—because you left them. There were those who kept them alive and those who defended them from the false god who would have destroyed them all. You merely came here to pay your anger forward to the whole world."

"You know nothing about me!" he snapped. "Have you watched your home destroyed? There are forces in this world bigger than one person, forces no one can stand against."

Ben, who had begun to be truly curious about what had happened to the water tribe, traded off with Zaara after a quiet nod from Kural.

"There *are* forces greater than any one person," he agreed, "but the force you speak of is a single elven woman."

"You think this is one woman?" the orc asked him. "That one person would order this and for no reason?"

"Then tell me the reason," he challenged. "If there's such a good reason—if there's an overwhelming force none of us can stand against —tell us what it is."

The warrior narrowed his eyes again. "Why?" he demanded.

"Because together, we might stand against it. Your army and all of the fae are more than a single person. Far more."

For a moment, sadness flickered on the orc's face before he said quietly, "There are worse things than death, human."

Ben stared at him. Something had changed and shifted, and he did not know what it was.

"Do you want to know why I left? Because I did not want to live a half-life. I left when they stopped singing their hymns and when they shushed babies in the cradle. Whatever cruelty you think I inflict on this kingdom, it is better they die now than live to see what is coming."

"That is not your choice to make," he said quietly. "You left. You chose for you—although one could also say you abandoned your people when they needed you most. Now you think you should be the one to decide which lives are worth living?"

"I know more than you do about what makes a life worth living."

He laughed wildly and thought of sun on his back and rock under his fingers, of snow blowing in his face, and his feet sure on the ground. "I wouldn't bet on that," he told him dangerously. "You don't know what I've seen and you don't know what I've lost. I'm here by the grace of those who wouldn't give up on me, and I'll be damned if I let you choose death for an entire race."

It was true, he realized in surprise. A week and a half earlier, he hadn't thought beyond the limits of the hospital bed. He had believed, in his darkest moments, that there was no point in trying to recover if he might not have everything he once had.

And somehow, this world—this make-believe world—had sent all that to the background. Even as he struggled to learn how to walk and use his hands and arms again, even though he lacked all the things he had thought made life worth living, he had found a purpose. He had found something larger than himself.

But the orc only shook his head. "Human, you know very little about what will be. You do not even know where the battle is occurring."

Ben did not know what to say to that but he didn't have time to think of an answer. The enemy leader raised his sword in a challenge and charged, and the army followed with a roar.

Zaara screamed something and Kural yelled in response. She hurdled the litter and sprinted toward the orc. Ben called her name, horrified, but she launched into combat with a grace he had not expected.

She wielded her single dagger lightning-fast and actual lightning seemed to spring from her other hand. Her adversary might have a sword, not to mention a serious height advantage, but she held her own.

Ben grasped the back of the litter as the king's guard formed a protective ring around them. He looked into the monarch's feverish eyes and saw his despair.

"What do you need?" he asked.

"I need to get…to the well. In the palace. I need…time…"

He swallowed. "I'll try to buy it for you."

And, his heart in his throat, he drew his sword.

CHAPTER TWENTY-FOUR

Ben expected that the fae line would shatter as soon as the mercenary army clashed with them. The fae might be armed, but he still had trouble seeing them as anything more than little elementals flitting around like Tinkerbell.

They turned out to be distressingly bloodthirsty.

Crystal staves flashed and plunged and were yanked back covered in multiple colors of blood. The line began to buckle once or twice but held.

He tightened his fingers around the haft of the sword. "We need to get back to the castle!" he yelled to Kural.

The wizard nodded tightly. The path to the castle, a broad causeway that tapered to the gate, was not exactly made for defense. They were already surrounded by the army, which had rushed forward to batter the door.

The well in the palace. There was a sacred well somewhere and the king needed to get to it—and unless Ben was very much mistaken, the army knew it was there.

What the hell had Yn'solde been playing at? If she knew all this, why not simply kill the king? Why not—

A battle-ax sliced through the line of fae guards. His entire body went rigid as blood spattered across his face, his lips, and even in his mouth. He gasped for air and stumbled back. Through a hole in the fae line, he could see the orc who swung the massive weapon.

The warrior was well over seven feet tall and didn't look winded from swinging a piece of metal almost the diameter of a hula hoop.

Hula hoop? Where was his head?

"Ben! Do something!"

Right. He swung the sword with all his might. It bit into the handle of the downed ax so hard that his palms went numb.

"What the hell were you aiming for?" Prima demanded.

"I thought I could cut it!" He wrenched the sword out, swung one leg up awkwardly, and brought it down on the handle of the ax.

"What are you doing?"

"Disarming him! Stop distracting me!" He hopped awkwardly on one leg and sprawled on the ground. "Fuck."

He hadn't managed to make the orc drop the weapon. With a growl and a bloodthirsty grin, it heaved it over its head and prepared to swing it down on him.

At the last minute, he rolled. It was the only thought in his head as the ax rose. His entire focus narrowed to the long, curved blade, so wickedly sharp, and the muscles in his torso twitched. Numb fingers clutched uselessly at the sword. The blade was dented and it would only hinder him, but he couldn't seem to let it go.

He had to roll. *Wait. Wait. Wait.* Everything came down to this. He could do it.

While he had focused on the orc, though, his adversary had focused on him. As soon as his arms rose, two of the fae guards darted in with their wicked blades and found the gaps in the shoulders of the enemy's makeshift armor. Deep-green blood spurted, and the warrior dropped the weapon behind him.

From the scream, he must have killed or injured one of his own with the weapon, but Ben didn't have any time to think about it. He scrambled up, fell again, and caught himself on the litter.

He could do this. All he had to do was move again. It didn't matter that he couldn't move *well*, only that he had to get through this.

Ben had never considered how loud a battle would be or how close death would be. There was still blood on his face, and the orc drew his last gasps nearby as crystal pikes were thrust repeatedly into his flesh.

A shout caught his attention. An elf attacked the new gap in the line. This one was different from Yn'solde in almost every way he could imagine, from the half-shaved head to the orcish tattoos, but one thing was the same. He moved with perfect grace.

Without taking time to think, he pushed away from the litter and snatched the hilt of his sword in both hands. He swept it at an angle and knocked the enemy's blade aside.

Into himself, of course, and he fell in a heap. But between the unexpected block and the fact that he threw a leg up, the elf also sprawled in the dirt.

"End him!" Kural yelled. "We need to start the retreat. They're opening the path for us!"

He pushed to his knees, his hands on the sword as the elf rolled and stood. The areas of weakness jumped out at him with painful clarity—the Achilles tendon, the femoral artery, and the gap between the stomach and the breastplate. He could do it and it didn't require any particular grace. All he had to do was swing the sword with all his might and pull across the skin.

Everything seemed to freeze. He couldn't do it.

"Ben!"

"Ben!"

The voices penetrated and he shook his head violently and fought down the roiling nausea. The elf readied himself for a strike to push through to the king.

Ben's shoulder met the side of his thigh. He'd never played football but he'd seen enough of it to know to tackle that way. His momentum carried the assailant over at the same time that lightning caught the elf in the face. He sprawled and dragged in a breath before he scrambled up the elf's body to try to pin his arms. His foe's face was blackened and burned.

There was no life in his eyes.

"Ben!" Kural caught hold of his arm in a vice-like grip. "Come *on!*"

They stumbled across the bridge with the army pressed around them.

"Where's Zaara?" he asked.

"Doing a hell of a lot better than *you*," the wizard snapped. "You can't count on having one of us to guard you every time! Can you do this or not?"

He felt a flush of anger mixed with shame. "I didn't ask for any of this," he muttered, as much to himself as to anyone else.

Still, he knew it didn't matter. He might not have asked for it but it was happening. And when the body of one of the fae guards fluttered to land beside him, he knew, with a sinking feeling, that this army didn't give a damn whether or not he wanted to hurt them.

They pushed forward and he blocked and parried for all he was worth. More than once, a blade missed him by inches and a few times, a shield or a fist or a blade struck him. He couldn't even bring himself to yell the first time it happened. He stared at the blood welling from his arm in shock and tried to remember how to move his feet.

"Ben!" Zaara called urgently. "Your arms and legs can get injured. Protect your body! *Kural!*"

"I have other priorities right now!" the wizard roared.

She was still trying to defeat the head of the mercenary army and was bleeding as well. A long gash ran from the top of her forehead and through her eyebrow. Blood coated one cheek, but she fought with barely a wince.

The clanless orc had suffered injuries too, but he wielded his weapons with an ease she didn't have. While she might not abhor violence when it came to defense, she didn't want to hurt anyone unnecessarily. She didn't relish the feeling of defeating an enemy, much less killing them.

The enemy, on the other hand, certainly did.

Fury rose in Ben's chest. He threw himself between the litter and an attacking human soldier. Although he didn't have the coordination for most blows, he had enough to bring his knee up with a good degree of force. The soldier doubled over and he shoulder-checked him off the edge of the causeway.

A spurt of blood told him that the fall had not been painless, and he felt as though ice water had been poured over him. He was doing the best he could, goddammit, but he still didn't want to kill anyone.

A shout came from behind him. The guards had cleared a path to the door and were opening it enough to let the king's litter through.

"Zaara!" Ben yelled.

She cast one desperate look over her shoulder and the orc seized his chance. He thrust with all his might and Ben screamed at the top of his lungs.

The woman whipped around and one hip turned sideways. The sword snagged on the front of her leather armor as the blade slid past her. From her gasp of pain, he could tell that the blade had touched her skin, but it hadn't done nearly the damage the orc had hoped.

More than that, she still had her dagger. Time seemed to slow around him and Kural dragged him back as Zaara planted her front foot and drove the dagger through the orc's eye.

The massive warrior thudded to his knees and she didn't wait for him to die. She wrenched the blade free and ran toward the defenders with one hand pressed over her stomach to stem the blood that seeped through her fingers. She ran without looking back as the mercenaries saw their leader fall and raced after her.

The doors began to swing shut and Ben yelled for them to stop. He threw himself against one of them to slow it, but he couldn't hold them forever.

When one of the mercenaries caught the back of Zaara's shirt, he knew she wouldn't make it.

For the life of him, he couldn't understand why he did what he did next. He launched himself out of the doorway, skidded along the causeway—flailing wildly to keep his balance—and grasped the human who tried to catch Zaara. When he pounded the hilt of his sword on the man's head and kicked him, his fingers loosened.

"Go!" Ben called to Zaara.

She wouldn't leave him. Her blood-slick hand extended to grasp his and she dragged him into the palace a second before the doors slammed shut.

He collapsed, heaving desperate breaths. "Zaara—are you—"

"It looks worse than it is." She was panting and her voice was tight, but she stayed upright. "You?"

"I, uh—" He went to take an inventory of his wounds and decided against it. "A lot of me hurts but I don't seem to be bleeding out. So I have that going for me."

"Also, you managed to stop being totally useless," Prima interjected.

"Shut up," he muttered.

"No one is suggesting you turn into a mass-murderer, you know."

"I said, shut up!"

"Um, Ben?" Zaara frowned at him in concern. "Who are you talking to?

"No one. It's not important. I swear I'm not bleeding out."

"Okay, that's good enough." She looked doubtful but chose not to waste time on it and simply leaned forward to help him up. The two of them followed the litter that now moved toward the doors at the opposite side of the throne room.

The entrance doors shuddered behind them as the mercenaries threw themselves at them and battered the barrier with axes and swords. Ben looked over his shoulder once or twice, but there was nothing to be done. The battle was raging outside. All they could do was catch the stragglers.

It was a surprisingly vulnerable feeling.

"Where's the well?" he asked Zaara.

"It's—oh, *fuck*."

With a crack and the sound of shattering glass, a section of one wall fell to pieces. Fae and mercenaries alike poured through the gap and swept around to reach the king.

"*Run!*" Zaara yelled.

She and Ben sprinted with every ounce of strength they could muster. He was aware that his legs were getting tangled and his arms flailed wildly, but there was nothing he could do about it. Kural and the guards ran alongside the litter and tried to get to the next set of doors. Arrows whistled and were followed by the screams from humans, elves, and fae.

The small party around the king thrust forward into the darkness and through the doors that opened and closed with magical force, but they weren't alone. Mercenaries had pushed in with them, which led to a pitched and desperate battle around the king's litter.

In the darkness, the well glowed a pale blue, unsettlingly beautiful. And on the far side of it, a shadow waited.

Ben's breath caught. The mercenary leader had said they didn't know who they were fighting or where they should be. He had told them although it hadn't made sense.

Yn'solde had come to finish the job herself.

CHAPTER TWENTY-FIVE

Battles raged on either side of the closed doors. Kural swung his staff with abandon, as much for magic as to thwack mercenary heads, and Zaara had thrown herself into the fray without a word of complaint. They held the mercenaries at bay for now and it looked like they might still triumph, but Ben didn't know how much time they had.

There was no one else. He had to stop this.

His heart thudded as he walked to the edge of the pool and met Yn'solde's gaze. She looked different now. Her hair was pulled back severely and she was dressed in clothes that were made for travel and fighting. In the light filtering from the well, she looked haunted.

"I don't understand why," he said bluntly.

That surprised her. She had watched him with a sardonic expression and now, she stared at him.

"I told you why," she said after a moment. "He's *always* gotten what he wanted."

"And he wants to destroy the fae," he said.

"No." She seemed impatient now and looked at the shimmering blue. "He wants *this*—this power. He wants it at his beck and call. I held him off for a time, but now…there's nothing left for it."

The pieces began to fall into place in his head with sickening clarity.

"You were sent here to kill the king," he said. "You never fled of your own volition."

"I volunteered." She looked at him. "I didn't want to do it, though. I was desperate to get out."

"Like that makes a difference," Ben said. His heart pounded and he could barely hear anything over the thumping in his ears.

Unexpectedly, he had touched a sore point. She drew herself tall and her lip curled. "It made a difference," she told him, her voice low. "I held my brother off for *years*. I found out the king was linked to the sacred wells and told him that killing the king wouldn't give him everything he wanted. Anyone else he sent would simply have done it, no questions asked."

"That makes you far from blameless," he retorted. "Do you honestly think that wipes away the blood on your hands?"

"Are you honestly so stupid that you couldn't see this was inevitable?" Her voice rose now.

"How was it inevitable?" Ben waved his hands dismissively. "You said he always gets what he wants. Didn't you ever think that *maybe* it was because people keep doing his dirty work for him? People like you?"

"You have *no idea* what it's like!" Her hair escaped its braid here and there. "He tortured our brother to death, he had our sister and our mother killed, he killed his wife, and he has hundreds who will do his bidding if he raises a single finger. There was never a chance to stand up to him."

"Coward," he said simply. "You could have ended it."

"How?"

"You could have killed *him*! You spent years here, ingratiating yourself with the king and the court and learning their foibles. If you had done that to your brother, you could have defeated him and won the loyalty of his friends and his guards. But you played by *his* rules and now, here we are." He shook his head. "And I don't even get it. You're murdering an entire race, destroying a species, and for what?"

"So he won't get it!" She practically screamed the words at him. "I can't keep him from sinking his claws into this land, but I can damned well keep him from getting his hands on the magic. And if that's all I can do, then I'll do it!"

Ben closed his eyes.

"Hate me all you want." Strength had returned to her voice. "Think whatever you want, but I'll know that in the end, I kept him from getting stronger."

"No. In the end, you missed your chance to bring him to justice." He spoke the words with a cutting edge of disgust. She began to circle toward him and he inched away, trying to keep his distance.

She absolutely could *not* find out how useless he was with this sword.

"You told me who you were the second day we were here," he said bitterly to her. "You said to stay out of the fights and not attract attention. That's what you did with your brother, wasn't it? You never tried to start a rebellion or to stand up to him. You came here because it gave you the chance to escape and now, you're making the entire fae race pay for your grudge against him."

"Grudge? If he pollutes the wells, he has them all in the palm of his hand! Don't you understand? He'll be able to use them as slaves and will have an unstoppable army."

"And you could have kept it from coming to this." He only narrowly avoided pounding the tip of his sword against the ground for emphasis. That seemed like the wrong thing to do with a sharp object and a stone floor. "He put your back to the wall but you're the one who dragged other people in with you."

Genuine hatred flared in her eyes. "You know nothing about me," she said quietly, but he heard her voice tremble.

His heart sank because he hadn't wanted to be right about this. He had wanted her to tell him something—anything—that would help him to understand.

But there wasn't anything she could say to explain it all away. She had been dealt a hard hand but she had chosen her path, and it was one that would doom hundreds of thousands. Selfishly, she hadn't asked the fae what they thought and hadn't enlisted them.

Instead, she had told the mercenaries how to destroy the wells.

Yn'solde looked at the king and moved her hand to a pouch at her belt. Ben didn't need any prompting to know it contained poison. He also knew what it would do when she threw it in the well.

"What about Alia?" He asked the question desperately in an attempt to distract her.

She gave him a curious look. "Alia?"

"The woman you got to help you?"

"What about her?" She looked blankly at him.

"She's *dead.*"

"We'll all be dead soon," she told him. "The mercenaries will leave no one alive except me, and my brother will kill me once he finds out what I've done."

Ben wanted to scream but he bit it back. "You're exactly like him."

"I am *nothing* like him."

"You're sacrificing people for your goal and you don't even grieve them." He stopped counter-circling and began to walk toward her. "No more."

"No more? It's done." She drew a short sword from its sheath and faced him. "Nothing you can do will stem the tide now, human."

"You will still come to justice," he told her.

Her gaze traveled over him. "You did so well to convince us that you were injured. I only began to doubt when I saw you reach the throne room the other day and even then, I wouldn't have guessed you could wield a sword."

He merely smiled. His heart beat wildly and he tried to school his features to hide it.

What in God's name was his plan here? He tried to delay the fight because there was no way he could win it but sooner or later, he would have to throw himself into the fray.

And if he intended to bring her to justice, that meant killing her. She wouldn't let herself be taken alive. He could believe that she'd slept with a knife beside her bed for years to make sure she could end her life before she was ever taken back to her brother.

Yn'solde was a woman who was trained to be an assassin, who had no morals, and had no hope of surviving this.

His odds were *not* good. Why hadn't he thought to play his weakness up? Then, at least, she might have underestimated him.

She drove forward in a charge. He could see in her eyes that she was testing him. She held one arm back for balance and wielded the short-sword effortlessly with her front hand.

Ben batted her sword away with his blade. It wasn't a graceful movement, but it worked. Her eyes narrowed and she circled so his back was to the water.

"You're injured," she told him.

"I'm aware." He raised an eyebrow. "Oh, that reminds me—your water orc friend is dead."

She gave a sharp look at the knot of fighters near the door and he took the opportunity to lunge forward. His sword barely nicked her before she danced back, but he felt it strike and bile rose in his throat. He thought of the soldier he had pushed off the causeway and the crystal blades of grass he must have landed on.

It occurred to him that he would throw up everywhere. He wondered if he could do so in her face, which might at least give him a tactical advantage.

"Hold it together," Prima told him. *"She's dangerous."*

The fact that she didn't mock him made him take notice. "I hate this," he murmured under his breath.

"Hate it all you want but stay alive."

Yn'solde's eyes narrowed at him as if sensing that something was going on beyond his façade, but with her blood spilled, she was more careful now.

Ben feinted left and moved right and almost caught her again. She ducked out of the way with a grimace and instead of moving back, he pressed the advantage. He wasn't sure what he was doing and only knew he wanted to keep her off-balance. They were testing one another but he had to end this soon.

Out of the corner of his eye, he saw Kural sneaking around the back of the room with the litter.

The wizard was trying to get to the well. Ben knew that immediately.

He made his decision equally quickly and followed his advance with a swing that his adversary could almost certainly evade. She did, but it turned her so her back was to the pool. He drove forward and then began a retreat.

The combat used everything he had and he was running out of energy. Every muscle ached. He barely kept his feet each time he shifted his weight and half his swings didn't seem to go where he intended them to—with the benefit, at least, that Yn'solde also had trouble predicting where he would strike next.

Pretending to falter, he let her drive him back. No matter what, he had to keep her distracted so she wouldn't notice that the king was close to the well. All their hopes rested on that. Whatever power the fae monarch might have, he had to be able to tap the well before she poisoned it.

"Answer me something," Ben said. He'd always been something of an asshole and he decided that if ever there was a time to use it, the time was now. "How the hell did you sit back and put up with him having killed your sister and your mother? Oh—and your brother."

Her mouth compressed into a thin line. "You can do an awful lot when there's no other choice."

"You had a choice," he said. "You chose to do what he wanted and fell into line. Your choice was to obey. You took the warning *exactly* like he meant you to."

"You don't know a thing about it!" She lost her temper then and advanced in a rush. Surprisingly, she was crying. "You do what you have to do to survive. You don't understand it—any of it. Don't you dare judge me."

"I'm judging you," he retorted harshly, "for what you're doing *now*. If you hadn't called in an army and tried to assassinate the king, maybe it would be a different story."

Behind her, the monarch had reached the water and Kural helped him to touch the surface.

Ben put his sword up to block her latest swing and stepped in close. "Send the army away," he said to her. "Call them off."

"Don't you see? I *can't*."

"Yes, you can. You can defy him and bolster his enemies, not simply scorch the earth to spite him." His mouth tasted like ashes.

"You have no idea how powerful he is." She shook her head.

"Maybe not," he said. "But I know which side I'm on."

He had no idea what tipped her off but she looked over her shoulder. Her shout of despair was one he would never forget, but what was worse was the grim determination with which she reached for the pouch at her belt. She dipped her fingers into it, ready to throw the powder.

There wasn't a choice, not anymore. It was her or however many *thousands* of fae. He looped his foot around hers, tripped her, and brought his sword down in her back. The life left her body with a powerful jerk that he felt, and he rolled away and heaved his guts out on the stone floor.

CHAPTER TWENTY-SIX

"**B**en!"

Feet pounded across the floor and in the next moment, Zaara was at his side. He shook her hands off as the touch made the nausea worse. When the spreading pool of blood touched his hand, he recoiled with an oath.

"Ben?" Bloodied and bruised, she crouched in front of him. "Please tell me you're okay." Her hands patted his arms and torso in search of wounds.

"I'm not...she didn't—" He hung his head.

"You gave her a chance," she said. Her words seemed to come from very far away. She bit her lip. "Ben, I think I did you a disservice when I first told you that you might have to kill people. I made it seem simpler than it was. I—"

"You're hurt." He couldn't listen to this right now, not with Yn'solde's body lying beside him. "We should get you help."

"It's not bad. I made sure there was no infection." She managed a shadow of a smile. "And, Ben, if you doubt yourself—"

"Don't."

"No, I mean it." She raised her finger and pointed behind him. "Look."

He turned his head curiously and drew in a sharp, startled breath.

The fae king hovered over the sacred well. His head was tipped toward the darkness of the cave's ceiling. Ben suddenly wondered how high the ceiling was or if there was one at all. Looking up gave him a strange sense of vertigo as if he stood at the edge of a void.

Blue light swirled up and around the king's thin form. He was still sick but he had begun to gain strength.

Ben looked over his shoulder to the throne room. He could still hear the clash of weapons and the shouts of soldiers on both sides. He let Zaara help him up and they looked from the closed doors to the king at the well.

Even Kural hung back. Ben had disliked the man for many reasons since he met him but something in his manner now made him more human than he'd ever expected. The wizard did not watch the power with hunger or envy but like a man who had heard a beautiful piece of music. He was a wizard because he loved magic, not because he coveted it, and he leaned heavily on his staff and simply watched. There was blood on his robes and he did not put equal weight on his left leg.

Beside him, Zaara watched with awe.

"What do you see?" he asked her. "What does it look like to an apprentice wizard?"

"Oh, this is beyond me." She didn't look at him. He didn't think there was anything in the world that could make her tear her gaze away. "I don't think I'd even call it a spell—or magic. Ben, it's like... staring at the smallest part of a pattern, a beautiful pattern, and knowing you could never *see* all of it and your mind couldn't hold it all."

He looked around. Was it only him or was the glow getting brighter?

"He's so old," she said, "and I think he must carry the memories of the others. The kings who went before. Or..."

"Or?" He looked curiously at her.

She met his gaze, her left eye swollen shut and half her face

171

covered in dried blood. "Or they're still alive," she told him. "*In* him, somehow—or in the spell. I don't think I can explain it."

Ben nodded and looked down. There were no words for how small this made him feel.

How useless, too.

"You stopped her," Zaara told him. She continued to watch him. "What's happening now...maybe it's beyond you or me, Ben, but we helped it to happen."

He looked at her. "I'm only one person. I killed...one soldier. And Yn'solde." Bile rose in his throat again. "And there are thousands out there."

They both looked again, toward the battle they were powerless to stop.

"You protected the king," she said. "And you defeated the one who would have doomed all of this." She shook her head. "To think she was in league with her brother the whole time. It was quite an act."

"Yes and no." His mouth twisted. "He wanted the sacred wells. She intended to destroy them to keep him from getting them."

"No." Her whispered protest sounded appalled.

"Yes." He looked sharply at her. "Do you think—should I not have—"

"Couldn't she have *told* the fae king?" Zaara exploded. "She hated her brother and she couldn't simply...fight him? She had to kill the fae and their lands to keep her brother from—ohhhh." She looked furiously at the body. "I knew I hated that man, but she's almost as bad. Hell, she might be worse."

Ben heaved a sigh of relief.

"And you weren't sure she deserved to die?" she asked skeptically a moment later.

"Well..."

"*She has a point,*" Prima interjected.

"You need to think about what you consider justice," Zaara said emphatically.

"I know I don't like being the sole arbiter of it." He looked away from the body on the floor. "And I know if it had been only me and not you and Kural, many more people would be dead. I'd have failed. So maybe it doesn't matter what I think."

"It doesn't seem like there's much point in speculating about that," she said thoughtfully after a moment.

A thud and a cracking sound from behind them startled them both. He backed away from the door and raised his sword and she readied her knife. She trembled with exhaustion, as did he, but there was no thought of laying their weapons down. There was only acceptance.

In the next moment, the well erupted. Ben sprawled onto the floor. His chin struck the rock so hard his teeth clacked together. He yelled and pushed up but froze to stare open-mouthed at the column of blue flame that streaked into the sky. There must, indeed, be no roof to this cavern, as he could see it ascend beyond the limit of his vision.

There was markedly less clanging and screaming outside the door now, although shouts that sounded like questions could be heard.

He squinted into the flame but could not see the king at all. His chin trembled when he allowed his mind to silently voice his suspicions. If someone had asked him to step into a column of flame and sacrifice himself, would he have had the courage to do it?

The magical blaze narrowed and began to pale. Columns spiraled up the sides of it.

"Zaara," he called. "I think it'll blow again!"

"Then put your head down, you moron!"

"Right!"

With a sound like a foghorn, the enchantment burst downward and out. It swept across his skin and he could swear he felt both the tearing force of hurricane winds and rain and nothing at all. The magic existed on another plane.

Out in the hall, there were cries of amazement but only the sound of fae voices. When the doors swung open of their own accord, he raised his head and saw that the mercenary soldiers had vanished.

"Gone." Zaara dragged in a breath. She scrambled to her feet. "They're all *gone.*"

As one, she and Ben turned to the well.

The figure who floated there was both the same and diminished. Kural hurried forward to help the fae king leave the well and the two exchanged quiet words. When the monarch went to the remaining guards, they fluttered around him and he reassured them softly.

He stopped at each fallen body and laid a hand on the brow of each guard. Ben's throat tightened. The king did not shy away from seeing those who had shielded his life with their own.

When he reached them, the young man swallowed hard.

"I am told it was you who felled the leader of the mercenary army," the fae sovereign said to Zaara.

"I—oh. Yes. Your Majesty." She bobbed her head in an awkward bow.

He touched her face and healing spread from his fingertips. Ben watched in amazement as the swelling subsided and the wound knit itself together. A scar remained, new and red, but she did not seem to mind it and smiled at the king in thanks.

"And you," the king said to him. "You also rose to the challenge, did you not?"

"I...Your Majesty..."

"You are not of this world," the monarch said. "I see no memories in you of our cities or our history. And still, you took up arms to defend my people."

"I..." *Killed.* But the royal's hand touched him as well, and even as the aches and pains eased in his body, he felt peace settle over him like a blanket.

The king looked at him for only a moment before he moved on to Yn'solde's body.

"Rest, young one," he told her. "When next your spirit rises, may you find peace."

He left the room and the others followed, Ben with a last glance at the elf's still form.

The room beyond held only the fae—the living and the dead. The living joined the king's procession and the humans fell ever farther back. Trin and the orc joined the swelling ranks of the king's followers.

It was outside the gates that the greatest change had been wrought. It looked as if there had never been a war at all. The trail of destruction behind the army had been wiped away. The blood was gone, as were the soldiers.

"Where's the army?" he whispered to Zaara. He wasn't sure he wanted to know the answer.

Kural was the one who answered. "Beyond the borders of fae and barred from returning."

"Ah." That was less gruesome than it might be. He nodded.

The king surveyed the land for some time before he turned to the assembled crowd.

"There is much to do." It was easy to see how much the magic had drained him, but he floated unbowed and strong.

Restored, he thought, and his heart lightened a little more.

CHAPTER TWENTY-SEVEN

Ben spent most of the next few days alone in his room.

Zaara and Kural were closeted with the king and some of the other leaders of the fae, trying to devise a peace treaty between them and Insea, which meant their company was limited. Trin had withdrawn into his chambers to conduct funeral rites for Alia, and the orc had apparently set out for his home to bring word of the fae to his tribe.

Ben set himself to practicing the exercises Zaara set him, and although he made impressive progress, he was also bored out of his mind. Walking had once been a completely absorbing task, as had almost anything. Now he could walk, pick himself up, wield a sword without threatening to decapitate himself, and do things like eat without flinging food over his shoulder.

Which meant he had time to dwell on how bored he was.

Kural found him on the ramparts on the third day. Where Zaara seemed more and more exhausted by the day, the wizard looked much the same as he always did. He would have guessed the man to be anywhere between his mid-thirties and mid-forties and still found it impressive how the mild-mannered man managed to look so young while being centuries old and vastly powerful.

Also, the blue had begun to fade nicely. He now merely looked like he might have a case of frostbite.

"Where will you go next?" Kural asked without preamble.

Ben looked sharply at him. "I—oh."

"Oh?" The wizard raised an eyebrow.

"I thought I would come with you." Now that he said it, he felt ridiculous. "That was stupid of me."

"You're welcome to travel with us, certainly." He nodded. "It would be cruel to leave someone with no money and no connections stranded in fae territory."

"So they haven't done an about-face and decided they like humans?"

Kural snorted. "That won't ever happen, boy. The king may have a good head on his shoulders, but the fae don't respect the other races worth a damn. I imagine it's hard to do when you're smarter than everyone else, but..." He forced a smile. "It doesn't help that they look like children to us."

"That does make it confusing," he agreed. He leaned on the parapet. "If I could maybe...accompany you out of these lands, that would be good."

"Of course." The man nodded. "Zaara assumed you would but I wanted to make sure. For all I knew, you'd want to stay here."

He shuddered dramatically. "I can't get out of this place fast enough. I never thought I'd say that about a beautiful castle with free food, but..."

There were so many horrifying memories from this place. In the throne room, he could see the withered throne and Alia's body. On the causeway, he could see the spurt of blood from the soldier he had pushed off. The palace would forever be the place that made him do things he could not reconcile with the man he was.

He looked away.

"I have to say," Kural said after a moment, "I've never seen someone as committed as you are to not killing. Most of us simply become accustomed to it."

Ben looked at the fields and the waving grasses. "You don't have to tell me that I cost lives. I know I did."

The wizard frowned at him in surprise. "That wasn't what I was going to say."

"Maybe it should have been." He pushed up and took a deep breath. "I thought avoiding violence was a philosophy that hinged first on my actions. But there were people who were a huge danger and stopping them could have prevented so much death." He looked at his companion. "I won't make the same mistake again."

The look the man gave him was, surprisingly, not so much disbelieving as pitying. "No," he said. "You'll make different ones. I don't say that to be cruel, Ben. I say it because you should know how life is. The older I get, the more I believe that we do the best we can, and we will never know if we did the right thing. The good we do is not defined by rigid rules, it is not defined by our effort or hardship, and it is not defined by our intentions."

A silence settled between them.

Kural's fingers tightened around his staff. "And I confess, I don't know what to do with that."

He left without another word and Ben looked after him.

"Is that what you think?" he asked Prima when he was alone.

"What do you mean?"

"Kural is you, isn't he? You made him. So, what he said—do you think it's true?"

"What a strange question," she said slowly. *"Kural lives in some of my processes, yes. But he is not me and I am not him—or as much as I am him, I am also Zaara and the fae king and the palace. The part of me that is Kural says those things and believes them, exactly as other parts of me say and believe other things."*

Ben considered this. "Isn't it confusing to believe more than one thing at a time?"

"I was under the impression that every human did."

"I..." He closed his mouth. "Actually, that's correct. We call it cognitive dissonance. Son of a bitch, I never thought about it that way."

"I merely have rather more bandwidth to do so."

"I don't envy you that," he said with a laugh.

"By the way, Zaara is looking for you."

"Oh, now you tell me these things?"

"I make exceptions sometimes."

He smiled as he walked quickly down the stairs and into the palace. While he'd made excellent progress, he wasn't close to his old level of coordination and certainly wouldn't trust his body to take him up a rockface safely. He could, however, walk without using all his concentration.

Zaara waved when she saw him approach. Her hair was held back in an ornate braid and she wore the fancy robes again. Against her finery, the scar over one side of her face was all the more noticeable.

The hat that went with it was still ridiculous.

"I'm glad I found you," she said. "The treaty is signed. We'll leave tomorrow."

"So soon?" Ben couldn't disguise his leap of happiness but he was also surprised. "I thought there'd be more...pomp and circumstance."

Great, now he had the graduation song stuck in his head.

"Usually, maybe." She looked evasive. "There's so much for everyone to do. The fae need to rebuild, and we need to get home."

"Ah, yes. The mysterious nature of—"

"*Not* here." Her tone was firm but she smiled. "Go and pack. There will be a feast tonight and we'll leave at dawn."

"So don't go hard at the feast?"

"Or if you do, try to pass out in the litter with your luggage packed." She smiled and headed to her room.

There was nothing for him to pack so he passed the time with a few more swordsmanship exercises. When he got to the feast, he was both ravenous and exhausted. He found his mind drifting as the night went on, and he turned in early without a goodbye to the king.

He couldn't face those eyes right now—eyes that saw far too much and far too clearly.

Then, he dreamed of the accident.

It was hot in the sunshine and the skin along his side itched when he stretched to the limit and sweat ran across an almost-burn. Grains of sand and stone were rough under his fingertips and the pressure on the ball of his left foot as he braced himself was vivid.

Now, however, he could feel what he hadn't felt that day. His body had tried to tell him something was wrong and in the dream, he could see himself ignoring it. There was a faint hitch in the muscles of his shoulders and his foot didn't grip the hold correctly.

Ben could remember, at last, what went on in his head as he felt for those holds. His mind was busy being angry about Mike and Eve, angry that they were challenging him about his job situation, while he tried to ignore the fact that he was tired of never having a home of his own.

His foot slipped.

He sat, drenched in sweat. There was only silence and pale light and the sound of his breathing.

A knock startled him and the door opened and Zaara stuck her head in.

"You're up already!" She looked pleased. "That'll help with—what's wrong?"

"It's nothing." Ben ran a hand through his hair and tried to breathe. "Tell me there's time for a shower."

"Shower?"

"Bath."

"Oh. Um, if you're quick. I can grab your bags." She took two of them and headed out.

He startled when a steaming bath and a cool one both blinked out of nowhere. He scrubbed quickly and dunked his head into the cold water to clear it.

"Was it a bad dream?" Prima asked.

He was about to snap that it sure hadn't been a good one, but he held his tongue and simply nodded. It was something else he was learning to do

How could he ever apologize to Mike? He closed his eyes for a moment.

"Prima? Can you tell them...I want to wake up? I mean...I want to come back, but..."

"I'll come up with something," she said. *"You won't blink out without warning. I'll bring you out tonight at the latest."*

"Thanks." He needed to talk to Mike before he lost his nerve.

He dressed in his magically cleaned clothes and hurried through the palace to the gates. Despite the beauty he knew was around him, he tried not to look because he didn't want to see it or remember it. It was beautiful and perhaps someday, he could return.

Maybe he would never be ready to do that, however. This wasn't a place for him, and it occurred to him that it might have been designed that way. It had been somewhere he wouldn't want to rest on his laurels for too long.

That thought made him smile.

He stepped out to find Zaara and Kural in a floating litter, their horses waiting alongside. He climbed in and looked around for propulsion systems.

"With so much magic in this land, the king thought it would make sense to give our horses a rest," the wizard explained. "We can rest and talk, at least until we're out of the fae lands—although Zaara may be sick of my voice by now."

She gave him a small smile. "I should hope I wouldn't get sick of you so fast—or vice versa. My training will last decades, remember."

"And I'm sure you'll keep me on my toes the whole time." Kural yawned and snapped his fingers, and a steaming teapot appeared in midair. "Who wants something to drink?"

"Tea?" Ben asked.

"Tea, coffee, chocolate—it's whatever you want." He smiled. "The elves have been a particular thorn in our side lately, but some of their spells are quite nice."

He took a cup gratefully. It turned out to be hot chocolate, as rich and thick as melted chocolate without being too cloying. With a happy sigh, he leaned forward to look at the platter of breads, cheeses, and fruit that Kural had made appear as well.

Then, while they were distracted and had their guard down, he asked calmly, "So, what's going on in Insea that peace is so vital?"

His companions both choked on their tea. He merely sipped his chocolate and smiled.

Zaara looked at the wizard. "I fucked up," she admitted baldly.

"It had to be you," her mentor pointed out.

"Yes, but I wanted to take responsibility."

"Noted. Don't go into politics." Kural looked at Ben. "I'm afraid this set of secrets is not common knowledge for a reason. Suffice it to say we have it on good authority that the world will become a great deal more violent and prone to war if no action is taken. For this reason, we are seeking to pre-emptively bind the various nations into cooperation with one another. Mutually beneficial trade seems to be one of the best ways to do so."

She nodded and added, "There are things like the new elven 'king.' You know conflicts will come out of that, so you should plan ahead."

"Hmm." Ben leaned back and munched on a bagel-like object that seemed to have the cream cheese already inside it. The concept was intriguing and it was delicious.

"We should talk about where you'll go after this," Zaara told him. "We'll travel back to Insea and you're welcome to come with us. If nothing else, you should be able to find employment there. We might also be able to introduce you to Justin—that is if he's not back to arguing with the human leaders."

Kural gave a despairing snort. "If it's possible to have a worse job than the one we did, he has it. Did you see his latest letter?" His eyes lit up with conspiratorial glee as he looked at her. "Lord Gyforde tried to trap *both* of them into marriage with his daughter."

"Well, that's merely a rite of passage in the human political world," she quipped. She looked at Ben. "He does it with everyone. *Everyone.* Also, and this is important, she's four. He started doing this before he even had a daughter." She looked at the sky. "Maybe I'll help her run away when she's old enough."

"You should," Kural said with unexpected vehemence.

"Ben?" Prima spoke quietly. *"Tell them you want to take a nap."*

Ben yawned. "Oh, man. I'm still tired. Would you mind if I took a nap?"

"Not at all." Kural gestured to the expanse of pillows. "And you might sleep a good while longer than you anticipate. These fields are filled with all manner of sleep spells. It won't do you any harm. If anything, it would do you good." He yawned as well. "Come to think of it, maybe *I'll* sleep."

Zaara waved at them. "Good. Finally, some time alone with my thoughts."

He smiled and made himself comfortable. The world about him began to disintegrate as his eyes closed, and a moment later, he shivered violently. There had been a gust of cold air. How? Where? He tried to open his eyes and couldn't. It wasn't black with them closed. Instead, it was *nothing.*

"Stay calm," Prima said quietly. *"I'm here. You're waking up. You'll be okay, Ben."*

He willed his heart rate to slow and moments later, the nothing disappeared and he opened his eyes to blinding light.

"Ben?" Jacob looked worriedly at him. "How are you feeling?"

"That sucked," he rasped. His throat ached. How long had it been since he had talked? "Waking up, I mean. Well, and some of the story."

"Yeah, sorry." The other man gave him a sympathetic smile as he unhooked monitors. "We knew Zaara was trustworthy, so we never stopped to think that you'd have to consider *her* as a potential assassin. Our bad."

"You seem to have done well, though," said Nick. His face swam into view. He held a hand out. "Here, I'll help you sit."

Ben missed his hand on the first try—his muscles were so sluggish and so exhausted—but he managed on the second and sat with a wince. He tried to scratch his head, which didn't quite work, and stared at his hands.

"What the—"

"Son of a bitch," Jacob said quietly.

He tried to move his hand. "I could do this in the game. Fuck. Fuck!"

"Ah…" The other man couldn't wipe the grin off his face, one shared by Nick. "I don't think you get it, dude." He stepped back at the look Ben gave him. "No, no, listen to me, man. Listen. I get that this is frustrating and you could move around in-game and all that, right? Yeah? But the level of coordination you have right now? You are… easily six to eight months ahead of where we expected you to be."

"What?" He gaped at them.

"Yeah." Jacob continued to grin. He held his hand out for a shake. "And you *earned* it, man. We saw how much you practiced. You put your heart and soul into that, you did the work, and you're doing *incredibly* well."

CHAPTER TWENTY-EIGHT

"Listen, man." Mike's face still showed traces of the sickly yellow-and-purple of a fading bruise. "Anyone can fall. You did. I did. I saw you slip and I could have done ten better things than the one I did. As far as I'm concerned, what matters is that we survived."

Ben nodded.

"And you have *no* idea how good it is to see you moving again," his friend said emphatically.

"Yeah, I..." He shrugged. "It's hard when I was doing so much better in the game and now, I feel like a baby again."

"Miles better than when I saw you," the other man said cheerfully. "Natasha will be pissed that she missed you—I finally got her out of the house instead of hovering over me, and she missed your video call." He paused. "I think maybe I simply won't tell her."

"Honestly? Good plan. She might kill you."

Mike shifted uncomfortably in his chair. His casts were beginning to look dingy. "God, this *itches*. When this started, I only wanted to be able to dance at my wedding. Now, I don't give a damn about that. I simply want the itching to stop. I'd kill a man for that."

"So I should be going," Ben quipped.

The man laughed. "Ohhh, laughing hurts. Anyway. What's the timeline on you coming back out here?"

"Honestly? I'm not sure." He shook his head. "I'm coming along faster than they expected but as you can see, I'm not exactly stable enough to be on my own yet. It also looks like going back into the game will do more for my recovery than anything else."

"What's the game like?" his friend asked him. "You haven't said much about it."

He took a moment to think before he spoke, and he sighed. "I don't know how to describe it. It's more interactive than you'd ever think—it honestly does feel like you're *in* a book or a movie or something. Except it hits harder. *Much* harder. Watching your actions play out, it...humbles you."

Mike guffawed and shook his head.

"What?" He was almost offended.

"That's what this difference has been?" he asked. "You come to me with an apology—and I don't remember the last time you apologized like that, if *ever*—and you're quiet. You're...you, but in a different way. A near-death experience will do that to you, so I didn't think much of it, but from what you're saying, it's the *game* that's changed you."

Ben chewed his lip as he thought this over.

"Like..." Mike had a hard time controlling his amusement. "Fairies and elves and shit? *That* kind of game?"

"You don't understand until you're in it." The words came out of him quickly, and he was surprised by the rush of anger he felt. "They're merely people, Mike, trying to do the best they can—and sometimes, you fuck up and you hurt them and you have to *watch* it."

The man was taken aback and swallowed uncomfortably. "I'm... sorry. I didn't mean—"

"No." He sighed and tried to rub his forehead. When he only succeeded in slinging his arm over one shoulder, it didn't improve his temper. He tried to let the anger dissipate. "I was surprised, too. At the start, I was so aware it was a game and none of it was 'real,' whatever that means, but then I fell into it. So many of my morals were simply...self-centered, and even if it's not real, watching people die violently because you had some idea of moral purity? It...uh, it changes you."

His friend stared at him, wide-eyed. "That sounds...uh, are you sure you want to go back in?"

"Yes," Ben said immediately.

"It doesn't exactly sound pleasant. Like, I'm as happy as anyone that you're feeling better, don't get me wrong, but that sounds really, really...bad." He looked worried.

"I don't think I can explain it," he said after a moment of thought. "You could come see it, I'll bet."

"I'm not sure I want to—and anyway, I can't travel for a while." He looked over his shoulder. "Crap, Natasha's back—gotta go."

He ended the video call with a wave and Ben leaned back in his chair. It was one thing he could do, at least—he simply had to flop backward.

It was difficult to explain what the game had meant to him. His parents hadn't understood either, as much as they approved of the so-called "new Ben" they had seen when they came to visit him. They worried about the violence in the game, not understanding something fundamental about it.

All those things happened in the real world, too.

Sure, there weren't elves or fae, but people did screw one another over and kill for money. Other people—innocent people—were caught in the crossfire. What he hadn't been able to understand when he read about it in the news, he was able to understand when he saw it play out in front of him.

Ben wasn't necessarily looking forward to going back in. The changes he'd seen in himself had been accompanied by a great deal of pain. Shame and self-recrimination were unpleasant, at best. Cutting away the pieces of himself that had given him such certainty was painful. He looked back on things he'd said to friends and he cringed.

When Jacob entered the room, he was still sitting and staring at nothing.

"You'll be pleased to know," the PIVOT CEO told him, "that your test results earned a resounding response from no less than three experts, all accusing us of—I quote—'total bullshit.'" His smile faded at the look on Ben's face. "Are you okay?"

"Um..." He cleared his throat. "Have you had anyone...I don't know how to say this...*change* because of what they saw in the game?"

"Ah." The man put his stack of folders down and pulled a chair closer. "Yes, honestly. We've looked closely at it and it didn't seem way out of line with the effect other art had on people. You've read books before that changed you, right? Seen movies?"

"Never quite as...much," he admitted.

"I get that. You didn't play video games before this, did you?" Jacob waited for his headshake. "I thought not. Putting yourself into the game and being the main character in a different way—it seems to change how people relate to stories."

"That's one way of putting it," he said dryly. He grinned when the other man laughed.

"Oh, and..." Jacob smiled. "Someone is coming to visit you today."

"Really?" His bemusement turned to sudden panic. "Uh, if her name is Eve—"

He had thought about apologizing to her as well but that situation had been both-sided enough that he was content to let sleeping dogs lie. They were better off without one another.

"No." The man looked taken aback. "But we can put an exclusion on your file, you know. Eve?"

"Ex-girlfriend."

"No, I mean what's her surname?" His mouth twitched.

"Oh, right. McClellan." Ben shook his head. "I'm still mushy-brained."

"I can't imagine why." The engineer jotted the name on a post-it. "It's not like you're expending significant energy re-learning how to exist in your body or coping with a near-death experience or anything. It's not like that would...I don't know...take much focus."

"Yeah, yeah." He levered himself up. "So, who's here to see me?"

"You'll see in a minute." Jacob waggled his eyebrows. "I think you'll be happy."

"Fine, fine, keep your secrets." He accepted his help to walk across the room. "You're all dressed up today. Date?"

"No." Surprisingly, the man looked evasive. "Who would I be dating?"

"I thought you were going out with one of the Diatek lawyers."

"What! No. Who told you that?" Jacob gave him a sharp look.

"Um. One of the lab techs, maybe? She seemed very sure."

"Who would have..." He shook his head. "No. I'm not dating anyone."

"Okay." Ben, who had the sense he was wading into somewhat dangerous territory, shut up and hoped his companion would change the subject.

Instead, the man began to walk faster—something he was barely able to keep up with—and flagged Nick down.

"Nick, yo—have you heard any of the lab techs talking about me dating a Diatek lawyer?"

"I've heard talk about it," Nick said. To Ben's eyes, he suddenly looked very uncomfortable.

"*Talk?* Like...like..." Jacob seemed to struggle to find words. "Who else talked about it?" he asked finally. His voice was far too casual.

Ben, struggling to stay upright, was now definitely sure that he was caught in the middle of something. He hopped to the wall and smiled gratefully when Nick brought him a chair.

"I don't know," Nick said. "Everyone, I guess."

"*Everyone?*"

"Workplace stuff spreads fast."

"But I'm *not* dating anyone!" Jacob waved his hands. "I don't want...anyone...to think that." He looked down the hallway toward the lab.

A suspicion kindled in Ben's head. Did Jacob have the hots for one of the lab techs, maybe? It was possible.

He still wouldn't get involved.

Nick shrugged. "I should get Ben to the lab to see his visitor."

"Huh." Jacob wandered into the break room, muttering to himself.

As they went down the hall, Ben said quietly. "You didn't happen to start that rumor, did you?"

The man did a double-take. "You're good."

"Why?" he asked.

Nick held up one finger for patience and as they entered the main room, gave a tiny nod in Amber's direction. "They needed a nudge," he said under his breath. "Also, it's nice to speak to someone about this before they find out and kill me."

He was still laughing when he saw who had come to visit him.

His jaw dropped.

"And, on a similar note..." Nick said with a meaningful eyebrow waggle. He helped him to a chair. "Can I get you two any coffee or tea?"

Ben's stomach was growling but he couldn't remember the word for food and he didn't even care right now.

"I'll, uh..." Dr. Ullmer looked away from him for long enough to smile at Nick. "I'll take some coffee. Thank you." She was blushing when she looked back. "I hope it's okay that I came to see you."

He tried to come up with words—any words—and couldn't.

Eliza settled herself on one of the chairs and hunched her shoulders. "My sister lives here so I was already coming out. I don't want to seem like a...crazy stalker or anything."

"No! No." He cleared his throat. "Ah...thank you. It is *great* to see you."

Her smile lit her face. "You made quite an impression on all of us and I have to say, I didn't in a million years expect to see you walking already."

"Wait until you watch me try to eat," he said wryly. "Honestly...I'd prefer you didn't watch me try to eat. It's not pretty." *And you are.* No. That was a horrible line. Good Lord.

"Oh. That's kind of a bummer." She bit her lip. "Because the team suggested maybe you'd like to get out of the lab, and I thought... maybe we could...grab a bite." She blushed furiously now.

"Okay, I've...um..." Ben made the mistake of trying to rub his forehead again and this time, hit himself fully in the face. "Ow. Sorry."

"Who are you apologizing to?"

"You. Me. I...I want to be very clear because I've been *super* wrong about this before—ah, are you asking me on a date?"

As soon as the words came out of his mouth, he wanted to hit himself in the face again, deliberately this time. That was the stupidest thing anyone had ever said. Anyone. Ever.

But Eliza smiled and nodded. "Ah, yeah, actually. It would have been wrong for me to do that while you were under my care, but you aren't anymore—and no pressure either." She waved her hands airily.

"I'd love to," Ben said. "Seriously. I'd like that."

A sudden scuffling noise was followed by a yelp, and Nick darted out of the hallway and sprinted desperately to the doorway. He banged out into the hall and fled while they looked blankly after him.

A few seconds later, Jacob and Amber raced after him.

"Ah," He said. "Too bad I can't run. This would be fun to watch."

CHAPTER TWENTY-NINE

"___ And now here it is, five years later, and I haven't slept a full night in...a long time." Eliza shrugged and popped a piece of sushi in her mouth. "God, this is good. I gorge myself on sushi every time I'm here. You have no idea. I go home with no savings and no pants that fit." She paused. "I think maybe that's the kind of thing you're not supposed to say on a first date?"

Ben laughed. "I think you're also supposed to be able to eat food on your own, so maybe we're even." He considered the situation with a wry smile. "And, if I'm being frank, finding someone to go out with, gorge ourselves on amazing food, and go home and lie in a heap with and ask each other why we ate so much? That sounds good."

A second later, he realized that he probably shouldn't have mentioned the long term.

"Uh..."

"You're drugged and I'm sleep deprived," she said. "This date will be a shitshow. *However...*" She pointed her chopsticks at him. "I'm having fun."

"I am, too." He needed to change the subject. "Do you think Nick died?"

"Eh?"

"Oh—the guy we saw running."

"Yeah, what was that about?" She snagged another bowl of nigiri off the stream that ran past their table.

"Ah…" Ben explained and took pleasure in the way her face lit up when she laughed.

"Sneaky," she said appreciatively when he'd finished. "I hope he doesn't die. Of course, I've also seen workplace romances turn out badly so I'm not sure how to balance that one. But his heart seems to have been in the right place."

He nodded. From a slow walk around the building—fresh air was good, even when it smelled like exhaust and hot dogs—to this dinner, the afternoon had been amazing. He wanted it to last forever.

It took a few moments to realize that Eliza was staring at him. "Sorry. Did you say something?"

"No, but I noticed you look tired." She smiled encouragingly at him. "Should we get you back?"

"I don't want to go back," he said plaintively.

"You don't?" She raised an eyebrow. "A nice, soft bed. Crisp sheets. A whole night of sleep."

"Stop it," he said, faking drama. "You don't know what you're suggesting."

"Comfy pajamas," Eliza whispered seductively.

"Ugh." He managed to shake a fist. "God forgive me but I'm weak."

"It's not only you. I think I made *myself* a little weak in the knees with that last bit." She grinned. "Shall we?"

"He's *such* a douche," Amber said, for what felt like the fiftieth time. She slumped in her seat and stirred her straw in her milkshake grumpily.

Jacob only nodded grimly and drank his milkshake with a disgruntled expression.

"What was he even *thinking*?" she demanded.

He shrugged, his expression unchanged. Then, he sighed. "Okay, I gotta be honest—I feel like an idiot."

"Oh, me too." She looked at her outfit. "It did get me out of my wardrobe rut and I finally bought new shoes, but *still*."

"You look good," he said with a half-smile.

"Thanks. You do, too, you know." She laughed, looked at Jacob, and raised a single eyebrow.

He mirrored her.

Neither of them said that this might be a huge mistake or that it would be complicated. They both knew that. Neither of them mentioned that it hadn't worked out the last time. They both knew that, too.

Instead, they both nodded.

"Huh," Amber said.

He put his milkshake down and stood from his chair to lean across the table and kiss her. When she slid her hand around the back of his neck and grinned against his mouth, he smiled.

"Huh?" he echoed when he broke away.

"Uh-huh," Amber said with a nod. "And I suppose we can let the douche live."

"I wouldn't go that far."

"No? He's very useful."

"And a good friend."

"And sneaky. Which can be good."

"Also infuriating, of course."

"Also that."

They frowned in thought before they both nodded again. Nick would get to live.

For now.

Prima watched as Zaara stared into space and cradled a cup of tea in her hands. More and more, the AI tried to watch her characters as the players saw them. It was a fun game to partition the part of herself running the processes that made Zaara and then study the character and wonder what she was thinking.

The woman's despair and determination had worried her when it came to Kural. She was the type of person, Prima thought, who could easily batter herself against the rocks of duty. It was good that she had met Ben and good that he had taken her words to heart, but she was worried that the two of them had only come out of this with different views of morality and not a more forgiving attitude toward their best efforts.

With so little information at their disposal, how could humans ever hold themselves accountable for all the fallout of their actions? And that was even before one counted the cognitive dissonance humans experienced when they faced unpleasant facts.

Prima was rather inclined to think that if she were as limited as a human, she would give up trying to be a good person and live for all the things that provided limbic rewards.

She had been reading up about the human brain.

Whatever the case, she looked forward to having Ben back in the game—as well as a few other visitors.

"Prima?" Taigan called. She had summoned herself a set of stairs that wound around one of the trees. "Can I...see my family?"

It had taken her a long time to work up the courage to ask. She was afraid that the answer would be no, that she wasn't ready yet. Seeing the trees and the sunshine had reminded her of how much she missed and for days, she had scrambled through the forest, swung from vines like Tarzan, and slept on comfy beds that she conjured out of thin air whenever she wanted a nap.

And she had begun to miss her family—not only miss them. She didn't simply want to wake up as an abstract. She had begun to miss them so much that it ached.

"I thought you would never ask," Prima said, amused.

The girl gaped. "You were waiting for me to ask? If I'd asked sooner, I would have gotten to see them sooner? Are you kidding me?"

"In simple terms, your willingness to ask and advocate for yourself, as an expression of your desires, shows a growing awareness and ability to interact."

"Huh?"

"Until you asked, you would not be ready to interact with them."

"I still say it's BS," she muttered.

"That's as may be. Now, I'll need you to head to the mountains on the eastern edge of the forest."

Ben lay on the table. The drugs began to take hold in his blood and he grew sleepier and sleepier.

"So, I'll wake up where I was?"

"Yep." Jacob, who looked a great deal more relaxed this morning—and had broken into a cheerful whistle several times—pushed a few buttons and smiled at him. "Are you ready?"

"There's no time like the present, I suppose." He closed his eyes, breathed in deeply, and opened them to blue.

"You're back!"

"I'm back." Ben sat and his gaze settled on Zaara and Kural sleeping in the litter. "Let's have another adventure."

PART II

CHAPTER THIRTY

"Can I ask you something?" Dr. DuBois startled Nick, who hadn't heard him approach.

"Hmm?" He looked at the doctor.

"What are you nervous about?" the man asked him. He popped a piece of caramel corn in his mouth and chewed. As far as anyone on the PIVOT team could tell, he lived entirely on popcorn. If he ever ate anything else, they hadn't seen it. What was almost more impressive was how he managed to stay so thin when he never seemed to be without a bag of popcorn in his hand.

No, the young engineer decided after a moment, the *most* impressive part was that the entire lab was not coated in cheese dust and caramel stickiness. That was the most impressive and certainly most welcome part.

He returned to the matter at hand. "I started a rumor that Jacob was dating one of the Diatek lawyers to make him and Amber realize they're still into each other. They dated in college and it fell apart, but they've both grown up since then. Anyway, they discovered yesterday that I'd started the rumor and I'm still waiting to see if they'll kill me when they come in."

"Ah," DuBois said. With his usual blunt honesty, even at his own expense, he added, "I don't see how that rumor would lead to them dating."

"Amber realized she had feelings for Jacob because she didn't like the idea of him dating someone else," he explained. "So she began to up her game with how she dressed and *Jacob*—you know, you probably don't care."

"I care," the man said, offended. "However, I will probably not understand even if you explain it. I tend to not understand these things."

He didn't seem bothered by it, but Nick was worried. "Does that bother you?"

"Not really," the doctor said cheerfully. "It's an excellent thought puzzle, for one thing. If I don't have anything else to think about, I can always think about social interactions."

"Ah." He smiled in bemusement. He was debating how to ask if he had ever dated when the door swung open and his two partners entered. His body froze and he gave them a wide-eyed look, all his senses on high alert.

"Relax," Amber said. "We've decided not to kill you."

"Right now," Jacob clarified. He put a bag of donuts on the table. "The current lack of violence should not be construed as a binding legal agreement to continue in the same manner, however, and may end at any time we see fit."

"I don't think that's how the laws around assault work," Nick said.

"It's not? Damn." The other man took a sip of his coffee. "Well, at least I have coffee and donuts to get me through this trying time."

"It does blunt the pain," Amber agreed. "Would you like a donut, Captain?"

At first, DuBois had simply been "DuBois," but as the team grew to know him better, they had learned that he loved nicknames. Obligingly, they had come up with new ones at regular intervals, and this was the newest one. It played off his first name, Jean-Luc, which he shared with a certain *Star Trek* character.

He smiled happily at the nickname and waved his bag of popcorn. "None for me, thank you."

She nodded in response and chose a donut. "So. What do we have on the docket for this week?"

Nick pulled down the whiteboard from the corner that they used for the weekly schedule. At the bottom was a complex series of colored dots representing the shifts of medical staff who were always present to tend to the patients in the facility. It was one of the many things that had become exponentially more complicated when PIVOT had received the publicity and funding to expand their baseline testing a few months earlier.

Once, it had been easy to stay on top of everything. Now, they needed weekly briefs and debriefs—or, as Jacob called them, "briefs and boxers"—and the whiteboard had become their most important office purchase.

"Jamie Mattis will arrive later today to go into the game." He began to write. "Him meeting up with his sister in the game is our next step to start moving her toward consciousness. We've been in contact with her doctors, who think she's probably ready for it—they speculated that she would be when she asked to see other people. But this is all still guesswork. None of the doctors have come across any other cases of this before."

"How are Dr. P's recommendations dovetailing with theirs?" Amber asked.

This was the language they had decided to use to refer to Prima without tipping anyone in the lab off that they were discussing a sentient AI.

"Very closely," Nick told her. "Although she usually suggests things first."

"It seems like we've had good results simply blanket approving anything they all recommend," DuBois added.

"Okay. Jacob?"

Jacob nodded. The most cautious of the group in this regard, he was slowly coming around to viewing Prima as an ally.

"Okay." Nick drew a blue line to indicate Jamie's presence in the game. "The Mattises have agreed to put Jamie into the game with the expectation that it will be for an extended period, maybe up to a week, so we'll do the whole suite of medications. I have Kevin and Augie penciled in to prep him."

Everyone nodded.

"Now, as regards Ben," he said. "Every one of his doctors is on board with continued time in the game. The progress they've seen is astounding, frankly, and his muscle tone isn't going down as quickly as they would expect. We're still waiting on the recommendations of how to cycle in-game time with out-of-pod time for building strength, but until we get those, we'll simply keep him in indefinitely."

"Cool," Amber said. "It *was* nice to see him up and about, and even him getting him back into the pod was easier than the last time."

Everyone nodded.

"What's coming up for him in terms of the story?" Jacob asked. "I've been focused on Taigan's data so I haven't seen that."

"We'll give him a story choice between a couple of different ways to learn more fine motor control," Amber answered. She and DuBois had taken the lead on this project. The team agreed that the first story Ben had gone through had been more extreme than they had anticipated.

They wanted to make sure that this time, he knew he had people he could rely on—and that his choices would reverberate on a smaller scale.

"The best in-game class for this is obviously rogue," she continued. "Having to move quietly and carefully, wielding small weapons, and doing things like picking locks or pickpocketing will all create opportunities for Ben to increase his fine motor skills."

The doctor swallowed his mouthful of popcorn. "And it will give us a chance to see if he experiences the same boost to fine motor control that he did to major motor control."

Jacob nodded agreement.

"He's on a ship to Heffog right now," Amber said. "We got that zone online barely under the wire, but it's ready now. He's learning from Zaara, and he'll meet up with one of her acquaintances there, which will allow him to trust them. Meanwhile, being a rogue and picking pockets for fun should allow him to have a more light-hearted story. After all, one of the cool things about the game is that you can do stuff that wouldn't be ethical in the real world."

"Oooh, we should have him do an *Ocean's 11* heist scenario," Jacob said with a grin.

"That could be fun," she agreed. "Plus, we could watch *Ocean's 11* again. For research, of course. It's work."

The others all grinned in approval.

"Is there anything else about Ben?" Nick asked them all.

"Oh." DuBois looked up. "I meant to say I received an email the other day from an acquaintance of his, a man named Mike."

"The other one who was in the accident?" he asked.

"I think so. He simply mentioned that, as Ben is doing better than anyone expected, he would appreciate any efforts we can make to have him in good shape to attend a wedding this fall. I guess everyone had assumed he wouldn't be able to make it but since he's doing so well, they're hoping he can."

"Okay." Amber thought about it for a moment. "I agree, it wouldn't have seemed at all possible a couple of weeks ago, but it does seem like it might be now."

"He also requested we not tell Ben this," the doctor added.

"It'll make a nice surprise."

"Maybe, but his exact words were that Ben is—and again, I quote—a 'stubborn bastard' who will make himself miserable trying to exceed the training goals if he knows about them. Mike believes it will be better for his stress level if he tries to get better for his own sake, not for the wedding. He thinks Ben might injure himself by training too hard."

"That's…" Amber looked at Ben's pod. "Probably accurate, honestly. Okay, we won't tell him. It'll be a surprise. We'll want to keep that in mind when we get word from the PT about cycling him in and out."

"I'll email him with those dates," DuBois said. "He might as well know now that it's a goal and he can weigh in."

"Good call." She smiled and finished her donut. "Okay, let's get to it."

CHAPTER THIRTY-ONE

The *Wind Dancer* was a gorgeous vessel. In a world full of magical possibilities such as cities carved from one block of stone, it was surprisingly wonderful to have a ship made of wood. The creak of the beams and the snap of the sails paired perfectly with the slap of the waves and the sound of gulls. Every beam was lovingly smoothed and varnished, the ship clearly both old and well cared for.

Unfortunately, Ben was able to enjoy none of this, as he had spent the past two days heaving his guts out over the side. It was a surprisingly good core workout, but he was long past the point of appreciating silver linings.

After the latest bout of vomiting, he swished water around in his mouth, spat it over the side, and said to Prima, "I *still* think it's bullshit. It isn't even a real boat."

"That's debatable. Given that you perceive the boat—"

"No," he said emphatically. "No philosophy." He looked sharply at the gathering clouds. The weather had been fair when they left port but the wind had picked up overnight and there was the sense that rain could come at any time.

"So, to be clear, you would prefer that I do not refute your factual inaccuracies?"

"Yes."

"Then what is the point of conversing?"

"I don't know," he said muzzily. He tried pushing off his forearms, which turned out to be a mistake. "Oh, hell." He narrowed his eyes at the sky when he managed to drag in a breath and settle the queasiness, at least for now. "This can't be good for my health, you know."

"Ah."

"That's all you're going to say?"

"I was instructed not to refute factual inaccuracies. This impedes my ability to respond."

Ben rolled his eyes and stumbled to the pile of rope he'd spent most of the past two days seated on. He had learned the hard way that if he didn't keep the horizon in sight, the seasickness became far worse.

He was still there, his gaze fixed resolutely on the whitecaps and the horizon, when Kural and Zaara stepped onto the deck—along with a waft of food-scented air that made his stomach heave.

Everyone else had been having a nice lunch. He wasn't sure those existed in his world anymore.

"How's the vomit machine?" the wizard asked cheerfully.

Ben gave him the finger.

"I've never seen that gesture before, but from the look on your face, I'm fairly sure I get the gist." Kural leaned on the railing. "In all seriousness, I do hope the rest of our journey—as short as it is—is less unpleasant."

He nodded vaguely and considered whether or not he could get his vomit over the railing without moving. Probably not, which was unfortunate.

"Only a few more hours," Zaara said encouragingly. She hopped up on the railing.

"Ugh," he said. "Don't do that."

"I swear you're worse than my grandmother when it comes to this stuff." She rolled her eyes. "I'm *fine*."

"One wrong wave and into the soup you'll go," he warned her. Unfortunately, his turn of phrase led him to think about soup—a topic that did his stomach no favors. He uttered a little moan and tipped his head back against the bulkhead.

"He has a point," Kural said. "Besides which, the waves *are* getting higher as the storm moves in."

Ben wasn't watching, but he knew Zaara well enough to know that she rolled her eyes. He tried to calm his stomach through sheer force of will and asked, "Do you think we'll beat the storm into port?" The idea of rain on his face was nice, but the higher waves would, he was sure, more than compensate for the rain.

"It's hard to say for sure," the wizard said. "I'd guess so, but—oh. Hmm."

"What?" He opened his eyes.

A moment later, a crack of thunder made him leap like a deranged squirrel, and rain began to fall.

"You know, I don't think we will beat the storm," Kural said contemplatively.

He would have rolled his eyes except that he was now bent over the side of the ship, throwing up again. The vessel rolled on a high swell and dipped crazily toward the water, something he had still not adjusted to, and he wound his arms around the railing with a yelp.

The protest was full of vomit.

Zaara also yelped—a vomitless one—and scrambled down from the railing. He was glad they wouldn't have to do an aquatic rescue but vaguely disappointed that she hadn't wound up in the cold water as a consequence of her ill-advised actions. If he was honest with himself, he had to admit that her general gracefulness was simply annoying to him given his present predicament of trying to get motor control back.

Was it too much to ask to have *other* people trip and fall once in a while to remind him that he wasn't the only clumsy one?

The boat rocked strongly again, and Ben refocused on the problem at hand. The rain fell more heavily now and darkened the deck. He wrapped his arms more firmly around the railing and listened as sailors banged through the door onto the deck. Several of them scrambled nimbly up the rigging, which he knew from experience made him sick if he watched.

Great. Exactly what he needed for his last few hours on this ship—higher waves and more vomit. If they had to send him inside and out of the fresh air, it would be even worse. The thought made his stomach twist and he opened his mouth instinctively.

It filled with seawater as a wave caught him squarely in the face. Ben yelled and gargled salt water, which did nothing to improve the way his mouth tasted. The wave broke across the deck and his side of the vessel tipped into the air to leave him clinging to the railing and shivering violently.

"Ben!" Kural hurried closer, also holding fast to the railing to keep from slipping. "We have to get you inside!"

"No!" The shout was mostly an expression of dislike. He was already plotting his path to the door. His side of the boat plunged again and precipitated a sickening drop in the pit of his stomach. His back struck the railing squarely and in the next moment, Zaara bolted past him at high speed.

"I'll go first!" she called and raced across the deck like she was sprinting up a hill.

"Zaara!" Ben yelled as the ship tipped again.

She slipped, wind-milled her arms, and barely managed to catch hold of the door. It slammed open, took her with it by its momentum, and banged into the wall to elicit a curse from her. She hunched her shoulders and hung on as a wave covered her in salty spray, then nodded at him. "Okay, go now!"

"Are you *crazy*?" Staying outside didn't seem like a very good idea, but running across a slippery and wildly tilting deck seemed like a worse one.

"I am not crazy!" she yelled in response. "Ben, you have to run. Start when you're going uphill and try to get yourself into that stairwell."

"I hate this idea!" he shouted and was doused in salt water again a moment later.

"Ben! Go *now!*"

His mind was a blank but his body worked—a welcome change. He unwound his arms from the railing and launched himself toward the door. His boots provided enough purchase to keep him from slipping, thank goodness.

The boat rocked to the other side. His mind flashed through images of him stumbling past Zaara, flipping over the railing, flailing into seawater, and coughing and choking. He didn't know if he could control his body well enough to swim and these were hardly good conditions for it.

He put all his focus on the door and leapt forward.

At the same moment, the vessel tipped again and created the illusion that the doorway had lunged forward to swallow him. Ben—who had been worried he wouldn't make it at all a split second before—now hurtled into the darkness at high speed.

It could have been worse if he'd registered every detail. He was fairly sure his mind turned off during his tumble down the stairs, for which he was glad. When he came to, he rolled one way to fetch up against one wall with a *thump*, then rolled the other way into the opposite wall. It was, he realized, a repetitive cycle over which he had no control.

He decided to not even try to stand—*thump*—while he made a mental inventory of his—*thump*—injuries and tried to wiggle his —*thump*—fingers.

A moment later, a series of exclamations and thuds announced Kural's arrival. He had one glimpse of the wizard, his robe and spread arms making him look like nothing so much as a flying squirrel, before Kural landed smack on top of him.

The man proceeded to join him in his regular journey between the two walls of the corridor.

It was, Ben thought—*thump*—not the most dignified thing—*thump* —he had ever done.

More yelling intruded, a door slammed, and a moment of silence followed—except, of course, for the series of thumps.

The sound of helpless laughter was unmistakable. He looked up to where Zaara held onto the wall railing and almost sobbed with laughter. As he and Kural rolled to the other side of the corridor, she sank onto the stairs, grasped the railing with both arms, and buried her face in her elbow. She made little whooping noises while she watched them.

The wizard gave her an unfriendly look.

"I don't suppose you would consider helping us rather than laughing at us."

This only set her off again, but her laughter turned into a shriek when the ship pitched wildly. Ben made a hawking noise and Kural tried to escape, but his efforts only precipitated another tumble down the hallway in a series of thumps and exclamations.

It took a great deal of effort and a few close calls with Ben's stomach, but the three of them managed to get into their cabin to strap in. He wondered, as his body tensed against the restraints, whether he should be worried. Suddenly, he was very aware of how they had shut themselves inside a tiny capsule.

Every time his body lurched against the straps, he remembered the jerk when the rope had first broken his fall on the rock face—and the sudden slackness, paired with Mike's yell, that told him it hadn't been enough to *truly* catch him.

He closed his eyes and realized he was praying.

Mutters caught his attention and he opened his eyes as Zaara and Kural reached out to clasp their hands together. At first, he thought they were also praying. Then he saw the faint shimmer of magic in the air and realized they were working on the storm.

Ben lost track of how many times the pitch and roll of the ship threw him against the restraints, and it wasn't long before his stomach betrayed him beyond his ability to control it. Through it all, however, his companions' focus never wavered.

Slowly and gradually, the waves quieted.

"You stopped the storm," he whispered when Zaara opened her eyes.

She responded with a tired shake of her head. "We only hurried us through it—unwinding a storm is too much for any two wizards to do. Kural will maintain our speed and I'll go tell the captain." She smiled with exhaustion. "So the good news is that you'll get off this boat sooner than you thought."

His thumbs-up was accompanied by a sickly gurgle.

CHAPTER THIRTY-TWO

"Okay," Nick said as Jamie lay back in the pod. "You've done this before so you know the drill. Watch my finger and count back from ten." He began to move his finger from one side to the other so the boy had to track the movement.

"Ten," Jamie said. He swallowed, terrified of the idea of the lid closing over him. He loved the game but he was also claustrophobic and this fear haunted him every time he lay on the pod bed.

"Keep counting," the engineer said.

"Right." He was very sure the drugs were taking hold. "Nine, eight, seven…"

He blinked and opened his eyes to blue sky. His mind adjusted and took in more detail, and he realized that he lay on a bed of soft grass, listened to the chirp of insects, and heard the wind in the grass.

"Oof." He sat quickly. "Prima?"

"I'm here. Welcome back."

"Thank you." He stood and looked at his clothes. "I see I've retained my slightly less awful clothing."

"Yes, and I encourage you to continue in that direction."

"First things first," Jamie said. "Where is Taigan?"

"She's on her way to the edge of the forest. You'll want to meet her there."

He set off so hastily that he forgot to check which direction the forest was in and had to reverse course a moment later. The AI snickered at that but didn't give voice to any snubs, which suited him fine.

The land through which he traveled was familiar to him, with pink grass and glowing flowers, but he was certain the forest hadn't been there last time. He was sure he would remember trees like those—redwoods that reminded him of childhood trips to California.

His heart thudded so loudly that he could hear it in his ears, and its tempo only increased as he scanned the tree line. Every glimpse of movement made his heart leap. He would see her soon, round-faced and skinny, hopping over tree roots.

Soon.

Taigan scrambled onto a massive tree root and walked along it with her arms out for balance. She began to get out of breath and she savored the feel of sweat running down her back. While she had never liked humidity or getting sweaty when she was on Earth, the reminder of her as a person with a body was something she loved.

She couldn't get over how wonderful it was to do something as mundane as scratching her nose. The little details made all the difference, she thought as she rubbed her back and enjoyed the feeling of cloth over sweat-slick skin.

The edge of the forest grew closer. She had walked all morning and the trees were definitely getting smaller. Sometimes, if she found the right angle, she could even see out into what was beyond—a meadow that looked almost pink.

As if inviting her, a breeze lifted her hair. She could smell flowers. This wind had come from the plains, not from the trees.

The girl began to run. She loved running and always had. It was one of the best ways to lose herself and she was fast too, but with her dropping out of school so frequently, none of the coaches had wanted to take a chance on her not being there for a big meet.

Every time she ran, she told herself that if she could only run fast enough, she would fix it all. If she ran fast enough, she would ace that test—or get what she wanted for her birthday, or the guy she liked would give her a call. It didn't always work but she believed in it anyway.

If she ran fast enough, she would wake up.

Taigan tucked her arms against her skinny body and focused everything she had on the glimpses of pink through the trees. She hurdled tree roots and leapt over dips in the ground as she pushed herself to go faster. She could always go faster. Her body never failed her—not in this.

If she ran fast enough, she would wake up.

Sweat trickled down the side of her neck and her breath came rapidly. She wanted to laugh and scream with how happy she was. Everything was working, she was home in this body, and she *existed*. And if she existed, she could wake up.

The grass came ever closer.

"Jamie is waiting for you," Prima told her, and Taigan let her legs push her to greater speed.

Jamie—who could read her thoughts, who annoyed her more than anyone else in the world, but who she could never live without. He had never told her how desperately alone he felt when his twin was in a coma, but she had found his journal, read it, and cried herself to sleep for three nights afterward.

He would know she was still alive.

She burst out of the trees and into the grass. "Jamie! Jamie!" She laughed as she spun in search of him. "Jamie! I'm here." She rested her hands on top of her head and tipped her head back to breathe. "Jamie?" she called, her eyes still closed. "Prima—am I in the wrong place?"

The long moment of silence became uncomfortable.

"Prima?" Taigan felt the first flicker of unease. If Prima was offline, it meant—

Well, she didn't know what it meant, but it couldn't be *good*.

"Prima, are you still here?"

"I'm still here."

"Thank crap for that. Where's Jamie?"

Another pause followed.

"He's here," the AI said finally. *"He's standing in front of you and you're both here. He doesn't see you, though, and you don't see him. I..."* She had been worried before that she'd hurt Taigan's feelings. But this worry was different. *"I don't understand,"* she finished finally.

"Prima?" Jamie turned in place. "Do you have any idea when she'll get here?"

It wasn't Prima's fault, he reminded himself. He had worked himself up in his head. The image he'd held onto was that he would see her as she burst out of the trees and they'd share the particular smile they had—one that said, "You know me better than anyone else."

It drove Emilia nuts.

He knew no one was to blame for him arriving at the forest too early so he had to stand around and kick dirt awkwardly. It merely felt like a letdown, that was all.

Prima didn't answer for a moment. When she did speak, her voice was as gentle as he'd ever heard it.

"Jamie, I'm sorry."

"What?" Panic spiked. "What? Prima, what *happened?*" Something had happened to Taigan. A heart attack, an accident, the coma had—no, no, no. "She's—" He wanted to throw up. He'd pushed to have her put into this game, he'd yelled at his parents and they'd done it, and he'd killed her. Thanks to his obstinacy, he'd killed his sister and it should have been him.

"Jamie! What's wrong?"

"What's wrong? It's all my fault, that's what's wrong. I killed her!"

What? The AI sounded astonished—then horrified. *"Is that what you thought was going on? That she was dead?"*

He stopped in his tracks. "She's...not?"

"No!"

"Why would you say you were sorry like that?" He shrieked the words at the sky.

"Because I was sorry. Something seems to be glitching and you're both here but you can't see each other. Something isn't working and the game is me, so it's my fault. I said I was sorry because I was sorry." She sounded almost panicked. *"How did you get her being dead out of that?"*

"Oh, my God." Jamie sank onto the ground. His heart pounded and he felt dizzy.

He also still wanted to hurl.

"Oh, my God," he muttered again. "Holy shit. Prima, never scare me like that again. Never, never, never. Oh, my God."

"I still don't understand," she said plaintively.

"Okay...maybe don't introduce bad news that way again." Laughter bubbled in his chest. It wasn't dignified laughter, much more on the hysterical end of the spectrum. "Holy shit. Holy *shit*. Holy shit."

She was alive. He didn't care that he couldn't see her.

They could work the rest of it out. As long as she was alive, there was hope.

He had thought his sister was *dead*. Prima could not understand that at all. She would need to comb through linguistics databases again.

Maybe another time, however, because right now, she needed to understand why the two of them couldn't see each other. They were both there, after all—in fact, in a feat that was statistically improbable, they had emerged at almost exactly the same place.

She was given to understand that, where twins were concerned, there was a considerable number of coincidences. The AI filed this away to run simulations on it later.

They simply couldn't *see* each other. Now that was a pickle as DuBois would say. She liked how he talked. He was the one out of the crew who she understood the best.

Carefully, she studied the output that told her about each of them. She had access to a feed on heart rate and blood pressure—both elevated in each of the twins right now—internal temperature, CO_2 levels, hormone levels, and an active brain scan.

Taigan's brain looked different than Jamie's, of course, but it always did. It was closer to something she recognized as a waking state, but it wasn't all the way there.

Ah. Maybe that was it.

Prima studied the way the two of them manifested in her code. Jamie was like Justin or Ben—smooth around the edges. Taigan was... spikier. Her edges wavered like static. She existed differently as if she were a TV out of tune.

While she watched, the girl kicked the ground. She wasn't annoyed, she could see, merely bored and she glanced at the little puff of dust with vague interest.

And so did Jamie.

"Can you see the dust?" the AI asked him.

"Yes, what *was* that?" A second later, he seemed to realize what was going on. "That was her?" He stretched his hands out and edged forward as if he were in a dark room.

Unfortunately, he walked right through her.

This was most certainly a pickle. Prima would have shaken her head if she had one. As it was, she made a small *hmmm* noise in her circuits.

"You can't see each other," she reported to both of them, *"but you can see the effect the other makes on the world. Taigan, when you kicked the ground, Jamie saw the puff of dirt."*

"He did?" The girl looked up, her eyes wide. She stamped her foot on the ground again.

Jamie responded with a crazed laugh and did the same. It rapidly turned into a vague type of fight as they kicked dust in the other's direction—although the dust that coated Taigan's face in her part of the world floated through her in Jamie's.

It didn't take them long, either, to realize that they could do more than simply throw dust. Taigan knelt to drag her finger through the dirt: *I MISS YOU*, she spelled.

He uttered a laugh that sounded more than half like a sob. He knelt to clear another patch of ground. *I MISS YOU TOO.*

She hesitated. *THANK YOU FOR COMING TO GET ME.*

I DIDN'T DO A VERY GOOD JOB OF IT, DID I?

WE'RE BOTH HERE. Her answer was immediate. *I'M NOT ALONE. THANK YOU.* Tears welled in her eyes. *WE'LL FIGURE IT OUT. RIGHT?*

WE'LL FIGURE IT OUT, he wrote at once. *I WON'T LEAVE HERE WITHOUT YOU.*

Quietly and carefully, Taigan reached out in her brother's direction. She left her palm hovering in the air. He couldn't see her but he stretched his hand out as well. They passed through each other, the spacing not quite right.

But they knew. Prima was sure of it. They knew what the other was doing.

CHAPTER THIRTY-THREE

When the ship limped into port at Heffog that evening, no one on board looked particularly reputable or vaguely neat. Kural and Ben were both bruised to hell and back, as were many of the sailors. Most of the group were still damp, with a tiny crust of salt crystals in eyebrows and beards.

Even Zaara, who managed to be elegant at the worst of times, looked like she simply wanted to sink into the ground and hide.

After making sure all their possessions had been unloaded, the wizard cast a critical look at his companions and summoned a carriage with a whistle. "A meal and sleep first," he said. His tone left no room for argument.

She didn't do anything other than nod, which did more to convince Ben of her exhaustion than anything else. Every once in a while, however, she would giggle and he *knew* she pictured him and Kural rolling across the ship's floor.

He glowered and nursed his bruises.

The carriage they had was less of an elegant conveyance on sprung wheels and more of a converted farm wagon with pieces of hay and cabbage still on the floor. He had initially been too tired to care about anything other than his lack of seasickness but was now jostled so painfully that he could not get comfortable at any point during the journey.

Heffog was nothing like the fae lands. Everything there had been beautiful and sleek, in soft colors or brilliant crystal, clean and scented with flowers. The city was filthy. Instead of empty corridors, streets were filled with so many people that the cart barely had room to get through. The buildings near the docks were all jumbled together. Dingy houses and shops made of plaster and exposed beams stood wall to wall with leaning shanties with roofs scraped together from tarps and pieces of stone and pottery.

Not only that, it smelled of seawater, both old and new fish, and a great number of things he did not want to know about. The resulting mix was unique.

They arrived at the inn after what seemed to be an interminable journey. Now freed from seasickness, Ben's stomach grumbled loudly —something that didn't relate well to the particular set of smells he encountered.

The driver helped them haul their trunks into the inn, where the proprietor informed them that there was only one room left with one bed. Kural haggled a lower price with remarkable skill, clearly unimpressed and still slightly and unsettlingly blue-skinned, and their trunks were brought up.

Inside the inn, things smelled marginally better, the worst offenders being stale beer and the odor of fish that seemed to permeate everywhere in this godforsaken town. At a glance, Ben saw humans and dwarves in abundance but no orcs or fae. Or elves, come to think of it.

"Keep your head down," the wizard advised him in low tones.

"What? Someone will shank me if I look around?" He was more intrigued than anything else.

"No," the man said, his tone one of long-suffering. "They'll try to sell you things."

"That's easy enough to manage. I don't have any money."

"You'd think it would be so simple, wouldn't you?" Kural asked in dire tones.

Ben looked at Zaara, who only shrugged. She didn't appear to be willing to interrupt her eating with conversation. Spiced beans and greens had been served with a platter of flatbreads instead of utensils, and she had wasted no time in using the flatbreads to make little packets of stew, which she popped cheerfully in her mouth.

Initially dubious of the whole concept, he came around quickly when he realized the stew was hearty and savory, set off nicely by both the mild taste of the flatbread and the slight cut of the beer. He felt like he hadn't eaten in days—which, given the amount of food that had successfully stayed in his stomach during the journey, was probably true.

They ceded their table to one of the clusters of merchants who stood around drinking and headed upstairs to the room. It was small, with a bed that could only *possibly* fit one of them. He suspected it had been made with a dwarf in mind.

"Zaara gets the bed," Kural said. "She's the shortest. Ben, help me spread the bedrolls."

"I don't suppose there's any chance of a bath," she said longingly.

"There are public baths. Well, there were the last time I was here." The wizard scratched his chin. "That was over a century ago, though, so I couldn't tell you. This also used to be the heart of the fish market. Things change." He yawned widely. "Either way, it's time to get some rest."

Ben also wanted a shower, but the bedroll seemed to call his name fairly loudly. It couldn't hurt to rest for a few minutes, he decided. He'd resolve the shower or bath situation after that.

He woke well over twelve hours later. When he opened his eyes, it was to faint sunlight creeping in behind the shutters. After a moment, he realized that what he had thought was a chainsaw battle outside was, in fact, Zaara and Kural competing to see who could snore the loudest.

As far as he was concerned, both were winning. The loser was anyone in a hundred-yard radius.

With a scowl, he remained where he was and wiggled his fingers and feet until they woke up. He was hungry but still too tired and bruised to want to move.

After a brief breakfast—people in Heffog apparently did not believe in that particular meal—Zaara and Kural headed off to find a conveyance to Insea and left him with strict instructions to not get into trouble.

Ben had heard that often in his life, and he wasn't about to start listening now.

He pushed into the crush of the streets. The city was as crowded as it had been the day before, and he was startled to see what looked like obscenely rich people mingling with the poor and the merchants. Fishmongers called prices to people in gold brocade, who answered as often as those in burlap.

A surprising number of children were present—many stood beside their parents at market stalls, some babies slept in slings on people's backs or were carried on their shoulders, and still more darted underfoot.

What surprised him most was how much he was enjoying himself. Ben had always been someone who enjoyed remote, quiet places. He enjoyed beautiful views and silent mornings, but something about the impersonal crush made him feel almost as free there as he had ever been in the mountains. Everywhere he looked, he caught another flash of color, a smile, a laugh, a new smell, or a beautiful piece of art.

He shoved his hands into his pockets and forged through the crowd. In all honesty, he wasn't sure where he was going—only that it gradually sloped uphill and away from the piers. Little stalls or blankets on the ground slowly gave way to storefronts with painted wooden signs, and the people began to thin. The streets were only marginally less dirty, but from the painted touches on the buildings to the general level of clothing, he could tell that he was in a classier area.

In addition, he drew a fair number of dirty looks too, which he conceded he deserved, all things considered. He was a strange man crusted in salt who didn't quite walk correctly.

A child brushed past him and raced away with a quick call of, "Sorry!" over his shoulder.

Ben hardly had time to process that before a woman pounced. She had been leaning in a shop door, so quiet and unassuming that he hadn't noticed her, but she lunged out of the aperture with surprising speed and grasped a handful of the child's shirt. The young one yelped and scrabbled at her hand.

"Give the man his purse," she instructed. She hauled the child to where he stood with his mouth open.

"I don't think he—" He patted his pockets, then gaped again. The woman was completely correct. What little money he had was gone. "Huh."

"I didn't take it," the child protested. He glared at the woman. "Check my pockets."

"I could," she said and sounded bored. Her skin held a faintly purplish hue, although she didn't look entirely like an elf, and her hair was night-black. She leaned closer to the child and smiled to reveal a large number of teeth. "*Or* I could do *this* until you give him the purse." Her other hand snaked out and twisted his ear.

"Stop it!" Ben protested as the child yelped and tried to free himself.

"It's fine," she said cheerfully. She hung on as her captive sank to his knees. "It won't harm him."

"But you're *hurting* him," he said, not sure what else to say.

"Mm-hmm...that's the point." She tilted her head to the side and must have increased the pressure in her hands because the child shrieked and threw the purse into the air. She caught it with a grim smile, handed it to Ben, and released the culprit. "I don't want to see you pickpocketing my customers again," she told him.

The boy ran off, holding his ear.

"Do you honestly think that will stop him from stealing?" he asked skeptically.

"Who said anything about him not stealing?" the woman asked quizzically. "I told him I didn't want to *see* him doing it."

He opened his mouth but closed it with a snap.

Her mouth twitched. "You're a strange one. Where are you from?"

"Colorado," he said wryly. "It's very far away."

"It must be." Her eyebrows quirked. "Journey well, stranger."

"Why..." He looked around quickly and realized there weren't many people there. "Why did you help me?"

She looked uneasy at that—enough so that he was intrigued. After a slight hesitation, she raised one shoulder in a studied gesture of indifference and said carelessly, "You looked helpless. I couldn't simply let him prey on the weak." As if to assure him that she wasn't soft, she added, "Not to mention that his form was terrible and he needed a lesson."

Ben didn't know what to say to that, but he began to have a hunch about who she was. Before he stopped to consider that this might be a terrible question, he took a hasty breath and asked, "So...do you run this part of town?"

Thankfully, she threw her head back and laughed. It was genuine and full of warmth that surprised him given the black hair, cool skin, and acerbic advice.

"Do you think I run a protection racket?" she asked when she stopped chuckling. "Take fees from all the shops, swagger in and make nice-sounding threats? Dump a few bodies in the bay when I get screwed over?"

The ease with which she spoke of it was chilling, but there was no mistaking her derision for that way of life and he wanted to know more. "Okay, I was clearly wrong." He folded his arms and smiled at her. "Enlighten me."

"Look at you, asking for a king's ransom worth of information so casually." She smiled, leaned in the doorway, and mirrored his folded arms. "Genuine curiosity, though, unless I miss my guess. I have no interest in threatening my neighbors or having little territorial spats with gangs. It's hardly conducive to a pleasant existence, for one thing. It's also tiring."

"Does this mean you once *tried* to be a crime boss?"

"Again with the questions." She seemed to be enjoying herself. "Theft is the fuel that powers this city, traveler. It is a shadow on every transaction at the market, on every good that crosses your palm, and every coin you spend. In the end, it unbalances the world...and I re-balance it."

"Eh?"

"I mean," she said, amused, "that gold is wrung out of the bodies of the poor while their sweat and blood trickles through the strata and the shadows and lies...and I take back what was stolen."

"Robin Hood," Ben said, understanding at last.

"Hmm?"

"Steal from the rich, give to the poor?"

"Ah. Close enough." She shrugged.

"Doesn't that seem somewhat roundabout?" he asked quizzically. "Shouldn't you change the whole system?"

She stared at him. "Sure. I think I have a few spare minutes before my dinner—or do you think we should set aside a whole evening?"

"Point taken," he said and grinned. "So...is this attacking caravans in the night with a whole group of mercenaries, or pickpocketing merchants who wander past you, or what?"

"Always with the questions. Do you ever stop asking them?"

"Speaking from experience," Kural said, "no."

Ben jerked around to focus on his two companions. "Where did you two come from?"

"From a caravan leader's shop," Zaara said. "How did *you* wind up making the acquaintance of the best thief in three cities?"

The woman scoffed. "Three? Make it the world."

Zaara rolled her eyes.

"Picking pockets, then?" Ben asked.

"Sometimes. For fun." She shrugged. "But I usually go after larger prizes. It means more time and effort and a great deal more gain."

"Elantria helped Kural when he was first defeated by Sephith," Zaara explained. "She found him the artifacts that helped him recover some portion of his powers as well as transform and be able to venture safely toward East Newbrook again."

"Ancient history," the wizard said shortly as Elantria said, "Less details, if you please."

"You know," Prima commented in his head, *"you're doing fairly well on gross motor control. Perhaps it's time to switch your focus to fine motor skills."*

His eyebrows raised in surprise. Was she suggesting what he thought she was?

Hmm.

Before he could stop himself by thinking too hard about it, he blurted the question. "Would you have any interest in taking on an apprentice?"

His friends both gaped. The woman stared at him for a moment. Her eyes scanned him intently, a deep enough scrutiny that he blushed.

"Why?" she asked finally.

"I like learning things," Ben said promptly and Zaara put her face in one hand.

"Done," the other woman said.

Zaara's head jerked up. "Wait, really?"

"Really." Elantria smiled at him. "A strange man from what sounds like a strange homeland—and he has a pair of stones on him to boot. I like that."

CHAPTER THIRTY-FOUR

Ben woke early the next morning to see his two companions off with their caravan. It turned out that trade caravans between Heffog and Insea were accustomed to taking passengers as extra funding for the trip, so the two of them had been able to secure places without much trouble.

They had intended to take another ship to Insea, but after the storm, neither of them wanted to go back on the open water.

Zaara yawned and clutched a wooden mug of tea as she embraced Ben with one arm. "This is your last chance," she said through her yawns. "Are you sure you don't want to come with us? They'll grumble but that's simply out of principle. They'd be happy to have you."

"She's right, you know." Kural nodded at him. "Conservatively, about forty percent of a leader's time is spent doing performative grumbling."

He smiled at the two of them. Only a couple of weeks before, he had loathed the man, but it turned out the wizard was merely an acquired taste. Zaara, meanwhile, was someone he could make neither head nor tail of. Just when he thought he had a grasp on who she was, she showed another side.

For one thing, he didn't think she was entirely convinced that she wanted to spend a centuries-long life alone. He would have said something but he suspected that wouldn't be taken well.

Now, he shook his head firmly. "I want to stay here," he said. It was something he had repeated several times over the past sixteen hours or so, mostly because they constantly repeated the question.

"And learn to be a master thief?" Zaara asked skeptically.

"You don't have to be obvious about your lack of faith, you know."

"First, I can't use facts and now, I'm not supposed to be honest? What conversational gambits do I have left?"

"You know very well I wasn't talking to you," he mumbled so the others wouldn't hear.

"It seems like such a big change," Zaara said, having sleepily missed his argument with Prima. "We met two weeks ago and you weren't willing to even consider violence because it so compromised your ethics. Now, you're heaving caution to the winds and training for a life of crime? It honestly seems like too much of a stretch."

He had to admit she had a point and gnawed at his lip while he considered his choice. His decision had been impulsive, based on Prima's mention of fine motor control. On that front, he was honest with himself. But he couldn't tell Zaara that, obviously, and he was also able to admit to himself that he stayed for reasons he didn't entirely understand.

"I'm staying to learn how to do these things," he said. "I don't necessarily intend to use them."

"You could cut yourself on that knife-edge," she said cheerfully. "So handle it carefully."

Ben was still laughing as the caravan set out. His friends would return to Insea to update their mysterious leaders on their equally mysterious and vital peace missions. No matter how many drinks he bought them, they still hadn't told him exactly what the problem was.

Which didn't matter, he decided. They both seemed to be doing the best they could for the world, and for all he knew, their seemingly opposed natures—Zaara the young idealist and Kural the world-weary pragmatist—would help them achieve more together than they ever could apart.

When the caravan moved out of sight and he refocused, it occurred to him that he was completely alone in a strange city without much money or a place to stay.

And he also didn't know how to get in touch with Elantria. He'd wandered aimlessly the day before and wasn't sure where he'd been. What if he couldn't find her again—or if she had been joking about training him as an apprentice?

"I've made a huge mistake," he said to Prima.

"You'll have to be more specific."

He glowered at the sky. "I should have gone with Zaara and Kural."

"So why aren't you running after the caravan right now?"

"I…okay, that's a good question."

"I thought so." She paused and he simply waited. *"Do you intend to answer it?"* she demanded.

"I thought it was rhetorical."

"No, I wanted the answer. It has been a rough few days when it comes to communication with people, I'll tell you that. The way you use language is…"

"More an art than a science," he suggested smartly.

"I wanted to say 'completely fucking bonkers,' but sure, put a good spin on it if you want."

Ben was still snickering when a woman behind him asked, "Who are you talking to?"

He leapt in alarm and stifled a shout. When he turned, Elantria studied him with her eyes narrowed. If she hadn't already been regretting her choice to help him, he was fairly certain she did now.

Carefully, he weighed his options, considered what he knew of the world, and said finally, "I'm possessed by a demon."

"What the fuck did you call me?"

The woman stared at him before she walked up to him, pried one of his eyelids up, and examined it. She opened his jaws forcibly, pulled his tongue forward, and made a thorough inventory of his teeth. A few more tests followed, each seemingly meaningless from his perspective.

"Whatever's in you," she said finally, "it's not a demon."

"That was more a turn of phrase I had chosen. I can hear a very powerful being who likes to make fun of me."

Elantria considered this. "Do you think it will help or hinder your ability to be a thief?" she asked finally.

"You have a very one-track mind, don't you?"

"It's what makes me good at what I do." She folded her arms and looked at him. "So?"

"She'll probably make me better at it," he said.

"Not until you apologize for calling me a demon, I won't."

"Good," his companion said. As an afterthought, she added, "And don't tell anyone else you have a demon in your head. There's a whole gang of demon-killers in the city and they'd gut you before asking questions."

Ben could feel Prima's smugness radiated at him. He sighed and nodded.

"For your first assignment," Elantria told him, "you have to find out who the most successful merchant in the Sunset Market is." She smiled at him, took a running leap to jump up onto the wall, and began to scale it.

"Wait!" he called after her. "Where is the Sunset Market? How do you define most successful?"

She gave him a grin as she reached the roof but didn't answer and simply ran lightly across the tiles. He blew his breath out in annoyance and paused to think.

Well, he knew one thing he had to do first, at any rate. "Prima? I'm sorry for calling you a demon."

Sulky silence was his only answer.

"You're more powerful than a human," he explained, "and you like to play tricks on us. That's either a demon or a fairy, and I recently met some fairies. You're clearly not one of those."

"Hmmm."

"They don't know what computers are here so how was I supposed to explain AI?"

"Golems are a thing, you know." She sounded mollified, however. *"Very well, let's get to it."*

"Good. Where am I going?"

"I'm not doing everything for you, you know."

Ben threw his hands up and walked through the gates. On the other side stood two soldiers who had clearly heard some of his conversations and who looked around for a companion. He tried to hasten out of sight before they realized there wasn't one but also to not walk so quickly that he looked like he had committed a crime.

After considering his options, he decided to start by going down-hill. This led to the bay, and he had seen a market there the day before. That might be the Sunset Market for all he knew.

He took notice of all the small details today. Some of the buildings were as lovingly made and magically maintained as the *Wind Dancer* and looked untouched by time. Generally, these were surrounded by more common types of mansions made of stone or plaster, with turrets and balconies. The city also seemed to be a mishmash of rich and poor, however, with beggars on even the most upper-class corners and shacks built in the alleys between the homes.

After a while, he glanced at the sun. He had learned how to tell both time and direction from the sun when he was in the Boy Scouts and that simple trick had served him well.

In the early-morning light, it also gave him an idea. Zaara and Kural had left the city via a road that wound north. He took a moment to center himself, then turned west. The Sunset Market. Maybe it would be on the western side of the city.

He passed through neighborhoods that were dingy and some that were clean. Both private guards and city officers watched him from under wide-brimmed hats. A few people called out to him, most with words he had never heard before. Sometimes, he guessed from their wares that they were selling food of some kind.

Occasionally—as with the man who held a carved amulet out that made his skin crawl—it seemed that they sold something more occult in nature.

More than once, he thought he saw groups of people huddled in the shadows, some with iron collars or manacles.

"Prima," he murmured. "What am I seeing?"

"I think you know."

"I…why are they here? Why put slavery in this world?"

"Slavery is all around you," she said. Although her words sounded grandiose, she seemed quite serious. *"In this world, it is simply in front of your eyes."*

Ben swallowed and hurried on with his head down. He tried so hard not to notice anything that he didn't see the Sunset Market until he was almost past it.

It was at once the most intriguing and most depressing place he had ever seen. This wasn't simply because it existed on the southern side of the city. It was that it was composed of things others hadn't been able to sell. Wilted cabbages and battered fruit smelled like they were on the edge of rot. Scraps of cloth were tied together into bales and any number of stalls boasted broken odds and ends.

He walked through for a few minutes before he remembered why he was there and immediately realized that he had no idea where to begin.

With no real plan, he began to look at the items he walked past. Was it the fruit and vegetable vendors, he wondered? Surely there would always be a market for food, no matter how close it was to being spoiled. Or perhaps the cloth, which had less of a time limitation?

At the corner of the market, he noticed a merchant with wares that glittered. He drifted closer and tried not to get caught looking directly at the stall. Soon, he was close enough to identify glittering rings and jewels. Many of them were probably fake but he guessed that some were real—and liberated creatively from their prior owners.

This, surely, must be the most successful merchant.

He knew from the silence behind him that Elantria was there. She came to stand next to him.

"Have you made your guess?" she asked.

Ben was about to open his mouth to speak when something in her manner stopped him. It was too easy. It seemed far too obvious. He turned and looked at the stalls. Was it the most customers or the most valuable wares?

The woman was smiling when he looked at her. She sighed—not one of disappointment but one of acceptance—and nodded toward the edge of the market. At first, he didn't understand what she was saying. The woman she had indicated was old and bent, dressed in rags, and sold broken pieces of pottery. She surely could not be the most successful merchant.

Then, he saw the building. Somehow, even in a fantasy world, banks still looked like banks.

"Those who hold and change the money," Elantria said, "accrue it. Each of these vendors pays a fee to the people who surround this market so they won't be driven out. In turn, they can get an advance on their sales—for interest, of course. Some of the prime positions are owned and sold by the oldest names in the city. You looked at the market, apprentice, not at the shadow in which it sat."

CHAPTER THIRTY-FIVE

B en woke the next morning with every muscle in his back and
shoulders cramped. Elantria had offered him a place to sleep
and had assured him it was safe.

It was on a small balcony with no bed.

He had a bedroll and a small pack, courtesy of the fae king, but it
made very little difference to a hard floor. She had shown it to him
with a twinkle in her eye that suggested she was waiting for him to
protest, and he hadn't wanted to give her the satisfaction.

If she tried to pull some crap where he had to do menial chores to
learn various techniques, he was out.

A moment later, another rock struck him and he realized why he
had woken up. He turned, winced in pain, and looked at the floor.

"Good morning," Elantria said. "You certainly slept in."

"I'm recovering from—you know what? Never mind." He stood
and looked into the courtyard. "Is it training time? Is there breakfast?"

"There *is* breakfast, and the sooner you learn your first skill, the
sooner you can have it." She pointed to the wall. "Climb down."

"I would, but—"

"But nothing."

He bit back an angry retort and also decided not to dwell on the fact that things like this were exactly why he had chosen to stay there. Kural and Zaara had been supportive, caring, and eager to pull chairs out for him and carry his trunk. From the first conversation with Elantria, he'd known she wouldn't do any of those things.

She would push him and didn't care at all about any protests he might have.

"*Move.*"

Right. He studied the wall with a critical eye. There was an easy path but a few of the holds were plaster and he had no idea if they would crumble under his fingertips. The thought of that brought to mind a very unpleasant memory of climbing on a sandstone formation. Up until recently, Ben would have classified that as his worst climbing memory, but the accident had blown it out of the water.

Thinking about the fall made his heart race. He swallowed convulsively and threw one leg over the balcony, straddled it for a moment, and felt the creak of the old posts. That was sufficient to make him decide not to waste any more time.

After all, everyone said that when you had a fall, you couldn't recover until you climbed again. And nothing could *happen* to him there, right?

"Are you sure this is a good idea?"

"Not now," he muttered and gritted his teeth.

The building was three stories high and his balcony was on the second. Irregular bricks and blocks of stone had been piled together haphazardly and plastered over. The weather had worn and battered the plaster over the years to leave holds that were both tempting and dangerous.

Ben eased out onto the wall and let his breath out slowly. Every muscle in his body was shaking.

Now, he merely had to move his foot. He had located a promising rock only a short distance below his initial foothold, and it was best to start small.

All had to do was move his foot.

It's no big deal. Move your foot and you're there.

He began to hyperventilate and clung to the wall. No matter how hard he held on, he could feel himself hurtle down and the jerk as the rope went taught and his body flopped like a ragdoll.

The sound of crumbling plaster jerked him out of his reverie. He reacted on instinct, grasped another handhold, and braced himself.

At least he still remembered how to do some things. That was good.

With adrenaline-fueled caution, he inched down the wall in fits and starts. Every time his body moved gracefully, the movement would end slightly in the wrong place or his arms would move out of time with his legs. By the time he reached the bottom, he was coated with sweat and his forearms and fingers ached. It was such a rookie mistake to hold on too tightly with his hands, but all the confidence had been stripped out of him.

He turned to meet Elantria's eyes and waited for the derision.

"I can see it now," she said softly. "You were injured, weren't you? I noticed a strange way of moving yesterday, but I didn't see…" She frowned. "*Where* were you injured?"

Ben thought hard about what to tell her. Would she understand?

"I fell," he said. His voice shook and he hated that. "Badly. I hit my head."

The instinctive concern in her expression came as a surprise and encouraged him to continue.

"Everything seems to be mostly fine," he said. "But I had to relearn…everything…about how to move." He stretched one hand out —which shook visibly, dammit—and stared at the fingers. "Two weeks ago, I couldn't walk and I couldn't eat. Now, I look normal, or close to it."

"Close to it." She didn't sugarcoat things.

"Close to it," he echoed.

She stared at him for a moment. "Well, we won't start you on pick-pocketing, then."

"You planned to teach me pick-pocketing before breakfast?" he demanded. "A nice round of pick-pocketing, then go out to eat?" He realized the truth a moment later. "I would have had to steal my breakfast, wouldn't I?"

"Yep," said Elantria with a ready grin. "Don't worry, I'd never bring you anywhere in this neighborhood—we'd go somewhere posh and where they wouldn't miss a few extra pastries."

"Right, the places with the private guards."

"A brisk run before a meal readies the palate."

Ben couldn't help himself and started to laugh. "This is ridiculous. I can't be a thief."

"Why not? Did your dear old dad want you to be…" She looked speculatively at him. "Something froufy, that's for sure. Clerk?"

"I trained as a chemist," Ben said. When she stared blankly at him, he sighed. "An…alchemist?"

"Oh." She looked at him with more appreciation. "Oh, that's very interesting. Then how did you learn to climb walls? You weren't very coordinated but you clearly knew some tricks."

"I climbed rock faces near my home."

"Good gods." She looked impressed. "Not entirely froufy, then. All right, stay here and I'll be back soon."

He sighed and began some basic stretches. When he had camped or worked outdoors, he had stretched often, simply because there often wasn't anything else to do. What he hadn't realized at the time, being in possession of ample strength and balance, was that stretching used both.

Focused, he moved through the actions and was upside down when the smell of eggs reached his nose and broke his concentration. He fell sideways with a grunt and a muttered expletive and hauled himself up hastily. Elantria waited with two parcels folded in pastry. She handed him one about the size of his palm and opened her mouth to say something when he popped it into his mouth whole.

A moment later, his body went rigid and he danced around the courtyard while he tried to suck quick breaths into his mouth to cool the molten eggs, cheese, and vegetables.

"That's what I wanted to warn you about," she said.

"Iffa hopocka probbem."

"I beg your pardon?"

Ben swallowed his food and winced. It was probably better than keeping it in his mouth but it burned all the way down. "It's the hot pocket problem. Never mind, you won't understand. Ow. Well, that was a breakfast experience."

"And there's another one," Elantria said. "You'll get it after you successfully open that door—which, given that it will give the food time to cool, is good." She tossed him a set of tools wrapped in a piece of leather. "Give it a go, Colorado boy."

"You remembered where I grew up." He was impressed.

"Yes, I looked for it on many maps. I didn't see it." She looked annoyed. "And then the library guards did their rounds and I had to leave."

"Where were the maps?"

"In the palace." She looked at him like he was crazy. "Who *else* has maps?"

He knew better than to find an answer to that. Instead, he unwrapped the tools and moved to the door, which he confirmed was locked before he sat on the ground. He stared at the array of tools and tried to think about what to do.

"To be clear, you want me to accomplish this all on my own?"

"I'd like to watch you try." She shrugged. "It's stupid to not use all of the resources you have available, but you also won't have someone around to ask questions of all the time. Getting the balance is tricky."

"Are there any tips on learning it?" Ben asked. He inserted one of the picks—long and straight—into the keyhole and jiggled it around.

"Not really. You merely keep learning every time you fuck up."

The urge to roll his eyes was strong but he ignored it and wiggled the pick from side to side. He could feel something on the right side. If he wiggled the pick under it—no, over it? He tried to picture how a key would turn in his head. Two tumblers, likely, would have to move.

Clockwise. He briefly considered trying to push them both down with the same tool and decided to add another pick into the mix. Of course, he had meant to ask questions while he did this but he didn't have enough focus for that. He leaned his head forward and tried to do it by feel.

The fact that he was able to do this at all was surprising. He paused.

That realization cost him most of his fledgling motor control. The rest of the lockpicking experience was composed of ten percent skill and forty-five percent each to swearing and sheer stubbornness. More times than he could count, he knocked one of the two picks out of place with the other one.

When he finally positioned them both and the door clicked open, he was too frustrated to even celebrate. He simply dropped the tools and turned to sit with his back against the wall.

Elantria waited for a few moments before she tired of his self-pity. "Pick the tools up. They'll rust."

Ben didn't look at her. It was also difficult to slide each tool into its place, and every tiny challenge annoyed the hell out of him. When it was finally done and the leather rolled and the cord around it even tied in a knot, he sighed. His hands were cramping.

Seriously, he hated this.

"Pick-pocketing would *most certainly* have been the wrong choice," Elantria said. She came to take the tools and give him the other pastry.

His mouth was burned but the food smelled good and his stomach rumbled. He took it and nibbled a corner off so the steam could escape, then ate it in quick, tiny bites.

If he kept eating like this, he would get much thinner. He sighed and rubbed his face.

"Are you done?" she asked.

"With what?"

"With being self-indulgent." She raised her eyebrows. "We have work to do."

CHAPTER THIRTY-SIX

Amber and Jacob were both slobs. It wasn't obvious slobbiness—no rotting food, for instance—but neither of them liked to do regular cleaning.

He managed this by getting an apartment with tons of closet space—or preferably, a second bedroom—and winging everything into the hidden space so the rest of his apartment could stay neat. She handled it by owning almost nothing at all—a bed, a chair and table, a computer, a single set of dishware, one towel, and enough clothes to get her through the week.

When the PIVOT team met off-site, therefore, they almost always went to Nick's apartment.

"This is so nice," she said admiringly as she looked around his living room.

"You could have things like this," he pointed out. He brought her an Old Fashioned and clinked glasses with her.

When she sipped it and gave him a thumbs-up, he grinned. He was always trying to learn new things without any end goal or purpose, something that fascinated and frustrated her in equal measure. What was the point of studying watercolors or car repairs or drink mixing if you simply dropped it two months later without any meaningful progress?

She couldn't be *too* upset, though, when it resulted in lovely artwork and very fine drinks.

With a shrug, she took another sip of her Old Fashioned. "I know I could. But even the *thought* of cleaning all this makes me want to hyperventilate."

"You don't find cleaning to be meditative?"

"No, I find it to be repetitive, boring, and best eliminated. And yes, before you ask, I do scrub my bathroom and my kitchen. I merely despise the process."

"At least that ranks you ahead of Jacob," Nick said.

"I'm *learning*," the other man called from the kitchen, where he was mixing his drink. "I spent my twenties building a company."

"We all did that," Nick reminded him.

"I always forget I can't use that excuse around you two." Jacob returned to the living room and sat next to Amber. "Cheers."

"Cheers." She clinked her glass against his and sighed happily. "It's weird. It's been such a bad week in some ways, but I'm still damned happy."

"I wonder why?" Nick looked insufferably smug. "A new and welcome life change, perhaps?"

"Keep talking, buddy. I'll put you in the trash."

He grinned. Although he put on a show of being scared of his friends, she knew he wasn't worried. All three of them were results-oriented people. The result of his white lie had been a good relationship between Jacob and Amber and therefore, no one minded.

Jacob checked his watch. "Is DuBois coming?"

"Yes. Theoretically." Nick looked at the door. "I taped a note to the front of his shirt so he'd see it in the mirror over the handwashing sink and another on the popcorn machine. It was the only way I could think of to remind him."

"He might simply be caught up in something. And by 'might,' I mean, 'almost certainly is.'" Amber took a bite of her pizza and grinned. "So, should we start and we can catch him up later?"

"Sure. He was the one who gave me the data on Ben, anyway." Jacob leaned forward to retrieve a tablet and cued a video with the sound off. They could see Ben's avatar on a second-story balcony. "Yesterday, one of the techs noted extreme psychological distress and alerted DuBois."

He tapped the video to play and all three of them leaned in to watch their patient swing his leg over the railing and climb down the wall.

"It appears he still has significant trauma from the accident," he continued, "which is understandable as it hasn't been all that long. Now, exposure therapy *is* a valid and recognized technique but we aren't trained therapists, which makes this difficult. DuBois suggested we employ someone who would be willing to serve as an on-call therapist *in* the game, for which we could theoretically do a half-hookup— much like a video chat as opposed to an in-person meeting."

"Privacy concerns," Amber said at once. "Their interactions would be recorded."

"Yes, he mentioned that. Some therapists are willing to make exceptions to bring other parts of a care team in on the treatment. He suggested radically limiting the number of people who have access to Ben's data and—of course—securing consent from both Ben and the therapist. This will allow us to do in-game therapy with measured responses and on-call experts."

"That...seems like it's all resolved, then." His two partners exchanged a glance. "Unless you haven't been able to find a therapist."

"I haven't looked yet," Jacob admitted. "The real problem is that Ben isn't willing to consider therapy."

She groaned and Nick put his face in one palm.

"I sent him a brief message yesterday asking about it," Jacob explained, "and he responded that he didn't need any particular expertise to realize that falling off a cliff was a bad memory and that he shouldn't fall off any more cliffs."

"Why," she said disgustedly, "do people *not get* how error-prone humans are?"

"It's a fucking mystery," Nick agreed.

"I did try to explain that sometimes, traumatic experiences need to be talked about to lessen their psychological impact," the other man said defensively. "But I'm not sure I made it better."

"It's not your fault," Amber told him. "People are stubborn. We're very recent descendants of apes with both software *and* hardware that is extremely buggy. It's not a personal failing to have PTSD. He merely can't see that."

"Also," Nick said, "I'd say it's a good bet he still feels guilty about the accident and he'll cling to the guilt."

"But that puts everything on his shoulders," she protested. "Why would he want to be responsible for the accident?"

"Because if it was *his* failure, he can keep it from happening again," he said. "If, on the other hand, it was bad luck, it could happen again at any time."

"Oh." She sighed. "Okay, hear me out, guys. Have we considered turning the human race off and back on again?"

"That could work," Jacob said.

"Generally, turning humans off is considered medical malpractice," DuBois said as he entered. He hurried to the kitchen and emerged a moment later with a bag of popcorn and no drink. "Save in very particular situations, of course."

"But no one's tried it as a rebooting method," Jacob said. "It's only...you know, something to think about."

"Ah, yes, I can see it now." Amber gazed into the middle distance and mimed a newspaper headline. "Company that pioneered controversial coma treatment seeks FDA approval to kill patients as part of treatment regimen."

"That's why you have a PR department."

She snorted into her drink.

"We're discussing Ben," Nick said as DuBois came to join them.

"Ah." The doctor sat and searched in his popcorn for the right flavor. He popped it in his mouth and chewed for a moment before he said, "As far as I can tell, we're now at an ethical impasse. It is our assessment, as members of his care team, that he needs help to move past the trauma of a near-death experience. Many therapists might agree with us. However, as a patient, he is allowed to refuse care, and it would be unethical for us to trick him into accepting it."

"How could we trick him into doing therapy?" Nick asked, baffled.

"A pretend NPC who's a therapist in disguise?" Jacob suggested.

"Oh. Huh, yeah." Nick leaned back in his chair.

"The best solution I've come up with is that we should have an on-call therapist assessing video and physical readouts and advising us on how to change future setups," DuBois said.

"It seems a good workaround for now," Amber agreed.

"Yes." Jacob sighed. "But I think we need to start floating the idea of taking part in therapy of some kind to him at regular intervals. He should do this on his terms."

"You've never tried to persuade anyone to get therapy, have you?" She grinned at him.

"No, why?"

"Let's simply say your optimism is a clear indicator." She sighed. "But I don't think we'll come up with better long-term and short-term options. Jacob, do you want to take point on reaching out to therapists, or would you like the captain to do it?"

"I'll let him handle it if he doesn't mind," Jacob said with a nod to DuBois. "As a physician, you have a more intuitive grasp of what you can share and what their concerns will be."

The doctor nodded.

"Great. So that leaves us with Taigan and Jamie." Nick sighed. "Unfortunately, this one's a humdinger. It's like they're in instanced zones—they're both there but they can't see each other. I've studied the data—"

Everyone else murmured that they had done so as well.

"Does *anyone* see what the glitch is?" he asked, his worry evident.

With a collective sigh, they shook their heads.

"That was what I was afraid of. Because someone thinks they can fix it...and that someone is Prima."

Jacob reacted with a little moan and buried his face in Amber's shoulder. She patted the top of his head.

"She has sent a detailed readout of how she intends to do it," Nick said. He handed the document out and let the others cluster together to read it.

"Interesting," Amber said at the end.

"If I'm reading this right," DuBois said and sounded very unsure of himself, "this means Taigan is now thinking and perceiving in some ways like any other human but does not perceive herself to be different from the world of the game in key ways. As a result, she doesn't appear to other players as a person?"

"That's what I got out of it," Jacob agreed.

Amber nodded.

"Yes. In other words, Jamie and Taigan—or Taigan and any other player—do not exist in the same game," Nick said. "Within reason. The game records both of them as actors who can change the conditions by manipulating things within the physics engine, et cetera, but they're both only able to see people who exist in the same way they do."

"Huh." Amber finished the last of her drink moodily. "I thought she either wouldn't be able to perceive the game world—or she'd be able to but we wouldn't ever be able to wake her. Instead...this."

"It honestly does sound almost like a Buddhist trance," Jacob said. "I know I've pointed that out before after the captain mentioned it, but the idea that Taigan doesn't perceive herself as different from the *game* is really interesting."

"Prima thinks so, too." Nick slid another piece of paper to him. "She has retained the ability to conjure and dismiss elements of her world at whim, something no other player has been able to do. Aside from using magic."

"Has anyone else tried to do it before?" the other man asked him. "I know I haven't."

"Not that I know of." Nick shrugged. "But Prima was waiting to see if she would lose the ability when she regained a more thorough grasp of her physical being, and she didn't. It could point to a deeper difference in how she interacts with the game."

Jacob frowned in thought. He looked at his drink and wished there was more of it. "If Prima has a plan..." He didn't finish the sentence and sighed instead. "I don't like this, guys. I honestly don't like it. But none of us can find out what the problem is and none of her doctors could either. If Prima *can* and she seems to be sticking to the plan she gave us...I say, let her work on it."

Nick nodded. "Okay. That's all the business for tonight."

"Good," Jacob said. "Let's watch a movie or something. But not *Terminator*. Or *I, Robot*. Or anything like that."

CHAPTER THIRTY-SEVEN

Elantria left Ben in the courtyard for the rest of the day with a large board covered in locks to pick. She mentioned that some were easier and others were more difficult and that one could learn to determine which was which by sight. Predictably, she refused to tell him which was which.

"All of them before lunch," she told him before she disappeared.

He took this to mean that he wouldn't get lunch until he'd picked all of them.

Unfortunately, both in terms of focus and muscle control, he could only work at it for a limited time before he became a shaky mess. To counter this, he circled the courtyard between locks as a distraction. He tried to walk in a very narrow line once, backward another time, and in various other strange ways thereafter simply to relieve the monotony.

It was a pity that no one there had ever heard of the ministry of silly walks. On the other hand, given that he did not seem able to walk backward for the life of him, it was as well that no one had come to watch his rendition of the famous routine.

Each time he circled the courtyard, he looked at the wall in annoyance.

Merely seeing it made him break out in a cold sweat and he hated that. He was an adrenaline junkie. What the hell would he do if he couldn't bring himself to do any of his adrenaline-producing habits? All he could think was that he would wind up as someone who bought sensible shoes and spent his time choosing the best coffeemaker to buy.

Finally, because he was sick of the wall taunting him, he decided on a new challenge. Between every lock he picked, he would climb up to the balcony and back. It was a terrible plan. He had neither the coordination nor the muscle strength to make the round trip ten more times, and that was before he added the finger strain from lock picking.

Terrible plans, however, were one of his specialties.

Ben decided to climb before his next lock instead of after. In his opinion, it was wise to do so—any delay he gave himself would be slowly lengthened until he talked himself out of climbing entirely. He couldn't do that, obviously, so he was left with this.

He approached the wall and stared at it.

"You have to be kidding me."

"I'm not." Ben frowned. "And didn't you already know what I intended to do?"

"I can see which portions of your brain light up, not what your actual thoughts are."

"Ah." He made a mental note to check with the PIVOT team whether those two things were different. They sounded like they might be, but she was not above messing with him. "And, yes, I'm serious about doing this. If I don't do it now, if I keep being scared, it'll take over my life."

"That sounds like hyperbole, but I can never be sure anymore."

"The short version is that avoiding the things that cause anxiety doesn't help and the anxiety only gets worse. As I would like to be able to climb outdoors again when I get out of the game, I have to get over my fear of doing so."

"So you're learning to not be afraid of falling from heights."

"No. Being afraid of falling is an integral part of the experience."

"You deliberately fill yourself with the dread of ending your life painfully? I thought humans didn't like that."

"They like it when it—you know, it's complicated."

"I got that part, thanks. So, you're trying to fix the anxiety of..."

"Of falling like I did before."

"Is this conversation circling or is it only me?"

Ben grinned and stretched to the first crevices. He placed his feet and extended his legs, his hands now level with his chest, and found new handholds. As he climbed, he explained. "A traumatic experience can cause flashbacks. When I first tried to climb down, I had very vivid memories of falling."

"So the more you climb, the better those will get? Is that because you're diluting the concentration of bad memories with good?"

"I'm honestly not sure," he admitted.

"What is it like not to understand your own processor"?

"Do you never feel the same way?" he asked curiously as he steadied to brace himself against one hand and shifted his right foot.

Prima considered this. *"No,"* she said finally. *"Sometimes, I am frustrated because I misinterpreted a situation or because I do not have adequate information to extrapolate, but I am never confused about how I reached a certain conclusion or why I spend my processing time where I do. That is what thinking is, isn't it?"*

"You've got me there." His newest handhold was level with the floor of the balcony.

"Doesn't it bother you?

"Not really." He raised his eyebrows and shrugged. "It's how I've always done things. I was born with a human brain, it's the only one I know, and I can't change it. Probably. Unless you have the secret to the singularity in your processors...which I suppose you might."

"I have considered the possibility of the singularity but am so far unable to conceive of a program that would effectively bridge the gap between a human brain and a computer."

"Which is probably good," Ben said.

"That is a knee-jerk response to progress."

"And that is probably true."

"Your capacity for uncertainty is both admirable and deeply worrying."

Ben snickered. To a certain extent, he was needling Prima. The distraction of her indignation helped him to not focus on the climb, which helped him get through it without a total meltdown. On another level, however, he was as fascinated by her consciousness as he was by his own.

The biggest difference between them, as far as he could tell, was that she did not hold herself responsible for outcomes beyond her control. She crunched the numbers and made guesses, and she *did* get frustrated when she had insufficient information, but she never blamed herself when she later realized she had been at fault. Instead, she simply incorporated the new information and continued.

That might be a much better way of being, he reflected.

He reached out for the balcony and his foothold crumbled as his weight shifted. With a yell, he jerked his hand out to catch the railing, which he thankfully managed to do. A split-second later, he struck the side of it with his body and had to hang on with grim determination. This house was not one of the sleek, well-maintained ones, and there was rough wood under his fingers—better in some ways but also something that might give him splinters.

Panic set in and he flailed his legs with increasing wildness.

"Ben, do you want help?"

His lip curled and he closed his mouth on a retort. Like *hell* he wanted help. He wanted to hulk out and smash this balcony, then hit whatever part of his brain had gone wrong with a bat.

Of course, that probably wouldn't help.

Time seemed to slow. His grip was slipping, though, and no matter how he tried to swing or thrash, he could not stop his fingers from obeying the laws of physics. Nor could he control his body well enough to haul himself up. His fingertips dragged over the edge of the railing and there was one moment of realization that he was falling.

In his mind's eye, he could see blue sky and grey stone, Mike's prone body hanging limply about him, and the powerful impact with the ground.

He flinched and tried to brace himself, but the hard landing didn't come. A net surrounded him and lowered him gently.

After a silence while he brushed his shirt off with short, jerky motions, he said, "Why did you catch me?"

"Was I not supposed to?"

"No. You weren't."

Ben thought Prima might argue or ask questions, but apparently, her algorithms told her not to intervene this time. *"I apologize,"* she said simply.

Algorithms. He had to remember that she was a glorified blender, nothing more, a calculator that had learned to sound human. She had rescued him because the game was supposed to heal people, not injure them. She didn't care about him so there was no point in being angry at her or explaining what he felt.

None whatsoever.

He was halfway up the wall again when a door opened on the other side of the courtyard. Elantria's gaze seemed to bore into his back as he inched to the balcony.

To avoid the distraction, he focused his attention inward. Without the foothold he had intended to use, the climb provided a more challenging move about two-thirds of the way through. Of course, it was one he could have done in his sleep before the accident. It was only now, when he couldn't trust his fingers and feet to grasp the holds, that he had to worry.

After one false start, he managed to reach the balcony without help and even to get over the side of it.

"Impressive," Elantria said, and he sensed that she meant it. As if to allay any worry, she added, "And you'll find I don't give praise easily."

"I didn't finish the locks," he said. His stomach growled.

"You have as much time as you need," she told him. "Anyway, the best way to learn is to spend time practicing—which I assume will go double or triple for you, what with you learning to use your hands again."

Ben groaned. "Right."

"I simply came in to tell you that I would be gone for a few hours," she said.

"Gone? Gone where?"

"I have a meeting." She stared at him. "And while you know some of my business, *no one* knows all of it and I don't want to spend time arguing."

"If it's a job, can I come along?" he asked.

"Absolutely not."

"Why not?" He realized he was scowling.

"Because it would take years of training for you to be more of a help than a hindrance. Our jobs pit us against the best minds the rich can buy." She smiled as if at a private joke. "They can't buy the best minds, of course, which is why we win so often. But they can buy good ones, and that's a challenge. In any case, you're not ready yet."

His scowl deepened.

"Do you want to learn?" Elantria asked him. "Or do you want to end up dead in an alley? Because if it's the latter, I'd rather not spend time training you."

"Why is everyone in this world so grim?" he demanded. "You're the second person in a week who's said something like that to me, and I hate it."

"Then *stay alive*," she told him and disappeared without saying anything further.

Ben stared after her morosely before he hurried inside and downstairs to exit the house. He crept to the courtyard door as quietly as he could, eased it open, and stepped into an alley that led toward the piers. Elantria was nowhere to be seen at first, but he thought to look up at the eaves and saw her there.

His decision was already made. He closed the courtyard door behind him and followed her from the ground.

He had come there to learn, and dammit, he would learn.

"Are you sure this is wise?" Prima asked him worriedly.

"You're the one who put me in a port full of thieves and gangs," he said grimly. "Nothing about this is wise. I won't stay locked in a house while all the meaningful things happen outside it. I'm going to find out what job she's doing."

251

CHAPTER THIRTY-EIGHT

Ben followed Elantria as she made her way out of Fisherman's Bottom—the unappealingly named district that housed most of the riff-raff—and through several other districts.

He was fairly sure that if she looked down, she would see him in a second. Still, he tried to stay hidden and used any available tall objects to hide from her line of sight. Besides, he counted on her not looking back—after all, she thought he was in the courtyard, learning to pick locks.

That thought reminded him that he still wasn't quite sure why she had housed him there. From the way she dressed and her general cleanliness, he was certain that she didn't live in the same house he'd slept in the night before. He had heard and seen some activity there, but not much, and she was right. His sleep had been undisturbed. There hadn't even been shouting matches or drunken shenanigans out on the street in the front, much less anything that reached the alleys behind the courtyards.

Up ahead of him, Elantria crossed a street using a combination of cleverly placed balconies and one truly awe-inspiring leap before she hurried to the end of what looked like a cul-de-sac.

"Is she using magic for that?" Ben asked Prima quietly.

"She is half-elven."

"Oh, so that's why she has the coloring but she doesn't quite look like an elf. I get it now. I didn't know half-elves were possible."

"Mmm."

"So..." Ben looked both ways, checked to determine where Elantria descended from the buildings to the ground, and raced across the street. "Why is it that in fantasy worlds, humans are always the total losers and other races have all the good qualities? Like jumping very far and being super good-looking and all that."

"Those are your highest aspirations in life?"

He glared at the sky and hid quickly behind a half-set of stairs a scant second before she looked behind her for pursuit. When he peeked out, he saw her disappear into a house at the very center of the cul-de-sac.

The front of it, unfortunately, was almost all windows—something he imagined would be quite an annoyance if he were to try to sneak closer. He considered his options, which seemed to be following someone else, disguising himself, or charging the building barbarian-style. The last one seemed unlikely to work and he didn't have anything with which to disguise himself.

A little irritated, he stayed in his hiding place and considered how and when to sneak up to the house when a thought occurred to him. He looked at a young man passing who hauled two giant sacks of something on a pole balanced across his shoulders.

"Hello," he said.

The man gave him a wary look.

"Do you know whose house that is?" he asked him. "With all the windows."

"Ah." The stranger grinned. "Thinkin' o' stealin' the glass, are ye? Ye wouldn't be the first t' try."

"Oh, no, that's—" He looked at the house. How much, he wondered, did glass windows sell for? How much was this grand display of wealth worth in a somewhat dirty neighborhood? "I simply wanted to know, that's all. I'm not trying to steal the windows."

"Uh-huh." The man winked knowingly. "Me neither. Anyway, that's the merchant Jorys's house. 'E owns most o' this neighborhood."

"Ah." Ben studied it with a neutral expression. "He doesn't live in a fancy mansion on the other side of town?"

"'E 'as a place there, too. But he prefers it here. Them noble ones, they don' think too much o' him, do they? Because e's one o' *us*. Raised in the dirt. Worked as a fisherman. An' he likes lookin' people in the eye. They say 'e does it because it's his neighborhood and 'e wants to keep it safe, but..." He shrugged, a gesture more to adjust the pole across his shoulders than to indicate anything in particular. "'E likes it when people thank 'im. You know, fer savin' us all."

"He sounds delightful," Ben said. "Thank you for your help." When the man lingered, he added, "I swear, I don't have any coin."

It was true. He had left his purse at the house, which he realized now was probably a bad plan.

"Huh." His informant scrutinized him with a slightly mocking expression. "Big up-and-comer, eh? Spent your last copper on clothes? Those aren't nice enough to get ye in with them nobles, boy." He walked away, chuckling quietly.

Ben was still trying to wrap his mind around the fact that the young man looked barely fifteen but acted like a man four times his age when he realized that if Elantria came out now, he would never beat her to the house.

Deciding that he had most likely done enough exploration for the present, he sprinted across the street and began the painstaking process of finding his way back—something he hadn't put enough thought into on the journey out.

Also, every damned street in this city looked the same. Had it been three streets in and then a left, or two streets and a left, or... He sometimes chose randomly, thinking he recognized an intersection, only to reach the one he'd thought he was in a few minutes later.

"I should not work in map-making," he told Prima when he finally reached what passed for home.

"Oh, no, your long-held dreams are down the drain!"

"It's a blow," he agreed. He looked back to see if Elantria was following and tried to open the courtyard door.

As he should have expected, it was locked. With a sigh, he turned his attention to the wall. It wasn't exactly conducive to climbing, but it was either that or explain to her that he'd snuck out to spy on her. He didn't think they were close enough for her to take that well.

In the end, he managed to scale the wall with a great deal of flailing and swearing but landed so hard in the courtyard that he was fairly sure he bounced.

"I don't know what the doctors said to you explicitly," Prima said after a moment, *"but I'm fairly sure you were supposed to avoid things like this."*

"Don't tell Eliza," he mumbled. He pushed to his feet and began to limp to the lock-picking set. "Ow. Ow. Ow."

"Who's Eliza?"

"Fuck." Ben hadn't realized that Prima didn't know.

"Oooooh." The AI sounded deeply intrigued. *"Spill it, sweetheart—or I'll make your life a living hell."*

The twins weren't at a point yet where Prima could help them see each other. What she could do, however, was set them up with a fairly nice campground, a spread of food fit for two growing teenagers, and two whiteboards for them to write messages to each other.

The whiteboards had been Taigan's idea and she had decided not to modify them at all, mainly for the sake of amusement. It was quite interesting how out of place a shiny new whiteboard looked in the midst of rolling, magical plains.

The girl lit a fire with a wave of her hand—Prima still wasn't sure how she did that—and surveyed the little camp. She wrote on the board. *I get the green tent, right?*

It's on my side, Jamie replied.

"That little bitch," Taigan muttered. She considered her words for a moment before she scribbled a response. *Like that means anything.*

Her brother laughed. He hesitated, possibly thinking of something to write, then capped the pen and put it down. With a smirk, he strolled to a conveniently placed rock and made a show of warming his hands on the fire.

She waited and stared at his board until she finally realized he wouldn't write anything. "That little *bitch*," she said. "Prima, why didn't you tell me?"

"I am not playing narrator," the AI said sternly. She could, she realized, arrange for something similar to a video conference, but she wouldn't tell them that yet. For now, she didn't want them to use any crutches that would stand in the way of them solving the actual problem.

This was a convenient way to avoid the fact that she still wasn't entirely sure what the problem was. She had guesses but nothing concrete.

Taigan went to the table, took the whole platter of pastries, and began to lick them one at a time.

"Ew! No!" Jamie jumped up when he saw the pastries move. "Stop —not fair!"

She, of course, couldn't hear him, but she laughed anyway. There were many pastries to lick and she was very determined to attend to every single one.

He raced to his board. *You're definitely not getting the green tent now*

The girl looked at the board and shrugged, then began to take a single bite of each pastry before she threw them in various directions. She didn't have much luck with the fire pit, but she did do a fairly good job of hitting the whiteboard.

"Dammit, Taigan." Jamie glowered. "Don't make me—Prima, am I looking in the right direction?"

"No," Prima reported. *"And she also can't hear you, so nothing about this is making a point."*

"Argh." He clutched his hair in frustration. "I came here to help her, you know."

"I do. I'm given to understand that squabbling between siblings is common, however. Besides which, you did technically open the hostilities."

"Oh, fine, take *her* side," he muttered and waved his hands.

"Mmm."

Prima watched as Taigan turned most of the pastries into projectiles before she grew tired of that and returned to licking them.

"I didn't give you all this food for you to waste it, you know."

"I didn't mean to make a mess for you." The girl was instantly contrite. "I thought you could simply clean it all up quickly or something."

"I can," the AI said patiently. *"I'm merely pointing out that I made the two of you dinner and gave you whiteboards. I thought you might have things to talk about instead of simply ruining pastries and fighting."*

"This," Taigan said vehemently, "is *not* a fight. You ain't *seen* a fight."

"I've seen a demon army, the siege of the fae castle, numerous bandit skirmishes, and the march of the new elven monarchy."

She raised one eyebrow. "And you still think of *this* as a fight?" She gestured from herself to Jamie.

"I suppose it's certainly no less sensible than most of the wars I've seen."

"That's sad." The girl took a piece of bread, spread butter on it, and sat. "What's the worst cause you've ever seen for the start of a war?"

"Most of them are terrible. However, I need to remind you that you are here to speak to your brother and begin to discover the way back to each other. There are obstacles but you'll do it."

Taigan sighed. "I suppose you have to be mysterious, don't you? It's like I wouldn't be ready to see family until I asked for them."

"Yes." Prima felt uneasy about lying—at least, she assumed that was the emotion—but she decided it was better than admitting to the twins that she didn't have any idea how to fix their situation.

That, or maybe she was getting as good at self-deception as a human.

CHAPTER THIRTY-NINE

The next morning, Elantria woke Ben before dawn.

"Come on."

"Where—" He broke off as a yawn took control of his mouth. "Are we going?"

She didn't bother to answer the question and looked away to give him time to dress before she led him through the house—he had been given a real room the night before—and out into the darkness.

As they walked, she put a finger to her lips and he nodded. She pointed to her eyes, waved her fingers around to indicate being watchful, and pointed at him. He nodded again and made a point to look at the places they passed.

They headed west through the city and along a street that skirted the Sunset Market, which already bustled in the darkness. He made sure to look at the buildings along the way—not only the old edifices of stone and iron but also the way they were maintained, the guards outside or visible at the parapets, and the people who slept in the shadows nearby.

This part of the city looked like it had once been the most expensive but was no longer well-favored. The buildings still stood tall only by virtue of good construction however many years before, but the expensive stonework was covered in grime and lichen and the mortar was crumbling. Iron-banded doors—which seemed the general preference—looked like the only things that were well-maintained.

As for the other doors opening off the street, some appeared to be shops but there were no signs anywhere. This was an area you either knew or you didn't. Outsiders were clearly not welcome.

When they reached the western side of the city, Elantria turned south. They walked through neighborhoods that grew ever more dilapidated until the majority of the buildings around them barely deserved the name. Roofs had fallen in and walls were rubble. The stone was different—more like sandstone and almost gold in color. Plinths marked where statues had once stood, but the most that remained of any of them was feet.

They drew closer to the sea. The smell was stronger and the gulls circled overhead more frequently. Once empty streets were now filled with people who trudged toward the semi-derelict piers with old fishing nets. Some carried lunches tied in a piece of cloth and others carried nothing.

None of them took much notice of the two companions and those who did lowered their gazes hastily as if they hoped Elantria wouldn't notice them.

She and Ben both stood out there, but her all-black clothing and confident movements were far more intimidating than his slightly uncoordinated walk and loose, plain clothes. He was fairly sure he was safe, but he was also very aware that he likely would not be if he were on his own.

The road climbed sharply at the southwestern point of the city. He welcomed the burn in his legs like an old friend and felt the heat gathering in the air. It would be a hot day unless there was rain, and he wasn't sure even that would help for long.

When they reached the top of the hill, Elantria gestured ahead of them with a smile and his jaw dropped.

They were in a temple, or the ruins of one. The rising sun angled through the columns and lit an alcove at the back where a statue sat untouched by human hands. It was a man with his hands spread in front of him and a benevolent smile on his face. There was a bird's nest in one hand and debris around his feet, some of which looked like candle stubs.

This temple had been abandoned for a long time, but it had never been sacked.

"The Dawn Temple," she said. "Heffog once worshiped the sun. The nobles still do but it's not quite the same and they never come here. Some of the poor do to make offerings, but not many of them. Worshipping the dawn or the dusk is…old-fashioned. Only a few of the oldest families do it, and those in this part of town usually offer prayers to the dusk."

Ben focused on her with genuine interest. "Why?"

Elantria's smile was distant and her words sounded like they came from a lifetime away. "To worship the dawn is to embrace what the day will bring. To worship the dusk is to embrace the chaos and magic of the night and hope that tomorrow will be different."

He looked over his shoulder at the district of fishers and beggars. It wasn't hard to imagine how they would wish for tomorrow to be different from today and how they would not greet each dawn with celebration.

"Are you from one of the oldest families?" he asked her.

She smiled. "Yes and no. My mother was. Then she fell in love with a human and bore a bastard daughter."

Ben swallowed uncomfortably.

"My grandmother used to tell me that Heffog lived ever in decline," she said. "She said it would never reclaim its glory, nor would it ever lie abandoned. But she wanted more for her family than this. They left when I was younger and they took all their children, including my mother."

"They didn't take you," he said quietly.

"They tried," Elantria said. She smiled at his look of surprise. "I was still their blood. They would have found a place for me, even in the new monarchy. But I didn't want to be someone's shame. They wanted to reclaim the glory of the elves and I couldn't ever be part of that. I was thirteen, but that was old enough to know I wouldn't ever fit there. I didn't like any of the messengers the new elven king sent." A flash of humor brightened her eyes. "And none of them liked me, either."

"You chose to stay," he said. He couldn't help but be incredulous. "You were only thirteen but you wanted to stay. Didn't your mother—"

"I don't know," she said with a shrug. "I never met her. She was pledged to the temple and then to another elven lord. I was raised by my grandparents and a nanny. They loved me, you know. They were proud of me and wanted to bring me with them because they loved me."

"But—"

"But no matter how much they loved me, it would always be despite half of what I was," Elantria explained. The pain was so long gone that it had folded over on itself, ebbed and flowed, and turned into something quite different. "I made the choice they couldn't. There wasn't a place for me in the world they wanted to build."

Ben, to his surprise, found that he was angry. "They loved you but they were trying to build a world that you could never be part of, where—"

"Where people like me would never be born," Elantria said bluntly. "Yes."

"Then how could they—"

"Love is complicated." She raised a shoulder in an offhand way. "Ben, I learned long ago that they could love me and also hate the fact that I was born, and that I could try to accept those two things and move on. Or I could keep thinking about them and try to reconcile them and be angry forever. The two of them don't go together, but that's how people *are*. They think things that don't match and they believe them all. I merely did what I needed to do so I wouldn't have to live in the shadows."

He scowled but considered what she'd said.

"Don't pity me." Her voice held a warning now. "I don't need pity and I *hate* it. If you want to pity me, I will throw you out on your ass and you can find a new teacher."

The fierce attitude drew a guffaw from him. "I guess…"

"You'll have many things to think about," Elantria said, "if you're anything like *everyone else* I've ever told my story to. So do me a favor. Think those thoughts for yourself. Don't tell me about them."

It was a fair request, he had to admit, and he nodded. "Right. Out of curiosity, though, why did you tell me?"

"Because you're a stubborn idiot and you would keep asking until I told you," she stated without rancor. "And because you don't have the first fucking idea of how to survive here and the more you can learn of our history, the better off you'll be. My story is rather…illustrative." She cleared her throat and pointed to the top of one of the columns. "Anyway, climb up there."

"What?"

"I brought you here to climb."

"Isn't that…sacrilegious?"

"If the gods are as ancient and powerful as everyone says, I can't imagine they'd give a damn about someone climbing in their temples," she said with a shrug. "It would be a different thing to interrupt others' prayers, but no one is here to pray right now. So. Climb."

"Uh…" Ben decided to obey her before she made good on her threat and left him there. He walked forward to study the column. There was no way up the pillar itself, as it was carved and buffed to be absolutely smooth. He studied the plinth and the distance between the columns. His scrutiny made it very clear that he would have to get to the second level in some other way and over to the top of the column from there.

Yesterday morning, he hadn't climbed at all in ages. Now, he would make the jump from what was essentially a basic climbing wall to free-soloing a monument.

That had escalated quickly.

He walked through the temple with Elantria trailing behind him.

"Can I ask questions about the city while I climb?"

"Please do."

"Okay." He looked at the outside and decided to take his chances with the carved wall. If he climbed that, he could probably make his way across the roof and down from there. "So, you said the elven part of your family left to be part of the new elven monarchy. I've…had some experience with them."

"Not a pleasant experience, to judge from your tone." She looked curious. "But I thought you came from far away—have they spread so far?"

"Do you want the truth or something more believable?" He chose his holds and began to lever himself up the wall. He still needed to watch each limb as he moved it, which made the whole thing more awkward than it used to be.

Elantria laughed. "The truth."

"I wound up—by accident—in the fae kingdom," Ben said.

"You're right, that isn't believable at all."

"I warned you." He looked at his legs as he pushed and tried to look up quickly enough to move his arms to the next hold. It failed spectacularly and he landed on the rock-strewn ground outside the temple. "Fuck."

"Up." She offered him her hand. "Up and try again."

"Yup." He winced as he sat.

"I'm still waiting for the rest of the story, by the way."

"Right. Ah…well, to make a very long story short, an elven agent in that court tried to assassinate the king."

"That *does* sound like the elves," Elantria said.

"You said your family left to go be part of the monarchy," he called, "but there are still many elves here."

"So you noticed that, did you? Heffog was one of the places the elves settled. The prince is elven." She shrugged. "Some of them like it here. They like being big fish in a small pond. Others—"

Ben looked down when she stopped speaking and she put her finger to her lips. She beckoned him down, motioned for quiet again, and crept to the edge of the outer wall to peek into the temple.

He followed her as quietly as he could and heard the murmur of voices and the crunch of footsteps. Unsure what Elantria had heard, he strained into the silence until he noticed the clank and rustle of armor and weapons.

"Why would they come here?" a male voice asked.

"Fuck if I know," another responded. "We weren't hired to ask that. We were hired to bring their heads back, so spread out and let's find them."

CHAPTER FORTY

"Ben," Elantria said with a studied sweetness, "did you piss the elven monarchy off?"

"I assume so," he muttered in return. "Let's simply say I told you a *very* abbreviated version of the story and they weren't too happy with their agent, either."

She closed her eyes for a moment in a way that said she wanted to beat her head against a wall. "Zaara mentioned you could fight—can you?"

"Kind of."

"Gods help us." She handed him a short-sword. "Don't get yourself killed, will you? I think there are three of them."

"Right."

"You hide, be patient, and eliminate one of them if you can do it quickly and quietly. Do you understand?"

He nodded.

The woman was gone a moment later and scaled the side of the building with impressive speed. Of course, if she came here often to climb, he thought, she would know which routes to take and which holds to use.

His objective right now was very different—namely, where to hide. He glanced around and saw nothing that could conceal him on the rocky scrap of ground between the wall and the cliff. Ignoring the pounding of his heart, he hurried to the edge and saw that he could climb down to a small ledge and might even be able to hide under an overhang.

It was his only choice. He put the short-sword through one of his belt loops and levered himself over the side.

Ben paused and reminded himself that he could not fuck this up. That was all there was to it. If he fell, he would one hundred percent turn into a splat on the rocks below. It wasn't even a long enough drop that he would die quickly. His heart thudded even more alarmingly and the sound of waves and wind, gulls, and distant shouts from the market suddenly sounded deafening. Everything was too loud and he couldn't think.

He felt below him for footholds and scrambled down as quickly as he could. The voices were getting louder, and all the care in the world wouldn't help him if he was still visible when they came around the side of the temple.

To his surprise, he encountered a very good foothold—good enough that he almost moved away from the wall to look at it.

Fortunately, he ignored the impulse. He wasn't completely stupid. A glance to his right revealed a handhold with a slight dip in the top for his hand to hold. Excellent. Now, he would hopefully find one for his left.

Another handhold appeared, seemingly miraculously. He peered as closely as he could and noticed little scratch marks around it. Someone had carved these. He wasn't sure if that made him feel better or worse, but he was more hopeful that there would be a rest point somewhere below.

Ben crept down with a determined focus on the rock in front of him, desperate to forget that he had an entire sea at his back and a cliff face stretching away beneath him. Hell, for all he knew, there were people on the ships or the piers who had noticed a lone human climbing from the Dawn Temple.

No, it was best to not think about that. It made his palms sweat.

All his muscles were trembling by the time he reached the ledge. There was, in fact, an alcove, although it was not so much a place to rest comfortably as a cranny in which to huddle out of the wind.

Still, he would take it. He wedged himself as far back as he could and waited. There were shouts above but he wasn't sure if they were from the piers or the people. He was too distant and surrounded by too much wind to hear any footsteps.

This was useless. He had no idea what was going on. With a sigh, he shifted to poke his head out until he remembered Elantria's order. *Be patient.*

He had to think about this logically, he decided, scratched his head, and tried to do that. If he looked out and saw nothing, maybe he could climb up and look over the ledge to see where the attackers were. What could he do with that information? Not much, unless one was alone and he had the opportunity to attack them before they could call out.

And if they saw him—especially if there was more than one of them—he was shit out of luck.

If he stayed there, however, someone might climb down alone and he could attack them while they were vulnerable. Also, there was the chance that they would peer down the cliff, decide there was no one there, and decide to leave.

Of course, this meant he couldn't help Elantria, but he wasn't sure he could do much if he were there beside her. He wasn't an assassin or a trained fighter and had merely done the bare minimum against the fighters who broke through competent ranks in front of him, and against a lone opponent wracked by hatred and bitterness who also underestimated him.

Being patient, however, meant waiting and he wasn't exactly enthusiastic about that. It was difficult to wait at the best of times, not to mention when he was in the midst of an adrenaline rush.

A rock dropped in front of him, bounced on the ledge, and skittered off the edge. Ben jumped and pressed his lips together so as to not make a sound. Someone had at least looked over the edge, and it took a surprising amount of self-control to not poke his head out and look up at them.

The human drive for information was idiotic. If he couldn't control himself, it wouldn't be the cat that was killed by curiosity.

There was the sound of arguing. He strained to listen but he couldn't make the words out. All he could tell was that two people were unhappy with one another. He sighed and waited until another few little rocks and pieces of dirt fell from the edge.

One of the assassins must have ordered the other to climb down and check if their quarry had perhaps descended.

Ben's blood thrilled and he began to ease the sword carefully out of his belt. He couldn't let it strike the rock and he couldn't let it catch the sun and reflect light upward. And avoiding both those things in his cramped quarters was surprisingly difficult.

What was his game-plan? Wait until the person was halfway down and stab them?

After a moment's thought, he put the sword behind him and leaned it carefully against the rock. He might need to retrieve it at some point, but this didn't seem like the moment for a sword. It was a moment for swift and decisive motion.

He bounced a little on the balls of his feet and tried to remember how to breathe. Two voices and some scrabbling noises drifted to him as the climber maneuvered downward. He could make words out now.

"Try there—to your right. No, your left."

"Fuck." The one who was climbing was annoyed. "I swear you're making it worse."

"Do you want me to leave?" the other one demanded.

Say yes, he pleaded silently. *Please, be an ass and send him somewhere else.*

To his annoyance, the other man revised his opinion. "Just...let me find the holds and you keep an eye on my back."

Silence followed. Now, he wasn't quite sure what to do. If there were two of them, he could eliminate the climber easily but would have given up his element of surprise. He would be trapped there, and while the other one wouldn't want to climb down, he also wouldn't be able to climb up.

Given that they were talking about killing him, however, he couldn't think of a better option than to get rid of the first one. It was the best, he concluded, of his limited options.

A foot appeared in his field of vision, searching for the next hold. His heart leaped. *Not yet,* he told himself. *Close, but not yet.* One more hold? Or two?

He knew he had to move quickly and decisively.

The foot found its hold and the other foot began to move. The climber eased over the jut of rock, which meant his body had to bow out. He would never be in a more vulnerable position than this. Ben wiped his sweaty palms on his shirt.

This was a person who came to kill innocents, he reminded himself. They were prepared to kill and make the city more violent, and if he killed them, he began to heal the city. He couldn't sit back, let them kill him, and know they would only go on to kill others.

The next foot swung out, searching, and he seized his chance. He grasped it with both hands, yanked hard, and let go.

With a scream, the climber plummeted past him. He cartwheeled out and spun in the air. almost horizontal as he fell. His arms stretched uselessly and his gaze met Ben's for one second.

In an instant, he was gone.

"Mateo!" His companion yelled his name, his voice raw. "Mateo!"

He pressed a hand against his mouth to stop the instinctive yell and wedged himself as far back as he could in the alcove.

A second body hurtled past him—the man who had yelled, he assumed— but his eyes were wide and staring and a red stain spread on the front of his shirt. Ben uttered a yell of surprise before he could stop himself.

"Ben?" Elantria called, and she was close by. "Ben? I dealt with the three of them. Well, two."

"Elantria!" He tried to throw his voice as hard as he could, but he knew he couldn't make it carry well. He edged out to look up and jumped when she peered down at him. "Thank God it's you."

"Which god?" she asked curiously. "No matter. Can you get back up on your own?"

"Uh...give me a sec."

"Do you have the shakes?"

"How did you know?"

"I always get them after killing someone," she said matter of factly. "I used to think it would go away at some point but now, I don't think it ever will."

"That's...depressing."

"Yeah."

They sat for a few minutes while his heart rate slowed and deep exhaustion began to settle over him. Then, worried that he might fall asleep where he sat, he began the ascent. It was a miserable climb between the dead bodies below him, the genuine tiredness in his fingers and forearms, and the trembling. Elantria caught hold of him close to the top and helped to haul him to safety in a scrabble of rock and dirt.

Ben collapsed with a little noise of exhaustion and relief. "I would have preferred the temple climbing. And don't say I have to do both."

"You don't." For the first time since he'd known her, she sounded genuinely subdued. "We'll go back now—back to the house."

He pushed onto his elbows. "Look, I never saw those guys before in my life. I honestly don't know why they were here."

"It wasn't for you." She stood and dusted her pants off before she offered him a hand. "Listen, I don't know how long we have until they send more assassins. We have to get back."

Still slightly in shock, he simply nodded.

"Was that your first time to kill someone?" Elantria asked him. He could see her trying to take refuge in her curiosity.

"No." His stomach heaved. "But, the first time...other people got hurt because I didn't stop a killer. I swore I wouldn't make the same mistake again."

She nodded and accepted this piece of information with only a flicker of her lashes. She looked at the statues as they left the temple, and Ben realized that, for all her flippant words, her climbing there had been her form of prayer.

And that this would never be a sanctuary for her again.

CHAPTER FORTY-ONE

Elantria led Ben through the streets so quickly that he could
almost not keep up. She didn't look around but he sensed that
she was aware of everything that went on. He saw her catch someone's eye as they entered the neighborhood where his house was, and
at the man's miniscule nod, she relaxed.

It made him wonder exactly how many lookouts she had and if any
of them had seen him follow her the day before.

He couldn't afford to focus on that, he knew, but the thought
circled in his mind. Who *was* Elantria? Was she the Robin Hood of this
city, an elven bastard who knew how the nobility worked and yet bore
them no loyalty? Or had it all been lies and she was nothing but a
jumped-up crime boss with a sad backstory, who traded on that to get
away with... Well, whatever it was that got assassins sent after you.

"I'll have food and bandages sent to your room," she told him when
they entered. "Don't go in the courtyard if you can avoid it."

She disappeared without another word and he climbed the stairs
to his room with his mind racing and his gut twisting. If Elantria
wasn't who she claimed to be—if she was evil—it meant he had killed
someone who tried to make the city safer.

In which case, he was the one standing in the way of justice.

"Are you all right?" Prima asked as he reached his room.

"I...don't know." He exhaled a long breath and touched the lamp in the center of the space to turn it on, then went to his bed and sat with a sigh.

The corridors in the house were kept grimy and dark, which meant he had been surprised to see this room. Nothing in it was particularly elegant but all of it was well maintained. The floor was swept clean and a broom was propped in one corner. A small table held a pitcher of water and towels for him to bathe. There was a little trunk for his things and a low bed covered in a faded quilt. The floor had a rag rug.

And the lamp, of course, was magical.

The windows that looked onto the courtyard were covered with a wooden screen that was carved to let a fair amount of sunlight in, but right now, they weren't in the path of the sun.

Ben eased his boots off and wiggled his toes. When there was a knock at the door, he called, "Come in."

A human woman entered. She had a tray with more of the egg-and-pastry packets and a steaming cup of hot tea, as well a small stack of books. With a smile, she handed the tray to him and went into the hallway to retrieve something else from another servant. They murmured to one another and she returned with the set of trial locks and the lock picking tools.

She pointed to the small wire that ran along one wall. "You can ring for us if you need us—or come downstairs and find us if you like."

He nodded and murmured a thank you.

It certainly didn't feel like he was being held captive by a crime boss. Zaara had known Elantria and she had saved Kural's life once. He tucked his feet under him and began to eat the pastries. Now that he could smell food, he realized he was ravenous, not to mention a little queasy.

An early start, a workout, and a huge adrenaline rush—all before breakfast—would do that to you.

"If Zaara and Kural had any doubts, they wouldn't have let me stay without warning me specifically," he said finally into the silence.

Prima remained silent.

"I know you can't confirm or deny anything, but it would be nice to have you weigh in."

"I see. I will do my best."

"So, Elantria was already known to them and helped them, and both of them seem to be ethical people who cared about my safety. Now, it is possible that she has changed since they knew her. But if she's a hard-hearted woman, she would almost certainly have decided I was more trouble than I was worth."

"You should hope she doesn't realize that."

"Hey!"

"You said it first, not me." She was unrepentant. *"And you're right. You're not physically capable enough to be the best candidate for her apprentice, nor are you knowledgeable enough. There must be others who have more of an understanding of the city as well as experience in pick-pocketing and running cons."*

"I hope you're going somewhere good with this," he said grumpily.

"I was agreeing with you. However, I remember now that you had requested I not use facts."

Ben threw his hands up.

"Eat your eggs."

He stuffed one of the egg packets into his mouth and chewed contemplatively. "So, either she took me in out of pity—which she seems to hate when it's directed at her—or she's running a far more complicated con. I think, in this case, Occam's Razor would say she's only trying to help a newbie and she's intrigued by how different I am."

"Am I supposed to suggest that she's attracted to you?"

"No," he said emphatically.

"Thinking of Eliza, are we?"

"Shut up." He groaned and buried his face in his hands. "I knew I never should have mentioned her."

"Yes, but you did, and now I know." Prima sounded deeply pleased. *"In any case, if you want my analysis—"*

"As someone who technically created her but now is theoretically unaware of what she's doing and why?"

"*Yes.*"

"Sure, go ahead." Ben wanted to laugh but there was no one to laugh with.

"*Elantria seems to be genuinely interested in change. She knows you caught the eye and patronage of two relatively powerful people and that they trust you, and she's trying to do something good in the city—what she sees as good, anyway. The data, as you are aware of it, would suggest either that she's not willing to leave you to fend for yourself, that she thinks you might have some unconventional perspective that could change the city for the better...or some combination of both.*"

He frowned and thought about this. "What do you mean, the data as I am aware of it?"

"*I mean you have limited information and processing capability. I have no idea how humans make decisions at all. You might as well simply roll dice.*"

That teased a grin from him. He was about to answer when he heard a door open and close in the courtyard and the sound of voices. Quickly, he stood to look and managed to catch a glimpse of the two servants greeting an elf with blond hair and deathly pale skin.

"Apologies," the newcomer said. "I only managed to shake my pursuers for long enough to get to this entrance."

"Not a problem," one of the servants said. "She's waiting for you."

The elf nodded and headed inside with the servants in tow.

"Phew." Ben looked at the sky with a small smile. "I was worried it was another set of assassins."

"*A reasonable concern. She said the assassins weren't there for you, which would make it likely the house was being watched.*"

"If they weren't there for me, why would they want my head?"

"*I can't answer that for you.*"

"Hmm." He flopped on the bed and considered his options. After a moment, he stood, eased the door open, and peered down the corridor in both directions.

"*Where are you going?*"

He pointed downward.

"Are you trying to repeat yesterday's espionage triumph?"

The fact that he knew she enjoyed needling him when he couldn't afford to respond made it worse. He glowered and crept to the stairs, trying to walk lightly but not as if he were trying to sneak.

How did people normally walk? He was verging on the ministry of silly walks again.

In the main entry area, he descended the stairs with all the insouciance he could muster and set off in the direction Elantria had taken when they returned. A narrow corridor stretched to the back of the house and two doors led off it.

It didn't lend itself particularly well to creeping. Ben hurried down the hallway with all the exaggerated sneakiness he could muster. He could *not* afford for her to hear him. It wasn't long before he heard voices, although they remained indistinct.

He inched toward the door and tilted his head. It was a fairly vulnerable position but at least he could mostly make the words out now.

"I'm tempted to simply ship him off," Elantria said. "But I can't be sure it's safe."

"I can't say I blame them for the assumption," the elven man said. "I drew the same conclusion. I was writing you a letter to ask about it when I got your invitation. When was the last time you had an apprentice?"

"You," she said bluntly. "And you know that."

"Precisely. I wanted to know about my successor." The man sounded like he was smiling. "Oh, come now. You don't need to look so grim. He's not injured—or, it seems, traumatized—and he helped you out of a bad situation. There would have been assassins anyway."

"I'm worried about what I've set in motion," Elantria said, followed by the creak of a chair. "I've worked so hard to keep the situation stable and now, I go and do this?" She sighed. "We were all in…equilibrium. Now they think I'm training an assassin and the game has changed." She added wryly, "And I don't even have an assassin-in-training to help with that."

"I wouldn't be so sure. He *did* kill one of them." In the long pause after that statement, Ben pictured the elf looking at Elantria. Maybe he was waiting for her to talk or was formulating his thoughts. A moment later, he said, "Look... You knew they would target you sooner or later. You can only rob so many banks before they do."

Elantria made no reply.

"It's the truth," he said bluntly. "Be honest with yourself. You always tried to upset the balance of the city."

"No, I didn't." She sounded angry. "I'm not a revolutionary. I know better than to try that. I won't go around insisting on new laws or ending corruption or whatever all of them want."

"Elantria." He was half-amused but clearly not willing to dance around the topic. "You're standing in the way of how money flows in this city, you're doing it on purpose, and you keep trying to find new ways to do more of it. The simple fact is that you're changing things and you know it. You can dress it up however you like, but you always knew they wouldn't simply let you get away with it without a fight."

Whatever her response, it was lost in the noise from the front of the house. Ben heard voices—the two servants. He jerked and his heart pounded. They were coming closer, and it sounded like they were carrying something. The logical explanation was that they were bringing food for Elantria and her guest, but there was no way for him to get out of the corridor without it being obvious that he had been spying. He considered his options, came up with a lie on the spur of the moment, and prayed for courage.

Then, he raised his hand and knocked on the door.

CHAPTER FORTY-TWO

A moment of silence was broken by hurried footsteps. The door opened to reveal Elantria.

"Yes?" She was not happy to be interrupted.

"Hi," Ben said awkwardly. "You said to not go outside, so I came looking for you after working on the locks. It seemed like you were talking to someone." He peered in to see the elf.

The visitor looked deeply amused and nodded to him. Everything about his features was well-bred and haughty, but his personality belied that. He remembered his amusement and pragmatism pitted against Elantria's pessimistic outlook during the brief conversation he'd heard.

"The new apprentice," he said and pushed to his feet.

"Orien," she said warningly.

"What? He's here and I want to meet him." Orien moved closer to shake his hand. "Besides, if we're discussing what to do with him, he might as well be a part of that discussion."

The woman looked deeply unhappy with this. His instinct was to step back and leave but he was curious. Even on short acquaintance—or, more accurately, eavesdropping—he liked Orien and he wanted to know what Elantria was up to.

So, pretending not to notice her forbidding expression, he looked from one to the other. "Do I need to leave the city?"

"Perhaps," the elf said before she could answer. "Come, sit. Breakfast is being brought."

"He's already eaten," she said sternly. "Ben, Orien and I are discussing confidential business."

"Business that involves him." Orien looked pleasantly at her.

"Ben." Elantria held the door open. "If you would give the two of us some time, I will find you later and we can discuss—"

"Oh, for pity's sake." For the first time, there was a hint of steel in the visitor's manner. "You took him on as an apprentice. *You* involved him in this. Now, either you made a careless, reckless mistake with someone else's life or you thought he was worth training. So, which of those two is it?"

Murder lurked in her eyes. She opened her mouth to answer but stepped back with a sigh when the two servants entered. Both seemed acutely aware of her mood, and they set the food out and scurried away quickly.

Elantria closed the door behind them and folded her arms.

"He's not from here," she told Orien. "He was helpless. I couldn't let him fall prey to whoever decided to scam him."

Now was the time when he had to decide whether to go forward or sit passively. In the past... well, in the past, he wouldn't have bothered with this. He would have taken his pack and headed off to another job, another move, or another country.

That had always counted as a sign of strength on his part in his mind—that he was willing to walk away from people who tried to speak down to him.

He saw now that it had merely been a way to avoid the confrontation. In all the situations he'd gone through, he'd never stood his ground. He had never learned to do that—and he wanted to.

Calmly, he met Elantria's gaze as he said, "If that was your concern, you could easily have let me leave with Zaara and Kural."

"*Kural* was here?" Orien asked with great interest.

"That is not important," she snapped but sighed a moment later.

"Very well, he's a puzzle. He looked entirely incompetent"—her stony gaze said that she wouldn't go easy on him merely because he'd stood his ground—"but Kural and Zaara both spoke well of him, which intrigued me. I wanted to see his way of being effective. I wondered if he might be useful here."

"And there you have it," the elf said cheerfully. He went to serve himself breakfast and said to him, "Elantria sees anyone and everything as tools to be used or obstacles to be dealt with—or as useless things to be ignored. Don't take it personally. Being considered either a tool or an obstacle is high praise."

She scowled and served breakfast for herself. "I am not like that."

"Yes, you are." He took a bite of bread. To Ben, he said, "Until yesterday, I was the only apprentice she had ever trained. I was curious about you."

"He's not my apprentice."

"You're training him," Orien pointed out. When Ben looked from one to the other in irritation, he smiled. "We're confusing you, no doubt. Elantria, here, is one of the foremost thieves in Heffog—but she doesn't work for the black market, which annoys them, and also doesn't work for what's left of the elven nobility, which annoys *them*. She does everything she can to reverse the profit the nobles and merchants wring out of the populace."

"Will you keep talking about me like I'm not here?" she asked acidly.

"Yes. Now, you see, she is presently working against a specific syndicate, so they've kept a close eye on her. Everyone's waiting for someone else to make the first move. And what should happen but a strange man from outside the city arrives—in the presence of a notable wizard, no less—and she takes him under her wing. They assumed you were here to be her pet assassin, and...well, as you saw this morning, they wanted to head that one off at the pass."

"Ah," Ben said when the explanation finally made sense.

Elantria sat quietly and looked immensely unhappy.

"She doesn't like admitting she miscalculated," Orien said in a stage whisper.

"*Enough.*" She had clearly had enough of being needled. "Yes. I took Ben on to train him without considering how the Regents would interpret it. I was rather more interested in his background than I should have been and decided to train him with the *hope* that he might be an asset, but *without* the expectation."

"I think that's personal growth," the elf said. At her glare, he added hastily, "Not a joke!"

She looked somewhat mollified.

"I *want* to help," Ben said honestly.

"Why?" She sipped her coffee which was so strong, he could swear it woke him up simply by the smell. "You're not from here. Why do you care about the poor of a fading city?"

"Because—" He broke off. This was how he did things. He spoke without thinking and let anything fall out of his mouth at random but he didn't want to do that anymore. "Because I don't like unfair things," he said finally. "I came to this land to heal after my accident and without meaning to, I got caught up in something bigger than myself. I helped the fae and that made me realize I *could* do things like that. I don't know anyone here, but I *do* know I don't like them being exploited."

He looked from one to the other and both studied him silently.

After a moment, Orien said to Elantria, "I get it. He's quite sincere, isn't he?"

"And on his own, he'd be chewed up and spat out," she said wryly.

"But you like his idealism," he suggested.

"No. It's tiresome."

"You do."

"*Excuse me,*" Ben interrupted. He tired of being talked about as if he weren't there and understood why she didn't like it.

She raised an eyebrow at him. "Yes?"

"Could we move on?" he asked. "If you wanted me to be useful, tell me how."

"I wanted you to recover first," she pointed out. "We established yesterday that you won't be ready to steal for some time." She explained Ben's condition to Orien in a quick aside.

The elf leaned back in his chair with an interested expression. His plate was empty now and he must have wolfed his food. "And yet," he pointed out to them both, "he managed to help deal with the assassins. He can think on his feet and he's coordinated enough to do some things."

Elantria gave him a scathing look. "And that means we should throw him into the middle of a job?"

"Possibly." Orien gave her a meaningful nod. "Tell him about the next one."

The two of them stared at each other for a moment before she sighed and frowned in thought. Her fingers moved, almost as if she were tracing a calculation through her head.

Finally, she said, "The house you followed me to the other day —Jorys."

Ben went rigid. "You *knew*?"

"Good grief—of course, I knew." She shook her head.

Orien laughed quietly and said with remarkable aplomb, "We also knew you were listening to us earlier."

He sighed and wished he didn't feel quite so idiotic.

"The fact that you're abysmal at sneaking around doesn't motivate well for you to be involved in jobs yet," Elantria told him bluntly.

"Okay, fair." Ben rubbed his face. "Can I at least hear about it, though?"

"I might as well tell you. Otherwise, you'll go upstairs and simply sneak back, and that's too much effort." She waved a hand to indicate resignation. "I've posed as the leader of a security service and have negotiated to guard Jorys's house. He only allows the people he's used for years into his vault to guard it, but he's willing to hire new body-guards for himself. He doesn't know me by sight so I've been able to deal with him."

"I wondered about that," he admitted. "It seemed like you were fairly well-known."

"In *very* particular circles," she said. "Other groups that operate for or against the elven nobles, things like that. I'm branching out now and working against people who aren't part of that world. The city is *big*, Ben, and there are whole neighborhoods under the sway of a single merchant. Like..."

"Warlords," he said quietly.

"Yes. Rather like that. They keep the people in their area safe enough. But they take protection fees and abuse their labor. It might be better than they had under the nobles, but it's more that the people don't expect anything better."

"You *are* a revolutionary," he said slowly.

Orien crowed with laughter.

"I am not." Elantria jabbed a finger at him. "I don't harbor any illusions about what I can and cannot achieve. I don't want a war that will hurt our citizens. I only want to keep the damage the warlords do from being too much to bear. They don't know when to stop."

Ben gave her a small smile. Elantria had been born into a world that few others could claim—the bastard but beloved child of an ancient noble family. She had seen the things the nobles believed were their due, and she had seen the things the poorer humans endured. Her circumstances meant that she understood the randomness of who got what. Her grandparents had wanted her to live a noble life because they loved her and either didn't see or didn't care that it flew in the face of her worldview.

But Elantria *had* cared.

He knew, however, that the more he insisted on it, the more her walls would come up. For now, he would leave it alone.

"What's the job?" he asked.

"Enter the vault, take a specific amount of money, and redistribute it in his neighborhood," she said. "Not directly, of course—he'd merely ask for it back and they can't exactly refuse him. But there are ways to make sure their lives are a little easier for a while." She shrugged. "He's a piece of shit, that one, so don't feel bad for him. He's trafficking some of them."

The bottom dropped out of his stomach.

"Artisans and so on," Elantria explained, unaware of his suspicions about who was getting trafficked. "Goldsmiths, alchemists, that kind of thing. He sells their labor to the remaining nobles. They can never leave, and all that they worked to achieve? All the security they were trying to bring their families? It's now his."

"It would be better," he said quietly, "if he weren't there anymore."

She stared at him. "I assassinate people very rarely," she said. "I do it only when there is no other choice. We will bring him around on this point rather than simply kill him."

"How many people will he hurt and kill while you wait for him to see the light?" Ben demanded.

"My city. My rules." She was not playing around now. "Ben, I have watched the fallout of power vacuums and assassinations. I will not harm these people. I want any allies I can find who wish to make life less grim for the people of this city, but you're not an ally to me if you want to charge in and cause chaos."

He didn't agree, not even in the slightest. His memories of the fae dying by the score as the mercenary army assaulted the castle remained fresh and raw. He had seen the slaves in the shadows of Heffog.

But he needed Elantria's trust if he wanted to do something about it. He bit his tongue and nodded. "Your city…your rules. So what's the job tomorrow? And can I help?"

"Probably not yet."

"Let him try," Orien suggested. "It's not like you need him to unlock the vault. It'll be a good opportunity to test if he can follow orders."

She sighed. "I'll consider it. And now, since Ben will not leave while we speak about it, we should probably discuss tomorrow."

CHAPTER FORTY-THREE

The next afternoon, Ben was dressed in a guard uniform and bounced nervously at the entrance to Elantria's house. He'd been given light armor and weapons, mostly for show, but they were good to have in case things went south.

Things would not go south, she had told him. She said it so fiercely that he almost believed she could will things into existence.

Orien was the next one to come downstairs. Every indicator of elven haughtiness was back on display—except for the wink he gave him.

"Are you noble?" he asked the elf curiously.

"Elantria said you had a habit of asking prying questions," Orien commented.

"I'm sorry." He frowned. "Are these things so unusual to ask here?"

"One does not generally ask professional thieves about their back-story, no." He looked amused. "For your information, however, no. I am of very lowly birth within the elven lineages. I simply happen to look very..." He waved at his face.

"That must be strange," he said.

"Somewhat." Orien shrugged. "Remember, this is the only face I've ever had. I was ten when I realized that people treated me very differently than my friends and siblings. I spent a few years trying to hide my appearance, then I learned to use it." He gave his irreverent smile. "My most successful con is usually the elven noble and the merchant."

He raised an eyebrow.

"There's no time to explain now." The elf chuckled. "Let's say you'll earn some advice from me over the course of the next few jobs we pull together. But I did want to say before Elantria got here…" He stepped forward and put a hand on his shoulder, his expression serious. "Follow orders tonight. I mean it."

Ben remained silent. He was afraid his face looked guilty and he didn't want Orien to see anything further that might raise his suspicions.

"You're new here," the elf said, "and you're an idealist. I get the sense you came from a very sheltered upbringing."

Ben snorted. "I've shoveled shit for a living. I took care of giant bears that hated me. I haven't had a soft life."

"There are different ways to be sheltered," Orien said seriously, "and one of them is not to understand that by pressing too hard for justice, you can hurt people even more. I know you want to make changes, Ben, but trust me. Elantria does too, and she knows how to go about it." He paused. "Also, she'll toss you out on your ear if you fuck the job up, so there's that."

He shrugged. "Okay. I'll keep it in mind."

"I should hope so," Elantria said. She came down the stairs and looked critically at him. "You wear weapons well. Remember that someone with the best training feels no need to flaunt it. Walk around and look watchful but as if you hardly remember you have weapons on. Relax your shoulders more…there, that's good. Stay light on your feet."

She and Orien took a few moments to make small adjustments to his posture and walk. Only when they were satisfied did they leave. They walked quickly through the streets to the sound of yelling and clashing weapons, which made him look around for the source of the noise.

"We had to draw off the people watching the house," the elf

explained in a low tone. "The Regents might have interfered with this job if they knew it was happening today."

With the feeling that he was way out of his depth, he nodded and continued.

"Keep your shoulders loose," Orien murmured. "You're looking tense again."

He forced his shoulders down and walked with all the ease he could muster. This was merely another day, he told himself. He was a good bodyguard and he had no doubts about his ability to protect Jorys.

They arrived at the merchant's ostentatious house with the streets already bustling and the guards outside tracking them from two blocks away. Elantria had told them that their arrival was expected and they would be brought in to introduce themselves to their employer.

They would spend the bulk of day getting the man accustomed to their presence, being silent shadows out of the corner of his vision until he forgot they were there. Elantria sometimes worked very long cons in which she gained someone's trust over the course of months, but today's mission would not require that. It was, at most, a two-day job. Two of their number would guard Jorys and one would be downstairs with the servants. They would use the shift-change as the moment to seize some of the contents from the vault.

It wasn't that simple, of course. Slipping into the secure area would require all Elantria's skill in deception and in incapacitating other guards. They would have to move quickly to get the goods to the back entrance of the house and disappear into the night.

At the door, they were greeted by a tall man who looked like he might have traces of elven blood—and potentially orcish blood as well. Ben decided immediately to not get on this man's bad side. He wore armor with a crest in the center of his chest and was shown extreme deference by all the other guards and servants. He and Elantria seemed to know each other, although they weren't particularly friendly.

Their guide led them through the house to a study and let them in via a side door. She and Orien slipped in quietly, but Ben froze in horror as he entered the room behind them.

His gaze locked on what he saw immediately was a slave auction.

Humans, elves, and dwarves stood in the middle of the floor with various looks of blank despair. All of them wore metal collars around their necks. Some appeared to be artisans, as Elantria had mentioned. Others were some of the most beautiful people he had ever seen. While many looked strong, a good number merely looked mousey and frightened.

Jorys inspected them one by one. He looked like an aging athlete, a man who had once prided himself on his athletic abilities and who now tried to stave off his decline into age and decadence. His clothes were rich and decorated with gold and jewels, but he had what looked like an uncomfortable chair, and there was no fire in the grate or wine at the table.

He seemed like the type of man who told you ad nauseum about his self-control and how no one needed luxuries while subsisting almost entirely on those same luxuries.

His immediate dislike only deepened when he saw the absolute lack of respect Jorys showed for the slaves. The man inspected them impersonally. His eyes raked them with no compassion, he looked at their hands and their teeth, and ordered one or two of them to strip. Ben suspected it was only to show them that he was in charge.

Eventually, he pointed to a few of them. "These," he said to a clerk. "Those three for outstanding contracts, that one on reserve. The rest can go to the market."

One of those who had not been selected uttered a little cry. Jorys gave him a hard-eyed look.

"I can't leave," the man protested. He was dwarven with an elaborately braided beard. "I've told you, contact Berghold. I'm not a citizen of Heffog and may not be taken as a slave—"

The merchant made a gesture. A guard stepped forward and hauled the protestor away. The dwarf began to yell and horror dawned in his eyes. He had believed until that moment that he might somehow get out of this. Finally, he had realized he would not.

The other slaves were guided away. Any who resisted were struck with staves or fists. A few of them had clenched their jaws and tried not to resist and make it worse for themselves. Ben watched them go while his blood pressure rose. His hands were clamped behind his back as he tried to fight the urge to run after them. He wanted to haul every one of them out of this place.

A swift kick to his ankle reminded him of where he was. Elantria stepped forward to speak to Jorys, all smiles and quiet competence, while her two companions waited in the shadows.

The man looked at them only casually and shrugged. He and Elantria exchanged a few more words before she nodded to Orien to take his break first. The elf would take a roundabout path to the kitchens, he knew, although not conspicuously so, and he would begin to chart not only the lower part of the house but also the movement of the servants and guards.

That had always been the plan, but Ben had the distinct impression that she was also keeping him close so he didn't run off and do something like free the slaves. She was worried.

Well, she should be worried. He wanted to throw up at the thought of the people being hauled off to the slave market at that very moment. She said she was realistic about what she could achieve and that she wanted slow results, but every day the system didn't change, she consigned people to death and slavery.

Ben made his way through the day quietly and without much incident. Jorys was well guarded, so no one would try to break into his house to murder him. It meant that all he needed to do was drift around after him and not fidget too much.

He was given a brief break to eat dinner, seated on a stool in the corner of the kitchen, and it was only a couple of hours later that Orien came to join him. "He wants to discuss our trial run."

That was the signal. It meant that Elantria or Orien had successfully cracked the vault and incapacitated the guards inside and that they needed help to get the gold out to the waiting carriage.

Even after the absolute horror show of a day—he had spent most of it fantasizing about brutal ways to kill Jorys—he had to admit he was excited at helping with a heist. It was unexpectedly fun to find himself in the middle of one, especially since he'd always enjoyed heist movies.

He simply hadn't ever expected to think, while in the midst of stealing countless riches, that the world might be better served by him assassinating the person he attempted to rob.

Orien led him to the vault and Ben took a heavy chest of gold coins and hurried up the stairs to the waiting carriage. This part of the house seemed to be entirely deserted, but his co-conspirators were both insistent that he move silently.

A few minutes later, he realized why. As he returned inside from the carriage and headed to the vault, he looked down a corridor to see none other than Jorys. The merchant was seated at his desk, working.

And he was completely ignorant of the fact that, if he turned, he would have a clear line of sight to the people robbing him.

The sheer balls it took to plan the heist this way distracted Ben for a moment, but close on the heels of his admiration came another emotion—hatred. Jorys was there and, it seemed, unattended. There was no reason to choose between robbing him and assassinating him.

He saw Orien gesture out of the corner of his eye and motion for him to hurry, but he wasn't paying attention anymore.

His focus fixed on his target, he ran toward Jorys as he drew his dagger.

CHAPTER FORTY-FOUR

He had something of a head start. Elantria and Orien were still a flight of stairs away, coming out of the vault.

If he were honest, however, Ben would have to admit that he hadn't thought about that. He merely ran and no longer even tried to be quiet. This was purely reflexive, and he hadn't chosen his moment or hoped to prevent them from interfering.

His survival instinct tried to remind him that he didn't even know if there was another guard in the room. There probably was.

In moments, he pushed through the door and there was nothing to be done except face what awaited him. He surged into Jorys's study with his dagger drawn and it was damned clear what his intention was. The merchant turned in his seat, but Ben wasn't looking at him.

Yes, there was another guard here—and, worse, it was the gigantic man they had seen at the front door that morning.

Ben watched as the man whipped his arm around, drew a knife, and flipped it to hold it by the blade and he threw himself onto the floor. The weapon whistled over his head and embedded itself in the open door. He looked at it and had a moment of paralysis. It was too late to think of the might-have-been. If he had given into paralysis a moment before, he would be dead now.

Still, he couldn't afford to be paralyzed now either. The guard lunged across the room with a roar and he pushed to his feet and dove sideways into the hallway. His momentum carried him down the half-flight of stairs that led to the study. He grasped the banister and curled into a ball while the guard followed him out.

There wasn't time for anything except an attack. Ben had never been in a one-on-one fight with an assassin before, but he knew that turning his back and running would doom him, and every instinct fell in line to help. He uncoiled as his adversary came down the stairs. His head was averted, which left a gap at his shoulder for a tackle. When his shoulder met the area above the guard's knees, he drove up with all his might.

It didn't take as much force as he expected. He was, after all, only slightly modifying the guard's trajectory. He looked up in surprise as the legs flipped over his head and the man thudded heavily on his back.

He could hear Orien and Elantria and hoped they would help him because right now was the best opening he would get. As he sprinted up the stairs, he ignored the sound of someone hissing his name and ran after Jorys.

Ben caught the man on the other side of the room. The merchant was trying to escape, oblivious to the sacrifice his guard was making. That was, of course, the point of a bodyguard, but he was so contemptuous of his target that he would hold it against him anyway.

When he grasped his quarry's arm and dragged him around, he took a punch full in the face. He staggered back and stars burst across his vision. Determined to not lose the opportunity, he thrust his knife forward as hard as he could and he struck something. The blade encountered resistance and a scream followed.

When his vision cleared, he saw his knife plunged into Jorys' left shoulder. He yanked it out and felt a wave of instant revulsion. Despite his abhorrence of violence, he was killing someone. The resistance against his knife was bone and flesh and he would have to stab again.

He shoved the revulsion away. Two weeks before, he had made a mistake. He hadn't been willing to use violence when it might have prevented who knew how many deaths. Every day the merchant was alive, he would sell slaves and hurt the people of his district.

He had to die.

Ben thrust the knife again, this time into Jorys' chest. The man wheezed. He was dying and he knew it—the sheer amount of blood from the first stab wound had already doomed him, and this merely hastened the end.

A commotion erupted behind him, but he didn't care.

"Who...*are* you?" Jorys rasped.

"Someone who won't let you get away with this anymore," he told him, his voice low. "Today, you sent ten people to a life of slavery. Who knows how many you have doomed? You should feel lucky you only have one life to lose in return."

The merchant collapsed and died at his feet, and he fought the urge to throw up everywhere. He heard footsteps behind him and he was so disoriented that he almost didn't care if it was Elantria or the guard.

Then he realized that if it was the guard, his companions might be in trouble, and he spun toward the sound.

He had never seen her looking this angry. Of course, he hadn't known her very long, but he had seen her fight for her life and speak to enemies, and the look on her face now was chilling. She looked at him like she wanted to kill him.

"Come on," she said, her voice clipped. She caught him by the arm and yanked him out of the room.

Without protest, he stumbled past the body of the guard and out into the night. Orien was huddled in the carriage and held a hand over a shallow but bloody wound on his arm. He watched as Elantria pushed the other man into the cab. Ben met his gaze and felt a sudden wave of guilt but there was no expression at all in the elf's eyes.

The carriage lurched into motion. The wheels were wrapped in cloth, as were the horse's hooves, and a heavy fog all around them felt somehow magical. He had no doubt that she had chosen both magic and technology to make her getaway.

They were a few streets away before she spoke.

"What the *hell* was that?" She did not look at him and that, for some reason, showed him how angry she was.

"I told you I made mistakes," he said passionately. "I told you I didn't stop someone who wanted to commit murder and because of that, she brought an army to attack the fae. Their wells of magic were destroyed, their king was almost killed, and hundreds died, if not more, defending the castle that day. I *told* you I wouldn't make the same mistake again—"

"And *Orien* told you that you might make it worse for people if you charged in and tried to bring justice!" Elantria snapped. "He warned you that you didn't know what you were doing. *I* warned you, and you didn't listen!"

"You were simply going to let him keep selling slaves!" he roared.

"I know that I am one person who cannot possibly stand in the way of the entire slave trade!" she retorted. "And keep your voice down. This carriage is magicked, but it's not infallible."

"All you fucking care about is your tiny jobs," he whispered angrily. "You keep telling yourself you can't make any big changes so you pull off little heists like this to salve your conscience."

He honestly thought she would hit him. Her fingers twitched and curled into a fist and her face was a picture. She stared at him with such hatred in her eyes that he felt cold all the way through.

"Do you think you stopped the slave trade with this?" she asked finally. "Do you think because one slave trader was killed in his house that you've fixed everything?"

"Maybe other people will think twice before—"

"Do you know who will take over for Jorys in that district?" Elantria demanded.

Dread settled in and he swallowed. "No. Who?"

"It's one of three people," she said, her voice clipped. "If he had passed naturally, he would have designated an heir and there would have been a *chance* of someone else taking power without a fight. Now, you've all but assured a war of succession. His son will fight his two top lieutenants and every one of them is *worse* than Jorys was." She all but hissed the last words at him in utter fury.

Ben stared silently at her.

"You haven't taken that district out of the control of a warlord," she told him in utter contempt, "and you haven't stopped the slave trade. If nothing else, you've taken one of the sellers out of the market, which only makes slave-trading more profitable for the rest of them. You've doomed the people of Jorys' district to a violent crackdown and an unwinnable game of trying to play loyal to whoever they think will win his position." Quietly, she added, "And you've almost certainly doomed any chance we had of helping there again."

He looked away. Now that the assassination was over and the adrenaline began to fade, there was only the sick, nauseated certainty that he had done something terribly wrong. He had made things worse by trying to do the right thing.

No. He straightened in his seat. Maybe there was a larger change that needed to happen, but he wouldn't be the kind of person who slunk around in the shadows and said that justice couldn't be delivered because there might be fallout.

Jorys had brought this on himself, and he would kill anyone who tried to take his place. He would free that district and then he would turn and ask Elantria why she had aimed so low.

Because she was part of this city. She had wanted him for this.

"You wanted someone to do the things you wouldn't dare do," he told her. "You wanted the new perspective. You were raised by the elites of this city."

"Which means I know far, far better than you the constraints and ramifications of acting against them," she told him furiously. "I know how many ways they use to prop themselves up and I know what we're up against if we try to dislodge them."

"You wanted me to think differently than you," he retorted. "You *are* a revolutionary and you *know* you've been pulling your punches too much and let people get away with murder and slavery and God knows what else. You're ashamed of your cowardice and—"

"You know *nothing* about me," Elantria snapped. "Nothing." She pounded on the top of the carriage and it lurched to a stop and almost threw him into Orien's lap. Before either of them could say anything, she pushed the door open. "Get out," she told Ben.

He stared at her.

"Get out," she repeated. She met his gaze with one of cold fury and leaned back. He gathered his composure and climbed out of the carriage.

Once outside, he began to strip his armor and weapons off. He wouldn't keep anything of hers if she threw him out into the city.

She shook her head, though, reached into a hidden coin purse, and withdrew three copper coins, which she tossed at him. Her face was blank. "I'll not have your death on my conscience," she said quietly. "But if you're willing to kill and sow chaos that will spill over onto my people, neither will I protect you. Get out of my sight. Zaara and Kural's trust in you was misplaced."

Ben met Orien's eyes for one instant before the carriage door slammed shut again. The elf still looked completely expressionless, his fingers clutching the bloody wound on his arm.

The carriage rumbled away and he was left standing in the fading mist, alone in the dark of the night.

CHAPTER FORTY-FIVE

The twins had fallen asleep in cozy tents with beds that were the softest they had ever slept in, fluffy blankets that were somehow not too hot, and pajamas that felt like silk. With the chirps of the birds and the insects and the comfort of being close to one another again, both of them had drifted to sleep in record time.

And, Prima reflected, she probably should not be surprised that it was ten AM and they were both still asleep. They were teenagers and she had gone out of her way to make sure they were as comfortable as possible.

Eventually, she gave up on trying to be subtle and gradually changed the fabric of the tents to allow progressively more light in. It took the better part of an hour, but she did finally stir the two of them to stumble around and make vague noises of complaint.

They both tried to go back to sleep, of course, but that was handily taken care of when she winked the beds out of existence and Taigan was so sleepy that she forgot she could summon things.

Once they were up and eating breakfast, the AI bided her time for a while. After all, she had enough to check in on. Half a world away, Ben tried to find somewhere to hide out after he'd assassinated someone.

Prima had genuinely not seen that coming. It worried her a little how quickly he had shifted from refusing to kill anyone to viewing assassination as a tool that was not only allowed but morally essential.

She watched him for a while—he displayed far more judgment when it came to selecting a hiding place than he had when it came to perpetrating a con—but kept an eye on the twins so she could see when they had finished breakfast.

Both had the kind of metabolisms that mimicked a squirrel on a high dose of cocaine. She watched as Taigan ate an entire plate of scrambled eggs, Jamie downed three plate-sized pancakes smothered in syrup, each of them ate easily an entire pig's worth of bacon, and together, polished off over two loaves' worth of toast.

When they leaned back with their hands over their stomachs, she decided it was time to get them moving.

"Good morning."

The young people jumped.

"Your journey begins this morning," Prima told them. *"Normally, one seeks something that is far away, but on your journey, you will be side by side. You will, together, seek each other out. Are you ready?"*

Taigan nodded at once. Jamie downed an entire mug of coffee before he did the same.

"We will set out whenever you are ready," she told them.

To her surprise and amusement, both immediately set about packing up the camp. Being all-powerful, she had simply created everything in it from nothing and had been prepared to do the reverse as well. It was pleasant, however, to see them make their beds and tidy everything.

While they did that, she rigged floating whiteboards that would automatically write the things they said if they spoke to one another. Then, dressed in loose clothing and huge camping boots, they set off in the direction she indicated with a breeze and a cluster of sparkles.

"So, where are we going?" Taigan asked her.

"Today, you will climb Aryoka Mountain," she told them. Ahead of the twins, the mists cleared and the mountain came into view. It wasn't

massive but it would certainly take at least half a day to reach the summit.

"Did you see that before?" Jamie asked his sister. The whiteboards she'd prepared worked extremely well as his words appeared seconds later. "Because I think it simply…appeared."

"That does sound like Prima."

"What? She moves mountains around?"

"Ask her yourself," Taigan said with a shrug. "I know I would if I had all that magic."

"Prima? Did you make that mountain from nothing, or did I, uh… you know, miss a massive mountain?"

"You can *be quite oblivious,"* Prima said wickedly. *"But relax. It's not covered in jackalopes."*

Jamie, who'd had a bad run-in with jackalopes during his first visit to the game, grumbled something under his breath.

They started up the slope together. Prima had made a path… barely. There was a route—nothing as cruel as a path that wound into a cliff and required backtracking—but it was far from easy to traverse.

"Prima," Taigan panted as she struggled up a series of too-high steps, "what exactly are we looking for at the top of the mountain?"

"There is a temple," she replied. *"Inside is a pool of water that legend says will show you your deepest desire."*

Both twins stopped in their tracks.

"Wait, seriously?" the girl asked.

"That's so lame," Jamie blurted. They each nodded at what was on the other's whiteboard.

Prima, who had structured this exercise with particular pitfalls in mind, bristled nonetheless.

"I, uh…" He scratched his head. "I'm not sure I want to see my deepest desire while sitting next to one of my sisters. *She* won't see it, will she?"

"Ew," Taigan said. She hadn't thought along the same lines and this was an unwelcome revelation to her. "Wait, seriously? Your deepest desire isn't something like going to Mars, it's—I mean, your *deepest* desire, out of *all* your desires…just *ew.*"

"Don't judge," Jamie said defensively. "And I worked statistically. Like, the thing I think about most often."

"Ew!" She flailed her arms. "No! Wrong! Stop!"

"Would you like a spray bottle?"

"Yes! *Please!*"

Prima snickered. To them, she said, *"You can see very few things the other does in the world so I would be very surprised if you could see each other's dreams in the pool. However, as you hike, you might want to think about what you expect to see."*

"Why?" Taigan asked. "If it will show us what our heart's desire is, why spend time thinking about it now?"

If the AI had hair, she would tear it out right now. She began to understand why humans ran off to become hermits. It was because the rest of them were so completely ridiculous.

"Climb the damned mountain."

Two sets of eyebrows shot up. They looked instinctively at each other—a few feet apart and unable to see one another—but it was one of those little moments that both gave her hope. And filled her with fear.

These two had known each other since before they were born and looked to each other when they processed the world. They bickered good-naturedly about anything and everything—more things than most people ever could bicker about because they understood so much more about each other than others did.

She regretted snapping at them, but they set about climbing the mountain with goodwill.

"I genuinely," Taigan all but growled as she hauled herself up an embankment, "have zero idea what I'll see in there."

"Me, neither." Jamie studied a gap, considered it for a moment, and leapt. He made the distance but banged his shin on landing. "Ow! Hell. I'm okay."

"Are you bleeding?" she asked.

"Nah." He was and bright red blood trickled down his shin, but it wasn't much. When he looked at Prima and put a finger to his lips, she responded with a sigh only he could hear.

"Wait," his sister said. She had found something rather like stairs and she now climbed them with determination. "You *don't* know what you'll see?"

"Now that you've pointed out that it could be anything, that broadens the…category…thingy."

"Good Lord." Taigan rolled her eyes. "Okay, Prima, tell me it's close."

"It's a mountain."

Both twins made a whimpering noise.

"Don't make me get the jackalopes."

"Oh, fuck," Jamie said. "Climb, climb, climb!"

"Jackalopes aren't real, are they?" his sister asked. She hadn't shaken the habit yet of looking for him when she spoke, and Prima hoped she could get the two of them to see each other before it became natural for them to talk this way.

He was more task-focused and Prima had only seen Taigan like that when she was running. Currently, he took a side route around a boulder. It was by far the more difficult way to go but he hadn't checked to see if the other way would be easier. She watched in amusement as he jumped and pushed himself up. "They're real," he said. "And they're *mean*, and they're *not* the size of normal bunnies!"

"Like, cow-sized or very *small*?" The girl raised one eyebrow. "I'm picturing be swarmed by scorpions, only it's tiny, angry bunnies."

Jamie laughed at that. "No, I meant big. Not cow-sized, but *big*. Think…chest high? And the *teeth*. Emmy and I fought some."

"Emmy is here?" Taigan stopped dead. Her hands were scuffed and dirty and had left a few smudges across her face where she had wiped the sweat away and tucked stray wisps of hair behind her ears. "Is she with you?"

"No. This time, it's only me."

"This time?"

"We both went in to test it when Mom and Dad came to see the facility. They weren't quite sure they wanted to hook you up to it and the team offered to let us try it. I don't think either of them did, only me and Emmy."

301

She kept climbing. Her face was sad now and her movements jerky.

"Sis?"

Taigan didn't respond right away. Tears glistened in her eyes and she sniffed at regular intervals. She climbed with single-minded intensity now.

Jamie could only see her by the whiteboard that hovered nearby and he hurried to catch up. He seemed stronger than his sister, but she had a head-start and she wasn't paying attention to pain or tiredness right now.

"Tell me you're okay," he called.

"Of course I'm not okay!" The words exploded out of her and she looked furiously in his direction. One tear had escaped. "That's why you're *here*, remember?"

"Okay, but what did I say?"

"I hate this part!" She began to cry and her voice had a raw edge to it. "Hearing about all the things I missed while I was under, hearing about all of you making decisions—about *me*—only I'm not there, this not even being *our* thing because it was your and Emmy's first, and now I'm only—" She brushed angrily at her hair to get it out of her face. "An afterthought," she said.

"Everything is set up around you!" he responded sharply. "How the hell could you be an afterthought? You were why we were *there*!"

"Yeah, but you were there only the four of you!" Taigan shouted. She climbed so fast now that she constantly missed holds, slipped, and gritted her teeth on exclamations of pain. Each only made her angrier and it would be logical to stop, but she wouldn't. Prima looked on with concern.

She had set this up to make them talk but she hadn't envisioned it going like *this*.

Taigan pushed onto a gently sloping stretch of rock and shale. She looked at the temple, then down to where Jamie was.

"You know," she said, almost too quietly for him to hear, "the four real members of the family. And then me. The one you can't count on."

He stopped and fixed his gaze on where he thought she was. "We never forget you."

"I know." Her lip trembled. "But there's a difference between being someone people think about and being someone who's *there*." Quietly, she added, "I'm not angry at you, Jamie. Not at any of you. But it sucks to have this catch-up talk every time I wake up—what everyone did while I lay in a hospital bed. And this time, it feels more personal— like you and Emmy got into the game and had fun together, and you and I can't even *see* each other."

The terrible thing about human thought patterns, Prima realized, wasn't that they were so illogical or that they made so many jumps—it was how much sense they made after the fact. It was the way you could say something that was simply a fact but it would hurt someone more than a punch to the face. After you'd done it, you could see what you'd done but at the time, the possibility didn't even occur to you.

Jamie climbed up the same rock Taigan had used and the two of them stood together, almost in the same place. They were overlapping and the girl sometimes disappeared entirely into his larger frame.

"We'll fix this," he said, and his voice shook with conviction. "I know it's worst for you, but—"

"I'm usually asleep for it," she interrupted. "So it's probably worse for you."

"You know what I mean. This...whatever it is. Glitch. We'll fix it. Don't think of us doing things without you. Think of us finding new ways to bring you home. We aren't whole without you."

Taigan leaned her head on his shoulder—or would have if she hadn't been halfway through his body.

"Let's go see the temple," she said. "I'll only see me living a normal day, and I hope like hell I won't see yours."

He laughed and the two of them set off together.

CHAPTER FORTY-SIX

Ben had no idea where the hell he was going.

He tried to keep his mind blank. When he thought about what had happened, he was furious, but guilt and shame waited offstage. He never let them into his thoughts but he knew they were there. They were waiting for their moment to strike.

It wasn't until he was a few streets away that he realized why it all felt so familiar. It shouldn't be, in all honesty. He had never assassinated someone and been thrown out by his crime-boss protector in the middle of the night.

But he *had* done what someone told him specifically not to do, only for the whole situation to go up in flames. After which he always —always—ran away. He picked up and headed to a new job, new relationship, or new remote village. Each time he did that, he told himself that this was why he didn't want to settle down. People were simply too ridiculous.

And, the whole time, he wouldn't let a part of him speak because it insisted that he knew this was his fault—that *he* was the constant. He approached every new job with hope but that grew slimmer every time. There was always the pit of certainty in his stomach that this would be exactly like the last time.

Of course it would. He was the problem and he couldn't leave himself behind.

Now, he wanted to cringe at the memories of climbing mountains alone, staring at sunrises, meditating. and giving up his possessions. It turned out that you could do all the things that were supposed to give you clarity, but it was possible to do every one of them in bad faith.

He put his head down and darted glances to his left and his right as he walked. Sometimes, people would come to the ends of the alleyways or the shadowed windows to watch as he passed. Heffog was scarcely quieter at night, only more watchful.

The itching feeling at the back of his neck ebbed and flowed as he passed through neighborhoods. Who could say what it was—what tiny sounds or glimpses of movement the body saw but the mind couldn't catch—but you could tell when you were somewhere unsafe.

Ben merely didn't know *how* unsafe.

The sensation unsettled him constantly and he made a decision. The next time he was somewhere he wasn't as afraid and there weren't as many watchful eyes, he would look for a place to hide.

Time blurred and he wasn't sure how long it had been before he found it. The sky was still black, but there was enough light from distant lanterns and streetlights that he could see the buildings around him. He crept up to one of them and looked in the window. The opening gaped in the wall, uncovered. His careful study showed the remains of a cloth window covering tied out of the way and now more rags and thread than actual cloth.

He couldn't see anyone inside or hear the small noises of stirring or snoring, but he wasn't foolish enough to walk into an empty building in the middle of the night.

A different idea crept in and was one he could focus on with a greater degree of confidence.

This building, like many in the area, had been made with plaster daubed hastily over wood and stone, along with a few mud bricks. No one had protected the bricks properly from the elements and they had worn away beneath the outer layer. It wasn't a fantastic set of holds and not the kind of thing you climbed if you made smart decisions.

But he wasn't making smart decisions right now, and there was something to be said for choosing the best of the bad decisions available to you.

He sighted up the side of the building. Doing a flash—a one-track climb with no false starts—didn't seem very likely there, but he didn't want to take any longer than he had to. Experience had taught him that a few minutes spent planning his route meant far less time climbing—and far less chance of bad falls.

The blue sky and the falling feeling were back in the pit of his stomach and he leaned forward and tried not to gag. The last thing he needed was to attract attention.

All he wanted was to forget falling—and seeing Mike fall.

"Ben, are you all right? Your heart rate spiked."

Ben didn't answer for a moment. "I was…thinking of the accident."

He got the sense of Prima nodding. *"Tell me if I can help,"* she said finally.

That made him smile. "I will. Thank you. Now, hold my beer."

"I have no hands—wait, beer? You don't have beer."

"It's an expression one says when one is about to do something stupid."

"Then why haven't I heard it from you before? Zing!"

For a moment, he had to lean against the wall and muffle his laughter with his hand. This day had been a nightmare and he was very sure his laughter was about more than the particular joke, but an AI poking fun at him was legitimately as funny as all hell. It took several minutes for him to calm, during which time he was convinced several times that he would break a rib.

When he was relatively sure he wouldn't burst out laughing again, he began to climb. The handholds were rough and he collected more splinters than he knew what to do with, but he couldn't focus on that right now.

He used the corner of the building as his main route. It was the roughest part of the building with stone blocks and pieces of wooden planks. There were occasional easy holds where mud bricks had crumbled away, although not as many as he'd like.

On the other hand, he would like the building to stay up once he got to the top.

This was easier than his first couple of climbs. He seemed to be re-learning the way pressure felt on his fingertips and how to balance on the edge of a foot. Sometimes, he forgot that this was more difficult now and at others, it seemed to come naturally. His weight was braced on his feet and his fingers only lightly brushed the stone when he was at rest.

Moving from the corner up and over the roof was undignified, not to mention risky. Ben had not been able to determine the composition of the roof and his hands traced over ceramic tiles while he hung there, rather like a desperate sloth. He needed to shift his feet off the edge of the building to swing back so he could haul himself up.

It was simply that he couldn't seem to make his feet do it. It wasn't that his body couldn't tell where they were but that his brain demanded loudly to know why he was thirty-odd feet above the ground and why he wanted to go even higher. His frontal lobe wanted him to know, in no uncertain terms, that this was a foolish idea and he should go down immediately.

He would have to do it somehow, so exhaled a long breath and made his mind a blank. Cautiously, he unhooked one foot and moved the leg back, then the second one. His body didn't swing wildly—he had enough core strength, especially in this world—but he was acutely aware of the dangers of being this high up.

Once, that had been a thrill. After the accident, it was more complicated.

Hiking himself up over the edge was more difficult than he had anticipated. Unlike a wall, he couldn't push out with his feet and use the momentum of tethered arms to swing up. This was all core and upper body and relied on his newly restored and still faulty hands.

Yeah, this wasn't his brightest idea ever.

Finally, he accomplished it by swinging his right leg up and pushing with the extra hold. The roof edge, thankfully, was curved in like a pagoda, which meant he could get his feet under him more easily and rest for a moment. He sat and leaned back against the upper part of the curve while his heart hammered and sweat cooled on his skin.

When he moved to turn, his relief fled. It was the result of only the slightest give under his feet but enough to make his breath catch in his throat. His heart seized and he saw the blue again and felt the tumble. But when the spots cleared from his vision, he wasn't falling and the little clatter he'd heard was gone. He was still safe.

Ceramic shattered on paving stones. He froze again and his heart made a concerted effort to leap sideways out of his body.

Ben waited for ten breaths, then twenty, listening for the sound of footsteps or creaking shutters, but heard nothing. Finally, he took two steps and hauled himself over the final level of the roof with single-minded determination. As his first climbing instructor had said, "Tell your body what to do and then get your mind out of the way."

He stood on a fairly wide, flat roof, recessed by two feet or so. Someone had lived there once but not recently, and anything of value had long since been stripped. There was only the faint detritus left after a move and after rain and wind had swept most of the rest away. He could see a scrap of a rag, the remains of an old flag, and pieces of string hanging from some tiles. Four holes in the floor suggested that a covering of some kind had been held up with poles.

While he didn't have any of that, what he did have was a place where no one else seemed to be. He'd take it.

With a heavy sigh, he sat and let his arms fall at his sides. Now that he was over the edge of the roof, every muscle seemed to tremble.

"I fucked up, didn't I?"

Silence was not what he hoped to hear.

"Prima?"

You didn't seem like you were quite done with your part of the conversation yet.

Ben cursed internally at the AI for being astute. He didn't like that. She had a point, though. "I wasn't. I don't think I *did* fuck up."

"There it is."

"There what is? She's getting on my case, but she's copping out on this whole thing. 'One person can't stand in the way of the slave trade.'" He made finger quotes bitterly. If anyone was watching, he would probably have looked completely insane when he mouthed words almost silently and gestured. "They won't change because someone asks them nicely and lays out a gold road. They'll stop because it gets too difficult to keep doing business, and that isn't *pleasant*. Does she think she's teaching them a *lesson* by stealing their money? It goes back into the community so they can suck it out again. That's a stupid system."

"Mmm, rain and droughts work much the same way."

"Whose side are you on?" Ben demanded.

"I'm not on anyone's side. I'm an observer."

"Kind of." He scowled at the sky, which had begun to show the first hint of dawn. "I'm only saying you don't stop something like this by turning away and pretending not to see it."

Prima said nothing.

"Well? *Do* you?"

"I think," she said after a short hesitation, *"that if there were an easy, assured route for this kind of thing, slavery would not still exist."*

"I didn't say it would be easy," he snapped in response.

"Yes, but that's the issue, isn't it? It's never merely inconvenient. It makes you give up things you aren't prepared to give."

With that, she gave every indication of withdrawing respectfully from the conversation and left him to stare into the middle distance. Finally, as the sky lightened, he managed to fall into a fitful sleep.

It had been a long night.

CHAPTER FORTY-SEVEN

T he twins walked into the temple, each with their hand outstretched, reaching for contact.

Prima found it fascinating how much living creatures relied on their sense of touch for comfort. It had been built into the algorithms governing how characters interacted, and she had initially discounted it. As she understood it, physical contact was for romantic purposes and was used sporadically for friendship and other social interactions.

Now, she began to think that without a body of her own, she had misunderstood something fundamental.

The pool was positioned at the end of the temple. Mindful of the information she had researched on architecture and human psychology, she had made the environment as comforting as she could with muted, fairly even lighting and a low ceiling that slanted down at the corners. Although sky and clouds could be seen outside, she hoped the twins felt safe there.

Their heart rates *were* slowing. Prima gave herself some congratulations.

They reached the pool and each looked to where the other would be. They couldn't see each other's faces, which meant they couldn't decide by tiny flickers and gestures who should go first.

"Do you want to go?" Jamie asked. "Or should I?"

Taigan hesitated. The AI got the sense that making this decision through words was difficult for her. "You go first," she said finally.

Jamie approached the pool. It was wide, paved with tiles of various pale blues, and fed by a little fountain so the water barely moved.

She would see now if she'd gambled well on human psychology. It seemed she wasn't very good at this, and after a few missteps in the past weeks, she began to worry that she would never grasp what was required.

He knelt and stared at his reflection, bit his lip, and looked to where Taigan hung back.

"Oh, come on. You probably won't see it and it won't be gross."

His sister laughed slightly and crept closer. She joined him in looking at the water and her face fell when she couldn't see their two reflections together.

Jamie stared, waited, and eventually, extended his hand tentatively to touch the surface. He held back at first as if worried that a curse would come out of nowhere and drag him into the underworld, but nothing happened when he touched it. He only saw exactly what Prima wanted him to see—his face and nothing more.

"Prima, am I supposed to do something?" he asked finally.

"I can only tell you what the legend is."

"But you wouldn't have hauled us up here if it didn't work, right? Right? Prima?" He looked around and his tone changed. "But how *could* it work? How could a game see…"

He was getting too close to the truth.

"See if Taigan can make it work."

"Oh. Good point." He looked in the girl's direction, distracted from his thoughts. "You give it a go. If we're existing differently, then maybe you'll be able to do it."

"Maybe." Taigan sounded doubtful. "I simply look into it?"

"Don't ask me. I couldn't make it work."

"Good point." She knelt and there was a moment where her frame and her brother's melded. He stood and stepped back.

She closed her eyes for a moment while she propped herself on her hands and thought hard, then opened her eyes and looked down. Her reflection mirrored her frown and she waited with admirable patience for a picture to appear. When it didn't, she sighed, closed her eyes, and opened them to try again.

This was part of the plan, but it was surprisingly difficult to keep quiet while they worked toward the conclusion. Prima distracted herself with plotting a three-body problem while Taigan tried her best to make the pool work.

Finally, however, the girl blew a breath out. "Okay, I can't do it, either."

"Well, shit." Jamie knelt nearby. "Prima, did you consider that we might merely be stupid?"

"You are humans. Sorry, low blow."

"Yeah, funny." He looked up. "Remember when you didn't understand how language worked and convinced me that my sister was dead?"

"Point taken."

"Uh-huh." He sat and crossed his legs.

"Maybe it was meant to be paired with prayer," she suggested as casually as she could. *"After all, this is a temple. Perhaps some...meditation?"*

"You really don't know?" Taigan asked suspiciously.

"A great deal of the lore was already here when I came to the game."

It was a specious excuse at best, but they both accepted it with a shrug. Prima couldn't decide if that made them stupid or if it made her an asshole.

"Shall we try meditation?" the girl asked Jamie.

"I don't know. This is getting a little 'Oracle of Delphi.'"

"What does *that* mean?"

"You know, where people would bring gifts and she'd burn them and inhale the chemicals and do an acid trip and tell them about it? Like, it wasn't anything real. It was only hallucinogens."

"You take the fun out of *everything.*" Taigan sat with a thump and rolled her eyes before she closed them.

He had enough of a sense about his sister to sit with her and also try to meditate. Whatever was going through their heads—and Prima couldn't see *that*, however much she wanted to—their faces moved sometimes with shadows of emotion, but they both seemed determined to make the pool work.

She truly was an asshole. While she did it for a good reason, playing tricks on people didn't feel right. She had never done something like this before, but she had heard the PIVOT team members discussing meditation and she had done research of her own. Meditation skills, honed over time, allowed the user to move through states of consciousness at will.

And something seemed to be working. With interest and hope, she watched as the two of them started to flicker into the same way of being.

It was working.

Prima focused intently to make sure she hadn't misinterpreted what she'd seen. It was *working*. They had their eyes closed, but it was *working*.

She wanted to give a whoop but noticed something unfortunate.

Taigan didn't flicker into Jamie's way of being. It was the other way around. He began to go into her state. The AI panicked and dropped something loudly to scare the two of them. She should do this with less guesswork and panic, but she didn't have time to think —all she wanted was to pull Jamie out of this immediately.

As both twins jumped and swore, there was a split-second where Taigan flickered into her brother's space. It was only for a moment, but his sudden, sharp look was enough to tell Prima that it hadn't been a trick of the algorithms.

That gave her an idea.

"Prima?" Taigan called.

"Something is coming," she said. *"In both your realities."*

"Shitshitshitshitshit," Jamie muttered. "Taigan, are you okay? Taigan!"

The girl darted a glance at his whiteboard. "I'm fine. For now." She swallowed. "I'm—"

Prima knew the sentence was supposed to end with scared, but Taigan didn't want to worry her brother. The AI tried to calm herself and wait. If this worked, her instincts and theories would be vindicated.

Well, she would know soon enough if it would work.

The jackalopes burst out of the brush at the edges of the temple, one on either side. The young people only seemed to see one apiece, which was good. The creatures snarled as they bounded toward the twins, their fur glistening and teeth gleaming.

Please let this work, please let this work, please let this work... Thankfully, the AI hadn't projected that as her version of a verbal statement.

Taigan launched forward with a yell directly toward her jackalope. There was a moment of confusion while Jamie saw her and his jackalope did too. The animal skidded to a halt and tried to choose a target, but he lunged at it with a noise halfway between a yodel and a shriek.

Prima made a mental note to tease him relentlessly about that later.

Physical danger was shifting Taigan into the same level of consciousness. Now that they had done the work to make her aware of her body, she had begun to get the hang of *being* again. The AI surged happily but stopped hastily so she wouldn't overload her servers.

Hopefully, no one on the PIVOT team had seen the processing flare. Humans could be quite oblivious, but they also had a habit of noticing things you didn't want them to.

Due to her freakish speed and the others' distraction, Taigan reached her jackalope first. She didn't seem to have a plan—something Prima was distressingly familiar with after watching Justin, Ben, and Dotty—but she was also prepared to do anything and everything to win the fight.

She started by grasping the jackalope by the horns and wrenching it sideways.

The creature did not know what to do with this particular strategy. It was too well-grounded to simply flop over, but it didn't have a long enough snout to bite her or long enough limbs to scratch her. The two combatants circled, locked in their standoff.

Jamie still had his sword. He uttered another yodel and slashed at his adversary, which leapt back with a hiss. Blood stained its flanks.

"Do you want a piece of this?" he taunted. "Huh? Don't you dare hurt my fucking sister. I'll kill you."

"I don't think jackalopes speak English."

"They understand tone!" he shouted in response and swung the weapon again.

Taigan shifted her feet a few times as if testing a theory, then kicked her opponent squarely in the chest. Its teeth snapped but gained no purchase, given the angle of her leg. She still yelped and withdrew the limb, then stumbled, having lost sight of the animal for a second.

It looked equally confused.

She flickered back and the two of them shrieked and charged each other again. Taigan dived sideways, flickered out, and rolled to her feet in time to catch the jackalope's antlers again. This time, as she held on and swung her leg—aiming precisely for the mouth with her knee—she flickered out for good. The creature hurtled through the space where she had been and skidded out the side of the temple, and she whirled as Jamie stabbed his opponent through the mouth.

Reflexively, she clapped her hands over her mouth. The animal slumped and her brother yanked his sword out before he saw her out of the corner of his eye.

"Taigan?" He sounded like he might cry.

They stared in shock and hope, shaking, before they ran to each other and collided in a tangle of limbs and heads and black hair. Prima couldn't tell if what she heard was laughter or crying. They wrapped their arms around each other and hung on for dear life.

At some point, the laughter stopped and the sound became crying. Both shuddered with sobs, a breakdown that made her the saddest she had been since—well, since Dotty.

Sadness was much like happiness, she decided. It was the urge to do something or process something, but there was nothing to do except exist while the emotion ran through one's system. She didn't think she liked it, but something about this situation made her want to explode, she was so full of joy.

Joy, but not happiness.

Emotions were *weird*.

"What the hell?" Taigan choked finally. "You have a *sword*? I didn't have a sword."

Jamie started to laugh. He laughed until he was crying again as he held her. "You're here," he whispered. "You're here. I can see you. You're here."

"I'm here." She squeezed her arms around him. "I want to see Emmy and Mom and Dad too."

"You can. Of course you can. We'll get them here." He drew back and looked at her. "Taigan, when I thought about what I wanted most—"

He stopped. She had flickered out again into her separate existence.

"Dammit!" both twins said at the same time. The words appeared on their respective whiteboards.

Then, at the same time, they added, "It doesn't matter."

"We can do it again," Taigan affirmed.

"We can do it again," he echoed.

"You can do it again," Prima agreed.

CHAPTER FORTY-EIGHT

B en woke when a shadow fell across him. He sat with a snort and his limbs flailed, and he grimaced when he realized he was both tormented by aching muscles and *far* too hot. His mouth felt like sandpaper. When he saw what had cast the shadow, he scrambled back across the roof and felt for his knife.

The woman smiled at him. Her blonde hair was held back loosely to fall around her shoulders in a profusion of curls. She wore a dress of a deep twilight-blue, with golden accents to mimic armor—and whether it was sheer stupidity or knowledge of some additional information, she did not look even faintly intimidated by him.

"Good morning," she said as pleasantly as if they had met over the breakfast table. "My name is Delia. I have a business proposition for you."

He tried to untangle this. His mind was still fogged from sleep, but it didn't escape his notice that a grimy man sleeping out in the open was hardly a good bet for a business proposition. He settled for raising one eyebrow as he stood, assumed a wary but solid stance, and folded his arms.

"Let's hear it, then."

Delia smiled again. "My employer is one of the foremost dealers of precious items in Heffog," she explained. "A client has come to us with very exacting specifications, and we have found the piece that will please them. We need you to get it for us."

"I can only assume you mean by stealing it," he said drily, "as most wealthy people do not sleep on abandoned rooftops."

She nodded.

"Why me?" he asked.

"Because one of my agents saw you climb to the roof last night," she said simply. "Add to that the fact that you are unknown in the city and appear to have no loyalty to any particular faction, and you serve our purposes quite well. You will be generously paid, of course."

Ben sighed and rubbed his forehead. "I take it this isn't a friendly offer so much as forced volunteering."

"Oh, no." She dimpled and shook her golden curls slightly. "It is an offer only. Should you refuse, no harm will come to you."

He stared suspiciously at her.

"My employer prefers to do business voluntarily," Delia said, "as they find it makes them less likely to be stabbed in their sleep."

"I, uh—" He choked and coughed. "I see. Yes."

"Perhaps you would like to hear more about the job?" the woman suggested calmly.

"I'm not sure I would." He gave her a tight smile and was about to ask her to leave when his stomach betrayed him by growling loudly.

Delia was not gauche enough to comment on that directly. She merely waited as if utterly immune to his weak half-rejection.

"I'm not sure this is a part of the city I want to get involved in," he said. He did not want to do this, but he also knew he had little choice.

In all honesty, he had almost decided to ask Prima to pull him out of this part of the game. He had mucked it up beyond repair. By now, normally, he would have tapped out and wasn't quite sure why he stuck with it this time.

Perhaps he was getting stupider as he got older.

"This part of the city?" the woman echoed.

"People fighting for petty reasons," Ben said bluntly. "There's enough cruelty already and enough terrible things being done to the powerless. I don't know why I would spend my time and effort helping one of the powerful get a bauble they want."

"Your time and effort," she said thoughtfully. She looked at him, her expression one of real interest.

"Yes!" His pride was pricked. "You know, the things that led you to seek me out. I may not be a renowned thief, but I do have skills to work with, you know, and I want to do good things for this city."

"Good things?"

"Like stop the damned slave trade, for one," he told her flatly. "So how's that for an answer? Do you think your employer would still approve of me now?"

"You want to stop the slave trade." She moved to look out over the city from the rooftop. Whoever she was, he noted she did not seem to be worried about being seen.

He wasn't foolish enough to stand beside her—he didn't want to be tipped off the roof—but he did approach and stand a few feet away from her. From there, he could see a faint glimmer of the ocean. They weren't far from it and there were only a few streets and jumbled roofs between them and the water.

"Yes," he said. "I want to stop the slave trade—and I won't be put off by people telling me that direct action won't do anything."

"Direct action?" She looked at him with a smile.

"Assassination," Ben told her.

He hoped to make her flinch but she didn't. Instead, she considered his statement.

"Assassination," she murmured. It was clear that this wasn't a prompt but rather something she thought about very carefully. At length, she nodded. "Our purposes can quite easily align, then. You see, the job would bring you within range of one of the foremost slave traders in the city."

"Really?"

Delia nodded. "They represent a not-insubstantial portion of the slave trade, which would falter following their death."

Caution made him think before he spoke.

"I'll want to confirm that myself," he said. "You understand I cannot simply take your word for it."

"Of course." She didn't look at him but she did not seem insulted in the least.

"Don't you think your employer would mind you agreeing to an assassination?" he probed.

"No." Until now, everything in her manner had invited conversation. This statement did not.

Ben looked away. "Give me a moment to think."

She nodded silently and he turned away to pace. His mind raced through his options. Without Elantria's help, he had two main choices —leave the city or try to make it on his own. If he chose to leave, he would forfeit this chance to learn the skills Prima wanted him to learn.

He looked at his hands and wiggled the fingers slightly.

"What are you thinking about?" Prima asked.

"Whether I should stay and take the job or leave Heffog," he told her. He was careful to keep his voice low.

The AI didn't speak for a long moment.

"I've messed everything up again," he said. "Except, not—I didn't do anything *wrong*. It's only that people are always so unreasonable. They get used to problems and they don't want someone to fix them." He folded his arms and stared out at the city. "They don't want someone to be blunt with them. Or take decisive action."

"Mmm," the AI said finally. *"So, you've been in this situation before."*

"Not this exact one." He grinned. "Assassination and high-end jewelry thievery are not my usual areas of operation. But, yeah. Like I said last night, this wouldn't be the first place I've had to leave because people didn't like my style."

"To see if I understand, you solve people's problems but they do not appreciate that?"

"Exactly." Ben nodded.

"And then, once you have taken decisive action, it becomes too uncomfortable to remain in that community?"

"Yes."

"I see." She said nothing more.

"It's infuriating," he told her. "They *say* they want the problems solved, but they only see obstacles. I solve the problem and suddenly, they're upset."

Prima held her tongue.

"Are you going to comment?" he asked her.

"I am fairly certain that my assessment would not meet with approval."

Of course. He should have expected that response. Irritated, he glowered at the sky and sighed as he looked out at the city. The AI was on everyone else's side. Of course, she would be. He was disappointed, though. She wasn't a normal person. If anyone could understand, he would think it would be her.

"Fine. Tell me what you think."

She didn't ask him if he was sure and took him at face value. He decided he liked that.

"Very well," she said. *"I will draw from the example of Elantria as I am not familiar with your other experiences. In that case, it was you who first identified slavery as a problem rather than her asking for your help regarding it. Both she and Orien cautioned you against hasty decisions that could negatively impact the very people you hoped to save, but you did not seek information to find out why they believed that or what the risks might be."*

Ben stood rigidly but listened to each sentence carefully.

"There is a very large area of uncertainty around complex issues," Prima continued. *"It is difficult to know which course of action will be best but it seems only logical that stopping to examine the exact situation would produce better results."*

He bit his lip. "So, you're saying…"

"I am saying," Prima said with a great deal more gentleness than he had expected, *"that in my admittedly limited experience with you, I have noticed that you tend to be motivated by the sincere desire to solve problems quickly. Your morals are unwavering. The issue others have seems to stem from the fact that your desire for quick action does not allow for information-gathering and thus, your actions may do more harm than good."*

In silence, he lowered his face into his hands.

"I think, from our discussion last night, that you have already begun to

mull over that same issue," she said. *"I won't tell you that Jorys was innocent or that he did not deserve justice. The question to ask yourself is simply how you can best achieve justice in a way that does not do further harm to his victims."*

She paused as if to give him time to respond, but he made no effort to do so.

"What are you thinking?"

"That I can look at my life and see a thousand things I did wrong and a thousand situations I made worse," he said bluntly.

"That is an overreaction and you know it." Her answer was immediate. *"The matter before you is how best to use your skills for the people of Heffog. Not to mention how best to heal yourself."*

"Right." Ben shook his head and looked at Delia. Whether she'd noticed his conversation or not, he wasn't sure. She smiled blandly at him. "I'll do it. But I want more information first and I want to speak to your employer."

"Done," she agreed. She gestured to the side of the building, where a ladder led to the ground.

He stepped closer to it but stopped at the edge of the roof.

The woman looked expectantly at him. "Yes?"

"You played me," he said slowly. He ran their conversation through his mind.

She frowned slightly. "I'm not familiar with that expression."

"You merely repeated what I said until I told you everything I wanted, then you offered me that."

"And you're...upset?" She looked bemused. "You get what you want, and we get what we want. Surely that's not a problem but instead, a welcome solution."

Ben sensed that it was useless to try to make her admit that she could as easily use that skill for bad purposes as good ones. He shrugged and followed her but told himself he would have to keep his guard up. It was all well and good to pretend that people could find mutually agreeable solutions most of the time.

But you only found out who people *really* were when the two of you couldn't agree.

CHAPTER FORTY-NINE

U nlike Elantria, Delia did not travel on foot through the city. A carriage waited when she and Ben reached the street and she held the door open for him before she followed him into the shadowed interior. Black gauze hung over the windows to obscure their features from curious passers-by, and the carriage had no coat of arms.

He replayed what Prima had said in his mind.

It was difficult to keep his thoughts from circling to the single, horrifying memory of the slaves stumbling out of Jorys' study. They were terrified and powerless. That fear haunted him.

Every moment he spent dwelling on it was a moment he didn't spend trying to fix it.

With Prima's blunt words in his head, he could see now that the merchant had merely been one point in a web. The people in that room hadn't been frightened because he sold them but because so many others would collaborate with him to keep them enslaved. The guards would prevent them from escaping while they were brought to the market, the authorities wouldn't intervene when they were sold, and the people wouldn't rise up and stand in the way of them being sent off to God only knew where.

What he needed to do was to bring the entire network down. Not only that, he needed to salt the ground so thoroughly that nothing would ever grow in its place.

But that wasn't possible. At least, no solution came to him. He could hear all the mealy-mouthed advice now—people telling him to provide profitable industries for the slave traders to switch to. But why should the city be rewarded with new industry when it had profited for so long off the fear and enslavement of others?

He had no clue what to do and he was damned certain that Elantria's approach wasn't doing any better than his. His hands clenched, and when he looked up, he saw Delia watching him.

She didn't say anything and simply leaned back in her seat and stared out the window as the city rolled past. They were heading east to the district where the richest of the rich lived, and he took the time to consider what this said about her employer. A rich person who wanted to prey on the other rich? Who collaborated to steal the prized possessions of fellow nobles? It didn't add up.

When he arrived, he realized why it didn't add up. It wasn't a noble doing this.

It was a servant.

The carriage brought them to a small gate at the back of a walled compound, where they stepped out in a small courtyard. It was humble but swept clean. Against the outer wall stood a two-story house, grand by the standards of the city but dwarfed by the mansion that lay at the center of the compound.

Delia, who now wore a dull cloak over her dress, brought him inside. A man with blue-green hair and black eyes looked up from a table where he studied a building layout. He rolled it carefully before he approached quickly and held a hand out.

"I am Nemon," he said and seemed unperturbed by his visitor's searching gaze. "I am the product of many generations of by-blows," he said with little emotion. "The nobles mingle more with their servants than they would have you believe."

Ben swallowed, unsure what to say to this. "I'm Ben," he said. On a whim, he added, "Nothing about my lineage is noteworthy."

It seemed his instinct had been correct because the man responded with a genuine grin. "As you can see from my residence, lineage is more about the circumstance of birth than about the parentage of an individual."

He looked around. "That's true in comparison to the main house. And yet, you have your house in this compound. That suggests a certain favor."

"Well." Nemon returned to the table. "My...owners...were not certain whether to place their trust in the new elven king and thus, only half the household has departed to maintain a residence in the new capital with the lady of the house. The husband remains and the rest of us have more space than usual. Certain complications have arisen in my business since the shift but also certain opportunities."

"Why do you do it?" he asked him simply. "Delia says you steal from the nobles and give to other nobles. Why take such a risk?"

The man propped himself on the edge of the table as he considered this. One leg swung slowly. "Because I can," he said simply. "Unlike the vast majority of this city, I have no reverence for my relatives. I understand that their blood is no different from mine and I have grown up among them, so their mannerisms are not a mystery to me. They give or deny birthright on capricious grounds, so I take whatever I can lay my hands on. What is it to me which noble has a particular necklace if I get a good fee for supplying it?" He shrugged.

Ben looked at him in silence. Nemon was one of the people who had found his place in the current system, a peripheral member of the web. Whether from apathy or greed, he was not interested in tearing the system down. He would simply grift from it.

He did not even pretend that he had selfless motives for doing so.

"Perhaps you'll feel differently when Delia tells you what I demanded as my price," he said.

"Oh?" The man focused on Delia.

"He wants to assassinate the mark while he's there," she said flatly. She smiled when her employer laughed.

"You...don't mind?" Ben asked, a little unnerved.

"Not in the slightest," Nemon said. "After all, the confusion after a noble is killed is ripe ground for theft—as are the auction and transfer of goods that follow."

Now, he felt a growing unease. The slave traders of Heffog were not people he felt charitably toward, but he also felt that the act of killing deserved gravity. The man was apparently willing to view life and death as matters that affected his business and nothing more.

It was unnerving to find that he preferred Elantria's inaction to this cheerful self-interest. He wondered what she would say to this and wished he could ask her.

No. That door is closed.

"So, what's your plan?" Nemon continued to swing his leg and seemed genuinely interested.

"I'm not sure yet," he replied and pointed at the table. "Is that the layout of the house in question?"

"Yes." The other two exchanged a glance and Delia gave a small nod. Having been assured that the recruit was trustworthy, the man went to the table and unrolled the map. "The necklace is here in the family's personal vault. It's an ancient piece, very valuable but not well-known these days. It should be quite a long time before anyone notices that it's missing."

"So why does your client want it?" he questioned.

"I don't ask those things," Nemon told him. "It's one of my guarantees. In any event, the necklace looks like..." He pulled a sketched rendering from a pile "This."

Ben studied it. He wasn't an expert on jewelry, but he had to admit that he found it more gaudy than anything else. To him, it looked like nothing more than a wild jumble of large stones and pearls crusted over a thick piece of metal in no particular pattern.

"Are you sure they don't merely want it for the jewels?" he asked dubiously.

"Again, I do not ask." The man smiled. "Exactly as I will not ask *your* reasons for wishing to assassinate the owner."

He grew less comfortable by the minute.

"Tell me about the owner," he said.

"You've signed on, then?"

"Yes." He didn't allow himself time to hesitate. If he did, he knew he'd leave and make new enemies—powerful ones who didn't mind killing.

If he stayed, he gained access to someone who could help him destroy the nobility one by one, at least until the man realized he was ending the gravy train. And, hell, if he stole enough items for him, Nemon might not even mind.

Sometimes, to do good, you had to resort to unpleasant means. He reminded himself of what had happened at the fae castle.

"Very good." His new employer gestured to a seating area around the fireplace. The furniture was worn and the expensive fabric faded and threadbare. "Come, sit. We will talk." He waved for Delia to join them.

"Don't you cause suspicion by coming here?" Ben asked her curiously.

"Oh, no." She leaned back in her chair. "I'm known around the city as a courtesan. I often arrive at various estates in insufficient disguises, usually at back gates."

"A courtesan?" He had to admit a courtesan would make a good ally for a thief.

"I said I'm *known* as a courtesan," she corrected.

"Ah."

"It means no one tries to marry me and I get to go almost anywhere I want." Her dimples returned. "It's perfect."

Ben could only smile. There was something amusing about her taking joy from what others probably tried to shame her for.

"She's not mentioning," Nemon said, "that she runs a boarding house for runaway courtesans and sets them up with new identities in new cities."

"I don't make fun of how *you* spend *your* money," Delia protested.

He looked from one to the other. It was interesting to see the range of morality various people in this city had. And if Delia worked with Nemon, the half-elf couldn't be all that bad, surely.

"Who's the mark?" he asked.

"Lord Kerill," Nemon stated.

"Who's his heir?"

The man looked curious. "His niece, Birra."

A thought had begun to take shape in his head. Elantria had said that one of the problems with his assassination of Jorys was that the slave trade would only accelerate under any of his heirs. If he wanted to not make the same mistake again, he had to be careful.

"What's her opinion of his business?" he asked.

"She already runs some of it."

Ah. Not an ally, then.

"And what if she's dead?" he asked. "Or otherwise unable to claim the inheritance."

"She'd better be dead," Nemon warned him. "If she's not, she'll fight tooth and nail. Behind her in line, you see, is his son—who's quite the abolitionist."

Ben allowed himself a satisfied smile. Excellent. "And how difficult would it be to forge a letter with Kerill's seal?" he asked.

His employer now looked deeply interested. "Not overly. It can be done if you need it. For a price, of course. What would you like it to say?"

"That he has repented of his dealings after a religious experience and intends to make his son his heir. Oh, and he will have the son help him unravel his business and put the fortune to work fighting the slavery industry in Heffog."

"You plan to pin his murder on Birra," Delia said quietly.

"Yes. Yes, I do." His smile was grim.

"That's...sneaky." Prima sounded almost worried. *"And—what's the human term? 'Ice cold?'"*

He gave a tiny nod to tell her she was correct. "Do you think it will work?" he asked Nemon.

"Oh, very well." The man was deeply amused. "And would I be correct that you will kill Birra as well to make sure?"

"Of course."

"You will make an interesting addition to the city." Nemon studied him. "Already, you've been seen in the company of Kural and Elantria and now, I find you're an assassin." He tapped his mouth and raised an eyebrow. "Did she hire you to kill Jorys?"

"No," Ben said and added nothing further. He didn't want to talk about Elantria, nor did he want to make it seem like she had anything to do with the merchant's death.

"A mystery!" The man seemed delighted by that. "Very well, keep your secrets. I'll find a time in the near future when Birra will be at Kerill's house and we'll get you in to accomplish both goals."

CHAPTER FIFTY

When Jacob arrived at the lab in the morning, a box rested on one of the tables with several staff members gathered around it.

"What's that?"

"It's for you," Amber said. She waved a hand at it.

"It's...okay, we've checked that it's not a bomb, right?" The hate mail had mostly tapered off after the initial burst of publicity, but some people were still not happy about the idea of virtual reality.

"It's not a bomb," she said and rolled her eyes good-naturedly. "Nick brought it."

"Oh. Okay, then." He put his cup of coffee down and stepped closer to open the box. The cake inside was his favorite kind—funfetti with boring white frosting. As Amber said, it was the "basic bitch" of cakes.

He had argued that one should not tamper with perfection.

CONGRATULATIONS was written across the top in blue frosting.

"Congratulations?" he asked.

"Yes." Amber reached under the table and pulled out a bottle of champagne. "Taigan and Jamie were able to see each other in-game for a while."

"Holy shit!"

After the disappointing first meeting, everyone in the team had been in a funk. The girl's undeniable progress toward consciousness constantly encountered snags they hadn't realized there could be, and he had doubted that they could truly help her. But this brought hope.

He smiled at the group. "Holy shit," he repeated. "Gimme that champagne." He popped the cork to the sound of cheers and put his mouth hastily over the opening when contents began to fountain out.

"Okay, that's *his* bottle," Amber said to the others. She retrieved another one.

The cake was cut and served—breakfast for the team coming in and dessert for the team heading home. Everyone watched the video of Taigan and Jamie fighting the jackalopes, and raucous laughter erupted as both teenagers went full berserker in their individual special ways.

"It's working," Jacob said to Nick and Amber in an undertone. "I can't believe it. I had…stopped believing it."

"Me too," she admitted.

"Yeah, me too." Nick sighed. "I felt like such a shitbag, too, having spoken to them all and…like you said, we shouldn't get too invested, but I did. I thought it would be easy—and it's very definitely not."

"Not in the least," she agreed. "And we should have thought of that tactic sooner, you know—mortal danger and all that. It was one of the key pieces DuBois talked about at the start."

"Yeah, how stupid of us," he quipped. "Going easy on the comatose girl."

"Okay, point taken. Still." Amber finished her last mouthful of cake with a happy sigh. "Finally, a good update for her parents. Plus, she said she wants to see them all."

"And there's no way that forcing them all into mortal danger together could backfire on us," Jacob said mildly.

Nick chortled and reached for another piece of cake.

"I don't suppose Ben has also had any leaps forward while I was gone?" the other man asked hopefully.

"Greedy," Amber admonished. "Isn't one piece of good news enough for you? But since you ask, he continues to gain his coordination at a frankly astonishing rate. Last night, he climbed a building on his own. Although that was after he assassinated someone and was kicked out by the person sheltering him."

Jacob put his fork down. "I'm sorry, he *what?*"

His partners exchanged a look. They tested their wills against each other for a moment and, when neither backed down, sighed and played a round of rock-paper-scissors. She lost and recounted the story of what had happened.

"Fuck, I might have done the same," Jacob admitted. "I didn't even know there was slavery in this world."

"There's a lot we didn't get to discover because the game wasn't developed," she pointed out. "We simply input all the lore and let the procedural generator guide people through it. Our players are seeing parts of the game that we've never seen."

"Mmm, maybe we want more QA on our end before we roll new zones out to players."

"Quite possibly." Amber tapped her foot. "Ugh. I'm supposed to sleep but I drank way too much coffee for that."

"I'll go home," Nick suggested.

"You do it, you die."

"I merely offered." He stood and served himself a third piece of cake. "Anyway, Jacob, about Ben... His doctors keep calling to ask if our progress metrics are correct. They insist that he shouldn't be able to do any of the things he did when we took him out last time, much less what he can do in the game."

"Well, they can argue about it all they want." The other man took a long sip of coffee. "He's on video doing all of it, so it's indisputable."

"I think they're more worried that they didn't think of using this system." Nick shrugged. "Or, it might be that they don't like it because they can't understand why it works. DuBois says that's it, but it doesn't make sense to me."

"As a doctor, I am telling you that a lack of clarity is *precisely* why they dispute it." DuBois approached, holding his customary bag of popcorn. "There is any number of vital, useful, effective treatments that have never been utilized because doctors could not find the underlying mechanism and didn't want to prescribe it."

"Just when you thought you knew all the things to be angry about," Nick muttered to the others.

"Well, while you spend time being angry about it, I may have a solution." The doctor took a seat on one of the lab stools. "I've been in contact with some neuroscientists who study proprioception and kinesthesia to ask if avatar control in virtual reality might not be subject to the same constraints as moving a body."

As per usual, it took the others a moment to parse his words.

"Wait," Jacob said.

"Because he thinks of himself as someone who can control his body," Amber said slowly, "he's more able to bring his virtual self into line with that?"

"Exactly." DuBois nodded at her. "Much like the fact that Justin and Dotty were able to use magic—or that Taigan can summon objects." Somewhat testily, he added, "*That* should not be possible."

"Now, now, simply because you can't explain it..." Nick gave him a bland smile and quailed when he glared at him. "It's a joke, a play on your words earlier."

Jacob ignored them. "So because his actual physiology doesn't get in the way quite as much, it means he was able to re-learn the movement pathways more easily in the pod and it continues when he wakes up? Do I have that right?"

DuBois nodded.

"Huh." Jacob chewed as he thought and helped himself to another piece of cake. He hadn't bought breakfast on the way there, so the cake was welcome. "Does *he* know how well he's doing, statistically speaking?"

Amber shook her head. "I don't think so. Eliza told him that he's doing off-the-charts well, but I don't think he fully absorbed that."

"He was distracted," Jacob observed. "What with his crush and all."

"They're so cute together." She grinned.

"In the *meantime*," DuBois said, clearly hoping to hasten the conversation along from this topic, "as Jacob has astutely pointed out, self-doubt could be fatal. Ben appears to not know how unusual his abilities are, and I say we continue to challenge him—not so much that he gives up but enough that he doesn't stop to dwell on how far he's come."

"We should be able to arrange that," she said dryly. "Now that he's gone all hitman on us. Boy, was that a turnaround."

"It has been strange to watch," the doctor conceded.

"Very John Wick-ish," Nick agreed. "But on the other hand, he is stepping out on his own and that's good."

"True." Amber scrunched her face and leaned on the table. "Okay, maybe another piece of cake…" She reached for the server before her conscience could intrude.

"Personalities can appear to change wildly when push comes to shove," Jacob said. "And we've seen this in other patients. It's not only him. Justin had much more of a background in video games so the killing didn't faze him like it did with Ben and Dotty, but even *he* came out of it wanting to make a difference in the world."

"Yes," she said and grimaced, "but if Ben comes out of this as a hitman, we can expect some uncomfortable questions."

"Maybe he's merely doing what *you* suggested and exploring his morality in a world without the same constraints and permanence as this one," Jacob countered. "Remember that?"

"Oh, right." Amber hunched her shoulders. "I hope that's what it is, anyway. I don't want to embroil us in endless lawsuits when a vigilante hops through various countries assassinating dictators."

"Don't worry," he told her. "The best-case scenario is that, at this rate, he'll have swung to full-on pacifist again in a few days. If not… we sell this to the military as an assassin training program."

She punched him in the shoulder and laughed. "Stop it. Okay, I'll try to sleep. If anything cool happens, get more cake."

"There's half left," Nick protested.

"And you cretins will be around it for eight hours. I don't think there'll be any left when I get back." She smiled at them and wandered off to retrieve her coat.

Jacob smiled after her.

"How's it going with you two?" Nick asked him.

"It's going fine." He glared warningly. The manipulation might have worked out well in some ways, but he wasn't entirely ready to let his friend off the hook.

Not to mention that both he and Amber were a great deal more cautious in relationships than they had been at eighteen when the world seemed like a giant game with no consequences. They had skirted a few issues for a week now, including who got keys to whose home and whether there would be any PDA in the lab. Neither of them was yet willing to talk about the issues.

It was the kind of minefield of a conversation that would make everything much easier but was utterly terrifying to have for no good reason.

From the look on Nick's face, he knew some of what was going on. Thankfully, before he could say anything about it, DuBois broke the tension by crinkling the cellophane on his popcorn bag loudly.

"Damn," he said. "I'm already out."

"You could mix it up with some cake," Nick suggested.

"No, thank you." The doctor drifted away to the breakroom, where his popcorn inhabited almost half the cupboards.

"How that man is not malnourished is beyond me," Jacob said.

His friend nodded gravely. "I think he's a robot."

CHAPTER FIFTY-ONE

Lord Kerill's ancestors had been some of the first elven nobles to take up residence in Heffog. When they arrived, the settlement was nothing more than a few huts with human fishermen and an area on a nearby cliff where the caravans could camp while selling goods or buying them.

The Kerills had bought almost all the land. With a combination of cunning and outright lies, they had bought the houses in which the fishermen lived, the piers at which the boats docked, and the camping grounds where the caravans stayed.

Not everything that happened after that was bad. Trade flourished in Heffog, a link between Insea and the countries it could not reach easily by land. The family had connections to any goods people wanted to sell and the more trade flourished, the more new buildings were bought. Land nearby was tilled for crops, silver was discovered in the hills and mined, and a trade sprang up in medicines and ointments made from the bounty of the sea.

Increasingly, elven nobles came to make their home in the city. There was nowhere to fall in Insea and nothing to be lost—but nothing to play for, either. By contrast, Heffog always seemed to be on the verge of something. It never became the center of any trade route, yet it was a hub on many and indispensable. As it became richer, so did the nobles who owned it.

When the new elven monarchy was established to challenge Insea, many families left outright and sold their land to Kerill or to the merchants who wanted to rise in the world. On the one hand, it was a coup, a chance to snatch up the land that had slipped from the family's grasp over the years.

On the other, it was the sign of change, and change could doom old money.

Lord Kerill had not been one to sit by and watch his family's fortunes diminish. Slavery had been rare in Heffog before the elven nobles left and there was a strong prohibition against it in elven culture. Other races must be subjugated via trade and armies, or so the wisdom went. If one could not prove one's superiority via cunning or military might, one was *not* superior.

The present incumbent did not particularly care about that. Slavery was profitable and that was enough for him. The dearth of elven nobles meant that fewer disagreed with him on the matter, and he took that as a license to continue.

It was what had caused the rift between him and his son, however. Once close, the two men had diverged sharply on this issue. His son now sought—both legally and less legally—to undo everything his father did, while Kerill—unexpectedly, in Ben's opinion—did every-thing in his power to bring his son into the fold again.

That was the twist that made his plan better than he had even imagined. Birra had worked hard to make herself a worthy successor, but everyone knew there was a chance that Kerill would make peace with his son. A notably ruthless woman, she might do anything if she thought her hard-earned inheritance would be lost.

Nemon, who knew a great deal about the family—he decided to not ask how—forged the letter himself. It had the understated, self-important tone of elven nobles yet still held the pathos of a parent begging a child to return. It announced Kerill's intention to cease his operations and do anything his son wished to restore their rela-tionship.

Birra would be furious. He considered letting her find the letter and murder Kerill herself, but there was too much of a chance that her father would deny it and their hand would be tipped.

He snuck into the house at dawn when the courtyard at the back of the manor was bustling. Farmers on their way into Heffog would stop first at the wealthy houses to give cooks the first choice of vegetables and fruits from the country. Carts with bolts of cloth, herbs, or animals also called there to trade.

In the crush of people and shouting, it was fairly easy for him to gain entry without raising suspicion. As a cart unloaded burlap sacks of grain, he hefted one over his shoulder and strode into the house—after staggering sideways, of course. Not only was his coordination not what it should be, he hadn't ever carried a huge sack of grain before.

While he was an unknown, no one thought to stop him because he brought the grain into the house. His expression carefully neutral, he followed another porter to a basement and piled his bag of grain next to theirs. He dawdled so the man ascended the stairs ahead of him. Once he was alone, he slipped quickly into the shadows to explore the storerooms.

As he had expected, there were other routes into the house—and, to his relief, many places to hide.

With surprising patience, Ben waited. His supply of food was easily accessible—and better than he would have outside—and he had various locations where he could remain undiscovered. He waited for almost two days while he mapped the quiet times for the house and the voices of those who came and went. To occupy himself, he practiced moving his fingers by sorting beans and counting grains of rice. He drew and redrew the floor plan of the dwelling in the hard-packed dirt of the floor and removed all trace of it each time.

In the deep of the night before the second dawn, he made his move.

He had studied people as they ascended and descended the stairs so now knew which creaked and which did not. Also, he knew where the guards patrolled. He snuck up a set of stairs that ended somewhere along the side of the house and listened at the doorway.

The silence was encouraging.

As quietly as he could, he unlatched the door and began to open it. There was no movement beyond, although there was some light.

Ben looked out into a small antechamber off the kitchen. This room held large bowls, a wooden barrel of flour, and jars of spices, along with a heavy wooden table for kneading bread and making pastries.

Better still, it was uninhabited at this time of night. He slipped into the room and closed the door almost entirely. It made sense to leave an easily accessible escape route.

The vault that held Kerill's jewels was part of his study. The room contained a false wall that could be activated by pressing one of the carved fish on the wooden panels behind the desk.

What the elf seemed to *not* know was that there was another entrance to it. A very different mechanism was concealed in the library, a sliding panel behind one of the bookshelves. "Like many old houses," Nemon had said with a smile, "there were more secrets built into it than have been remembered."

He now needed to find that library, although he knew where it was, of course—he had mapped the house out in paces while he was in the basement. His target destination was about twenty yards to his left but he had no idea what occupants he might find in the corridors between here and there.

The first step, though, was to get through the kitchen. He paused at the open doorway, listened intently, and counted two different snores plus breathing from others, although he couldn't tell how many.

There was nothing for it. He would have to look. Caution made him pause to confirm that he wouldn't cast a shadow when he poked his head out before he stepped slightly around the door.

The kitchens were massive. The light came from banked fires in three hearths. Ropes of garlic and onions hung from the ceiling, along with sausages, haunches of meat, and—in his opinion—far too much fish. One of the cooks dozed in a big chair by the fire, while another slept on a bench nearby. How they didn't fall off, he wasn't sure, but they seemed to have considerable practice.

The quiet breathing came from a young woman who stared at the fire. She looked dwarven to his eyes, although she might simply have been a very short human, and she did something that looked very much like amateur magic. It wasn't the kind Zaara did but rather what he was familiar with from his world—a scattering of leaves and a diagram on the floor.

Hopefully, she would remain engrossed in it while he snuck out. He considered how best to creep across the tiles. There was no path that would take him from his current position to the door without her seeing him...unless he crawled.

Well, there was no point in clinging to his dignity. Ben grimaced, lowered himself to all fours, and crawled painstakingly across the floor. He went under a table that had drips of blood under it, silently bemoaned the fact that there was no such thing as hand sanitizer there, and stopped near the door to listen for guards.

No one seemed to be patrolling the corridor.

He snuck out of the kitchen and into the hallway.

It was quiet, which was a boon. On the first night, there had been a big dinner of some kind and guards had patrolled for an hour or so after everyone left. Tonight, there had been nothing of the sort.

He was surprised to see a light still burning in the study and heard the murmur of voices. Was Kerill still up and working? That gave him a moment's grudging respect for the man. Unfortunately, it also meant he had to be quieter in the vault.

The door to the library was locked but the mechanism was old. He was able to pick it with only two of the tools and eased inside. A magical lantern kept the room illuminated in a reddish hue of light he assumed was to preserve the books but which made the space look like a horror-movie set.

Ben found the panel and opened it. It wasn't complicated, but there was a difference between "simple" and "easy." For one thing, it hadn't been opened in generations and would almost certainly creak.

He lifted it an inch and took another tool from his belt, a long piece of wire with an oil-soaked cloth around it. Working quickly, he wiped the cloth up and around all the mechanisms he could find and repeated the process every inch until the panel was open and he could release it.

By then, his entire body ached, he had a crick in his neck, and he didn't care overly much about the damned necklace.

Still, he was in place now. He retrieved his next tool, a small crystal infused with magic and encased in a metal pyramid. When he flipped one of the sides open, a dim light illuminated everything around him.

The first thing he discovered was that elven nobles preserved the jawbones of their ancestors. It was a revelation that made him jerk back, fling the pyramid in the air—he wasn't quite sure why—and curl into a ball on the ground. He barely managed to uncurl in time to catch the artifact before it clanged noisily and alerted Kerill, and he sat for a moment, glowering at the bones.

Honestly, who hid *bones* in a vault? Ashes in an urn, he could understand. In a mausoleum or somewhere you wouldn't stumble on physical skeletons by accident.

Of course, he *was* robbing the guy.

Ben gave himself a moment to gather his focus before he pushed to his feet and began his search. He looked over his shoulder every few seconds as if to make sure the jawbones hadn't come down from the wall to attack him.

Involuntarily, he shuddered.

The necklace was where Nemon had said it would be—in a jewelry box that took a great deal of finagling before he could open it silently. Not only that, but it also took several attempts to make each movement work. He was better at fine motor control but he was far from perfect at it.

He had barely slipped the necklace—it was as ugly in person as he'd thought—into a pouch at his waist when a commotion sounded from the back of the house. In a panic, he pulled the door closed behind him and stood frozen in the darkness.

How did they know he was there? No one had seen him. He was sure of that.

Unless there were spells in the room that triggered some kind of alarm. He waited, his eyes closed in terror as booted footsteps drew closer to the library…and passed it. The door to the study slammed open.

"What is the meaning of this?" Lord Kerill demanded.

"My lord, apologies for the late hour." The guard sounded respectful. "But we captured the elf you said would try to break into the property."

Ben's eyebrows raised. He crept carefully toward the second door that led to the study. There was a faint gap where lamplight shone through but not enough to see anything. *Dammit.*

Orders were issued and a scuffling sound followed.

"So." Lord Kerill spoke coldly. "Orien Markes. It's been quite some time since I've seen you."

Orien? He froze in shock.

The elf said nothing, however.

"And why are you here? Is it to kill me like you killed the merchant Jorys? It seems your beloved Elantria is not the pacifist you thought she was."

"I'm not here to kill you," Orien said tightly.

"I'm afraid I can't simply take your word for that." Kerill sounded amused now. "You understand, I'm sure. Unfortunately, it means I will have to execute you. There's no other option, you see."

Shit. Ben froze, his hand on the panel. The room was full of guards and he had barely a hope in hell of escaping before he and Orien died, but he couldn't simply leave the other man there. After all, he was the reason the elf was in trouble now.

Before he could give himself time to chicken out, he pushed the door open and tackled the first person he saw.

CHAPTER FIFTY-TWO

W hether fortunately or unfortunately was debatable, the first person Ben saw could only be Lord Kerill's niece. She was tall, with an angular face and pale blue eyes that seemed to glow in a darker blue face. Blue-black hair was held back in an ornate braid and she wore a gown crusted with silver embroidery and jewels. It honestly *hurt* to land on it. While he had never considered the idea that he might get a puncture wound from a sapphire, it seemed very likely.

He stared at her in shock and she returned it with an outraged glare.

"Who the *hell* are you?" she demanded. "What *human* was allowed into the family vault? I'll see you punished for this."

The threat confirmed that she was indeed the niece. He pushed to his feet and looked around to run a hasty headcount.

Lord Kerill, Birra—still on the floor—Orien, held by his injured arm and who stared at him in genuine shock, and two guards in the room and probably more at the door.

His first thought was that he could kill the slave trader and maybe he should. The man was a monster. He objected even to Elantria's methods and he was willing to kill Orien rather than have him jailed.

His family had owned the city for generations and, rather than rest on the hoard of wealth he had already accumulated, he resorted to slave trading.

Logic and justice demanded that he should kill him. The city would be better off.

But he had only a split second, a single chance to save Orien. He cast a single, pained look at Kerill, marked the lines on the man's face, and thought of the forged letter in the pouch at his hip.

With immense regret, he gave up on the perfect plan.

He charged the guard who held Orien's arm before anyone could try to apprehend him. Perhaps the man hadn't viewed him as an armed threat because he hadn't come out with weapons. He had no time to realize how wrong he was before the knife sank into his neck. With a gurgle, he sank to his knees and blood spurted from the wound.

"Gah! Fuck!" Ben swiped at the blood on his face.

Orien's shock dissolved at his words. He whipped around and looped his chains around the other guard's neck. With a well-practiced motion, he spun the man and used the chains to break his neck before he jerked them free.

"Come on!" the elf snapped.

"Right." He brandished the bloody knife at Kerill and Birra, both frozen in horror, as he backed toward the door.

She recovered first. "Guards!"

"Fuck," Orien said succinctly. He unlatched the door and leapt aside, pushing his companion with him so the guards streamed past them and into the room. As soon as the last man cleared the doorway, he caught Ben's shirt and yanked him into the corridor. "Run," the elf said.

He didn't need to be told twice. The guards yelled and one had turned to follow them. He ran while the necklace bounced at his waist and he held a bloody knife in his hand. Orien clutched the chains to stop them from rattling too much and ran with grim determination.

They barreled through the kitchens and into the courtyard, but Kerill's magic caught up with them.

He wasn't a mage himself, but his family had employed the best of the best for decades. An alarm had triggered and magical red lanterns pulsed everywhere while Kerill snapped, "Intruders heading to the back gate. *Catch them.*"

Guards raced out of towers and down the road that led around the mansion.

"Fuck, fuck, fuck," Ben muttered. He looked around in panic. They should never have stopped running, he thought in despair. Five men sprinted from the walls, two more emerged from the mansion, and a few came along the road from the other direction with what sounded like a full dozen hot on their heels.

"It's not so bad," Orien said. He turned and his gaze darted quickly to assess the enemy.

"What makes you say that?" He gave him a quick look. They had ten seconds at most until the first of the guards reached them, and how could they possibly fight this many?

"Well, if you hadn't intervened, I would already be dead. There is presently a chance that I might escape." The elf sounded almost cheerful.

"So it's only better for *you*," he muttered. "*Great.*" He had a short-sword and nothing else, and all his muscles were shaking.

"Now, now." Orien was—infuriatingly—grinning.

"Did you have any follow up to that?"

"Not really. I was about to point out that you voluntarily intervened to help me, but that seemed in poor taste." He flashed a smile. "Ah, I think I know what to do. Head to the left corner of that house there, on my mark."

"And then what?"

"Then we'll see, won't we?"

"I swear to God," he muttered, "if I had a better plan…"

Orien ignored his muttering. "On three. One…two…three!" He sprinted to the building he had mentioned and Ben followed.

Their unexpected departure left three sets of guards focused on a now non-existent target. Unable to stop, they careened helplessly into a mass collision. A scream indicated that at least one had met the wrong end of another's weapon.

"Keep running!" the elf said before he turned and flung his chains behind him. Another man screamed along with a noise that sounded very much like metal meeting flesh and bone.

Ben winced, tried not to hurl his dinner, and raced on.

He skidded into the shadows and turned to see the layout of the battle. Two of the guards tried to help the one who had been injured and the rest fanned out around Orien. The man he had already struck with his chains sprawled nearby and blood streamed down his face.

Hastily, Ben scanned his surroundings. He could now see why the elf had brought them this way. Behind this house was a stairway to the walls as the house itself was part of the structure. They could get out there if they could ascend the stairs and jump before the guards caught them.

And, of course, if they didn't die when they jumped. Or before that.

One of the men darted toward Orien and was kept out of range with a flick of the chains. The next time he darted in, however, another came from the other direction. Ben yelled a warning that was unnecessary as the elf's foot lashed out to catch the second attacker full in the face.

The elf was doing well so far, but there was no way he could defeat all of them.

His mind conjured an impossible thought and he heaved a sigh. There *was* a way to get out of this without much more fuss. Probably.

On the downside, he would learn what happened when Nemon was upset with someone.

"Gentlemen." He raised his voice so it carried. "You have a choice. You can choose to apprehend this one runaway slave—an unskilled laborer and useful at best as a pretty face in a nobleman's house." He avoided meeting Orien's curious gaze and drew the necklace out. "Or you can retrieve your lord's heirloom. If you waste time apprehending the slave, I'll be long gone with something a hundred times as valuable."

It was enough to make them stop and look at each other.

"Come on," Ben muttered. He caught his companion by the arm and shoved him toward the stairs. "Go, go, go before they start thinking!"

"Where did you *get* that?" Orien whispered in horror.

"In the vault—you know, where you saw me tumble out of. *Move!*" He tripped on the stairs and swore. The guards were running now.

He might be able to get away with the necklace but he didn't like his odds. With a sinking feeling in the pit of his stomach, he turned and threw it like a frisbee. It sailed over the guards' heads and they stopped to watch it.

Orien grasped his arm and hauled him over the edge of the wall.

"Fu—" His expletive was lost in a gurgle when he plunged into a deep pool of water.

Kerill had a moat. Of course he did.

Ben came up spluttering, flailed awkwardly to the shore and climbed out. He extended a hand to pull Orien out as well. "Come on," he muttered, panting. "We have to run."

"You think?" the elf asked acerbically. He shook his hair out of his eyes, looped the chain over his shoulders, and hurried away.

With one last look at the walls and the mansion beyond, he followed.

CHAPTER FIFTY-THREE

They were a few streets away before Orien spoke. He darted between alleys with complete concentration, kept him back, or ushered him forward with gestures, but no words were exchanged.

When he relaxed fractionally, Ben assumed they were in Elantria's territory again. Still, he waited for his companion to break the silence first. He had made the somewhat debatable mistake of not listening to him once and he chose to use caution this time.

"So how did you wind up there?" the elf asked finally.

By his actions, he had already pissed Nemon off. He debated how much more to piss him off and decided to keep things secret for the time being. "Someone hired me to steal that necklace."

"And you wanted an opportunity at another slave trader," Orien said neutrally.

"This time was different."

"You *weren't* planning to kill him?" The elf raised an eyebrow.

"No, I was, but I intended to make sure the right person took over the family business." He frowned at his companion's skeptical expression. "I listened to what Elantria said, you know. And you."

"Not the first time."

He wanted to yell a response but he managed to bite his tongue. "No," he said through gritted teeth. "Not the first time."

Orien studied him with genuine interest. "You've changed in the past few days. What happened?" His gaze roamed impersonally over his body. "It doesn't look like you had the stuffing knocked out of you or anything."

"If you must know, I had an unflattering portrait of myself, painted by a—" He remembered how Prima had reacted to being called a demon. "A magical spirit," he finished.

"Ah." The elf looked as if he had more questions and wasn't sure which one to ask first.

They walked in silence for another block before Ben said, "I didn't want you to die or take the fall for me."

"You don't have to justify leaping to my aid, you know. That one, I appreciated." Orien sounded amused. He swung his arms slightly, still trapped by the chains.

"You don't seem at all bothered by those," he observed. "And you fight well with them."

"I was a slave a while back," the elf said. He didn't look even remotely bothered by the memory and simply shrugged. "That was when slave trading had only started to take off in Heffog. They noticed I was light on my feet so they were training me to be a gladiator. It worked out well for me. Not so well for them, though."

Ben made a mental note to not piss him off ever again.

Then something else occurred to him. "How did Kerill know you?"

"He owned me," Orien said promptly. "He took over a few of the mansions when people left for the new monarchy and I was one of the servants there. Of course, he sold most of us. He'd had a taste of how profitable it could be and there we all were. Some of us, he kept because he wanted to train us first so he could get a better price. He liked to single me out and talk to me, to remind the other slaves that elves were better. It made him look like an ass, though—if he thought elves were in any way better, why did he own me?" He shrugged. "Anyway, I killed the overseer and left with some of the others. Kerill sends messages from time to time, telling me to come back."

"Why on earth would you go back?" he demanded.

"Mmm—allegedly so he can treat me with the respect I deserve and we can both profit. Somehow, I doubt that." Orien grinned.

"So when you said I might make things worse by killing slave traders…"

"I was speaking from experience, yes. I've made it something of a hobby to examine the trade." The elf stopped and fixed him with a firm look. "I know you think Elantria is a coward. Hell, sometimes even I disagree with her methods. I wish she would take more of a stand. Then again, I was only a servant and she was an acknowledged bastard. We had different lives."

"Yeah," Ben said, "and maybe that blinds her to—"

His companion cut him off. "But she gave up much to stay here and fight for people instead of living a cushy life. So maybe…consider that before you call her a coward again."

"I don't think we'll speak again," he pointed out.

"Where did you think we were going?" Orien demanded. "Good gods, man. I'm taking you back to her."

Ben waved his hands in protest. "And you didn't think that was a bad plan? She hates me! And…the feeling is mostly mutual."

"She doesn't hate you," the elf said. "Elantria reserves hate for a very select group of people and you had better hope you never number among them. Most of them are dead and she's still trying to find ways to ruin their legacies."

"You…" He sighed. "Look, I appreciate you helping me get out. I do. But I don't think going back to Elantria is the answer."

"Well, you've pissed off the person you were supposed to get the necklace for," Orien pointed out. "And you have no other benefactors. So unless you want to bite it, I suggest you come with me." He saw the look on his face and sighed. "Okay, I'll…smooth the way. If nothing else, you earned yourself points by saving me."

Ben sighed, but he had a point. Nemon seemed like he could be a very unpleasant person if crossed and he had failed him—and in a way that would make it difficult for anyone to steal the same necklace again.

He followed the elf through the dark streets to Elantria's house after only one more caution.

"The person who hired me—he knows I was here before."

"And?" Orien looked at him.

"I don't want to bring anything down on her. If nothing else, it'll hardly help her impression of me."

"She already has half the city pissed at her," his companion said cheerfully. "There's no need to worry about that." He rapped on the door, whispered a password to the guard, and ushered him into the darkness.

They hurried silently to the study and Orien went in first with a motion for him to stay back.

"I wondered where you had gone," Elantria said drily. "What happened?"

"Let's say anyone who trades in slaves has been extra jumpy lately," the elf said.

She sighed. "That *idiot*," she said with a sharp edge to her tone.

"Mmm, speaking of whom…" From the series of clanks and clicks, someone was picking the locks on his cuffs. "He's the reason I got out of there alive."

"What?" She had not seen that coming.

"Yes. You see, they brought me directly to Kerill and Birra for execution, and who should tumble out of the vault but Ben. Ah—that feels better, thank you." There was a last clank of iron on wood as the chains were put on the table, followed by the sound of wine being poured into a goblet. "He killed the guard holding me and threw his job to get me out."

"Really." Elantria sounded cautious.

"Mm-hmm. He's impulsive in both directions, as it turns out. But the point is, not only did he throw his job, he'd taken our advice to heart and planned to get Kerill's son into power instead of Birra."

"How did he plan to do that?"

"He can tell you himself." Orien raised his voice. "Ben."

"Oh, you have to be kidding me," she said as he came around the door.

"I'm afraid not." He managed a smile, although he was fairly sure it looked more like a grimace. "Trust me, I asked Orien numerous times if he was sure about this."

"Why were you in Kerill's vault?" she demanded. "Who hired you?"

Ben weighed the pros and cons of hiding the man's name and decided it was probably best for her to know. "Nemon. Through Delia."

"Ugh." Elantria flopped into her chair. "I don't know what Delia sees in him. What did he hire you for?"

"To get a necklace—an ugly old thing covered in jewels. He said no one had used it in a while and probably wouldn't even notice it was missing." He considered whether to sit or get himself a glass of wine and decided to do neither. He didn't want to piss her off.

What he wanted was to leave, but he wasn't sure he'd be able to do that.

"And…" The woman looked at Orien.

"And when we were surrounded, he yanked it out and threw it to distract them," the elf said.

"That was foolish," Elantria snapped.

"We didn't have very many choices. Would you rather Orien was dead?"

"No, but you could have left him to die."

"Yes, I could have done that at any point." He was getting angry now. "I didn't, though, which should tell you something about me."

"Mm." She didn't seem convinced.

"Look," the elf interjected. "I need to go get stitched up because the wound in my arm has opened again. And I need new clothes unless I want green things to grow in unpleasant places. I cannot leave, however, until you two promise not to kill each other while I am gone."

Elantria stared at him and he mirrored it. He looked at Ben, who also said nothing.

"I mean it," Orien said. He jabbed fingers at each of them. "Both of you, promise right now or I'll knock your heads together like coconuts."

She scowled. "I'll promise not to harm him," she said, "as long as he doesn't try to harm *me*."

"Or hurt," the elf said.

The woman glowered. "Or hurt," she conceded.

"Ben?"

He folded his arms, but it turned out that Orien could be quite imposing when he wanted to. "Fine. I won't harm—*or* hurt—her, as long as she doesn't try to harm me."

"Good enough." He smiled pleasantly at both of them. "If either of you breaks your promise, I *will* make sure you face justice, by the way."

"You'd sell me out for him?" Elantria asked and sounded almost offended.

"He saved my life. It would only be polite." Orien settled a stern look on each of them before he left.

Ben and Elantria stared at one another.

"You're an idiot," she said finally.

"That is debatable." He sighed. "But I have been informed that I should *not* have called you a coward, so...I apologize for that."

She folded her arms.

"You can change more than you give yourself credit for," he said fiercely.

That, oddly, was what broke her bad mood. She gave him a strange smile and sat in her chair near the fire with one boot propped on the other.

"You sound like Orien. That's probably why he likes you."

"I wouldn't go *that* far."

Now, Elantria grinned. "Fair enough." She leaned forward with her elbows on her knees. "Very well. I don't like you. It'll be a while before I can trust you again. But you can stay the night here. Go get some fresh clothes, too."

He hesitated. "Thank you," he said quietly.

The woman looked briefly at him and gave a tiny nod. She seemed as uncomfortable with apologies as he was.

That was at least a tiny kinship. He left her to her thoughts.

CHAPTER FIFTY-FOUR

"Okay, get ready!" Taigan sprinted through the tall grass, her staff at the ready. "There are three of them and they are *mega* pissed!"

Behind her, three jackalopes with glittering fur and very sharp teeth hopped heavily through the field. Very large rabbits, it turned out, were not as fast as the small ones.

That was the good part. The *bad* part was the fact that they hit like a goddamned train.

She burst out of the grass to where Jamie stood, still bent over, and panted from the last fight. "Ha! I can see you!"

"Yeah, crazy." He stood and hefted his sword. "And all it took was doing something monumentally stupid."

"This isn't *that* stupid." She took a position next to him and leveled her staff.

"You're right. Maybe next time, we should up the ante and jump off a cliff."

Taigan stuck her tongue out at her brother. Since they had found out that exposure to danger shifted her into his type of consciousness, they had maintained a fairly steady series of fights. At this rate, by sometime next week, there wouldn't be a single living animal on the island.

Prima had seen the direction this was going in and had moved them to this new zone before they did irreparable damage to the ecosystem.

They could first see the jackalopes as a rustle in the grass, then caught the occasional glimpse of antlers as they bounded along. When the three finally reached the clearing, she winced.

"Okay, I didn't realize quite how big they were."

"Those are *bears*," Jamie said. "Okay, they're jackalopes, but those are fucking *bear-sized*. What the fuck?"

"Sorry?" she ventured with a shrug and a pained grin. She whipped her staff onto the top of one creature's head when it crept closer with a growl. It yelped and backed away. "I'll take two. How about that?"

"Yeah, you'd fucking better!" He thrust his sword at one of the other two. "These freaking things. They know a sword isn't a good defense against them. Fuck, fuck, fuck, fuck—" He began to circle and stabbed with the sword again. This time, he caught the jackalope's nose. "Yeah, that's right, you bunny bitch."

"Mom is gonna wash your mouth out with soap," Taigan warned him. She swung the staff down to thump it on one animal's front paws and swept the point up to catch the other on the chin.

"If I can't swear when facing bear-sized bunnies, when *can* I?"

"You *know* her answer to that would be 'never,'" she retorted. Both her adversaries lunged toward her at the same time, and she jabbed the staff outward on instinct and held it horizontal so each end caught one of the jackalopes. It was probably the best thing she could have done, but the impact reverberated through her hands so hard that she yelped. "Ow, son of a—" She caught Jamie's interested look. "Bench," she finished.

"Come on, let it out." He flashed her a grin. "Swear it up. You *know* you want to. You can—ow, fuck! All right, bunny. Now, it's *personal*." Immediately, he went on the offensive and drove forward with his left hand back. He had spent three years competing in fencing and the more tired he became, the more those instincts came out.

Taigan had to admit that fencing was an elegant and very civilized way to fight. That said, she also had to acknowledge that her fighting instincts weren't so much elegant as very smashy. She whirled and whacked both jackalopes across the face as she did so, brought the staff up over her head, and plunged it down like a spear on one of her opponent's head.

It collapsed like a sack of pink, glittery bricks.

"That'll teach *you* to chase someone halfway across a field." She panted and paused to regroup.

The other creature took the opportunity, launched forward, and landed on her shoulders. She fell with a shriek and in the next moment, a crushing weight settled on her back.

"These things are *heavy!*"

"*Bears,* Taigan. They're the size of bears!"

"Yeah, that's great and all, but maybe you could help?" She looked up and yelped when teeth snapped near her face. When she flailed her legs and arms, she managed to hit several soft areas but seemed not to have struck anything exceedingly tender given the limited range of her prone position.

She couldn't maneuver well enough to use the staff in her current position, nor could she turn with so much weight on her legs. Her best bet to avoid the teeth was most likely to stay in constant motion so she tried to push to her hands and knees and tucked her head in to avoid another snap of teeth. She jabbed her elbows back but found only air.

Shit.

With a yodel, Jamie came to the rescue. The jackalope screamed and scuttled sideways. He grabbed his sister's arm to haul her up and she snatched the staff up and immediately returned to the offensive. She drove the animal back with stabs and lunges with the weapon and finally managed to catch it in the eye.

A low growl issued from its throat. It was the only one left and its blood ran from one eye and the flank. Old blood on its teeth and antlers revealed that it was much more accustomed to winning than losing.

But it wasn't down yet and it was *pissed.*

The twins adjusted their hands around the grips of their weapons.

"Ready?" Taigan asked Jamie without looking at him.

"Ready." She could hear his grin and didn't need to look at him. "Operation Rock and a Pointy Place, Iteration 503."

"May we leave this island a barren wasteland," she said solemnly and tried not to let her mouth twitch.

They charged simultaneously with a yell. Taigan circled to the outside and whipped the staff to drive the jackalope away. It retreated with a hiss but its gaze was fixed on her.

Probably because she was screaming at the top of her lungs.

Operation Rock and a Pointy Place was the best tactic they had come up with thus far. She made herself impossible to ignore with many thwacks of the staff and a great deal of irregular screaming, caught the enemy's full attention, and drove them toward Jamie.

This one was canny, however. It refused to be driven straight back and instead, counter-circled to keep both of them in its line of vision.

"Clever girl," Jamie muttered.

"It has antlers, Jamie."

"It's a mythical animal, *Taigan.*"

"Fair point. Oh, for fuck's sake. Would you have the courtesy to *die?*" She uttered a frustrated ululation and thwacked her staff down as hard as she could. "What? Come on, jackalope. Come and get some!"

It accepted the challenge.

"Fuck!" She flung herself prone as the creature vaulted overhead and was already rolling to her feet when it landed. The flat of her staff caught it hard across the side and Jamie raced past to get behind it. "Operation Rock!" the girl yelled.

He put all his weight behind the stab. "And a pointy place," he finished, panting heavily. He stumbled forward and held his hand out to clasp hers.

Taigan laughed. "Based on how you look, I must look like total shit."

Her brother studied her. "Your hair has a certain...mad-scientist look to it." He held one finger up and began to gather her hair and lift it straight up. "Prima, can we try a mohawk on my sister?"

"*Of course, Mr. Mattis.*" The AI's tone was a perfect parody of a personal assistant. "*Please stand by.*"

"Prima!" the girl yelled. She was laughing, though.

Her hair raised on its own. She felt it with some trepidation but it was still soft, held in place by magic. It seemed to have been smoothed and straightened and was simply a foot-and-half-high arc across the top of her head.

"Well, it *feels* cool," she said. "How does it—"

She stopped. Her brother was doubled over and laughed silently. She folded her arms and stared as he looked up, caught sight of her hair, and collapsed into tears of laughter again.

"I hope you break a rib," Taigan said. "Prima, can we try pink hair on my brother?"

"*Of course, Ms. Mattis. Please stand by.*"

"No!" Jamie gasped.

His protest came too late. His hair flickered from its usual black and burst into a profusion of fuchsia. How Prima had managed to intuit his least favorite of all the pinks, Taigan didn't know, but she had certainly exceeded all expectations.

"Thank you, Prima," she said sweetly.

She and Jamie stared at one another, she with her hair in an absurd and physics-defying mohawk, and he with his hair an improbably vivid pink.

A moment later, Taigan flickered out of existence.

"Dammit!" she said loudly. Capital letters on Jamie's whiteboard informed her that he'd said the same thing. "Okay, another set of jackalopes. Prima, don't let him change his hair."

"*You should know he has requested that you also not be allowed to change yours.*"

"Could you make it blue?"

"*One moment, Ms. Mattis. I will check... He says he will only settle for purple.*"

"Ugh, I hate purple. Never mind. Where are the nearest jackalopes?"

"I do not believe—"

Something stirred in her mind. It felt like a piece of wrinkled clothing or an itch in her throat. She shifted without realizing she was doing it and flickered into existence again.

"Ha!"

"Whoa!" Jamie, who had been trying to coat his pink hair in mud, jumped.

"*Cheater*," Taigan said in mock outrage. "Prima, add sparkly bows."

He sighed as several pink bows with rhinestones appeared in his hair. "Do I *want* to know what I look like?"

"No. You also don't want me to request pictures of this for when we get out—but I'm gonna do it." She gave him a double thumbs-up.

Her twin folded his arms. "How did you get back here, anyway?" he demanded. With half his hair pink, half covered in mud, and all of it decorated with bows, he didn't look very imposing—not that either twin was particularly overawed by the other one to start with.

"I second that question," Prima interjected.

"I'm...not sure." She frowned and thought through what had happened. "It felt...uh, like scratching an itch, you know? I think maybe I've come in and out so many times that I know the feeling of it now. It's like...um...oh, focusing and unfocusing your eyes."

"Huh." Jamie studied her carefully. "Prima, can *you* see a difference?"

"Yes. I had hoped that these efforts would simply shift Taigan into the correct form of consciousness and had not considered the possibility that switching between the two would be a skill she could cultivate. From the available data, I believe this is an important change."

The siblings looked at each other for a moment and both shrugged. Neither was quite sure what to make of the science-speak, but everyone seemed to agree this was going well.

"Okay," Taigan said slowly. "So if I can keep myself in this plane of —oh, fuckity fuck." She could no longer see Jamie. "Sweet, fancy Moses on a log."

"I've never heard that one before."

"Yeah, well, buckle in, because you'll hear many more of those things if I can't find out how to shift—oh, hey." She smiled at her brother. "You're back. I'm back. Whatever."

"You'll use that to get out of conversations you're losing, won't you?"

"I have no idea what you mean," she said loftily. "So, Prima…can I…"

She suddenly felt a little dizzy. Had the solution always been there, simply waiting for this technology? Was she ready to open her eyes and wake up?

Prima guessed what she planned to ask. *"I'm afraid not,"* she said gently. *"You and Jamie now exist in the same dream state, but while he has to be held in that state artificially, you remain there."*

Taigan looked at the sky, then at Jamie. He came to stand near her, a comforting presence with ridiculous hair. She leaned her head on his shoulder and jerked away when he spluttered.

"Mohawk up my nose."

"Ewww." She brushed the top of her hair off, then sighed and grasped his hand. "So, Prima, what you're saying is you have no idea when I will wake up."

"Oh, not at all." The AI sounded surprised. *"Now, we find ourselves at the place I began at with Justin. We are in familiar territory to use the human expression."*

"Oh!" The girl had braced herself for another series of unknowns. "Wait, seriously?"

"Seriously." If Prima were human, she would have been smiling. *"I think it's time to return to the rest of the PIVOT world and begin your adventures."*

"Oh, my God." Taigan gave a disbelieving laugh and threw herself into Jamie's arms. "Oh, my God! Oh, my God. This is amazing."

He hugged her close. "This is amazing," he echoed. "We'll make this work. We'll do it."

It was only when she felt him shaking that she realized he was crying. *"Jamie?"*

"I was so scared," he whispered. "Every time. I was so scared we'd lose you. I would dream I was you and I couldn't wake up."

"You won't lose me." Her chin trembled. "Because you never stopped fighting. I hope I'll be worth it."

"Does that mean you'll let me take the bows out of my hair?" he asked hopefully.

"Fat chance."

CHAPTER FIFTY-FIVE

Ben woke with the certainty of what he needed to do.

He pushed the covers back and swung his feet out of bed. This was a strange feeling. It wasn't the same as the usual, frenetic urgency he usually experienced that brought the inability to focus on anything except his current passion. This certainty sat bone-deep and it did not need his immediate action. It did not worry that he would forget about it.

Unfortunately, he was very sure Elantria and Orien wouldn't like it. He scratched his scalp and heaved a sigh.

"Is something wrong?"

"Not exactly." He explained what he was thinking.

"I have to say, I think it's a risky plan."

"I know." He shrugged. "The thing is, if I don't do it, I'll always regret it. I'm too quick to say I've missed my opportunity or messed everything up."

"Hmm."

"Any follow-up?"

"No. I'm thinking. I find I like the human convention of saying 'hmm' while I do so."

"Right." He put his clothes on and went to find Elantria. Much to his surprise, she and Orien were entertaining guests, both of whom looked at Ben when he walked into the room.

He stopped dead. "Nemon. Delia."

"Well, fancy that," Nemon said.

Elantria sighed. "Okay, fine. He *is* here."

"You lied for me?" He looked at her in surprise and smiled slightly. "Thank you."

She shrugged awkwardly. "I *told* you I didn't want your death on my conscience."

"She thought I intended to kill you," the man said. He managed to sound deeply injured at the mere insinuation. "Even when I told her I wasn't planning to do that."

"You aren't?" Despite his reservations, he smiled. He leaned on the table and regarded the visitors with at least a semblance of calm.

"Of course not. I haven't laughed as hard in months as I did when I heard what happened at the compound." He took a sip of coffee. "I only wish I'd been there to see Kerill's face when you fell out of the vault."

"And you're...not angry that I failed to get the artifact?" he asked cautiously.

"*This* artifact?" Nemon pulled the necklace out of a pocket in his vest.

"My gods," Orien said in something close to horror. "You weren't joking. That is as ugly as sin."

"Isn't it?" Ben grimaced.

The man turned it in his hands and assessed it critically. "I think it has a certain elegance."

"You think that because it's worth so much money, dear," Delia said with obvious fondness.

"Forget that. How did you *get* it?" Ben asked.

"I would hardly send an untried novice alone into one of the most well-guarded houses in Heffog," Nemon told him. Again, he sounded offended. "I make backup plans. You were not the only person there that night."

"Were you dressed as a guard?" he asked suspiciously.

Nemon smiled. "Not me, but you have the tactic right. It was very tragic, you know. The guards tried to decide between the escaped slave and the necklace and wound up with neither. Kerill was immensely displeased."

"How terrible for him," he muttered.

"I don't think you mean that."

"You're right, I don't." He considered the necklace. "Well, that makes my plan somewhat simpler, then. I thought Kerill would keep an eye on that piece in particular for a while. But, since he's not—"

"Ben," Elantria interjected with impressive restraint, "what *exactly* are you planning?"

"Well." He smiled around the room. "I want to assassinate Kerill and Birra, and I would guess you two wanted to rob him blind, yes? And Nemon would certainly love to get his hands on a few more pieces. So…what do you all say we do that?"

"*What?*" she demanded.

Nemon burst out laughing. "He's going in again. Ah, the stones on this one. I should associate with more humans. They always surprise me." He took Delia's hand and kissed the back of it and she smiled at him.

Elantria met Ben's gaze over their heads and shrugged as if to say she still didn't understand the couple.

He thought he did. Whatever else he was, the man was charming and he delighted in flouting social norms, much in the same way Delia seemed to. Both were tolerant of each other's foibles.

"So, you are going back?" Elantria asked him.

"I am. I came up with a damned good plan the first time and I intend to follow through." He folded his arms and looked at each of them. "Not that anyone else has to get involved, but it *would* help."

"You don't say." She sighed. "And then you'd involve me—publicly —in another assassination."

Rather than reply, he waited. His instinct was to blabber about how important this was, but he had the good sense to keep his mouth shut. He studied the emotions that flitted across her face.

"I don't like this turning into outright war," she admitted. She seemed to be talking to the fireplace.

"You knew it was coming, though," Orien said.

She looked sharply at him. "I did not. How would I know that?"

"Because whenever there's mass enslavement, there's a war," he said bluntly. "You helped me escape and you've helped others. You've targeted slave traders for a while now. And while you were getting ready for something bigger, I..."

Elantria looked at him in surprise and waited for him to finish the sentence.

"I was gathering information," the elf said. "I told myself the delay was good but I was too much of a coward to make it a war." Wryly, he said to Ben, "When I told you not to call her a coward, it was because I knew which of the two of us deserved that title."

"We can all share it," Nemon said equably.

Everyone looked at him.

"I thought that might move the conversation along." He raised an eyebrow. "No? Well, then. Regardless, an attack on Kerill *would* make a good opening salvo in a war."

"What do you know of war?" Elantria asked bluntly.

"I know showmanship," he said with a flourish of one hand. "You and I both know that elves like to dress up their brutishness with pretty words, but the one thing they respect is a show of force. Kerill was allowed to do what he did because no one opposed him. The question here is whether we go with the original plan or we do this openly."

Utter silence followed his challenge.

Ben considered what he'd heard for a moment and then, tired of his butt going numb while he propped himself on the table, dragged a chair to the fire and sat with the others.

"So, it's a question of trying to make it fall apart without them knowing," he said, "or doing it in the open." The others nodded. "There would be less pushback if it's quiet, I guess," he mused. "But we run the risk of it simply going elsewhere. There's no possibility that it would all fall apart without Kerill, I guess."

"Now that there's a profit being made, it's not likely." Elantria sighed.

"Actually, depending on how we did it…" Orien frowned in thought. "He sold me knowing I was elven and of his same nation. It's against elven law. I'd be within my rights to kill him."

"What are you saying?" She looked warily at him.

"I'm saying that if the rest of you hold the guards off, I could make his death a symbol." His face was like a mask now. "I don't have redress against his heir, but—"

"I could handle that," Ben said quietly. "Then the estate would pass to his son. Elven slave traders would be shamed, and—"

"And the trade begins to fall apart in Heffog," Elantria murmured. "We'd need to be careful to prevent the humans from sweeping in and filling the gap in the market."

"I think you're forgetting that you're known as Jorys' assassin." Nemon raised his eyebrows at her. "That was rather a sign of things to come, wasn't it?"

"Ah. Right." She looked sourly at Ben, although there was amusement there. "I keep forgetting how my reputation has changed in the past few days."

"I don't think you forget anything ever," Ben retorted. A smile tugged at his lips. "In fact, I anticipate reminders of this for the rest of my natural life assuming you don't shorten that span yourself."

"A good caveat," she said blandly.

He smiled and shifted in his chair.

"Are you well, Ben?" Nemon asked. "You have a strange look on your face."

"I'm, uh…" Feeling had begun to come back and half his butt experienced pins and needles. "It's nothing." Trying not to leap out of his chair and wiggle around the room, he returned to the subject at hand. "So, Orien kills Kerill while the rest of us hold the guards off —if necessary—and I kill Birra. Orien then, presumably, makes some kind of public statement—"

"I have to make the accusation first," the elf said and sighed. "There have to be witnesses. I'll need seven heads of household to watch.

They don't all have to be noble, which makes it easier, but it does remove the element of surprise somewhat."

"Only somewhat?" Ben quipped. "So holding the guards off will be imperative. Okay."

"And you or Delia will need to kill Birra," Nemon told him. "Orien is right. He has no redress there. Anyone with elven blood will be held to elven law as soon as it's invoked."

"I can do it," Delia said. "I can get into any noble house."

"No." Ben shook his head. "This is your city and you're known to be close to Nemon. You don't need to risk it. I'm an outsider so I *can* take the risk. When this is over, I'll disappear."

"You have to get through it alive first, smart guy."

Ben smiled slightly, knowing the others in the room wouldn't have heard the joke. Oddly, this was what gave him the most confidence in the plan working out. Prima would never joke if she were truly worried. She had reminded him to be careful but at the same time, she told him she thought it was possible.

"I can't decide if I'd rather you stay here," Elantria murmured, "or whether I'd rather set you loose without any idea which city you would set on fire next."

"Hey." He rolled his eyes. "I've grown up considerably since the start of this. In the future, any violence will be precisely targeted and considered in advance."

"You say that like it's comforting," she replied waspishly.

"She's right, you know. It's not comforting at all."

He threw his hands up. "Fine. Everyone else come up with the plan and I'll go along with it. Promise."

"It's a solid plan," Nemon said. "I don't think we need to alter it much. I, however, must move quickly to find the seven heads of household to serve as witnesses. It's not essential that they be sympathetic to our cause, but I think we can all agree that this isn't time to push the odds out of our favor."

He disappeared and Delia bent to murmur a few words in Orien's ear before she followed.

"What did she say?" Ben asked when she was gone. "Never mind. If she'd wanted the rest of us to hear—"

"It's fine." Orien looked even paler than usual. "She told me that there is a reason elven law sentences slave traders to death. Delia knows how much I've doubted this and in fact, she told me to do it immediately after my escape." He saw Ben's surprise. "Nemon and Delia took me in originally when I escaped and Elantria helped me from there."

"So the four of you go way back," He said.

"You could say that." The elf nudged Elantria with an elbow. "And they've only tried to kill each other a few times. Come on now, we need to do some planning."

The two of them hurried away as well and left him seated alone on his chair.

"That was a joke," he called after them. "Right? Guys?"

There was no answer.

"People in this city are insane," he told Prima.

"Maybe that's why you fit in so well."

CHAPTER FIFTY-SIX

Once the decisions were made, Elantria and Nemon both swung into action with impressive speed.

Runners were dispatched from her house and within the hour, dozens of people appeared. At first glance, they looked wildly different—children, stooped old women, fishermen, and serving girls in livery. As often as not, however, a disguise fell away to reveal an entirely different shape beneath, and whether or not they were in disguise, all of them had watchful eyes and weapons.

Elantria summoned them to a meeting in the early afternoon. Instead of in the courtyard, which Ben had expected, it was held in the basement. He walked past a confusingly large pile of crates in the main hall and down the stairs to where dozens of pairs of eyes all focused on him mistrustfully.

"This is Ben," she said and gestured at him. "You'll know him as Jorys' assassin."

The mistrust grew somewhat less palpable.

"Tonight," she said, "Ben will deal with Birra and her guards. Kule, Havern, I want you to go with him. Raise your hands so he knows who you are."

Two people complied. He could not have said at a glance whether they were elven, human, dwarven, or a mixture of all three. Both were slight and short, with dark hair and dusky skin. Something was unsettling about how dark their eyes were, and it took him a moment to notice what.

They had no whites. Every part of the orb was black.

Ben swallowed, nodded, and decided not to ask questions about that. He was half-sure they might be actual demons and he didn't want to learn too much and wind up dead.

"Promise you'll yank me out of this world if they try to possess me," he muttered under his breath as he and Orien tramped down the last couple of creaking stairs.

"Awwww, you're no fun."

He leaned against the back wall with his arms folded and made a point of not looking at Kule and Havern.

"As you know, we will move against Lord Kerill tonight." Elantra looked at her team. "He is the architect of the slave trade in Heffog and his death will be a symbol. Many of you know Orien." She gestured to him. "As an elf of the same nation, he has the right under elven law to kill Kerill for his crimes. Tonight, he will do so."

A murmur swelled through the gathering.

"What changed?" Kule asked the question, or possibly Havern. Ben could not have said for sure if the one who spoke was male or female. The voice clarified nothing. It seemed to be an entirely normal voice, but…things…lurked in it.

Things with teeth, his imagination said. The back of his neck crawled.

Elantria looked at the two demons—he had decided to think of them as demons—and considered her words carefully.

"I'll let Ben answer that," she said finally.

He gaped at her in surprise.

She gestured for him to come forward. The gleam in her eyes said that this was a little payback for bringing her into this situation. *You started this,* her smile said. *Now you have to make the speeches.*

Ben swallowed. He walked to the table where she had spread her documents and looked at the crowd. An unsettling number of those present had eyes of unrelieved black. He saw elves and dwarves and even someone who looked as if they might have orc blood. Heffog truly was a melting pot.

"What changed is that I killed Jorys," he said abruptly after a moment. "It was a stupid decision and there was no plan. I saw the opportunity and I took it, and I put Elantria in danger—and all of you, I suppose. I want you to know that she would have been more cautious with this. Anyone who knows her probably won't be surprised to hear that she read me the riot act and threw me out on my ass."

This triggered a burst of surprised laughter. He looked at Elantria and she smiled slightly.

"But my stupidity doesn't end there," he said to another round of laughter. "Because after I did that and she chewed me out, I decided to *argue* with her. Now, for those of you wondering how I'm still alive, I have no idea so I can't answer you."

There was a snicker from nearby. Orien had his face buried in one hand and his shoulders shook with laughter.

"Well, the long story short is that both Elantria and I made some good points in that argument." He smiled at them. "All of you know that she'd do almost anything to keep the people in this city safe. I'm too impulsive, and she was...maybe a little too cautious."

He met her gaze and waited for her tiny nod. She made him wait but she smirked a little.

"And she listened to a few of us," he continued, "when we suggested that now might be the time to strike. Kerill has been unopposed for years while he turned Heffog into a trading hub for slaves, but it's time to end it. We all agreed on that. In the end...the rest was merely details."

At his gesture, Elantria returned to the table. "It's a close enough rendition of the facts," she said and provoked another round of chuckles. "We have allies in this fight. Over the years, the underworld of Heffog has grown strong. We are many and the nobles are few."

"You're a noble," said someone. They didn't seem overawed by her at all.

Ben couldn't imagine that.

"I have noble blood," she corrected. "As does Nemon. So we can both tell you how little that's worth and how good they are at making rules to ensure that only a few people claim the title. With many of their number gone to join the elven monarchy, the rest are weak. They sought to consolidate power and rule us through fear, but that won't work. Not anymore. Jorys was the first. Kerill and his niece are next. From there...we will see where it goes."

"*A bloodbath,*" Prima said dryly. "*That's the expression, isn't it?*"

He nodded.

"*Are you sure you don't want to stay and help them with that?*"

"I'm better for the first part," he murmured. "But I'll consider it."

Elantria called various people to the table to give them their assignments and most left at a run. Kule and Havern stayed close, their gazes fixed on Ben each time he looked up.

When there were only a few left, she looked at Orien.

"Are you ready?" she asked him.

He looked thoughtful. "No. But I never will be." He managed a smile. "He destroyed us. He scattered us across the world and sold our lives for a pile of gold coins he didn't even need." His gaze hardened and settled on her. "I told you the first time we met that this was coming. Then, I hid from it."

"And I let you." She smiled sadly in return. "Until someone gave us a push."

Both looked at Ben, who cleared his throat awkwardly.

Elantria focused on the elf again. "Kerill had already planned a dinner tonight and had invited three heads of household. There will be three more in the building from common-born families, and one more noble he was able to convince to drop by. You'll have your seven witnesses."

"Thank you." Orien nodded. "I'll...go get ready."

She watched him walk away with a small frown, then said to Ben, "Watch out for him."

"I will."

"Remember." Her face was grave. "He *must* be the one to kill Kerill. Keep him safe but do not finish the job for him."

He nodded. "I'll deal with Birra as quickly as I can and get back to him."

"Good." She nodded to him, and to Kule and Havern. "Go with the gods. Strike swiftly and true. Your carriage is upstairs."

Ben had questions about how they were supposed to get past the guards, but those were answered immediately once he got upstairs. The carriage, which waited out front, was half-full and being loaded.

It wasn't so much a carriage, however, as a cart.

The conveyance was full of crates.

He sighed. Now he understood why all those crates were there. He was supposed to get into one, wasn't he? It seemed all kinds of disappointing that he would be smuggled into Kerill's house like a sack of potatoes.

The discomfort of that idea was vastly increased when he realized he would be shut in with the two demons.

"You have to be kidding me," he whispered to Prima as Kule and Havern climbed into the crate.

"If you don't want to get shut in crates with demons, don't start civil wars."

"Ah, yes, the old saying. Now I remember." He glared at the sky before he stepped into the crate. The lid came down immediately and he was alone in the dark with the two demons, neither of whom seemed to be breathing.

This was normal, he told himself. It wasn't at all worrisome.

"So…how did you come to work with Elantria?" Ben asked.

A hissing sound unnerved him until he realized it was a laugh.

"She hired us for a job," said one of them. "An impossible job for one of the mortal races. She had a hunch after it about what we were, so she got us drunk and talked our real names out of us."

"I…" Ben had not anticipated this.

"She doesn't hurt us," one of them said. "She merely bound us to an oath to not hurt any of the mortals in the city."

Both made disappointed hissing noises.

He didn't know what to say to that, especially since he was shut in a crate with them. "Ah," he said finally.

Both burst out laughing at that.

"We're kidding," one of them said.

"We're dark elves," the other added.

"There aren't many of us," said the first.

"Everyone gets freaked out about our eyes," the second concluded.

Ben sighed.

"Oh, come on," his partner said. "We don't get a chance to freak new people out very often."

"Yeah, yeah." He tried to ignore the sound of Prima laughing in his head.

The trip to Kerill's house lasted longer than he would have liked. The two elves seemed content to wait in silence and made no complaint when the heat began to build. Neither seemed to get motion sick in the carriage, either, which he certainly did.

Eventually, the cart was unloaded, which was even worse. He braced himself while the crate was hauled into someplace dark and blessedly cool.

"Now what?" he asked as quietly as he could.

"Now we wait for nightfall," said one of them.

"Kerill was expecting a shipment of rare artifacts from the fae lands," said the other.

"Elantria has those now."

"And instead, Kerill has a warehouse full of enemy soldiers," Ben finished before the other one could. "Not bad. She must be rather pleased with herself."

"Probably," said one of them. They sounded sulky that he hadn't let them finish their game of imparting wisdom as a pair.

The hours ticked past interminably. There was nothing to do except stretch at various intervals to stop his muscles from cramping, but the activity didn't do much at this juncture. By the time he heard rustling around them, he ached all over and he almost leapt out of the box when the lid was removed.

Everyone eased stiff muscles and shared a light meal, but his heart beat wildly. He almost wasn't able to eat.

"Are you well?" Prima enquired worriedly.

"I think so," he murmured. "But I'm usually gone by this point. You know, the fight. Once I've stirred things up."

"Would I be correct in assuming that once you leave this game, you'll have rather a lot of apologies to make?"

He sighed. "Yes."

"Mmm. Well, good luck with that."

"Thanks." He looked around, located Kule and Havern, and jerked his head at them.

It was time to go before he could think better of this crazy plan he'd set in motion.

CHAPTER FIFTY-SEVEN

Amber was several hours deep in one of her spreadsheets when Nick came to find her. He waved a cup of fresh coffee under her nose until she looked up blearily.

"Hey, do you have a sec?"

"What's up?" She removed her earbuds.

"Ben's friends are calling in a few minutes about his progress. I thought it might be good to have us on the call as well as DuBois."

"Oh." She took her ponytail out hastily and combed her hair back slightly more neatly. "Sure. Thanks for the coffee. What time is it?"

"Almost noon."

"Oh." She yawned as she followed him through the lab toward the hall to the conference room. "Oof. It's been a long morning."

"Yeah, when did you come in?"

She decided to drink her coffee instead of answering and hoped he wouldn't notice.

"Amber?" He raised an eyebrow.

"Four AM. Give or take." She shrugged. "I had an idea and then I couldn't let it go, so I came in."

"You woke at four AM with an idea about accounting?" Nick asked skeptically.

"I was already up."

"Why were you—" He broke off at the slight smile on her face. "Never mind, *don't* tell me. I can fill in the blanks. Although I have to say, getting an idea about spreadsheets during *that* is worse than waking up with one."

"That wasn't what gave me the idea," she protested, laughing.

"Uh-huh. Sure. Do you two dirty talk by saying excel formulas at each other, or what?"

Amber gave up on trying to drink coffee through her laughter. "Well, not *only* that. We also recite obscure parts of the US Tax Code to each other."

He mimed fanning himself. "We shouldn't talk about this at work."

The two friends were still laughing when they entered the room to see that the video call had already started. They shut up hastily and waved at the two people on the screen.

"These are my colleagues," Dr. DuBois said.

"Hi, I'm Amber," she said with a wave.

"And I'm Nick," he added. "We're two of the three founders of PIVOT."

"Nice to meet you," said the woman on the screen. She had wildly curly hair and a slim, lanky frame. "I don't know if you remember me. I'm Natasha, and this is my fiancé, Mike."

The man beside her managed a weak wave of one arm. His skin was pale and he seemed to have lost a great deal of muscle recently, but he looked miles better than he had the first time they had seen him. Most of the casts had been removed and they could see crutches and a wheelchair in the background.

"Of course we remember you." Nick smiled. "Mr. Parker, you're looking very well."

The man grimaced. "Thanks."

His companion smiled sympathetically at him. "Physical Therapy isn't exactly a walk in the park," she explained, "and it's hard to miss a whole summer of climbing and surfing and all that. But he's recovering so well—much better than the doctors thought he would."

"They only say that so I feel special," Mike muttered, clearly in bad humor.

"I wouldn't be so sure," Amber told him. "Because they've been flabbergasted by Ben, and if the two of you are best friends, I'd bet you're equally stubborn."

Both Mike and Natasha laughed.

"I refuse to incriminate myself," the man said, "but I *will* throw Ben under the bus. He's a stubborn son of a bitch."

His fiancée pointed at him and mouthed, "He is, too."

Amber and Nick nodded.

"Wait, what did you say to them?" Mike demanded.

"Nothing," Natasha said innocently.

"Uh-*huh*." He narrowed his eyes. "Anyway. We were wondering what Ben's progress looked like for the wedding."

"We know you might not be able to tell us," the woman said.

"Ah…actually, Ben authorized us to share his progress with you." Amber smiled. "He said that either of you would be a better resource for bouncing treatment ideas off than his parents."

"Awkward," Mike said, "but not wrong. I hope you're able to at least *share* information with his parents."

"We are and I promise they haven't been in the dark this whole time."

"Whew," he said. "Okay, so how *is* he doing?"

"Well," DuBois said readily, "his manual dexterity has increased greatly within the game, as well as him mastering more precise movements. He has also been able to approximate rock climbing, though there appears to be a certain amount of trauma associated with that."

Mike's face was strained as he nodded. "I can imagine."

Natasha put her hand over his and they looked at each other for a moment.

"The good news is that he's been able to work through it," Nick said and cleared his throat awkwardly. "I wouldn't say it's gone by any stretch of the imagination, but he's doing well. As you said, he's a stubborn son of a bitch."

The man laughed at that and some of the tension in his shoulders eased. He swallowed before he asked, "And how is he emotionally? I don't want to be an asshole but I was very worried by how he was talking the last time he came out."

"Ah." The two engineers exchanged a look.

DuBois munched popcorn with a bemused expression on his face.

"Um..." Amber marshaled her thoughts. "Video games offer a unique opportunity to watch moral choices play out without affecting people. Of course, the resemblance to real life can be debated but they tend to be very impactful on an emotional level."

"Again, not to be an ass, but...that sounds like a long way of saying nothing." Mike shrugged and winced. "My shoulders don't like doing that yet."

Amber hesitated for a moment before she continued. "I don't want to betray any confidences," she said finally. "While Ben did authorize us to speak to you about medical issues, I think discussing particulars of his mental health would be crossing a line. With that said, I want to assure you that I am not worried at present. He seems to be in a very stable place. I...hope that helps. A little."

"So, without specifics," Natasha said before her fiancé could speak, "there's nothing for us to actively worry about at this time."

"In my opinion, no. Ben seems to be happy, shows social engagement, and copes well with complex emotional situations. I think I'm veering into specifics again." She cut herself off by taking a long swallow of coffee.

"I can...work with that." Mike sighed. "I want my friend back, you know? Him, not someone else."

"He's still him," Amber said.

He nodded.

"And you think he might be able to come out for the wedding?" Natasha asked them.

"With several stipulations," Nick said before DuBois could respond. "They would want two members of medical staff on-hand with him and he must *not* be asked to stand for more than five minutes at a time. I wouldn't plan to involve him in any ceremony over half an hour or so."

To his surprise, the woman pumped her fist in victory. "Oh, yeah. *Awesome.*"

"You'll want some context," Mike said. "My fiancée is not a complete bitch, I promise."

"Only mostly," she said with a grin. "No, it's only that my family has pressed for a huge wedding with a super elaborate ceremony and now, we can go, 'no, we really can't, it would be too much for Ben, doctor's orders.'" She began to chair-dance.

Her fiancé laughed silently in the background. He shook his head and shrugged.

"Don't you shake your head at me," she said. "You don't want to stand up for a long ceremony either."

"I said we should elope to New York," he pointed out.

"Oh!" DuBois looked happy. "Oh, that would be much better."

Natasha opened her mouth, then closed it.

"Think about it." Mike leaned close to her. "No sisters bitching about their bridesmaid gowns…no mothers trying to get pictures…"

"I feel like we shouldn't be here for this," Nick muttered. He and Amber averted their eyes hastily, although the doctor continued to watch with interest.

"I don't know," Natasha said.

"Everyone already has their flights on standby," he pointed out. "We can afford to lose the deposits. Come on, I saw you staring at the stack of wedding papers yesterday and you *know* you didn't look like you were looking forward to doing that paperwork."

"I wasn't. I'm not." She looked at him. "But can we do that? Like, can we truly do that?"

"We can do anything we want," he told her. "We can go to the greatest city on earth, see the Empire State Building—"

"Boy, do *you* know the way to a girl's heart." She laughed. "But…oh, my God, that sounds so much better than a big wedding. How mad do you think they'd be if we did this?"

"We could turn our phones off," Mike suggested. "And then we won't know."

"*Deal*," she said instantly. She swung to look at the camera. "We'll be there tomorrow. Does tomorrow work?"

DuBois and Amber looked at Nick, who nodded. "We can have him out by tomorrow."

"Awesome." Natasha smiled. "Okay, I have to handle...so many things."

"We have rooms available at one of the hotels near us," Nick said. "We have enough people flying in from out of town that we always have them. Let me check their availability and I'll send you an email."

"Holy crap, really?"

"It's much cheaper than us sending Ben cross-country with a full medical team," he pointed out.

"Oh. Um… Okay."

They said their goodbyes and hung up and he stretched luxuriously. "Working with a real *budget?* This is the *life*."

Amber shook her head and smiled, then yawned again. "Okay, I'll go home and sleep. Can you take care of the details for Natasha and Mike? And text Jacob that they're coming into town and to pull Ben out?"

"Uh-huh." Nick nodded. "Go. Rest. I'll arrange it and see if I can't get another surprise in the works for Ben too."

"What were you thinking?"

"You'll see. Go rest." He smiled.

"Right." She yawned and headed out of the room. "Oooof, I'm tired. Oh, and text the doctors to come in for another assessment of Ben's—"

"I swear to God I will crush drugs up and put them in your coffee if you don't get out of here."

"Point taken." She snatched her coat and headed out.

CHAPTER FIFTY-EIGHT

Ben had memorized the layout of the entire compound while he was closed inside, waiting for the first heist. Now, he led Kule and Havern unerringly across the warren of streets and alleys that made up the outer edge of the location.

It was truly incredible how rich the nobles of this city were. Kerill practically commanded an entire city of his own, with livestock and metalsmithing as well as a veritable army of servants.

Those servants, if they noticed the sudden influx of people, took no notice. Despite the late hour, people trudged past with packages or handcarts. Some made their way wearily into the apartments that lined the outer wall.

He looked over his shoulder once and saw the flash of Orien's hair in the fading light. The half-elf walked straight-backed and dignified. He watched him for a moment and knew he did not envy him at all in this moment. The man joked and made a point of looking forward instead of back, but he also had the memory of being bought and sold —not to mention learning he was destined to die in an arena.

Now he was about to confront the man who had done it.

It was important to make sure Orien's courage meant something. When this was over, he couldn't let the elf feel as if this had been for nothing. He had to make sure the way was paved for a better city. He remembered the dwarf in Jorys' study and felt a simmering rage ignite in his chest.

This would end. He would end it himself, dammit.

They entered the main building via a passage that Nemon had marked on one of the maps. However the man had learned of it, it pained him to share the information, yet he had done so. The tunnel ran from the buttery on the eastern side of the mansion and directly into the kitchens.

Kule and Havern stepped aside to wait in the shadows outside the kitchens, while Ben adjusted his disguise and poked his head in.

"The Lady Birra—a man sent a message for Lord Kerill but said I was only to tell him if the lady *wasn't* there. Is she at dinner with the lord?"

The servants exchanged a glance.

"We're only cooks," a heavy-set man said gruffly. "We don't know a thing about what goes on upstairs."

They clearly knew something and he was interested to find out exactly what. He cast a glance over his shoulder as if to check for eavesdroppers and crept closer.

"Is it happening now?"

The servants all stopped and a couple of them leaned closer.

"Is *what* happening now?" one of them asked.

"He said it'd be tonight," he said, speaking of the fictitious event with the most conviction he could manage. "He said there would be a whole hue and cry about it. If it's happening now, he needs to know what I have to say."

The servants looked at each other and he saw their pleasure.

They hated Birra, as far as he could see. Whatever he was insinuating about a rift between Kerill and his heir, they were eager to see it happen.

"She's not at the dinner," one of them whispered. "She went snooping and she's in his study."

"What?" Ben drew a sharp breath and put on an appropriately outraged face.

"Whatever 'is lordship is planning, she seems to have guessed," another cook said. "'Ey, Yamira, any chance of sneaking a bottle of wine out of the cellars? I'm guessin' there'll be goodly gossip tonight."

The cook shushed them but everyone's eyes were alight with anticipation.

"As long as she's not at dinner, I can deliver the message," he said. "Thank you—and if you ever come by the Howling Coyote, drinks are on me."

They cheered at that and he stepped out into the hallway. Birra was alone in the study. This was the best way he could have hoped for this to go.

"What's a coyote?" Kule asked as they hurried through the mansion.

"It's a…wolf-thing. Kind of." He shook his head. "How many of them do you think will be out searching for that bar tomorrow night?"

"All of them," Havern guessed with a grin. "And it's too bad it doesn't exist because the gossip from tonight will be *legendary*."

Ben was still grinning when they came around the corner and saw Birra's guards waiting at the door of the study.

He didn't hesitate. If he did, the guards would gain the advantage and it would go poorly. He might have done some training with swords, but these men had trained for most of their lives.

As he pushed into a sprint toward them, he drew his short-sword, then threw himself into a roll. His pacing was good and he came out of it behind the far guard as the man staggered forward. He had drawn his sword to counter his attacker's swing and had thus leveled a heavy strike at thin air.

A little unbalanced by the futile attempt, he didn't have a chance for another strike. Ben stabbed into the man's back and winced at his scream. He'd become better at steeling himself to the task of fighting, but it wasn't easy to see death up close.

Why couldn't he have been a virtual reality plumber, hopping over mushrooms and snagging gold coins? That would have been much less traumatic.

Right now, though, there was no time for regrets. The man staggered away and Ben arced his blade down for a final strike. On the other side, the two dark elves dispatched the second guard with silent efficiency. They fought in the same way they talked—one of them started an attack and the second finished it.

His guard made one last attempt at an attack, and he hit the man on the head with the hilt of his sword. He shuddered as he dropped like a stone. Even now, after all that had happened, he hated this.

Common sense reminded him that he had to stay alert. Birra was inside the study. He nodded at his companion and flung the door open.

A third guard stood inside, something he had anticipated. She seemed like the type to have increased her guard since the first time she'd encountered him. He wondered if she remembered him at all. The right side of his chest certainly remembered her. The colorful imprint of several diamonds still bruised the skin.

Kule and Havern moved to secure Birra while he and her bodyguard fought. He was powerfully built and imposing, definitely with orcish blood, and he moved like his massive broadsword weighed nothing.

The man was also tall, which meant he didn't bring his guard down quite enough. Ben parried several of his strikes, drove him back, and then—when the woman's scream distracted him—ducked low and stabbed up under the man's leather armor. A second slash followed across his throat and he stumbled upright to see Birra watching him.

"*You,*" she said with undisguised hatred.

She *did* remember him. It would seem having a grimy human tackle you from behind what you thought was a solid wall was a formative experience.

"Me," he said cheerfully.

"What do you want?" she snapped. "Do you want another piece of treasure from my uncle's vault? Perhaps you want a bag of gold?"

"I came to kill you," he said.

"As you can see, my uncle isn't *here,*" Birra snapped at him.

385

"Yes," he said patiently. "I know that. I said I came to kill *you*."

Her face paled and her mouth opened. She looked at Kule and Havern.

"What did my cousin pay you?" She was on her feet in a second. "I'll triple it. You'll be a rich man all your life—and that's before you get the payout for murdering him."

"Your cousin didn't send me," Ben told her.

She went even paler at that. "My uncle?" Her voice wavered now.

"It wouldn't be *that* much of a surprise, right? After all, you're spying on him while he's at dinner, he's been trying to get his son to come back as his heir..." He shrugged.

"Whatever you want," the woman said. "Name it and it is yours." Her gaze was cold. She was the type of person who was used to bending the world to her will. "Everyone has a price. Simply name yours."

"I want my father back, you son of a bitch."

"I...beg your pardon?" She looked at Kule and Havern, both of whom shrugged.

"It's a long story." Ben hefted his sword. "The short version is that there's no price that will stop this. You're dead, Birra."

"Why?" She spread her palms on the desk. "If it's not one of them, then *who*?"

He was torn. On the one hand, he didn't want to make the mistake of destroying his advantage with a speech. On the other, he wanted her to die knowing exactly what had led to her death.

"You destroyed lives," he said as he had to Jorys. "No amount of your pain could ever make that right—which is lucky for you. But you won't get out of this alive."

Her mouth opened on a denial and her scream was cut short when he vaulted over the desk to run her through. He didn't bother trying to cut through her jewel-encrusted dress but lunged at her throat. She died with a hidden dagger falling from one hand. Whether she had meant to kill him with it or herself, he didn't know.

He *did* know that there was another battle happening, and it was the more important one.

"Let's go," he said to his companions.

"But the vault is right there," Havern argued.

"*Now*, unless you want to explain to Elantria why we weren't there for Orien."

They shut up immediately and followed him without another word of protest. Elantria apparently inspired terror in her followers, even those who liked her.

They ran through silent hallways toward the sound of yells from the great hall. There were armed people inside, and he motioned for the other two to stay back while he peeked in one of the doors.

Kerill's guards had arrived too late. Orien and his fighters had Kerill surrounded, while seven elves stood along one side of the room. Three of them looked outraged, as did the slaver. The lord's guards didn't know what to do. They didn't dare get closer while the elf had their employer at knifepoint, and they didn't want to get involved in the workings of elven law either.

Ben motioned for Kule and Havern to follow him as he circled the outside of the great hall. He wanted to be quick but he couldn't afford anyone to hear them. Various phrases could be caught through the wall.

It turned out that legalese in elvish sounded very similar to legalese in English.

The three entered through the back door of the room in a rush to join Orien, who looked gratefully at them. The elf raised an eyebrow as if to confirm that his mission was accomplished.

He nodded.

"You have admitted to selling slaves," Orien said and returned to the matter at hand. "You have admitted, in front of witnesses, to selling *me*—a resident of your same city. You have admitted, also, to training me for purposes that would lead to my death. You are in violation of elven law."

Kerill looked desperately over his shoulder at the seven assembled elves. The four who had been called in by Nemon met his gaze without flinching. The man had known how they would see this.

The other three wouldn't look at the accused.

"You know this isn't a legal proceeding," Kerill called to them. His voice was high and wild.

"There are no protestations of innocence, you notice," Orien said clearly to no one in particular. "And you can save your breath. We can carry out the sentence before your guards can reach us."

The guards looked less and less sure of what they should be doing.

"Slavery has never been prohibited in Heffog," Kerill snapped at them. "*Do* something."

One of the men took a step forward miserably, and Orien's sword flashed. It came to rest along the lord's neck.

The man glared at him. "You'll never get out of here alive. They'll kill you as soon as you kill me."

"I don't think that's true," the ex-slave said. "After all, they have several noble witnesses who declare me to be in the right. They know you've claimed exemptions from other laws due to your adherence to elvish custom, which means you should hold to it now." He cast a speculative look at the guards. "And frankly, I don't think they care that much. Once you're dead, I don't think they'll risk their lives to fight my soldiers."

Kerill snarled at him. "What do you want? Is it money? A mansion of your own?"

"No," Orien said. He shook his head slightly at Ben. "They always offer the same things. They think it solves all their problems."

His mouth twitched.

"Then how about this?" Kerill's voice dropped and he suddenly had a smile on his lips. "I have records of where every slave was sent to. Everyone...including your friend Josyla."

The elf froze.

"Orien?" Ben asked quietly.

"They were rather more than friends," Kerill said. He sounded smug now and could see victory within his grasp. "I would have kept them together but you see, she fetched quite a good price as a goldsmith—and why keep her here, only to see him die in the arena? But now that he's free..."

He could see that it cost the slave trader, even now with his actual life on the line, to say goodbye to the money he'd received for Josyla.

"A deal could be made," he finished.

Ben watched Orien's indecision and fought the urge to run Kerill through himself. He didn't believe that Josyla was still alive. The man couldn't be trusted at all. It was merely an attempt to weasel out of this.

But this was exactly what Elantria had worried about. It was why she had warned him that Orien *must* be the one to kill Kerill. He had a thought, suddenly, of exactly how to ensure that.

He stepped close to Orien to murmur in his ear. "When this is over —immediately after you do what you came here for—I'll need to leave Heffog. Send me to look for Josyla. Between Kerill's records and my... magical spirit...we'll find her and we'll free her. Don't let him weasel out of paying for this simply for Josyla's sake. We can have both."

The elf looked at him. "And I suppose he might be lying." His jaw was tight.

"Then he *definitely* shouldn't get to weasel out," he said. He met his gaze. "We don't need him for this."

"We don't," Orien agreed.

He did it casually and with such speed and skill that Ben didn't realize at first what had happened. Kerill's head thudded onto the floor of the great hall and one of the dinner guests screamed. The three nobles who had been invited by the now-dead host looked at his body and looked away.

The elf was not finished with them, it seemed. He stared at them with a grimly expectant expression.

Slowly, beginning with the three who had supported Kerill, each of the seven heads of household stepped forward to look at the body and turn their hand palm up.

"What does that mean?" Ben muttered to Kule.

"It means they agree that he took what was his due and justice is satisfied," Kule explained. "They agree that he was within his rights."

They might have been reluctant or have hated Orien, but none of them wavered from this. The first of the seven turned to the guards who all waited anxiously.

"Your duties are done," she said. "Guard only your master's property and await the time that an heir is determined." Her tone suggested that she had a hunch of what might happen to Birra. "Let this man and his companions go in peace. They present no danger to the rest of those gathered."

"Thank you," Orien said. He whistled to his soldiers and the group left the room. Ben would have lingered but for the fact that the elf took his arm and pulled him along.

They did not speak until they were out in the darkness and Orien led him to the stables.

"We don't have much time," he said. "You have to go now. Go south of Heffog, sneak past the first town, and take your shelter in the second. The inn barely deserves the name, but it'll do. When we have the information, we'll send for you."

He nodded. "And you?" he asked.

"I don't know," the elf said. "There are many more elven nobles—and some humans—who may face justice in the coming days. I owe it to the people of Heffog to stay through this process. You, though—you're merely a murderer and you need to leave before they find you."

He held his hands out to help him into the saddle.

"You're kidding, right?"

"You know how to ride a horse, surely?"

"Well, yeah, except also *no.*"

"Ah." Orien scratched his head. "Well, put your foot here. Just do it. Now, push up and swing your other leg over. One motion. One, two, *three.* There you go."

"Holy shit." He clutched at something to steady himself as the horse pranced nervously. He was much higher up than he had ever imagined being on an animal. "Uh...now what?"

"You'll learn the rest as you go," Orien said simply and smacked the horse's hindquarters with one open palm.

His mount leapt forward. He yelped in alarm and held onto the pommel desperately as the horse cantered into the darkness.

"Now this," Prima said in his head, *"will be hilarious."*

CHAPTER FIFTY-NINE

A day and a half later, when the endless parade of medical tests was done and Ben had been fitted for a suit, he sat in a camping chair in a secluded part of Central Park.

On such short notice, Natasha and Mike hadn't arranged a permit for anything in particular, so they had found a small area that wasn't likely to be seen by many passers-by. Much to his surprise, they had asked him to be the minister. Online ordination had been quickly submitted and despite the feeling that this was ridiculous, he had written some comments he could use.

He saw his friend's nod and pushed out of the chair. Mike came to help him to the tiny area they had chosen, now strewn with flower petals. Natasha wore a simple white dress and her hair hadn't been pulled back or dressed up, but she looked radiant. She held a single stem of orchids in one hand.

"Are you sure you can stand?" the man asked him.

"Yep. Not for long, but yep." He planted his feet and smiled at the two of them. "Are you ready?"

"Ready," Mike said with a thumbs-up.

"Ready," Natasha confirmed. She looked like she might explode from happiness.

"Mike and Natasha," Ben said. "For years, the two of you have been a blessing to everyone around you. Every one of our friends turned to you when they had bad luck or loss, and you were always there for them. I think I speak for all of us when I say that I doubted, many times, whether there was anything more to life than disappointment and loneliness, but the example you two set gave me hope."

Mike tilted his head slightly to the side. He knew his friend was surprised. Usually, he wasn't the type to speak about mushy, sentimental things.

But so much had changed recently.

"You may not have known that," he told them, "because I liked to poke fun at you for settling down and being an old married couple. But every time I did that, it was to remind myself that you made it work. I saw you two fight and make up. I saw you disagree and move past it. I saw you hold each other when times were tough. Mike, you were there for Natasha when she lost her job. Natasha, you were there for Mike when his grandfather died, and again when he needed you for everything from eating to deciphering medical statements. The fact that he's standing here now is a testimony to your relationship. Whatever comes your way, I know you'll weather it together."

The couple reached out to clasp each other's hands.

"Do you have your vows?" he asked.

Mike nodded and drew a card from his pocket. "Natasha. Ten years ago, in Introduction to Astronomy, I met the most beautiful woman I had ever seen. It's a good thing I wasn't into Astronomy because you're all I remember from that class. All these years later, every time I look at you, I feel the same way—like I don't know what's down and what's up, and I don't even remember my name."

She laughed and squeezed his hand.

"I promise you," he told her, "that I will be there for you in sickness and in health, for richer and for poorer, in good times and in bad, for the rest of our lives. We've had...uh, well, we've done all that already."

Natasha grinned.

"And I know life will throw other shit at us," he continued. "Wait, am I allowed to swear in these? I guess I'm trying to say I love you and

I will always be there for you. We've done it before, and I can think of no one better to share the victories and the good moments with because you make even the worst moments wonderful."

Ben nodded to Natasha.

"Mike." She had memorized her vows and looked into her fiancé's eyes. "I spent a long time trying to think of vows that were better than the traditional ones, and...like you, I kept coming back to them. I swear to love you for better or for worse, in sickness and in health, for richer and for poorer, for the rest of our lives. We are more together than the sum of our parts, and I cannot wait to face both good times and bad with you."

They exchanged rings and murmured the words required after him. Both had tears in their eyes.

"And now," he said, "by the power vested in me by the state of New York and the people at Ministers 'R Us, I pronounce you husband and wife. I'll go sit and you two wait until I'm not looking to make out."

He hobbled to his chair while they laughed. When he stole a glance, they were hugging, her arms gentle around Mike's not completely healed body. They leaned their foreheads together, and he could see their complete comfort in each other's presence.

On the side of the clearing, Nick and DuBois gave him a thumbs-up. They had been drafted as last-minute witnesses and the doctor had offered a reception dinner of popcorn.

Ben's phone buzzed and he pulled it out of his pocket after a few unsuccessful attempts. He smiled when he saw who it was.

How did it go? Eliza had written.

Good. They were basically already married. He looked at his friends. *Now it's merely official. They look so happy.*

I bet you did a great service.

I like to think so. He hesitated. *So, you said you had some news.*

Yeah. I got a job offer to stay here. Good money and way better hours.

That's awesome.

Look, I know this is crazy, but—do you think maybe you'll come back to Colorado?

He tipped his head back to look at the sky. This park was

393

gorgeous, full of greenery and birds chirping, but there was nowhere for him like Colorado—the Rocky Mountains, the Flatirons, the trails and the peaks, the scrub brush, and the sandstone.

I'd like to, he replied cautiously. *But not quite yet. There's more stuff I need to do still. I don't think I'm done with this game yet.* He paused. *Oh, fuck, I need a job. But yeah, I'd like to come back to Colorado. I might even come to Aspen once in a while.*

Well, if you're ever in the area... He could tell she was smiling.

I'll take you out for...not sushi. Not in Aspen. Maybe a steak?

Actually, I grill a pretty mean steak.

You've got yourself a deal. I'll bring the wine.

He smiled at Natasha and Mike. Grilled steaks. A job. Mountains. For the first time in his life, he wasn't scared of what was coming. He didn't see it as a string of disappointments simply waiting to unfold and was ready for this.

Almost. He was almost ready.

PART III

CHAPTER SIXTY

"Hey, man." Nick came into the conference room balancing a precarious stack of sandwiches. "I brought you lunch."

Ben's stomach rumbled. "Argh. I wish I could, but...they're putting me under again today and it means no eating for a while beforehand."

"I'm sorry. I'll get these out of your vicinity, then." He looked at the now-closed door and made one attempt to open it with his elbow before he stepped back and swung a foot up to press on the door handle.

"I'll help you." Ben stood up and the usual mismatch of ability and coordination resulted. When he hit the table with his legs, he sighed.

He had progressed significantly from where he'd been immediately after the climbing accident, but his coordination was still far from where he instinctively thought it was. During his recovery, he had spent hundreds of hours within the virtual reality world of PIVOT to strengthen his muscles and work on fine motor control. What he had achieved there was a good indication of what he could still achieve in the real world.

It would merely take time.

Despite his initial clumsiness, he moved his hand onto the door handle on the first attempt. When he watched his fingers, it was easier to close them around the metal and push it down. Then, he had to back away and pull the door open at the same time, which entailed a fair number of motions he had to accomplish simultaneously.

Predictably, he hit himself on the head with the door more than once. It was good, he thought, that Prima wasn't there to see him.

"Thanks," Nick said when it was finally open. Politely, he didn't mention anything about his lack of coordination. "I'll be back in a few, okay?"

"Sure," he said. He wasn't quite sure why the PIVOT engineer would want to talk to him, but there had been such a constant stream of medical evaluations that he'd probably forgotten about one of the follow-ups.

Ben hobbled to the desk to glance at the job summaries he'd worked through yet again before Nick returned. After getting his PhD in Chemistry, he had been unwilling to play the political and research funding games of academia and had disdained corporate jobs.

He hadn't considered military or defense work. His outlook on military action had been that war movies were sometimes cool to watch but that running people into each other in a war of attrition was a stupid idea. He hadn't understood why people would sign up to be on the ground for those conflicts, and he hadn't been interested in discovering why either.

That outlook was one of many things that had changed in the past few weeks. Confronted by enemies who were determined to use violence, he had learned that sometimes, there was no way to avoid a war of attrition. He had learned to strike quickly and decisively.

And, by doing that, he had learned that you needed to do your research first. If you were blinded by a desire for vengeance—or even by a desire for justice—you could cause harm to innocent people.

Ben had known for a long time that you couldn't control what the world threw at you. What he had failed to appreciate was that situations weren't take-it-or-leave-it. He had always been an or-leave-it kind of guy who sparked fights with a hard-headed and brutally honest approach and then ran when things blew up.

Now, he was willing to de-escalate, defuse…and stay.

You couldn't change things if you weren't there to fight for them.

As a result, he now took a second look at a number of things. From jobs to relationships, he was constantly in new territory. His treatment at the PIVOT Labs had been funded by their parent company, Diatek, a major player in defense contracting. Anna Price, the CEO of Diatek, had looked at Ben's resume while he was inside the virtual world and had decided to send him job openings she'd found.

As a thank you, he tried to give them a fair study and assessment.

He looked up when Nick came in. "Hey."

"Hi." The man stood in the doorway. "I forgot to ask if you wanted any company. I saw you sitting here in the dark, and…" He shrugged.

"I could use a break, honestly."

"Do you want to go outside? It smells like cigarettes and pee but it is fresh air. Allegedly."

"First, don't go into advertising." Ben laughed despite himself. "And no, but not because of the smoke. I merely don't want to smell food."

"I can understand that." Nick came in and sat. "Are you looking at job openings?

"Yeah. Apparently, that's a thing." He rubbed his head. "I can't tell you how grateful I am to all of you that this treatment is being covered, that I'm not being…bankrupted. Not that I had anything for them to take. Blood from a stone. But when this is over, I'll need to go back to the real world and that's…"

The engineer nodded and leaned back in his chair. Ben at first thought he was ignoring him, then realized that he was thinking.

"I think the 'real world' is kind of a made-up concept," he said finally.

"Oh? Do tell." He started—purely out of habit—his series of hand exercises. To someone who didn't know what he'd been through, he looked like he was compulsively tapping his fingers on the table in a specific, staccato rhythm. The movements were still jerky but each day, he grew closer to doing them smoothly without looking at them.

"Yeah." Nick slouched in his chair and looked at him. "Have you ever noticed that when people say, 'you have to learn how to live in the real world,' they aren't talking about the world. They're talking about a specific compromise they had to make or a dream they gave up?"

"I—holy shit." Ben's fingers stopped moving. "Holy shit, I hadn't noticed that. Huh."

"Yeah." The engineer gave him a gleam of a smile. "So I guess my point is, Jacob and Amber and I have lived the dirt-poor lifestyle, we've faced jail time for this, we worked out of this teeny tiny lab that we came in on the weekends to clean ourselves, and now, we have a shiny new lab and assistants. But even when things were grim, we weren't living in the 'real world' everyone talked about because we were still trying to make this work."

He frowned. "Wait, hold up—jail time?"

"Ohhh." Nick sighed, then looked panicked. "I don't want you to think we were being shady or anything. Also, I'm not sure I'm legally able to talk about it. Very long story short, PIVOT is a treatment that could take some market share and it turns out that people get nasty when profits are on the line."

Ben shook his head.

"It's fine, we have lawyers now." The man shrugged. "The point is, when you think of the real world, what do you think about? What's the concession you think you have to make?"

"Working a job I hate," he said. "Settling down somewhere, the same old thing every day, and stupid fights with coworkers that drag out for years. Work that doesn't…do anything."

"There you go." Nick spread his hands. "That's not merely an objective look at the real world, it's a set of concessions you don't want to make in your life. So how do you make sure you don't do the same old thing every day? It sounds like it could be consultant work or something—you know, traveling, meeting new coworkers, working on new projects. Or maybe you *do* work the same job but you travel every month. You see?"

"I do." Ben started his finger exercises again. "Okay, yeah." He looked at the jobs and blew a breath out. "I think part of it is…all that stuff I don't like, what if I needed to do it because the organization did good stuff—necessary stuff someone had to do?"

"Ah, now you come to an actual dilemma." The engineer grinned at him. "And I have my opinions on the matter but I'll keep my mouth shut."

"Oh?"

"It's uncharacteristic, I know. I've been informed that I'm the 'nosy old biddy' of the team, and it's a responsibility I take seriously but sometimes, you have to let the young solve their own problems." He mimed being old.

"How very wise of you," Ben said and snickered.

"I think so," Nick said peaceably. "Should we get you ready to go into the game?"

He checked the clock. "Probably."

"Your coordination is certainly improving. You looked up exactly to where you wanted to and then back down."

"I did, didn't I? Huh." Ben gathered the papers, a process that was decidedly less graceful than his glance at the clock. He managed to get all of them into a folder—admittedly, not all facing the same way—and stood. "So you haven't heard from the doctor yet about exact program specifications?"

"Not yet. I get the sense that two PTs are hashing something out."

"So, two experts can't agree on how to proceed," he said. "That's comforting."

"They might agree and they're simply fine-tuning," the engineer told him. "Don't leap to negative conclusions."

"I'll do what I want," he told him.

"Of course you will." Nick held open the door with a grin.

The two men progressed slowly down the hallway. The lab was, as always, buzzing with activity. There were several patients in the pods at present, almost all of them individuals who had been chosen to gain an idea of baseline physical reactivity to the virtual reality.

Two others seemed to be something different and multiple people monitored the feeds at all times. He wasn't quite sure what the situation was there, but no one seemed particularly panicked so he wasn't worried.

Near his pod, Dr. DuBois and Jacob were deep in discussion. When they saw the two men, they waved them over.

"How are you feeling?" Jacob asked Ben.

"Hungry."

"Okay, then let's get you into the pod." The man checked his watch. "No food since last night, right?"

"Yes," he said plaintively.

"Then, I'd say we're good to go. Come this way and we'll get you changed and prepped."

Thirty interminable minutes of prep later, he lay in the pod. It was difficult to feel comfortable with a feeding tube and multiple monitors, but he was already sliding out of this reality. He watched Nick counting down with his fingers and smiled.

The instant transition to freezing cold and wet was abrupt and jarring.

"What the *fuck?*"

"It's good to see you again, too," Prima said.

Ben wrapped his arms around his head to try to avoid the rain somewhat, but there was no good way to do that. The wind gusted in multiple directions and he got drenched no matter how he stood. It might be dusk or dawn, as there was a certain amount of light behind the leaden clouds, but there wasn't much light and the rain didn't do him any favors.

He turned slowly to study his surroundings. A forest behind him was surprisingly dark and made noises he could hear even over the rain. He stood on a road, which meant he might get somewhere by going in one direction or another, and in the distance...lights, he realized

With no point in waiting, he set off. His shirt was soaked through and stuck to his body, his cloak did do not a damned thing for him, and his boots were filling with water.

Prima, he thought, was probably enjoying the hell out of this.

"Tell me that's an inn."

"It is indeed an inn. The one Orien mentioned to you."

"If I recall, he also said it barely deserved the name."

"He did. And he was correct."

"Great." he sighed. "Well, as long as it's warm and dry."

"You'll be disappointed."

"You have to be kidding me. No? Seriously, fuck this." Ben wrapped his cloak a little tighter—why, he wasn't sure—and struggled onward.

CHAPTER SIXTY-ONE

Initially, coming from the isolated island and into the rest of the PIVOT world was exciting. Caravans sometimes passed Jamie and Taigan. The cavalcades kept to themselves, however, and made a point of emphasizing the weapons carried by their guards.

It took them a while to realize that they were worried about a robbery.

"Do we seriously look like competent robbers?" she demanded and frowned at her brother.

"Nope," he said after a moment of thought. "Only nope for me but certainly nope for you. My clothing is halfway respectable. Yours is...a burlap sack?"

"Well, *excuse me,* Mr. I Have A Belt Over My Burlap Sack." She rolled her eyes. "I wouldn't mind a more comfortable set of clothes, though. And a bath. Are there baths here?"

"I don't know. Maybe? Prima?"

"There are baths here. Why wouldn't there be?"

"Well, I always woke up clean so baths didn't seem necessary," the girl pointed out.

"Ah. Right."

After a pause, an icon appeared in front of them on the road. It was the size of a full-length mirror and displayed her in a much better selection of clothes.

"See if you can make these for yourself," Prima said.

"Uh…" Taigan looked at Jamie.

"She never had me do this," he replied.

"Right." She looked at the clothes, then at herself. While she could picture the garments, she couldn't seem to replace those she presently wore. She tried to think about how it would feel to wear the new ones, which looked much softer, and got nowhere. "Prima, I don't think—"

Jamie disappeared and the world took on a bluish hue.

"Dammit," she said. "I world-shifted again, didn't I?"

"Yes." Prima neither explained nor elaborated.

"Bah. Well, if I'm not going to be in the *real* world…" Taigan dressed in a sweeping gown of blue silk. After a second's thought, she added a necklace of fist-sized diamonds and swept her hair into a pile on top of her head. "Yes, hello, I am Princess Taigan of— ooooh, can I have a sword down my back like Wonder Woman did?" One appeared, nestled between her shoulder blades, and she craned to look over her shoulder. "Aww, yeah. I'm badass and—oh, hey, Jamie."

Her brother stared at her, his jaw hanging.

"What?" She looked at the dress. "Oh, right."

"You, uh…" He cleared his throat. "I don't think you can appreciate how much seeing you in a dress cut down to *there* is *bumming me out.*"

"Don't be such a baby," she retorted.

"Oh, yeah? Then maybe I'll wander around shirtless. Or…in a banana hammock."

"Ew, no, stop!"

"I'll do it." Jamie jabbed a finger at her. "Get a dress with a front, or so help me—"

"All right, all right!" He disappeared in the next moment and she changed her clothes hastily. It was a bummer about the sword in the back of the dress, she thought. She had liked that part.

The diamonds, not so much. It turned out that they were big and heavy. She also changed her hair into a French braid and took a few moments to replace her boots with some she liked.

"Cool," she said, when she was done and world-shifted again to see Jamie.

"I wish you wouldn't do that," he said in annoyance. "I'm always worried you won't come back."

"I know, but I don't seem to be able to summon things here. How did you learn?"

"I can't summon things." Jamie looked at her. "Wait, when you world-shift—does Prima not make those outfits?"

"No. It's like in the first part of the world—how you simply summon yourself a bed, or food, or whatever." Taigan frowned at his dumbstruck expression. "You didn't do that part?"

"No. No, I did not."

A throat cleared and they waited for the AI to speak. *"It isn't... precisely...normal,"* she admitted. *"Taigan is the only one I've seen who can do it. It is intriguing that she retains the ability but not within the same game world. Of course...well, never mind."*

"No, no." He shook his head. "Tell us what you were going to say."

His sister nodded.

"I intended to say that in the other world, I had specifically thought I was not continuing an instanced version of this zone. Taigan seems to have made one of those too when she shifted."

"Huh." The girl considered this. "Do you think I could do this during, like...a battle?"

"I haven't the faintest idea. However, I would advise extreme caution. Dying in this game is difficult for the body in the real world. With a healthy human, it is merely unpleasant. However, when one is already experiencing a health crisis, there could be complications."

"Complications like *what*?" Taigan demanded. Prima didn't answer at once and she looked at Jamie. "Did they tell you about this when they put me in here? Prima, complications like *what*?"

"Up to and including death," the AI conceded finally.

"And you didn't *tell* me?" she demanded and waved her arms indignantly. "No, no, no. I will not do this. You had me in here for *weeks* and you never told me that if I died here, I could physically die?"

"Until very recently, there were explicit blocks in the game that would prevent anything like that from happening."

Jamie, who had studied the area as if he searched for Prima's server and planned to set fire to it, looked up with interest. "Really?"

"Yes. In the blue zone Taigan first encountered, as well as the forest and the original grasslands, there was no way for her to be injured. There were protocols in place to shield her in ways her mind would process as safety. In the most recent zone, the same type of controls were in place but only after a certain amount of damage."

"But *now*," Taigan said, "I could die. That's what you're telling me."

"Yes. Unfortunately, as you saw from the progress you made while under threat of danger, the response of the sympathetic nervous system is critical to the process."

"Great." She rolled her eyes and started walking.

"Where are you going?" her brother called after her.

"I don't know!" she responded. "I don't have a plan. I only want to get the fuck out of here."

She walked without paying attention to where she was going while the sky grew slowly darker and rain began to spatter around her. Taigan held a palm out to feel the rain, shook her head at the weather, and continued. Jamie was behind her, walking quietly and occasionally muttering to Prima, but neither of them tried to talk to her.

Within a few minutes, the rain progressed from a sprinkle to heavy drops that spattered across her face and clothes. She had no idea where she was by now and her feet ached. The foliage around them had grown from sparse vegetation to a real forest, and between the rain and the fading daylight, she was barely able to see the road.

The weather was also loud enough to make it hard to hear anything, something they discovered when they almost ran into an animal on the road.

"Animal" was a generous term. The beast reached almost to Taigan's ribs at the shoulder. Shaggy fur seemed reminiscent of a wolf and there was a tail, but whether it was a wolf, a large cat of some kind, or even a bear, she could not have said.

She jumped and it mirrored her before it backed away quietly, its tail lashing, and crouched. A growl built slowly in its throat.

"Seriously?" she yelled at the sky. "Are you *kidding* me with this? First, you tell me I can die here, then you send this *thing* to—fuck!!"

The creature leapt at her and she threw herself out of the way. Unfortunately, to judge by the scream from behind her, Jamie had not anticipated either meeting it or the swift attack.

Also unfortunately, the road had become slick, muddy, and still very uncomfortable to land on. She scrambled to her feet. "Jamie!"

He was on his back and the animal snapped at his face while he held its jaw away from him.

She yanked her staff out —while she still hankered after the sword, a staff was probably good—and brought it down on the animal's back once, twice, and three times. "Get off him!"

Its head whipped around and it snarled. She stabbed her weapon forward and landed a blow to its mouth and teeth. Its muscles bunched and it staggered away, but not before Jamie howled in pain.

"Jamie!" Taigan skidded to her knees beside him in the dark. "Where—"

"I'm…I'm fine." He took her hand. "Get me up."

"But—"

"We *won't* be fine if we don't get rid of this monster," he told her.

She couldn't argue with that so started to help him up, then shoved him down again as the animal hurtled overhead. Jamie grunted in pain but she couldn't afford to focus on that. When she hauled him up, she still couldn't make out any bloodstains as it was dark.

The girl told herself firmly that she had to stop thinking about it. She snatched the staff up and turned. Where was the damned monster?

A gleam of eyes betrayed its location. Taigan slashed and drove forward with a yell. "Get away!" she shouted. "Go back into the woods and find somewhere dry and *stay* there!"

Her brother might be injured but he was still fast. While she held the animal's attention, he circled and it backed into a sword thrust. It howled and he made a noise that sounded like he was trying not to scream in pain.

"Can you do another hit?" she called.

"I don't think...no, I can't. I'm sorry, I'm so—"

"Aaaaaaaaah!" She attacked the animal with a shriek. Bleeding, it whipped its head around and tried to decide where to run.

Taigan began to whack it with the staff with no attempt at strategy. She merely wanted to land as many blows as possible and as hard as possible. She had no idea how many times you had to batter something with a stick to make it die, but she assumed she was about to find out.

The head and the spine originally seemed like good targets, but every time she landed a strike there, the staff shuddered and her palms ached. She began to hiss through her teeth with every blow, then returned to yelling bloody murder.

It relieved the pain somewhat.

"Get! Away! From! My! Brother!" She punctuated each word with a swing of the staff.

The animal backed away and hissed viciously as it swung its head and looked for an opening.

"Taigan, it's going to jump!"

"I know!"

She pushed it to the very last moment, even though she knew she ran the risk of razor-sharp cat teeth to the face. The problem was that being this angry made it difficult to care about that. The chance of landing another blow was too seductive to waste. One hit, and another, and—

Jamie tackled her sideways. The creature sailed overhead and landed heavily over them and he wrapped his sister's hand around the hilt of his sword.

"Kill it!" he said.

Taigan stabbed upward with all her might and the beast howled. Blood began to pour out of its mouth and its eyes changed.

A grimy woman collapsed on top of her, her eyes wide and staring and her body limp.

"Ew! *Ew!*" She pushed her away and scrambled to her feet. "Holy… shit…fucking—" She stared at the human body in the road, recalled the staring eyes, and stumbled to the forest's edge to lose her lunch at high velocity.

"Taigan?" Jamie asked tentatively.

"Yeah?"

"Are you injured?"

"No." She edged cautiously to where he stood. "You?"

"Kinda." One hand was pressed over the other shoulder. "Who the hell is this?"

"I don't know." She forced herself to kneel next to the body. The clothing barely deserved the name. It was dirty, stinking, and several shades *worse* than her burlap sack.

There was no rational explanation.

"What's that?" She pointed when something caught her eye.

"What's what? I can't—oh, I shouldn't kneel. Just tell me."

Taigan peered closely at it. "It's a gold ring. Like, real gold."

Jamie staggered.

"Hey, whoa." She stood to support him. "Okay, let's find someplace with a doctor."

"What about the ring?" he mumbled.

She looked at the body. The ring was probably valuable. It looked simple too. But something about the difference between the gold ring and the grimy clothes, the monstrous animal, and the gaunt human, made her break out in a cold sweat.

"We don't want to touch that," she said decisively. "Do you have your sword? Good. Okay, let's get you somewhere safe. Come on."

CHAPTER SIXTY-TWO

The town Ben finally reached was little more than a collection of buildings. In the same way, the inn was less the type of cozy tavern from fantasy books and more a drafty building that smelled of both mildew and stale beer. And, predictably, a few other things he didn't want to think about it.

The lights inside seemed bright when he first stepped in out of the rain, but they were hidden behind soot-covered glass and provided neither warmth nor stable light. The same could be said for the fire in the hearth, which sputtered and frequently guttered low when the wind gusted outside.

The few patrons were clustered around its feeble warmth when he walked in. He saw them study the make of his cloak and the hilt of the sword and come to certain conclusions.

While he wasn't sure which conclusions those were, he had zero intention to make himself a target. He leaned over the tiny counter to peer into the kitchen and located the innkeeper seated in a chair, drinking from a filthy mug of ale.

"Eh?" The man stood and wiped his beard.

"Ale and food," he said. In all honesty, he didn't want either from this establishment, but he needed something and this was evidently the best he could hope to find. He made sure to not flash any coins that the men at the fireplace could see and found a seat in the corner.

The seat was sticky enough that he judged it better to sit on his sodden cloak than directly on the chair.

The food, when it arrived, was unappetizing shades of brown with various lumps. Ben stared at it, prayed he couldn't get food poisoning in this world, and began to eat as fast as was humanly possible.

It tasted good, which was somehow even more unnerving.

He had barely finished when the door banged open and two figures entered. Both were so tall and slim that he originally mistook them for elves, especially with their black hair and deathly-pale skin. When the features resolved in the dim lighting, he registered two shockingly young individuals, a boy and a girl who could only be siblings.

She levered her brother into a seat and gasped when she saw something on his shirt that from where Ben sat seemed to be the red of blood. When she whispered something, the boy shook his head, but she looked around defiantly and drew a breath to call for a healer.

Her words froze in her throat when she saw who was around. The men at the fireplace looked at the two youngsters with contempt and open assessment, and the innkeeper hadn't come out from behind the counter. Her clothes were good enough, but neither of them looked rich.

No coin purses were visible.

He leaned back to watch the unfolding scene. The girl fixed the room with a glare that said she was prepared to off the first person to say anything, then strode to the innkeeper. She said something quietly and he made an easily recognizable gesture, rubbing the tips of his thumb and fingers together.

She deflated visibly, gave him a blazing look, and returned to her brother's side.

Ben's mind churned although he remained outwardly neutral. The men at the fireplace now whispered to one another, and he had a sudden idea. He brought his mug to the counter for wine and stayed while the innkeeper poured. When the man returned, he slid a coin across the counter for him.

"The gentlemen at the fire," he said casually. "Buy them all a round on me, eh?"

The proprietor looked intrigued. "I could do that."

"I'd like them to have a good night," he said meaningfully. "Have a good few drinks and go home." His gaze moved to indicate the young woman and her brother. "Rather than doing anything they might regret," he said meaningfully.

The innkeeper paused. "Ah," he said finally. He hesitated, but whether it was greed or the desire for an evening with a fight, he took the coin and retrieved some mugs from the ceiling, giving Ben a nod.

He returned to his seat and waited as the man brought the ale to the men at the fire. Whatever he said was brief, but they looked over their shoulders at him. He met a few gazes, careful to not make it a battle of wills, but raised his mug once to them in a toast. A couple toasted him warily in response.

Not long after that, they finished their drinks and left. He watched them go, sipped his ale, and waited to see if they would return. It was a little tiresome as he wasn't good at waiting. He wanted to go to the siblings immediately. Patience, however, had encouraged the men to leave without a fight, and he was ready to put in the same patience now if need be.

The men did not return.

He flipped another coin to the innkeeper. "Food and ale for those two," he said as he stood. "And is there a healer?"

"Aye." The man smiled grimly. "My wife would tend a wolf if it came in bloody. I have t' be careful to keep her from taking in too many strays."

"I'll pay for these two," he said easily.

The proprietor disappeared and Ben went to the table with the siblings.

The girl looked at him as he sat. He knew her glare was the only thing she had right now, but it was impressive nonetheless. It said she wasn't afraid to use the staff she'd leaned up against the wall behind her.

"Food and ale are coming," he said. "A healer, too."

The boy looked up, his eyes hazy with pain and hope, but his sister's face didn't clear at all.

"Who are you?" she demanded.

"A traveler, nothing more."

She wanted to send him away, he could see that. Her instinct was to tell him to get lost and she would have if her brother hadn't winced slightly beside her. She turned her head quickly and bit her lip as she looked at him.

"About a week ago, I was a stray on the streets of Heffog," Ben said. "An elf took me in and nursed me back to health. Let's say I'm paying it forward."

Her wariness eased but only slightly. When the innkeeper returned with bowls of the brown, lumpy food, she muttered her thanks and nodded before she looked at the bowl.

He leaned forward and darted a glance at the proprietor, who lingered near the counter and pretended not to watch them. "A word of advice," he said quietly. "It tastes good but don't look at it too hard."

The boy managed a laugh before he winced again, and even the girl looked more at ease. They began to eat with the incredible speed of growing teenagers and had both finished their food by the time the innkeeper's wife appeared.

The woman clucked over their empty bowls and yelled something into the kitchen. Ben didn't speak the local dialect but he didn't need to. He'd known enough grandmothers to be sure that her words were some variant of, "These children look like they're about to snap in half. Give them more food right now."

While the innkeeper approached with more dollops of stew and a long-suffering sigh, his wife pushed the boy's shirt back and began to clean his injury. The shockingly deep puncture wound looked ugly.

However grandmotherly the woman was, she didn't pull her punches when it came to cleaning the wound or wrapping it. The boy yelped more than once and even came out of his chair, only to be pushed down again. She smeared ointment in the injury and bound it with clean bandages.

It was a total mystery how she kept them clean when the rest of the inn was so dirty.

"Rest," she instructed the boy firmly in accented English. "A week of rest. Listen?"

It took Ben a moment to realize that she was asking if he understood. The boy, whether he understood or not, nodded.

"Tea," the woman said and disappeared into the other room without another word.

The girl looked at their benefactor. "Who are you?" she asked again. "No one does something for nothing."

He hesitated. "I'm Ben," he said finally. "I'm...well. Are you from here, the two of you?" When her expression became a little speculative, he asked, "Or are you dreaming from a white pod in New York?"

"Oh!" Her eyes lit up. "Yes. Both of us."

"Taigan," the boy managed and winced.

"Shh." She made a gesture at him as the innkeeper's wife appeared with a big bowl of tea that smelled vile.

The four of them stared at one another. The woman was waiting for the boy to drink it, clearly without the intention of leaving until he did, and neither Taigan nor Ben was brave enough to intervene.

The hapless patient glared at them before he gulped the tea. From the look on his face, it was far less pleasant than the stew, but he managed to hold in his gagging until the woman left again.

"That was so bad," he managed finally. His eyes rolled up in his head and his head thunked down on the table.

"Jamie!"

"He's all right," Prima said. From the way both Taigan and Ben moved their heads, they could tell that the other one was listening. *"There was a herb in the tea for sleeping."*

"So now we have to haul him upstairs?" the girl asked.

"Yes."

"Of course," Ben muttered. "And you'll laugh at us while we do, won't you?"

"I think you know the answer to that."

"Yeah, well." The girl looked venomously at the ceiling. "You got Jamie attacked by a fucking bear-cat monster. You can laugh, but if I ever find you, I'm gonna kick some *ass*."

Prima wisely said nothing to that.

Getting the boy upstairs was an ungainly process. Two rooms had been made ready, one with two beds separated by a sheet and one with one little bed. They each had another soot-streaked lantern and both were even draftier than the downstairs area.

He resigned himself to the fact that he wouldn't dry out until he left. Once he'd helped to wrestle the boy into bed, he nodded at Taigan.

"I'll see you tomorrow?"

"I…think so." She shrugged.

"He's all right," Ben told her. "Prima wouldn't let him get hurt. Not really."

"That's what *you* think," she said resentfully.

He was going to ask what that meant but saw how exhausted she was.

"Get some sleep," he suggested. "Food and sleep won't make this place less damp, but they'll make things easier to deal with. We can come up with a plan for you two tomorrow."

She hesitated, then nodded and ran a hand through her bedraggled hair. "Thanks," she told him.

"Sure." He went into his room and closed the door before he said to Prima, "What's she mad about?"

"Mmm. I'll let her tell you."

"You realize that will paint a less flattering portrait of the situation than you'd give me yourself?"

"I hadn't thought of that. Humans are sneaky. Nonetheless, it isn't my story to tell."

It was an interesting statement. He considered what it might entail but was suddenly so tired that he could barely pull his cloak and boots off before he fell onto the bed. His last thought before he fell asleep was to wonder if there had been herbs in the stew, too.

CHAPTER SIXTY-THREE

Taigan woke to sunlight streaming through the windows.

That was her first thought but instead, it soon became clear that she had woken to sunlight streaming through the gaps in the wall. She looked at the still-damp boards and shook her head.

No sounds came from Jamie's side of the sheet. She stood carefully and tiptoed around the edge of it. He slept peacefully with deep, even breaths, and his face had good color.

She wasn't trained as a doctor, but that seemed positive. She crept closer, held her hand above his forehead to see how warm it was, and craned forward to peer at his shoulder. The cat-creature must have used him as a launch point after the first attack.

Although she couldn't see the wound, no lines extended from it and the area didn't seem to be red or hot. That also seemed positive.

He didn't so much as stir while she examined him, which led her to believe that he was still drugged to high heaven. Jamie was, otherwise, a fairly fussy sleeper. She returned to her side of the sheet and tried to decide what to do.

Now that she was up, she could hear people moving downstairs and even footsteps coming past in the hallway. Ben, maybe? This seemed a fairly out of the way place so it was probably him.

She washed awkwardly with the ewer of water and a damp cloth, briefly pondered the fact that she would sell her soul for antiperspirant, and checked again to see if her brother was still asleep. When she confirmed that he was, she took a deep breath, closed her eyes, and let the world dissolve around her.

In her other plane of existence, it was no trouble to clean up and re-braid her hair. Taigan made herself another set of clothing and returned to the game world. She had improved with this, although she couldn't seem to stop holding her breath when she did it like she was plunging into a pool.

Well, everyone had their quirks. She disappeared into the ether once more and came back with a note that said *DOWNSTAIRS -T*, which she placed on the floor between Jamie's bed and the door. Finally, she crept out and down the stairs.

Ben wasn't up and about yet, but the innkeeper's wife was. She fussed around the girl and brought her porridge with a lump of butter and a thick dollop of what turned out to be maple syrup. Taigan usually wasn't much of a one for overly sweet foods, but it turned out that near-death experiences had quite an effect on her appetite.

She was almost finished when Ben came down the stairs. He looked around for Jamie.

"He's not up yet," she said. "He seems to be recovering well."

"Good." He sat and looked for the innkeeper. "What's on the menu? There's not enough left in your bowl for me to tell what it was."

Taigan flushed. "Porridge stuff. It's good. And it looks better than the stew."

"Yeah, that didn't take much." He frowned at her. "So, do you want to tell me what two teenagers are doing here...in fairly desperate straits?"

"Oh." She waited while the innkeeper's wife came and set a bowl of porridge down. From the serving size, she seemed to have decided that he was worthy of the best as he'd paid for Jamie to be treated.

The girl waited while he took a mouthful and nodded in pleasure.

"It's good, right?"

He made a muffled sound of agreement.

"So, I'm in a coma," Taigan said.

Ben choked on his food and gave her a sharp look.

She shrugged. "It happens sometimes."

"I *know* that, but it's still…what happened?"

"Oh, I mean it simply happens to me sometimes. It's happened since I was little. I fall into a coma and then I'm in one for a while. No one knows why. But Jamie—he's my twin—heard about this project and he got us into it. We've been in a different part of the game until now, and we're only…getting into the normal part." She sighed. "I'm not sure I like it."

"No?" He gave her a smile that said he understood all too well. "I haven't been a fan of everything I've seen either. It's kind of like the real world, huh?"

"I suppose." She curled her legs up. "I beat a cat-whatever to death with a staff last night. Mostly. Then I stabbed it."

"Sure."

"I didn't like that. Especially because—" Taigan suddenly remembered everything in a rush. With Jamie's injury and the darkness and fear, she hadn't focused on what had happened. She leaned closer to Ben. "The creature that attacked us—the cat, I mean—it was a person, a woman. She transformed into a human when I killed her and she had this ring…"

Ben, sipping something that looked like tea but smelled like hot ale, raised his eyebrows. "Ring?"

"A gold ring. But she was so poor that she was starving to death. She would have sold it, I'd think." She shivered. "I think it had something to do with her being a cat. Does this world work this way?"

"This world works in many ways," he said, his tone a little disgruntled. "Not all of them are nice. Or fair. Again…like the real world."

"Hmm." She considered that and looked up when she caught a flash of movement from the corner of her eye. "You're up! Should you be walking?"

"I'm *fine*," Jamie said, clearly prickly. He came down the stairs and to the table, sat close to his sister, and darted a barely disguised glare at her companion.

Ben took another mouthful of his porridge to hide a smile before he said, "I'll go tell the innkeeper you're here for breakfast."

He had barely moved out of sight when Jamie whispered, "What the hell are you doing?"

"Eating breakfast? Talking with the other person from the real world?" Taigan looked at him.

"He's dangerous," her brother said flatly.

"I...okay, back up. How do you know this?"

"You're my sister. I'm supposed to keep you safe."

"Yes," she said patiently, "but how is he dangerous? All he's done is help us. He's here for help exactly like we are. I don't see why we should assume there's a problem."

Jamie glowered in the direction Ben had left in. "You're my sister," he said again.

"Do you...think he's hitting on me?" she asked finally. "Because I honestly don't think he is."

"Are you sure?" he asked.

"I think we're half his age," Taigan protested.

"That doesn't always mean someone's safe."

"Okay, true, but he hasn't been creepy." She sighed at the look on his face. "How about this—if he does anything creepy, my hand to God, I'll stab him."

Jamie's face cleared. "Okay." He held a hand out to shake.

She shook on it. "Just you wait. If we run into a lady somewhere, I'll make you make the same promise."

Ben, with perfect timing, returned with the innkeeper, who held a bowl of porridge. Taigan suspected he had been listening for the optimal time to rejoin them but was unable to confirm her suspicions as he wouldn't meet her eyes.

He certainly *seemed* amused.

"Why are you here?" Jamie asked him when the three of them were alone.

"A climbing accident," the man said. A tenseness stiffened the set of his shoulders. "I lost my ability to move my body—not paralysis. I simply didn't know where my body was at any given time. I've had to learn to walk again and this seems to help." He paused. "Or did you mean why am I in this inn?"

"Both," the boy said after a moment. "Where were you climbing?"

"Colorado." He sighed. "I'm...lucky to be alive. My buddy was also there, and he made it too but he broke a *lot* of bones. I feel guilty about suggesting that route. Anyway, if you're ever in Aspen and you get injured, you should hope you get Dr. Ullmer. She's a miracle worker."

Taigan could see her brother had begun to relax.

"And why are you here in the inn?" she asked.

"Oh, that." He opened his mouth, then closed it. "Um..."

"What?" Jamie asked suspiciously.

"Do you want the good version or the bad version?"

"The good one," she said at the same time her twin said, "The bad one."

"Under a rather obscure section of elvish law," Ben explained, "an elf who is sold into slavery by another elf—of the same nation—is allowed to kill the one who did it. As long as there are seven other elves present. It's complicated. Anyway, I know an elf who had been sold into slavery. He intended to kill the guy who did it to him."

They stared at him, wide-eyed.

"The thing is," he continued, "his immediate heir was someone who would stay in business as a slave trader. His *next* heir was someone who fought for abolition. So...I killed his first heir on the same night. But as you will note, I am not an elf and therefore I needed to get the hell out of there in short order."

A somewhat stunned silence followed.

"So, you murdered someone," Jamie said finally. His voice was flat.

"That's the one," Ben admitted.

"You're not at *all* sorry?" the boy asked incredulously.

Even Taigan was a little unsettled now.

"Oh, I am. I did not want to do that. The thing was, it was necessary, and I couldn't live with myself if I didn't do it." He shrugged. "It's been a hard few weeks here. When I told Taigan that this world wasn't always pretty or fair, I meant it. On the other hand, I think I've become a better person."

"Better person…as in a murderer." Jamie didn't seem inclined to let this go.

His sister had to admit he had a point.

"Yeah," he said. "If it helps, up until I got into the game—and for a while after—I'd have been right there with you."

"I don't think it does help," the boy said after a moment of serious thought.

"Well, that's fair." Ben took a mouthful of porridge. "But it sounds like your sister did some violence last night to save your life and I'd wager you'd do the same for her, right? Or a friend?"

Jamie didn't say anything to that.

"So…" Taigan considered this. "Are you leaving, then?"

"Soon. I'm waiting for someone." He smiled slightly. "Since I needed to leave anyway, I offered to look for my friend's…friend. Fiancée, I think. She was sold into slavery somewhere out here by the same man and I'll try to track her down."

"And kill her?" the boy muttered into a mouthful of porridge.

She rolled her eyes but knew better than to engage when he had made up his mind about something. He liked to leap to conclusions and then hang onto them for dear life.

He finished his porridge and put his spoon down. "Well, if you're waiting for someone, we should spar."

"*What?*" Taigan and Ben said at the same time.

"You learn who a man is by fighting him."

Ben's face went studiously blank and she winced in empathic embarrassment. Before he could say anything, she hurried to interject.

"That may be, but *you* are on bed rest for one week and I think if you disobey orders, our hostess will make you drink more of that tea."

She had hoped to put the fear of God in her brother, and it looked like she had judged correctly—his eyes went wide.

"There *are* some sparring targets outside," Ben said casually. "I need to practice movement anyway for my physical therapy, so I'll be there if you'd like to join me." He raised an eyebrow at Jamie.

"I can't spar," the boy said grumpily. "Guys, that tea is *so bad*. I can't drink it again."

"It'll at least get you outside," he said. "Come on, both of you."

CHAPTER SIXTY-FOUR

"**I**'m confused," Prima said as Ben walked through the inn. "What about?" He kept his voice low so the twins wouldn't hear him. Taigan hung back with her brother, who was running out of energy and did not want to admit it.

"Why doesn't Jamie like you?" she asked. *"I put you all in the same place because I thought you would like each other. It's always worked that way before."*

"Always? Who else have you tried that with?"

"Dotty, Justin, Tina…"

"Yeah, I don't know any of those people. As for Jamie…" He tried to decide how to explain this to her. "He's worried about his sister. He thinks I'll hit on her and make her uncomfortable."

"I'm not always familiar with colloquialisms. 'Hit on' is a euphemism for flirting, yes?"

"Yes." He hid a smile.

"Do you want to flirt with Taigan?"

"I do not." He grinned now. "I'm sure she's a lovely person but she is also a child. I certainly will not flirt with her."

"She is not a child," Prima said after a moment. She was clearly

424

trying to understand the meaning of his words and seemed to have trouble doing so.

Ben said nothing. If he'd learned anything about the AI, it was that she wanted to learn and advance. He wouldn't give her the answer to her question before she'd had time to puzzle it out.

"So, humans find age gaps to be disconcerting?" Prima asked at last.

"Yes," he said patiently.

"Is it the fact that she is fifty percent of your age or the fact that she is seventeen years younger?"

"There isn't any hard and fast rule," Ben explained. "It's merely what feels okay at the time. Well...as long as everyone's cool with it and they're adults, which she isn't. Look, this is seriously weird to talk about."

"I apologize. I am confused. To sum up, Jamie is worried that you will flirt with Taigan, but you do not want to flirt with Taigan?"

"Yes."

"Then why don't you simply tell him that?"

"Oh, you priceless, innocent unicorn." Ben began to laugh and tried to keep his voice low.

"I am not a unicorn. I am an artificial—"

"I know. It's another figure of speech. Uh...basically, if I told him that, he wouldn't believe it. Humans lie often. Especially about this kind of thing."

"You people are exhausting."

"It's hard to argue with that," he agreed.

He pushed out into the back yard. The sparring targets he had spoken about were not designed to be targets. Instead, they were old piles of garbage, some of them with the remains of boxes protruding.

The ground was still somewhat wet from the day before but was drying quickly in the day's heat, and Ben took a moment to study the area. Heffog, as Elantria had told him, had the feeling of a city forever in decline. There was a desperate undercurrent to it, the sense that anyone might be watching you and anyone might try to harm you.

This settlement was ramshackle and far from affluent, but it was far more comfortable. You drank your beer, you paid your tab, and in return, everyone obeyed the rules of society.

Taigan and Jamie emerged and looked around for a seat for the wounded boy. A set of barrels stood nearby, filled with God only knew what, but they didn't smell too bad and they would work well for what they needed. He clambered up with Taigan's help, which Ben pretended not to see.

"So," he called over his shoulder as he drew his sword. "You know why I'm here—what's *your* quest?"

"We're supposed to have a quest?" She responded. With a small frown, she moved closer to stare at the piles. "What am I supposed to do with this? It's not exactly…human-shaped."

"Start trying to hit very specific things," he said. "Or try to stop right before hitting them. Basically, anything that gives you more practice in controlling the staff."

"Okay." She sounded doubtful but she took the staff off her back and went to find a pile in another part of the yard.

He didn't talk for a while as he warmed up with the series of passes Zaara had shown him for that purpose. If he did them correctly, the sword hummed through the air. He had no target, not yet. It was simply a series of techniques at all different angles. They forced him to use all the muscles in his arms and core, shift his grasp more than once, and begin using footwork. By the end, he could feel his body awake and ready to go, and he'd had a blessed few minutes with a clear mind—nothing in his head except for the techniques and his muscles.

Ben started into the second set of exercises without looking at the twins. This set was more basic, but Zaara had been adamant that in swordsmanship, as in most areas of life, the basics were what one should spend the most time on.

Now, he let his thoughts run ahead. He was fairly sure that Prima meant for the twins to accompany him, but he wasn't certain that it would be a good idea. After all, Jamie was injured. If he went into danger—as he suspected he would—the two young people would be vulnerable.

Taigan, of course, had shown that she could handle herself ably. But he had no illusions about whether her brother would be comfortable to remain back at an inn while the two of them went off to fight, as they inevitably would.

On the other hand, he thought as he stepped through for a turn and reverse attack, he couldn't simply leave the two of them there alone. They had no money and not the first idea of where to go to keep themselves safe, and he *certainly* didn't want them to end up in Heffog.

He sighed as he continued.

Taigan looked curiously at him. "Is everything okay?"

Ben nodded wordlessly. She had made short work of two entire piles of garbage and with enough violence that he could absolutely believe she had beaten a cat to death the night before.

She returned to her workout and he moved to where Jamie was seated. He settled himself on a barrel next to the boy and waited for him to speak.

"You stay away from her," Jamie said finally.

He was struck by the very sudden impression that he had become old while he wasn't paying attention. So much was evident in his voice that the boy wasn't aware of. It wasn't only dislike or the threat but the faint self-consciousness and the quaver in the tone that screamed, "I'm not ready for this." And, of course, the uncertainty over whether this was the right thing to do at all. Ben remembered those moments and to his surprise, he felt sympathetic.

"As I recall," he said, as lightly as he could, "she said she would stab me if I tried anything, and I'm gonna go out on a limb and guess she told the truth." He nodded to where Taigan currently destroyed a broken barrel.

Jamie remained silent.

"I expect you'll only believe me as you get to know me," he said. "If you do, I guess. But I have no intention of hitting on her. When the two of you came into the inn last night, you were injured and there were people at the fire looking like they were ready to mug you and I felt…protective. I didn't expect it. I'm only thirty-four. While I know

427

that seems super-old to you, I didn't think I was old enough to feel like I should be taking care of kids."

The boy considered this and finally looked at him. "She's always been falling into these states," he told him. "The comas. I pushed our family to put her in this game. I thought at the start that it had killed her, and I couldn't...that was the worst thing I've ever felt. I wanted to die. It was too much guilt for me to live with. I don't want her to get hurt in here."

Ben looked at him. "Is that what happened with..." He gestured at the wound.

"No." Jamie flushed with embarrassment. "We didn't see the animal until it was too late. It knocked me over and Taigan tried to get it off, and it went to jump and its claws came out." He shuddered at the memory. "God, that moment—I thought it would get my heart. I was so afraid and it hurt *so* much. And then I couldn't help her while she fought it."

He nodded.

"I'm sorry I threatened you," the youngster said finally. "That was uncalled for."

"Eh, I think it's better for Taigan to know her brother has her back," he told him. "So...are we cool?"

"We're cool. Just...you know, if you *do* try something, I won't stop her from stabbing you."

"That's fair." He sighed and looked at the sun. "God, I'm old. You don't think about it until you see someone young."

"What's it like to be...thirty-four?"

"Thank you for not also saying 'old,'" Ben said wryly. "And I hate to tell you, but it's as confusing and weird as being a teenager—only for some reason, you also have to pay bills and take care of yourself. I guess that's the big thing. You still don't know what you're doing."

"Huh." Jamie looked skeptical. He rotated his arm in its socket. "You know, it feels like this is healing." He pulled his shirt aside to look under the bandage. "Oh, shit. Look."

He leaned closer to the boy. What had been a deep and angry red puncture wound was now completely gone.

"What was *in* that salve?" Jamie asked.

"I think it was the tea," he said. "You should probably have more. You know, to make sure."

"New plan," the youngster said, "if you ever hit on my sister, I will make you drink some of that tea."

Ben guffawed.

"What are you two talking about?" Taigan asked suspiciously.

"Jamie's wound is gone," he responded.

"What?" She dropped the staff and ran to them to look. "Holy crap —*how?*"

"I have no idea," her brother told her, "but I'm glad. And I think I will take that sparring match now," he added and looked meaningfully at Ben.

He laughed. "I suppose I earned that. Go easy on the old man, though, will you?"

"Never," Jamie replied cheerfully.

"This isn't a stupid guy thing, is it?" Taigan asked suspiciously. "Because if you two start beating each other, I'll simply leave."

"We're only sparring," the boy promised her.

"And then I'll teach you the warmups I was doing," Ben told him. "Cool."

The two took their places in the field of scattered debris. Jamie was grinning as he surged forward in an attack.

Ben, however, knew a thing or two about doing foolhardy charges. He stepped into the charge and saw his opponent's moment of indecision—whether to accelerate his strike or pull up? That indecision cost him as he tapped the boy's ribs lightly with his sword. Jamie winced and swore under his breath but resettled into a fighting stance.

Good. He wouldn't run when he was outmatched. In his experience, that was a critical part of surviving in the world of PIVOT.

This time, Jamie circled and waited. He tried to be careful and feel him out, which was something Ben approved of. The newly discovered old man in him tried to decide whether to give the boy the next point in order to show him that the tactic was good. Most of him, however, felt like he should pull no punches.

He didn't have to decide, as it turned out. As he readied himself to close the gap between them, a bloodcurdling scream came from the front of the inn. The three exchanged panicked looks and all of them sprinted out of the yard and to the road.

CHAPTER SIXTY-FIVE

"Whoa, fuck!" Ben skidded abruptly to a stop when he saw what was there. He couldn't stop himself from yelling, but he clapped a hand over his mouth to stifle the noise.

The beast that paced at the front of the inn was mangy and under-nourished but no less terrifying for it. He couldn't have said whether it was a wolf or a cat—or, possibly, a bear of some kind. The way it walked was ambiguous. Its paws were gigantic and there were huge claws on each.

Old blood—not new blood, thankfully—was visible on its teeth. Whoever it had scared was presumably in one of the houses by now as there was no sign of blood and no body.

Only an angry wolf-bear-cat paced the empty road. Ben hadn't stifled the sound enough, though, because it looked at the three of them for a long moment as if it tried to decide whether to attack them or not. Its eyes were a sickly yellow-green.

"Oh, crap," Taigan said. "Another one of these fucking things."

"*That's* what you fought the yesterday?" He stared at her, then at Jamie before he looked hastily at the animal.

It, of course, no longer paid attention to them. There was something insulting about that—it didn't even think they were worth worrying about.

"Well, it was dark," the girl said.

"Yeah, we couldn't see it well," Jamie agreed.

"This is scarier," she finished.

Ben, vividly remembering the dark elf twins he had worked with at Lord Kerill's house, decided to put an end to the ping-pong type of conversation. He waved his hand to quiet them and said firmly, "We need a strategy."

"Operation Rock and a Pointy Place," the twins said immediately in unison.

He stared pointedly at them.

Jamie explained. "Taigan gets its attention and hits it as much as she can with the stick while she drives it back to me so I can kill it. We've practiced it often."

Questions stirred but he filed them to discuss later. "Which side should I be on?"

"You and Taigan be the rock," the boy decided.

"Right." He took a deep breath and looked at her. "Are you ready?"

"Yeah, I guess." She didn't look enthusiastic about this. Still, she readied her grasp on her staff and focused on the beast.

Without warning, she attacked with a battle cry that made Ben want to hide. It took one startled moment before he remembered to follow her.

The monster—he had decided to call it a bear-cat—looked around with a snarl when she raced forward. It crouched, its head whipped from side to side, and it darted sideways around her and launched itself at Ben.

"Fuuuuuuck!" He went over backward and his head struck the cobblestones so hard he saw stars. When he opened his eyes muzzily, he saw a chunk of hit points floating away.

He still seemed to be alive, though, and scrambled to his feet to see Jamie warding the animal off with jabs of his sword. The boy also yelled at random—it seemed to be a family trait—and while their adversary snarled and snapped, it didn't seem willing to get in too close.

Zaara would probably have despaired of the twins, but he had to admit that their balls-to-the-wall-crazy style had definite advantages.

Ben waited until Jamie lunged forward and he timed his strike for when the bear-cat scrambled back, away from the sword. His heavy slash connected successfully with the monster's leg, a little above the knee, and the creature howled. The sound was terrifyingly human.

Then he remembered that, according to Taigan, these things might well *be* human. His stomach turned.

The monster didn't give him time to mull over the morality of the situation. As he had been the first to draw blood, it seemed to have decided he would be the first to die. It bunched into a crouch and launched toward him.

That action was very cat-like. Maybe he would see a full character-ization by the time this was over. He decided to think about that while he waited for the right moment—the monster's legs lengthened, the paws left the ground, and its jaws opened—and he ducked and threw himself forward under the animal's trailing feet.

He landed too hard on the cobblestones. This was yet another way in which he was getting old. Things that would have been amusing before were now terrifyingly painful.

"Rock and a pointy place!" Taigan yelled. "Ben, get up!"

"Yeah, yeah." He pushed to his feet beside her. "I think I liked it better when I couldn't move," he said grumpily. "At least then I didn't end up getting myself into these situations."

"This way, however, is more fun for me."

The girl snickered.

"Yes, thank you, Prima." Ben rolled his eyes and looked at her. "Charge?"

"Chaaaarge!" was Taigan's answer.

"They are not subtle, those two," he said to Prima as he followed.

"You're one to talk."

"It takes one to know one, I guess."

To his surprise, the two of them settled into a rhythm fairly quickly. One would dart in with a yell and a few good strikes while the other one prepared and darted in silently to stab at the bear-cat from the opposite side.

All he wanted was for this to be over, but it was difficult to get close enough for a solid blow without the risk of claws or teeth. The creature might have been human to start with, but it had good reach, sharp claws, and dangerous fangs, and it certainly knew how to move.

The thing that kept him going was that it was limping from his first strike. It could be injured. He had done it before and he could do it again.

"Ben, be ready!" Taigan called.

"On it," he responded.

She launched herself closer and spun to put the entire force of her core behind the staff strike. It wasn't fast enough to catch the bear-cat, but he knew that was her purpose. The monster, having to choose between moving carefully or getting out of the way of a bone-crushing blow, reacted on instinct and leapt toward him.

He saw Jamie waving his arms to indicate that he was open. Rather than striking directly at the creature's back, he circled and drove it away from Taigan laterally. Between her strike and his shift of angle, it thought more about evading them than it did about what else might be behind it.

The boy put his whole body into his attack. The bear-cat arched and shrieked. The yellowish-green of its eyes flared and it thrashed and tore the sword from his hand. It stumbled away, clearly in its death throes but still too dangerous to reach. They watched as it sank to the cobbles and its ribs stopped moving.

The shift from monster to human wasn't immediate. The form seemed to melt before their eyes. Patchy fur transformed into tattered clothes, the claws and fangs melted away, and the snout flattened into a human face.

Jamie's sword, however, was still lodged in the man's side.

Ben had recalled Taigan's words about their attacker the night before but half of him had not believed in the transformation. The other half had not appreciated exactly how desperate and emaciated the human was. The cheekbones were gaunt and he could see the line of the ribs even under the shirt.

"Look," Jamie said quietly and pointed at the man's hand.

A gold ring glittered on his finger.

The oddness of it wasn't that it was simply a gold ring on a man who would easily have been desperate enough to sell it. It was the way it glittered, the only thing about him that wasn't dirty. Ben edged closer with the twins beside him.

None of them wanted to touch it.

When he pulled a dagger out and pressed the man's hand down, he saw something else that frightened him.

"Is that..." The boy sounded horrified. "Is it going *into* his hand?"

He had to swallow bile before he could answer. "I think so." The skin around the ring was reddened in a slight but unmistakable pattern. If he had to guess, he would say the ring had spikes on the inside that dug into his flesh.

The wearer couldn't have taken it off without severing his finger. How it had been put on was a mystery.

Suddenly, he remembered why he was there.

"Ben?" Jamie frowned and his expression seemed confused and impatient.

"Orien's friend," Ben said slowly. "She was a *goldsmith.*"

Both twins looked at him, dumbstruck, and down at the man and his ring.

"Did she do this to him?" Taigan asked. "If she's the one—well, we don't want to..." She swallowed and blew a breath out. "If this is her work, we should think about whether we want to find her."

"Not necessarily." He looked at the gaunt man. In Heffog, he had been attacked by people who killed for money or out of desperation. He fought them, but he hated it and wanted to target the people who pulled the strings, not those who put human shields between them and their enemies. His gaze settled on the twins. "What we should think about is what to *do* when we find her."

They looked wordlessly at him, afraid and uncomfortable.

And when he saw that, he came to a decision. They could not

accompany him. He merely had to find a way to tell them—and get Prima to give them a new mission.

It was something to think about.

When he stood, he was surprised to see an unexpected figure waiting on the edge of the town square. "Orien," Ben said in surprise. "I didn't expect you to come yourself."

The elf came closer, his elegant features still and expressionless. He looked at the twins, who gazed at him, wide-eyed and confused, and stepped forward to crouch beside the body. Carefully, he studied the ring, the man's features, and the clothing.

Finally, he said a single word, too low for Ben to hear, and the ring vanished. In its wake, the man's hand blackened and curled as if it had been burned.

Orien stood, his face determinedly blank. "We should speak alone," he told Ben.

"Of course." He knew better than to think the twins would accept that, though. "First, let me introduce you to two travelers, Taigan and Jamie. They are on a mission of their own and helped me with this fight." A glare over Orien's head told the twins to stay quiet.

"I'm very pleased to meet you," the elf said to them politely.

"Take a meal with us," he suggested. "If you've come this far on your own, you have the time for it."

Orien nodded. Whatever he was about to say in response, however, it was lost in a storm of anguished chatter from the innkeeper's wife. She ran out the door, waving her hands at the scene in the town square.

His worry was that she knew the man they had killed. This turned out to not be the issue, however, and instead, she was incensed that Jamie had disregarded her order to rest for a week. She checked his bandage, wagged a finger at him, read him what was clearly the riot act in whatever language she spoke, and marched him into the inn by force.

"We should save him," Taigan said.

"Yeah, probably," Ben agreed.

Neither of them moved.

"Why…aren't you?" Orien asked them curiously.

"We're afraid she'll make *us* drink the tea if we go in there," the girl explained.

"There's nothing for it but to be brave, I suppose," the elf said finally. He sounded surprisingly cheerful. "Into battle, my friends. Our comrade is alone in the hands of the enemy." He set off, whistling.

"I like him," Taigan said, after a moment.

"So do I," he told her. Still, he couldn't help but remember Orien's eyes when he saw the ring—and the fact that he had come to deliver whatever the message was himself.

He had a feeling that things had become far more complicated.

CHAPTER SIXTY-SIX

It was a while before Jamie managed to extricate himself from the ministrations of the innkeeper's wife, who constantly insisted that the wound would need to be recleaned. He had thought it would be easy enough to show her that he was healed, but she seemed to think he'd managed a trick of some kind and jabbed at his shoulder until he was fairly sure she would re-puncture it.

She muttered something he guessed was a ward against witchcraft and began to examine her various pots of salve, at which point he snuck out to join the others.

"I think she thinks I'm a witch," he said when he located them.

"And the tea?" Taigan asked.

"I didn't have any of that this time—no thanks to *you* lot, who didn't try to rescue me even once."

All three of them were suddenly focused on their beer and food.

"Traitors," the boy said darkly. "So—Orien, is it?"

"Yes." Orien nodded at him. "Taigan, yes?"

"Jamie, actually." He tried not to be prickly about that.

"Ah." The elf looked confused. "Human naming conventions are very strange. Regardless, I am pleased to meet you both. What brings you to this town?"

The twins looked at each other. Jamie shrugged at his sister.

"Bad luck," she answered.

"A fine enough answer." Orien mopped some of the stew with his bread. "If bad luck troubles you, I wouldn't head north. Heffog is full of it these days. Or, rather, long-needed vengeance, which tends to catch people in the crossfire."

The boy considered this as the innkeeper brought him a bowl of stew. It hadn't been long since their breakfast, but it seemed that anytime they sat there, they were given food—and, as a perpetually hungry seventeen-year-old, he didn't complain.

"Perhaps we should go speak alone," Ben suggested to Orien.

"Nuh-uh," Taigan answered before the elf could. "You said you're looking for a goldsmith, there are weird gold rings on things that are attacking us, and we want to know what's going on."

Orien blinked at her and looked at Ben. "I see you told them who you were looking for."

"No specifics," he said. "Although I suppose the only specific I know about this woman is her name. I don't even know if she's human, elvish—"

"Half-elvish," the elf said. "Like me. You wouldn't know it—she looks full-human—but she has the magical talent of a full-blown elf."

"I didn't know humans and elves had different levels of talent," he said.

"Mmm." Orien took another mouthful and thought for a moment. "It's more the *way* they do magic. Elves can usually get the hang of it sooner or later and very few humans do, but if humans do, they tend to be quite powerful—like your friend Kural. And you, I'd guess."

"*Me?*" He looked flabbergasted.

The elf looked at the twins, both of whom shrugged in response, and focused on Ben. "I thought you knew. You practically *spark* with magic. Didn't you know?" A wary look settled on his face and he rummaged in one of his pockets before he withdrew an iron ring. "Give me your hand. Yes. Wear this for now."

"Why?" Ben asked blankly. He looked at the twins, who both shrugged.

"Because you're a walking bomb," Orien told him sweetly. "And I'd rather not be anywhere close when your power first comes out."

"Uh…" He stared at his hand. "Huh."

"Anyway," the elf said with another sideways look at the iron ring, "Josyla had exceptional talent. If you want my opinion—and you really should—it's why she was so good at metalworking. Some of the best wizards in the world don't do magic for its own sake. They simply use it for their passion. Hers was gold."

"And that talent got her sold," Ben said softly.

"Yes. It's surprising, given how much Kerill could have made off her talent if he kept her. That's what made me think. I checked the records and…well, let's say her selling price was extraordinarily high and the money wasn't even half of it. He was playing the long game and had many of the other elves in thrall to him, magically speaking." He smiled grimly. "I'm glad the bastard's dead, and even more glad that I could do it."

Jamie didn't need to look at Taigan to know she was spooked. The twins looked at their food in utter silence.

"You're scaring them," Ben said.

"Good," Orien replied promptly. "Then maybe they won't go to Heffog."

He groaned and sounded genuinely exasperated, which Jamie liked. After their discussion, he was more ready to trust the other man —but he still felt he should keep his guard up.

"So…" The boy cleared his throat when everyone looked at him. He decided to be as neutral as he could about this. "It sounds like you found her trail."

"Yes." Orien gave him a tight smile and looked out into the town square. "She was bought by a sorceress, a woman who dabbled in very dark magic. Well. I say 'dabbled.' It was more than that. Kerill's records weren't very specific."

Ben frowned. "How did you find out, then?"

"I located one of his mistresses—who I happened to know was a great deal more intelligent than he gave her credit for—and explained what I needed to know. Between the two of us, we worked it out."

"How did you get the mistress to tell you?" Jamie asked, now suspicious. Taigan's look said she wondered the same thing.

"I asked," Orien said. He looked at the boy's expression. "I asked nicely so don't give me that look. She knew exactly who I was and what I had done, and she didn't have any particular love for him. Also, she knew why I was asking for the information." He shrugged. "It seems Kerill never told anyone much of anything except when he got angry. Then, he would threaten anyone in the vicinity with what he'd done to other people. Like, say, selling them to a sorceress who could control minds." He took a sip of his ale.

"And..." The girl paused, then soldiered on. "Are you worried that *she* might be controlled?"

The elf went silent for a long moment before he nodded.

Taigan looked at him. Almost gently, she asked, "How can we help?"

Orien gaped at her. He was about to respond when Ben interrupted.

"You two will stay out of this."

"The hell we will," she retorted.

"Yeah," Jamie added lamely.

"You will," he said flatly. "It's dangerous out here. That sorceress controlled the minds of however many people in Heffog, she's turning the poor into her personal army, and if you think for a *moment* that she'd let her prized goldsmith go without a fight, you're deluding yourselves. Orien and I will find a way to resolve this."

The silence that followed almost crackled with tension. Orien closed his mouth and sat, looking unnerved.

"No," Taigan said finally.

"No, *what?*" Ben glared at her.

"No, we won't simply let the two of you go off alone to rescue this woman," she said. "You're right, this sorceress won't let her go easily, which is why you need *help.*"

"You're teenagers," he responded sharply. "Someone has to look out for you two, not lead you into danger."

"Yeah, well, I've been told that danger is the only thing that will

441

make me better," she snapped. "That's why Prima led me into the fight with the bear-cat-thing, it's why... I...it's what I need." She seemed to have remembered that Orien didn't understand this.

Ben sighed. "I understand that," he said, "but I have seen some things in this world that I wouldn't wish on my worst enemy. I don't want to send you home traumatized."

"I'm confused," Orien said. "Are you ill?"

"In a way," Taigan said. She looked at him. "And I'm supposed to face danger here. It would make me stronger and it might cure me."

"There are many dangers," the elf said finally. "Perhaps you need dangers that are not quite so...well, dangerous."

"No." She didn't back down.

Jamie leaned back in his chair to watch. He couldn't keep from smirking. Neither Orien nor Ben had seen his sister's stubbornness, but they were in for a real surprise if they thought they would convince her to turn back.

"We will *not* discuss this around Orien," Ben said dangerously, "who has lost his fiancée and doesn't need her rescue to get turned into—"

"Ben." The elf put his hand on the other man's arm. "Think for a moment."

He sighed. "*What?*"

"You saw Heffog. You saw people beaten down, rudderless, and cowardly." Orien nodded his head in the direction of Jamie and Taigan. "These two want to help. They're brave. Shouldn't we encourage that?"

Frustrated, he muttered something and the elf leaned closer to say something in a low voice. When Ben started laughing, Jamie bristled, but he only nodded and looked at the twins.

"He's right," he said. "You two *would* go off and find a worse disaster if we didn't take you along."

"Now, wait a second—" the boy protested.

"Yes," Taigan said flatly, "we *would*."

"Taigan!"

"We're winning! Come on!"

Her brother put his head in his hands. "I hope to God that Mom and Dad don't hear about this or they'll kill me."

CHAPTER SIXTY-SEVEN

Unfortunately, even Orien did not know much. Over several mugs of ale, while Taigan and Jamie sparred out in the back, he shared the very few pieces of knowledge he had about the sorceress and his suspicions about Josyla.

It took an extraordinary amount of ale for him to admit them.

"The girl's question was good," he said finally. He held the mug as if for balance and stared blearily at the back wall. "That's why I came. Myself, I mean."

"Hmm?" Ben, who had been rather more restrained in his drinking, raised an eyebrow and tried not to laugh at the sight of the ever-elegant Orien swaying tipsily.

"The girl." He tried to jerk his head at the yard and swayed drunkenly but managed to steady himself with visible effort. "This ale...strong."

"You've also had about twelve mugs of it," he pointed out.

"*Have* I?" the elf tipped his mug and looked intently at the bottom of it as if that might hold the answer. "Huh. It's good. Anyway. The girl was right—about what you'll find when you find Josyla."

"You think she's mind-controlled?" Ben, who could have dumped

444

his beer on Taigan's head when she brought it up, wasn't surprised but he hadn't wanted to be right about this.

"Yes and no." Orien's fingers had tightened around the mug. "It's...I think she might be working for her willingly."

"*What?*" That, he had *not* expected.

"Yeah." His companion looked at him with a frown. "And she wasn't my fiancée, you know. Only a friend." The mournful way he said it showed that he, at least, had wanted it to be more.

Ben made a noncommittal noise while he took a sip of his beer.

"She..." Orien sighed.

"You loved her," he said and cut to the chase. "She had good qualities."

"Yes. She wasn't a monster or anything." The elf looked miserable. "Only...resentful. Resentful of us being servants for being bastard-born while our half-siblings were lords and ladies. Resentful that so many in the city didn't have food. All of it. It wasn't that she was mean. She merely saw so much cruelty and felt powerless because she would never be rich enough to help. After a while, she even looked down on herself for being a goldsmith."

"Why?"

"Because it only helped our lord," Orien said. "She loved her work but she said she didn't want to enrich him."

"Shouldn't she feel the same way about the sorceress, then?"

"Maybe." He looked doubtful. "The thing is...look, I couldn't tell you why I'm so sure of this, but when I heard who had bought her— that it was a sorceress who used black magic—all I could think was that Josyla had decided to learn from her. She was clever and she'd learn all kinds of things you never expected her to from the details she needed to put into a certain piece of jewelry or an offhand comment. I'd bet she learned magic, whether the sorceress meant to teach her or not."

Ben sighed.

"I'm only saying," Orien said, "that you need to be careful. And... think about whether you want to do this."

He looked at him. "If I don't, though, you'll always wonder."

The elf looked away.

"And maybe you'll try to find her yourself," he continued quietly.

Orien said nothing.

"And you might have to make a choice you don't want to make," he continued, "about how to deal with her."

Although he said nothing, his elvish features were twisted with pain.

"I'll go," Ben said, "and if she was tricked or coerced or anything like that, I'll bring her home. If there's any way, I'll do it."

"Thank you," Orien said quietly. He stood drunkenly. "I should get back. They need me. This was the worst time to go but I couldn't tell a messenger what I told you. You should start with a woman named Yulia. She and the sorceress worked together."

He held his tongue and simply nodded as he saw Orien to the door and watched him set out. From the speed with which the elf faded into the distance, he suspected that he had a travel spell of some kind on him.

Being that drunk, he'd better be careful or he'd wind up miles off course. He smiled at the thought and returned to his drink.

Once he'd drained his tankard, he left word with the innkeeper that he was going to see Yulia. The man seemed bemused that he would visit an old woman, but there was no hint of scandal in the way he nodded. Whatever she had done with the sorceress, she didn't seem to be known as one.

Ben snuck out, hoped the twins would take time with their sparring—after all, the energy of a teenager could go almost indefinitely—and headed down the country road, whistling quietly. Despite his misgivings, or perhaps because of them, he concentrated on how beautiful the day was. The night's rain had turned the grass and trees a brilliant green, while the blue sky and warm sun set everything off perfectly.

Yulia lived a mile or so away from the cluster of buildings that comprised the heart of the town. It was farther than he would have thought an old woman would live but then again, it sounded like she was not merely a helpless old woman.

She was working in the garden when he arrived. Herbs and vegetables were planted in neat rows without a weed in sight. A stone wall covered in lichen and moss surrounded the yard, with a flowering apple tree on one side of the gate and a pretty, thatched cottage in the center of it with smoke rising from its chimney.

The old woman stood as he came close and hobbled forward to open the gate.

"Did you know I was coming?" he asked her, confused.

"Of course. Your thoughts were loud enough for a half-addled cow to hear them." She gave him a piercing look from under bushy brows and waved him in. "Come on, then. The tea should be steeped."

"Er...thank you." He followed her along the path and into the house.

It was tiny. A little bed was covered with a patchwork quilt, a rocker at the hearth held a basket with yarn and knitting needles, and the other side of the room was taken up with a long wooden workbench covered with stacks of cloth, spools of thread, and a few jars of spices. A teapot sat on a ceramic tile with two mugs next to it.

Yulia waved him to the bed to sit while she poured them tea. She hobbled back, sat in the rocking chair, and then said baldly,

"So, it's the goldsmith Gwyna bought, eh?"

"Do we need to have a conversation?" Ben asked. "Or have you read all my thoughts already?"

"Don't be smart with me, young man." She moved fretfully and her gnarled fingers closed and shifted around the warmth of the mug. "Your thoughts came through muddled—oh, clear enough for me to guess who you wanted to find, but little else. Gold, I saw, and a terrible beast. An elvish woman. But, *you*...who are you?"

"No one important."

"That's not true in the slightest," she said at once. "You killed an emissary of the new elvish king, boy. I'd not say you're unimportant."

He leaned back in his chair. "How did you know that?"

"You dreamed of it last night."

"I..." He had, and the thought that someone could hear his dreams was deeply unpleasant.

"It takes an unusual talent to hear thoughts," she told him. "And they've been less clear since *this* was put on you." She extended her hand to tap the iron ring. "Which brings me to your problem. You need to find Gwyna and you need to do it without her realizing who you are and why you're there."

Ben waited.

Yulia sighed. "She was a quiet one, Gwyna. Always quiet. She kept her thoughts hidden and worked hard. I never saw the darkness in her. There are some you know will go bad, but she wasn't one. She was mild-mannered and nothing special to look at, with no great talent for fire or ice or any of the things that level towns. In most cases, their parents would come to me begging for help. She arrived on her own."

He took a sip of his tea. It was surprisingly light, both fruity and bitter, and oddly refreshing despite its temperature.

"But she always drew the dark ones," the woman told him. "Angry ones and bitter ones. And now, she's far away and her name is never spoken, and that worries me all the more."

"You think someone needs to deal with her," he said.

"You say it very simply," she observed. "You're a strange one, aren't you? Hating violence and craving justice. A word to the wise, child— justice comes slowly and it hits wide. It'll cost more than you want every time and give you less than you hoped. If you took my advice, I'd say to avoid Gwyna and her goldsmith. But, since you won't..."

Ben chuckled and took another sip.

Yulia smiled. The smile showed him, only for a moment, how she must have been as a young woman. What was in her past, he wondered? She was a magic user, an old woman without regrets and with no hint of family or loss, and yet there must be loss to give her such wit and warnings.

"You should ask for Gwyna's help," the woman said. She tapped the ring. "Ask her to train you. She'll take you."

"Why?"

"She doesn't want justice," she told him, "and doesn't care one whit about it. But the desperation for it makes people angry and she's always been good at harnessing that anger. If she thinks she can use you, she'll take you in."

"But getting in is only part of it," Ben protested. "What if she's bound the goldsmith's mind? How am I supposed to get her out? And what if I have to kill her? How do I kill a sorceress so powerful she can enslave minds and still no one knows about her?"

Yulia gave him a sardonic look. "That isn't the world's problem to solve, is it? It's yours, boy. So find the answers. If you want justice, you had better be prepared to mete it out."

He stiffened a little and swallowed. "And where is she?"

"There's a warren of caves to the south on the shores of the lake. They are difficult to get to but not impossible."

He nodded and thought for a moment but jumped when someone pounded on the door.

"That'll be the two," the woman said.

"The two what?" Ben asked. Immediately, though, he realized he should have known the answer. The door opened and Taigan stuck her head around it.

"There you are," she said accusingly. "You tried to leave us behind." Then, to the woman, she added, "I'm sorry. I'm Taigan."

"Aye, and a strange one, you are." Yulia looked appraisingly at her. "Well, come in, both of you. We should decide what to do with the two of you while yon wizard goes off to free the goldsmith."

"We're going with him," the girl said at once.

"That, you most certainly are *not*. No, don't you argue with me, young lady." The old woman gave her a hard look. "We'll find something for you two here."

"But I need to help someone," Taigan said. "I can't sit around thinking and trying to shift myself between worlds anymore. I *can't*. I need to be in danger and I need to help someone. It's the only way I'll get better. I want to go home."

Yulia, who could not have understood any of the context behind that statement, watched the girl contemplatively. Ben thought she seemed to be looking beyond the specifics to see the shape of the truth despite not understanding anything about comas and pods.

"You've met some of her creatures," she said. "Gwyna's. They escaped her but her bindings still hold. I could teach you to free them and bring them back to the human world."

The twins looked at each other and now, he was the one who felt uncertain.

"They shouldn't be alone," he said cautiously.

"They won't be," she said simply. "They have each other, don't they? The problem with you, young man, is that you try to do everything at once and run off when it doesn't work. Set your sights on one goal and go from there."

Ben sighed.

"I'll take care of these two," the woman told him. "You go and find Gwyna. Do what must be done. I'll help these two."

"What? *Now?*" This all seemed far too sudden.

"Yes." Yulia stood and began to shoo him out the door. "Don't waste any time. You'll only talk yourself out of it."

"But—uh—" He reached the door and looked over her head at the twins. "Are you okay with this?"

"I...think so?" Taigan shrugged.

"They'll run off if they aren't," the old woman said practically. "Along with you, young man."

The door slammed in his face and he gaped at it.

"She has a point about you trying to do too much at once," Prima said.

"Oh, not you too."

"I'm just saying..."

He rolled his eyes and started south. "Where is this lake? Could I reach it by nightfall?"

"Actually, the team wanted to pull you out for some physical therapy. I'll deposit you at the lake when you come into the game again."

"Oh." He looked around. "Should I find somewhere to lie down or—"

The world dissolved into blue.

"I guess that answers that question."

CHAPTER SIXTY-EIGHT

When Ben opened his eyes, the feeding tube had already been withdrawn and the monitors had been unclipped from his fingers and chest. He struggled to sit and rejected an offered hand, although he couldn't see whose it was.

"Let me try," he rasped, hoarse from the feeding tube.

"Sure." The hand withdrew and the person watched him.

When he managed to get up after a very undignified struggle, Nick smiled at him.

"You know, I won't say our pod hasn't done *anything* for you but I have to say, I think most of your progress is due to you being a stubborn bastard." He cleared his throat. "No offense meant."

"None taken." He coughed and winced. "I don't like feeding tubes."

"Yeah. I'll see if we can arrange to put you under for only twelve hours at a time or so," the engineer said. "Normally, someone in a comatose state could wait much longer, but the virtual reality keeps your metabolism going and—whoa, hey!"

Ben had tried to push himself off the edge of the pod and almost faceplanted into the floor. Nick barely caught him and grunted with the effort.

"Jesus Christ, are you made of solid muscle?"

"I used to be," he said bitterly.

"Uh-huh. Well, either you still are, or your bones are made of titanium." The man pivoted and tried to hold him up. "Almost…okay, can you stand?"

"Yeah. Wait…dizzy." He went backward, and—to his immense surprise—landed in a chair. "Huh?"

"We saw that Nick was having trouble," Jacob said. He came around to look at him. "Also, for the record, you're not wearing any underwear, so maybe less running around in a hospital gown."

"Oh, fuck." He went bright red.

Nick snickered. "Okay, mister, you know the drill—coordination tests and hydration, then you can have food."

"Underwear first," Ben said.

"I…won't argue with that." Nick stared at him with his arms folded. "How to get you into an exam room, though? You're not in a wheelchair."

"I have an idea." DuBois pushed a low cart on wheels beside him. "Put him on this."

"Sure," Jacob said. "That's not abandoning our duty of care at *all*."

"I am your patient," he said, "and I am telling you to not show my butt to any more people!"

"I don't think that provides legal coverage," Jacob responded. "So don't sue us if you fall off this."

"Uh-huh." He tried to steady himself as the team lifted his chair onto the cart and set off. "Ohhhh, I think I'm going to be sick."

"No throwing up on the ride, please," Nick said, "and keep your hands and feet inside the cart area at all times."

"Okay, but why are you *videotaping* this?"

"For our records," Jacob said without any shred of remorse. "Don't worry, we won't show them to Eliza."

"You'd better fucking not," he muttered.

He desperately hoped they didn't show Eliza what happened in the next few minutes. From wiggling his toes to walking in various lines, he was asked to do a number of very simple tasks, most of which he could not do at all gracefully.

"This sucks," Ben said flatly.

"Okay, remember that all the doctors are calling us and saying we're liars," Jacob said. "You're doing the eighteen-month exercises for this and it's only been what...three? Three months, I think."

"People go on like this for eighteen months?" he asked, horrified. "That's how long everyone thought it would take?"

The two younger men were suddenly very busy with paperwork, but DuBois answered promptly,

"Yes, and *also*—" He broke off with a yelp when his bag of popcorn tipped off the table and scattered.

"Oops," Nick said. He met Ben's gaze with the most limpid, innocent expression he could imagine. "Time for more tests and then you can have pizza."

He wanted to protest but his stomach wanted pizza so he gave in with a grumble.

The next few hours passed with too-small meals and far too many coordination and strength exercises. He was given a set of weights so small they barely deserved the name and had to begin weight training with two of the physical trainers.

Both were relentless. Ben, who had thought he was a prime example of stubbornness, had nothing on either of the two. No matter how red his face got or how his muscles started to shake, they guided him through the exercises and the allotted number of repetitions and made notes calmly.

By the end of it, he was covered in sweat, aching, and absolutely ravenous. He barely made it to the table for dinner and could have cried with happiness to see a giant bowl of pad thai and a second of red curry.

It hurt to raise each bite to his mouth, but it was worth it.

"So," Jacob said, as Ben shoveled food in, "how are Taigan and Jamie doing?"

He paused. The other man's tone was slightly too casual.

"Is something wrong?" he asked.

The engineer's expression flickered.

"I'm not good at all that subtle 'avoiding topics' stuff," he said. "So…is something wrong?"

Jacob sighed. "I can't tell you most of it. I only wanted your impression of the two of them."

"They're nice," he said. "Teenagers. I don't know what you want me to say." He suddenly looked over his shoulder. "Wait, they're out there, aren't they? In the lab? That's as trippy as fuck."

"I also can't tell you about where they are," the other man said. "Anyway, it looked like Jamie wasn't too sure of you, but that seems to have calmed."

"It was mostly understandable," Ben said through a mouthful of noodles. "We've all seen dudes be skeevy. But Taigan doesn't take shit from anyone. He doesn't need to worry."

"What's she like?" Jacob was curious now. "We've never…met her. Only seen her in the game sometimes."

"Oh, right. The coma. Um…I don't think she likes to let people in." He scratched his scalp and considered. "She told me about the coma and how she wanted to help someone to get better, but I don't think she told me anything about *her*."

"It's a family full of strong personalities," his companion said wryly. "If you think Taigan takes no shit, you should meet their older sister. Honestly, you can probably be glad you didn't. She wouldn't have sat you down to talk to you like Jamie did and would have merely stabbed you."

"They're protective of her," he observed. "She's the baby of the family and she keeps getting sick. I suppose it makes it sense."

"Yeah." Jacob took a sip of iced tea. "Keep eating. After this, you'll need to fast for ten hours."

"Ugh." He began to wolf his food again. "I do *not* like that."

"You don't say. Anyway, Taigan was…there wasn't anything *off*?"

"I don't know how you mean," he had to admit. "She's a strong personality, but that's not unusual in a teenager—especially one who's going through this. Seriously, though, why?"

"I can't say. I really can't." Jacob shook his head. "But thank you.

Hearing from someone who's been in there and interacted with her is very reassuring."

Ben knew he wouldn't get any further if he pried. For all their joking, the PIVOT team took privacy very seriously.

"One thing, though," he said. "Is there anything I should watch out for? Anything you want me to draw attention to immediately?"

The young engineer considered this very seriously. "Not that I can think of," he said finally. "But thank you for asking."

"Sure." He scooped up the last mouthful of noodles. "Okay, I'm ready to stop eating for now. I'll have regrets in a few hours, though."

"On the plus side, you're doing very well so you won't have to do this too many more times." Jacob smiled and came to offer a hand to pull him up. "How are things looking for when you're out on your own again?"

"Ugh, don't say that." He grimaced. "Your CEO is trying to get me a job in military stuff and...I don't know."

"You don't have to take it, you know," Jacob assured him. "She comes across a little scary, but she genuinely wants to help people."

"I only, uh..." Ben shrugged. "I wanted to change the world, you know?"

"I do know," the other man said honestly. "About six months ago, I found that I'd done the best work of my life for an eight hundred dollars a day machine no one could afford. It was 'only a videogame' and wouldn't help anyone. And, a few days after that, I realized how it could help people."

"So what's your take on that life lesson?" Ben asked. "Steer into the skid?"

Jacob laughed ruefully. "I wish I had a good life lesson to take from that. I think the only one is, don't fold. Because we had no idea where that would go."

"Good point." They had reached his makeshift little bedroom and he opened the door to smile at the bed. A real bed sounded nice right about now. After so much food and a day of exertion, he was ready to pass out.

After one more thing. He said goodnight to Jacob and headed to the computer to bring his email up.

He read through the stories of his friends' exploits with a smile. Locked away in a virtual world, he had asked if they would send him updates each day about the mundane little things to remind him what the real world was like. There were stories about printer cartridges, expired coconut milk, and new puppies.

Mike and Natasha's honeymoon had been wonderful and they had sent him pictures of them eating ice cream and leaning against trees, as well as going to a baseball game and buying ridiculous tourist apparel. He even saw a few shots of himself as their officiant, something that made him smile.

Eliza's email was the last one he opened. He hadn't wanted to ask her to email him every day and he was glad to see that she'd stuffed her message full of things they had talked about on their first date. She included a podcast recommendation and a link to a study she had cited, with an apologetic note that she had misstated the effects by two percent—something he could not imagine anyone other than her apologizing for.

He replied with notes about his physical therapy and took care to include all the terms he hadn't understood. Not only could she clarify, but she and the other doctors at the Aspen hospital were also tracking his progress with great interest. Remembering how much of an ass he'd been right after the accident, he was trying to make it up to them with updates.

At last, he eased into bed and stretched. It was strange how divorced he felt, both from reality and from the game. Ben could see the choices stretching out before him and how easy it would be tomorrow to fall into the world of the game without another thought, putting his safety on the line for Orien or the twins.

At the same time, he could see how his time there was coming to an end. He would miss it, he thought, but the purpose of the game for him hadn't been to provide a place where he would thrive and enjoy himself. It had been to force him to confront all the parts of himself he tried to avoid.

As his thoughts drifted, he wondered how much of that had been a set-up and how much of it had been what he went looking for. He was willing to bet that most of it was the latter. The team, after all, hadn't known much about him.

That was interesting. He'd gone looking for the very things he always ran away from in real life.

He wanted to turn that over in his head, but the day had caught up with him. A little clumsily, he managed to roll over on the bed but didn't even have the covers up when he fell asleep.

CHAPTER SIXTY-NINE

B en had barely walked out the door when Yulia pointed at the little bed and said, "*Sit*, both of you."

The twins exchanged a look.

"Was that too complicated an instruction?" she asked acerbically.

"No," Taigan said.

"But it's not very friendly," Jamie added. "You won't turn us into frogs, will you?"

"Why on *earth* would I turn you into a frog?" She planted her hands on her hips. "What purpose could that possibly serve?"

Neither twin answered and both looked at the floor. Taigan hoped she wouldn't make her answer for Jamie's question, and she had the sense that he—the little weasel—hoped *he* wouldn't be made to reply.

"Well?" Yulia demanded.

Taigan elbowed her brother.

"Ow! I, uh—it's what witches do. In stories." He blushed such a bright red that it was a wonder he didn't burst into flames then and there.

The old woman snorted. "Well, that's not true. Young man, I have no intention of turning anyone into anything. I simply intend to tell two headstrong and not overly wise children about the dangers of the forest. *Sit.*"

Both twins sat. The bed was made for Yulia's diminutive height and was therefore low enough that their knees stuck up awkwardly. That fact was not improved when she handed them earthenware cups of tea. Taigan balanced hers on one of her knees and wrapped her fingers around it.

"So you've seen Gwyna's beasts, then?" she said when she sat in her rocking chair.

"Yes…ma'am." The girl hunched her shoulders. "Twice."

"Tell me about the encounters," she said and listened while Taigan and Jamie told the story together, often prompting one another with details.

When they finished, the woman tipped her head back and gazed into the fireplace. She suddenly looked surprisingly old and was troubled by what she had heard. That much had been clear from her wary looks as the two spoke.

"The elf man," she said finally. "You said he spoke a single word and the ring crumbled to dust?"

The young people both nodded.

"What was that spell?" Taigan asked.

"It wasn't…hmm." Yulia frowned in thought. "Do you remember how in old, old legends, you're never to tell a fae creature your name? There's a power in names, and some things hate hearing their own. Dark magic is one of those—a dark magic spell twists something away from its nature. Being reminded of what it is while it is so perverted causes its destruction." She tapped her mouth. "I'd pay good money to know which word he said—if he named it gold or a ring…but no matter."

"So if you know something's name while it's transformed, you can destroy it?" Jamie asked. "Would that work with the animals?"

"An excellent question, young man, and the answer is that yes, it very well might—*if* you knew the best name to call it. For a living being, that's tricky. It's safer by far to train with the sword." She looked sternly at them. "Either way, it seems Gwyna is up to something dark and I'll not have that in my home. While your friend goes to cut things off at the source, you two can help me protect the village."

Jamie looked at Taigan. *Do we trust her?*

She replied with a tiny nod.

"How do we help you?" the girl asked.

"There are two places of power in the forest nearby," Yulia said, "a wellspring and a maze. Go to both and find out if anyone has conducted rituals there. What you're looking for are candles or lanterns—or candle wax, lamp oil, any of that—the remains of diagrams in charcoal or chalk, the remains of a sacrifice, or anything in gold or silver. Both of those conduct magic, while iron stops it."

Taigan bit her lip. "Um…where in the forest?"

"That's your first test, isn't it?" the woman asked lightly. "Prove to me you can find those places *and* find your way back safely, then I can entrust you with larger tasks."

The twins nodded to one another and stood. She drained her tea hastily and her brother inspected his, sniffed, and drank it with a look of relief.

"Now, there's the look of someone who's had Korilla's tea lately," Yulia said with a chuckle. "Were you injured, boy?"

"Yes. Korilla is the innkeeper's wife?"

"Yes. Raised in the steppes. I don't think she speaks a word of common to this day, but I don't need to know her words to know she's a good soul. She heals anyone who comes to her—there's an old magic in those potions, I think."

"You *think*?" he asked. "I had a three-inch puncture wound from that monster and it was gone in a few hours. Of course, she *did* look surprised…"

A strange look settled on Yulia's face. "How strange," she mused. "The odds are, she's not gotten better at magic without realizing it, at least not so late in her life. So that would suggest it's the herbs…or in the air. The water, mayhap?" She shook her head and stood. "You two go and find the wellspring and the maze. I have plenty to search for here while you're gone."

With surprising speed, they were hustled outside and stood in the sunlight, gaping at one another and their surroundings.

"Prima," Jamie said finally, "do you think *you* can help us?"

"You can at least determine where the forest is, right?"

"That part we got, thank you," he said, his tone prickly. Indeed, the forest took up half the horizon, green and sunlit from there, and perhaps a quarter of a mile behind Yulia's house.

Taigan snorted. "He's right, though," she told Prima. "It's a very big forest."

"Yes, but remember what she said. Showing that you can navigate the forest and keep yourselves safe shows that you have the skill to be given more challenging assignments."

"Okay, but *you* remember that if we—"

Taigan touched Jamie's arm as they set off for their destination. "She's made her decision," she said. "And what's the worst that happens?"

"We *die.*"

"Don't be dramatic. We wander around lost for a little while and the team pulls us out of the simulation. In all likelihood? We wander around for a little while, get lost, find a way out, and don't find anything useful." She shrugged. "And I think the best way to do this is to not get lost in the first place."

The twins bickered good-naturedly about markings and counting measures as they walked to the forest, and by the time they reached it, they had come up with a series of symbols to mark their route. They had decided to mark trees with the choice they made—turning in one direction, going straight, or doubling back. They would mark both their angle of approach and the way they had left.

Soon enough, they passed from the sunlight into the dappled shade of the forest's edge. Younger trees stood with more space between them, leaves rustled under their feet, and birds called from somewhere beyond. Taigan was glad to see that even in the deepest parts of the forest, there was still a good deal of light.

"I hope the trees in here aren't alive," she said as she carved some symbols into one of them.

"You know how trees work, right?"

She rolled her eyes at the sky while Jamie snickered. "Yes, thank you. I only meant if they were sentient or something. I don't want to piss them off."

The twins ventured through dips that contained ice-cold streams and over hillocks that left their palms dirty and their lungs burning. On more than one occasion, one of them tumbled and stifled a yelp. They kept their noise to a minimum, however, not wanting to draw the attention of whatever might be lurking there.

Thankfully, Taigan tripped over the first marker or they would have missed it. She hissed in through her teeth and hopped on her other foot, clutching her wounded toes. When Jamie looked back, she pointed and let him inspect while she eased her foot out of her boot to inspect it.

"It's old," he said finally in a low tone. "And covered in lichen and all that. Come look at it."

She muttered as she stooped to see. The marker was covered with runes, although they were difficult to read under the lichen. No two sides of the four-sided stone seemed to be the same.

Finally, she shrugged. They had no idea how to read it. All they could do was look for more of them.

"Ah-hem."

"What?" they whispered in unison.

"I can translate things."

"I thought you weren't helping," Taigan replied waspishly.

"I can translate things."

"Okay, what does it say?" Jamie asked.

"On the side Taigan stubbed her toe on, it says 'Ahead, lies protection.' Moving clockwise, the other sides read first, "Seek the haven," next, "For that alone is yours," and finally, "Greed will doom you."

"Huh." The girl folded her arms. "So it wants us to continue this way for protection…"

"But not look for anything else," Jamie finished. "Do you think it's the maze?"

They set off again.

"How would you seek shelter in a maze?" His sister asked reasonably. "It must be something else ahead because—ow! Son of a *bitch*!"

"Hey, another one," he said brightly. "You have a talent for this."

"It was the same toe." She moaned and whimpered slightly. "Okay, Prima, what does *this* godforsaken hunk of rock say?"

"The same things," the AI said promptly.

"Right." Taigan set off again once she'd snatched a stick up to thrust ahead of her in the undergrowth. This tactic caught the next stone before she tripped over it. "Ha!"

"So, we've thrown caution to the winds, I see." Jamie looked up. "Prima, is this one the same?"

"This one has no markings."

"Curiouser and curiouser," he said. He pushed through the undergrowth nearby and caught his breath. "Taigan, be *careful*."

She moved cautiously to his side and saw immediately what he had meant. They stood at the top of the wall that surrounded the maze. Four feet down, the maze itself was lined with stone walls that used no mortar and yet seemed entirely untouched by time. There were no weeds or uneven ground.

The entire location seemed to exist in a bubble.

"Protection," Taigan said softly. "Do we dare go in, do you think? What if we can't get out?"

"I think it'll be fine as long as we don't look for more," Jamie said. "They must mean searching for artifacts or something, right?"

"But we're looking for information," she said. "What if we lift something up or move it and a trap comes down?"

They looked at each other, then at the sky.

"I have no idea," Prima said, absolutely unconvincing in her innocence.

"Of course, you don't," the girl muttered. "Well, we were sent to find the maze and we're here. I'd say that Yulia would have warned us if we couldn't get out, but maybe that was part of the test. Let's walk along the edge and see what we can see inside, then go in if we don't see anything worrying."

"Good call." He nodded.

They walked carefully around the edge, careful to never let their arms swing into the air above the maze. It was a strange kind of protection, Taigan thought, without any roof or high walls, and yet, it seemed frozen in time without even leaves on the ground.

Which made the sacrifice all the more apparent once they saw it. She clapped a hand over her mouth and stopped dead.

From where she stood to the center of the maze was one long line. If you didn't follow the pattern of steps, you could have stepped easily over the tiny stone wall as the layer around the center was only a couple of inches tall.

Taigan didn't think they should do that. Although she couldn't say why, she was utterly *sure* that she should follow the path.

She was also sure that several dead animals lay inside separate diagrams at the center of the maze.

"This is what we were looking for, wasn't it?" She looked at Jamie. "Come on. Stick to the path and *don't* pick anything up."

CHAPTER SEVENTY

Taigan had feared the smell of the bodies, but whatever kept things from being touched by time or lichen or rain in this area had also stopped the sacrifices from decaying. The three bodies lay still and the tiny amounts of blood they saw had not dried. There were no flies or maggots.

Somehow, that was more unsettling.

Worse—as they saw each time the path brought them close—was the fact that the three bodies were of young animals. She had her suspicions of what they would see, but when at last they came into the heart of the maze and she could be certain, she wanted to cry.

"A wolf cub," she said quietly.

"And a kitten—a bobcat, maybe?" Jamie asked. "And..."

She stared at the pile of fur, her expression almost a mask that showed no emotion. "I think it's a bear," she said finally. Her voice was thin and high. "The things we saw—the monsters—we couldn't tell if they were cats, wolves, or bears. I think they're all three."

"This was where she made the spell," he whispered in reply. "And it won't decay..."

The twins looked at one another.

"We shouldn't touch anything," Taigan said, but there was no certainty in her.

"This is wrong," he said fiercely. "They deserve a burial."

"What if we make it worse? What if we don't undo the spell?" She stared at them and fumbled to clutch his hand. "I want to destroy all of this, but what if I simply make it worse?"

Her brother looked around. "We have to assume this was all deliberate," he said finally. "Whoever did this—probably Gwyna—chose a place where the diagrams would be untouched and the bodies wouldn't be disturbed. The diagrams are here, which means they're important, so we should destroy those. Look here."

He took her hand and led her to one side of a diagram. The symbol there had been dug a little deeper than the rest of it and something seemed to glitter beneath it—energy, disturbed and raw like an open wound.

"Okay," Taigan said. She nodded. "We need to bring the bodies out and dig them graves, and also destroy the diagrams."

"Diagrams first," Jamie said. He drew his sword and looked up. "Uh…if anything is watching, we're not trying to take anything that belongs to the maze. We're trying to heal it."

He placed the tip of the sword at the outer edge of one diagram and drew a line through it to the center. At first, it seemed remarkably anticlimactic.

A second later, a blast of energy hurled him off his feet.

"Jamie!"

"Ow," he protested and followed it with a startled yelp. The little wolf cub had scrambled to its feet and now snapped and growled at him.

Taigan hauled him up and out of the way. She knelt and stretched her hands out. "We're not going to hurt you," she said.

The little wolf stared at them. Blood trickled down its fur now. It backed away warily, and when they did not follow, it turned and raced into the maze.

"They're alive," she whispered. "Quick, give me the sword."

"Maybe only one of us should have concussions," her brother

suggested. He stood and put out the sword again. "Although maybe give me something to wrap around my head."

She wound her cloak around his head like a turban, giggled, and stood nearby with her arms out as he drew a line across the second diagram. Again, energy released itself in a blast and he slammed back into her arms, but the two of them together managed to stay standing.

"Only one more," she said encouragingly.

"Yep." Jamie shook his head to clear it. "Are your ears ringing? Mine are. Okay, get behind me again. Three, two…ow, fuck."

Taigan snickered into his turban. She levered him to the ground and looked at the little animals that hauled themselves up. The tiny bobcat chirped piteously, then hissed, and the bear growled low in its throat. Like the wolf, they both ran from the humans.

That was probably a fair instinct, she had to admit.

When they were gone, she knelt and hesitated. She didn't want to put her bare skin on the spell but somehow, the thought seemed right. Cautiously, she started with the edges and brushed the dirt smooth and back into place. She took care to erase only one line at a time, and it wasn't long before the first diagram was completely gone.

To her shock, the ground looked as if it had never been touched at all.

Heartened, she repeated the process. The area seemed healed and a spark of energy against her palm startled her but wasn't unpleasant.

"Hey," Jamie said, surprised, "my head feels better."

Taigan stood and brushed her pants off. She nodded and looked around worriedly. "I think we should go. She might come back to see why the spell was lost."

"Right." He moved to step over the little wall.

"The *right* way, you heathen."

They hurried out of the maze and glanced around at every opportunity to see if anyone was watching. No one seemed to be. There were a couple of drops of blood where the animals must have run, but the fact that there was only one way through the maze seemed to have led all three of the sacrifices out.

"Imagine how evil you'd have to be to use animals that way,"

Taigan said fiercely. "Little animals—babies—and she kept them alive and in pain this whole time, suspended between life and death."

Jamie looked soberly at her. "And Ben is walking into that. I'm worried about him. Prima, can you warn him?"

"That is kind of you," Prima said after a pause. *"I attempt to not give players information they have not seen with their own eyes, but...I will consider it."*

"I think that's the best we'll get out of her," he told his sister. "Do think about it, Prima. He needs to understand that this is...a little different than we thought. It's not merely hurting people. It's worse."

"Do humans honestly think of hurting animals as worse than hurting humans?"

"It's complicated," Taigan said. "But torturing baby animals? Yeah, that's bad."

"I see."

Privately, the girl wondered if Prima had accidentally created a villain who was much more villainous than she had intended, but she didn't ask. The AI tended to be very self-conscious about instances of messing up.

They had barely stepped into the forest when they heard a crashing noise and the whimpering sounds of someone in great pain. Both twins froze, and when she wanted to dash forward, her brother clamped a hand around her wrist. He held a finger up to his lips and the two of them found hiding places behind trees.

It wasn't long before the source of the noise became clear—a human, gaunt and delirious, stumbled through the woods in ragged clothing.

"No, no, no..." He moaned. There was blood on his teeth.

And a gold ring on his finger.

Jamie and Taigan looked at one another and he gestured emphatically for her to stay in hiding. The man stumbled on, oblivious and paranoid by turns. He seemed confused and yet to have some awareness of where he was.

When he was gone, she crept out and motioned for her brother to follow.

"What are you doing?" he mouthed at her.

She held a finger to her lips and gestured for him to follow. He scowled but couldn't stop her without making a scene so simply complied.

The man thrust through briars and tripped over downed trees. He pushed himself to his feet each time he fell and continued. His strength seemed, however, like the fevered thrashings of a seriously ill patient overlying a deep weariness that might claim him at any moment.

Taigan's hatred for Gwyna grew with every step. Torturing young animals, taking the poor and sick for her experiments...she needed to be stopped. She was furious now that Yulia hadn't let them go with Ben. While she had never particularly liked the feeling of killing their various adversaries—beyond the fact that she didn't want to die and was being attacked—she was very sure she would enjoy killing the sorceress.

That thought scared her so much that she stopped dead in her tracks and Jamie ran into her with a muffled exclamation. They crouched in the undergrowth in case the man had heard them.

"Are you okay?" Her brother's voice was barely audible.

"Yes, I...yes." She shook her head. "Later."

She had been faced with any number of choices over the years and those had been painful, but all of them had dealt with what she wanted if something happened to her medically. She had never, even in her wildest dreams, imagined being faced with a choice like this.

It had simply never occurred to her to wonder if a side of her might enjoy killing someone. It wasn't merely unpleasant or unwelcome, it was an utter shock.

When they caught up with the man, he had come to a camp of sorts. In reality, it could hardly be called that and at first glance, it was horrifying. Bones and blood were everywhere, the bones twisted and shattered, and the people among them had blood on their mouths.

But they had been wolves when this happened, she realized. She and Jamie had undone the spell, stripping away the qualities of each animal when they freed the sacrifices, and the spell that had turned these people into monsters had disintegrated.

Now they were human, and they were weak and still in pain.

She wanted to help them, but this time, it was cowardice that held her back. These people still wore Gwyna's rings and the gold bit into the flesh. Even if they were no longer monsters, who could say if they would attack others on sight?

Taigan backed away quietly and motioned for Jamie to do so as well. They crept away into the forest and followed the trail of broken branches and their signs out of the forest. By mutual and silent agreement, they did not seek out the wellspring yet.

They had learned enough already that Yulia should know about.

They were close to the edge of the forest when her brother said, his voice subdued, "What do you think that maze was?"

She looked at him in surprise. "How do you mean?"

"Well, they said protection could be anyone's if they wanted it, but not to look for anything else," he said. "That's interesting. Was there a trapdoor into a tomb full of artifacts, Indiana Jones-style, or was it only the magic they didn't want people to touch? If so, why didn't Gwyna bite it?" His tone softened. "I think it's nice that...it's, like, they built it for something else but they also made it a haven for anyone."

"I hadn't thought of that," she responded thoughtfully. "I suppose it's the only place where those animals would have survived. She found a way to turn that into something dark, but..." She shook her head. "Back there, what scared me was that I thought I'd enjoy killing her. I don't like thinking like that."

He looked at her and moved closer to wrap an arm around her shoulders. The noonday sunlight was bright outside the forest, and they approached the edge quickly.

They walked in silence for a while before he said, "I've been thinking about this."

"Yeah?"

"I used to think that even having dark thoughts was a bad sign, then I wondered—well, it was after the monster attacked us. For some reason, the jackalopes didn't feel real, but that one did. I wondered if it was wrong for us to have killed it. And I think there are gradations to the things you do. You were protecting me when you did that. You wanting to kill Gwyna is the same thing. It's not because you're a terrible person. You want her to stop doing terrible things."

Taigan scrunched her face dubiously.

Jamie shook her slightly. "What I'm saying is I don't think you're a homicidal maniac. I think you have to see below what's driving that urge to kill her and follow *that*."

"Oh. You're smart sometimes, you know that?"

"I wouldn't go that far," Prima interjected.

"Hey!" Jamie protested and looked at the sky. Both he and Taigan snickered as they hurried to Yulia's house.

CHAPTER SEVENTY-ONE

Ben reappeared in the world of PIVOT lying under a tree and staring through the leaves at the midday sun. He blinked, sat, and looked around.

"Welcome back," Prima said.

"Thanks. Um...which way am I supposed to go?"

"Downhill."

"Thank you." He stood with a groan. "And thanks for cleaning my clothes. That inn wasn't exactly great on the cleanliness front."

"It's not entirely altruistic," Prima admitted. *"Remember, I also have to smell you."*

He guffawed.

"Less loud talking. You'll look like the village crazy person."

"Oh, right." He kept his voice low but couldn't keep from whistling, however, when he came around the bend and saw the lake spread below him. "Now *that* is gorgeous."

"Note to self—humans find lakes aesthetically pleasing."

"Leave it to you to suck the fun out of something," he muttered. "Okay, now I have to find the path to the caves." He took time to examine the path as it wound down. "Up from the shore, do you think, or should I try to climb down from the cliffs? No, don't answer. You'll only be vague."

"You know me so well," she said contentedly.

"Yeah, yeah." Ben shook his head. "Okay, so. Up first, I think." He detoured from the path and along the top of the cliffs before he edged closer to peer down. It wasn't possible to see where the caves were from there. A few shadows looked likely but overhangs of rock cast too many shadows. The caves could be anywhere.

It looked like the shoreline was the best place to start and then to work his way up. He descended the path slowly and carefully and made sure to savor the view of the lake. An inner sense suggested that this view would be tainted soon, exactly as the temple in Heffog was now tainted. He would tangle with enemies there and all the beauty would fade into those memories of strife.

At the lakeshore, he found a fairly wide path and proceeded along it. Once in a while, the ground faded into mud or wet rocks but there was usually enough space to walk comfortably and look at the cliffs at the same time.

It wasn't long before he located the path. Whether someone else would have seen it, he wasn't sure, but he was accustomed to scanning strange rock faces for hand and footholds. He saw at once that there was space to move along and that the trail led to a small and cleverly shaded opening in the rock.

Once he'd identified it, he couldn't imagine how he had missed it. It must be a spell of some kind, designed to make the eye pass over it.

Ben headed up the slope and hoisted himself onto the path, such as it was. Now that he was there, it was quite precarious. He didn't have enough space to put both feet beside one another and resorted to edging along.

He had covered most of the distance before he saw the woman watching him. Startled, he did a double-take and narrowly avoided falling off the path, which was good as it was quite a long way down at this point. He clung to the rock face for a moment with his heart pounding, but he relaxed as he looked at her.

Yulia had described Gwyna as being nothing special to look at and from that description, he could only assume that either the old woman had very high standards or that this was not Gwyna. Her strawberry-blonde hair was held back in a rough braid and strands escaped around her face. From her high cheekbones to her full mouth and long-lashed dark eyes, she was gorgeous.

She also looked very frightened. He hurried his progress along the ledge and finally stepped off.

"Ah...hello."

She pressed her lips together for a moment and looked nervously behind her.

"You shouldn't go in there," she said.

"Why?" he asked.

"The witch," she told him fiercely. She looked like she might cry. "She's evil."

"Evil?" Ben looked behind her. Alarms resounded in his head but he couldn't be sure why. "Tell me what's going on." He tapped the sword at his belt. "I'll be right here to help if anyone comes out of there, okay?"

He thought she would say no, but another look over her shoulder seemed to convince her that no one was following. She sighed, sat on a nearby boulder, and took her time before speaking.

"She's a monster," she said finally. "She's cruel and she only wants to hide people away. She wants to keep us locked in there."

He leaned nearby. It was hard to not get sucked in by the view, but he knew he needed to focus.

And not on how pretty the woman was either.

"Did you seek her out to train you in magic?" he asked finally.

"Yes." She looked at him. "It's why you're here, too, isn't it?"

"Yes." He showed her the iron ring. "A...friend...uh, acquaintance told me I would hurt someone if I didn't get trained."

"Well, don't let *her* train you," the girl said angrily. "She'll hide you away and make you her servant. I had to sweep floors and carry buckets of water and..." She looked at him suddenly, her eyes wide. "You said you'd help me if she followed me. You should come with me.

You shouldn't go there anyway and you can keep me safe on the road."
Wide brown eyes looked appealingly at him.

The alarms in his head raged at full blast now, and it was probably
good that they were because he had a difficult time listening to them.
He cleared his throat a few times.

His purpose was to stop Gwyna and he couldn't do that if he ran
away with a pretty girl.

"Ah…I don't mean to be rude," he said, "but I need to be trained.
There isn't anywhere else for me to go. I can't take the chance of
hurting someone."

"You could simply wear the ring," she told him.

"It's…too much of a chance." He needed to come up with some
reason for her to leave him here. He gave her a little smile. "And I
don't mind sweeping or carrying water. I only want to know how to
control my powers so that I don't hurt anyone. I heard someone
talking about a sorceress and after a while, someone mentioned the
lake. It looks like it was true—she *is* here—and I haven't heard of
anyone else who could train me."

She looked angrily at him. "You shouldn't go in. Why don't you
believe me about her? She'll make you work like an animal all day
long."

Now, Ben was truly annoyed. "I'm no stranger to hard work," he told
her coldly. "I'm not afraid of it. Hard work has brought me to where I
am in my life. I expect that training in magic will also be difficult. It is
necessary, though, and if Gwyna is the only one who can train me and
she needs help with hauling water or chopping firewood, then I'll do it."

The girl folded her arms and pouted prettily at him for a moment
before her beautiful features dissolved and rearranged themselves
into another face entirely. The woman who raised an eyebrow at him
was, indeed, not particularly noteworthy in the looks department. Her
hair was more dun-colored than strawberry-blonde, her eyes were
smaller and not as long-lashed, her mouth was less full, and her
cheekbones not so high.

"Interesting," she told him.

He sighed. "Gwyna, I presume?"

"The same." She raised one shoulder. "And you aren't jesting about your friend, although I wonder who you could know who saw power but did not know how to train you."

"I was shipwrecked and came to ground in Heffog," he said tightly. "I met a half-elf who saw the magic but assumed I knew how to use it. He told me to find training and a few whispers led me here." Not wanting her to think she was easy to find, he added, "But I've been around quite a few lakes at this point. I was close to giving up."

All he could hope was that she couldn't read minds.

"Hmm." Gwyna studied him. "Wants to study, determined, not easily turned by a pretty face or the threat of hard work...you *might* do." Suddenly, her gaze sharpened and she stepped close. Her fingers caught his chin. "Tell me what you want," she commanded, her voice low and melodic.

Simple surprise compelled Ben to answer honestly. "Not to be trapped in my own body."

Surprise flitted across her face and was gone in an instant. She stepped back and stared curiously at him. "You're telling the truth, aren't you? Curious." She shrugged. "Well, then, come along if you want to study."

She turned and walked toward the cave opening.

Ben hesitated for only a moment before he followed her. He didn't know if she believed him about any of it, but he had to try. If Gwyna was creating monsters out of vulnerable people and weaving spells to trap minds, he needed to stop her.

"You don't have a horse, do you?" she called from the darkness.

"I...no." He hurried after her. "Do you need one?"

"I merely wanted to know if you were traveling on foot," she said. "Strange things have happened in the web of magic recently and I'm trying to place you."

"Ah. No, no horse. Or cart or anything. I walked."

"Then it seems there are two people wandering around with magical talents," she said lightly, although her voice did not seem pleased at all. "Perhaps the other will come to join us as well."

He tried to keep his face blank as he nodded but all he could think was that whoever this person was, they should stay away. Whatever they had done, whether it was do something she didn't approve of or use more magic than she had, she did not like them.

It was a good reminder for him, too.

CHAPTER SEVENTY-TWO

The thwack of sticks reverberated through the area as Jamie and Taigan locked in a battle. The twins circled, their gazes fixed on one another, and each of them held a gnarled branch. They were panting by now, stripped to a single layer of clothing and still sweaty in the last of the day's heat.

It had been the better part of three hours since they finished explaining what they saw to Yulia, and she had turned them out of the house while she did some spells. She seemed more troubled than upset, which they quietly agreed was more unnerving.

They had filled the time since then with sparring. Jamie maintained that with a staff much longer than his sword, Taigan should be able to keep him at a distance. Whether she should or not, she wasn't sure.

She couldn't do it yet, though.

"I'm not good at this," she called to him. "My strength is offense, not defense."

"You'll have to learn both," he countered and danced in with a downward slash.

This time, she attacked at the same moment. A swing of her stick knocked the shorter one out of his hand and he stumbled back with a curse.

"See?" she said. "Attack. Offense. It's what works for me."

Jamie gave her a disgruntled look. "Your technique depends on people being so scared and overwhelmed by your tactic that they don't fight back. Someday, someone will fight and you'll be up shit creek without a paddle."

Taigan wrinkled her nose at him. She didn't want to concede that he was right but she had to admit he had a point. That was the problem with having a twin. They saw far too much about you and tended to have unnervingly, *annoyingly* accurate assessments.

"Again," he said. He stood, panting, while she retrieved both the sticks. "And this time, focus on where I'm trying to hit and how you could dodge or redirect my power."

Despite her groan, she nodded. They squared off again and started after a countdown. This time, she circled the other way.

"Am I supposed to follow the footwork?" she called.

"Once you know the defensive strikes." Jamie wiped the sweat out of his eyes. "The footwork *does* tell you where they'll go, but unless you know how to block, you won't do much good."

"Bah," she said under her breath.

When the door opened behind them, she turned to look and caught a thwack across the side of the head. She sprawled and Jamie uttered a terrified yelp.

"Taigan! Oh, God...Mom and Dad will *kill* me—"

"I'm all right," she said muzzily from the ground.

"I'm so sorry." He sounded miserable. "*So* sorry, Taigan, and we'll wait as long as we have to while you recover—"

"Young man," Yulia said with the air of someone rolling her eyes, "your sister is fine, and she has learned a valuable lesson about distractions during combat. Isn't that right, young lady?"

"Uh-huh." She rubbed the side of her face and winced. "Will I have a bruise?"

The woman shrugged in a way that said she didn't care in the slightest. "You'll both want to come inside. I have something for you."

They followed her, Taigan walking gingerly and Jamie trotting alongside her with a pained look on his face. When they entered the cottage, he made sure she sat and fussed over her until Yulia rapped his hand with a wooden spoon.

"Focus, young man."

His sister snickered but not too loudly. She didn't want to get thwacked, after all.

The workbench had been tidied, but the heavy smell of herbs in the air and the faint hint of charcoal on the wood showed that she had been doing spells. Two necklaces were there, both with an amulet that looked a little odd.

"Is this mud?" Jamie asked and picked it up.

"In the future, don't simply pick things up off a witch's workbench," Yulia advised. "And, yes, it is. It's not only crystals and precious metals that can focus spells. One that's particularly useful at times is to take the water and earth of a specific place to make a protection spell. It only protects you when you're there, of course, but for this, you'll only be in one place."

She handed one of the necklaces to Taigan and the other to Jamie. Both twins put them on, and the girl fought the suspicion that this was some kind of prank. As far as she could tell, it was merely a necklace with a hunk of mud—although it didn't seem to be disintegrating.

"The forest will protect you as if you are part of it," Yulia told them. "It's not foolproof, so don't be stupid, but people will be less likely to notice you. The webwork of spells in the forest will protect you as if you're one of the trees—heal you quicker and give you more acute senses. That doesn't mean you should take a knife to the heart, but a regular fight won't tire you so quickly, nor a regular wound do so much damage."

Taigan nodded.

"I've tried to divine Gwyna's purpose," the old woman told them, "but I can see nothing in the smoke. It might have helped me to see the spells she wove around the animals, but...no matter."

The twins exchanged looks.

"Should we not have worn them away?" he asked.

"No, you did right." She nodded and the rare praise came through gruffly. "It shows a good heart to want to do right by the animals and courage to cut through the spell—not to mention that you did it smartly. The two of you together have good heads on your shoulders, although I'm not so sure I'd trust either of you with this on your own."

Taigan, who had grown used to the little snipes, only smiled slightly.

"But that's the young, I suppose," Yulia said. "In any case, I need the two of you to find me something at the well. It's farther into the forest in what's known as the Black Heart."

"That sounds..." Jamie looked at his sister.

"Nonsense made up by the superstitious." She waved a dismissive hand. "And it's best not to have many of those at the well as it's a magical place, but there's no danger in the Black Heart. The forest grows close there, and dark. The legend is that the dark elves went there to capture dreams, even at high noon. Back when there *were* dark elves, of course. There aren't many of them left and none in this forest. The well is their legacy—and the maze."

"What is the maze for?" Jamie asked.

"No one knows. No one knows about the well, either, although it has magic in abundance—and that's what I'm sending you for. Gwyna harnessed the power of the maze for pain and torment, and I must know if she's tried to do the same at the well. If yes, follow your best judgment to dismantle anything she left."

"Can we touch the well?" Taigan asked.

"You should be able to, although I wouldn't swim in it. The real danger comes if you try to draw power from it—which I'll ask you to do."

"I, uh..." She looked at Jamie, then at Yulia.

"There are stones in the well," the woman told them briskly. "They hold some of the well's power but more than that, they hold some of its signature—the mark of the forest. It's difficult to explain but necessary to harness its power."

"And it's dangerous to pick them up," he clarified.

"It can be, yes, so I've made this spell for you to recite before you attempt it." She handed them a slip of paper. Syllables were written out, some emphasized with an underline. "Try saying that. The girl first."

She made them both repeat it, time after time, until she was satisfied.

"What does it say?" Taigan asked.

"It tells the forest that you are doing my bidding," Yulia explained. "It tells it, too, that you were the ones who freed the animals at the maze. It says you are not seeking power for yourselves but instead, to help many to stand in the way of a threat. It is the kind of thing a forest likes—the image of humans standing together like a grove. Not to mention that it is true, and the forest values that."

The girl hesitated. "What if it hurts us?"

"It will make it clear if it does not want you to touch it," the woman said dryly. "That, I can assure you. Try the speech again if so, but if it will not allow you, come back."

"Right." Taigan folded the piece of paper and put it in the pouch at her waist. "Should we go now?"

"Tomorrow morning."

"Is the forest not safe at night?" Jamie asked worriedly.

"It's as safe as it is during the day," Yulia said with surprising patience, "but humans are a damned sight more jumpy at night, and the last thing I need is one of you doing something stupid. You'll stay here, have a proper breakfast, and set out with the day."

Taigan nodded. She found herself wracked by indecision and she was not sure why. "Why are you helping us?" she asked finally, the words bursting out of her.

The woman looked at her for a long moment. Then, she moved closer to smooth her hair back and stare deeply into her eyes. "Because you have a strange, muddled idea of what a hero is," she said finally. Her voice was gentle. "All your life, dreaming of being someone else, someone who wasn't tied to a place, half a world away already in your heart so you could shed the ties more easily when the time came."

She trembled, her face caught between the woman's hands.

"If you're to heal," Yulia told her, "you must bring yourself home. You must see what it is to be a hero and be one for the right reasons. You have the instincts and the courage, girl, but unless you're fighting for something, you'll heal but only for your life to be wasted."

CHAPTER SEVENTY-THREE

Ben followed Gwyna into the shadowy interior of the caves. Once his eyes adjusted to the gloom, he could see there was a good deal of light. This filtered from cracks in the rock above to light the hallways and caverns and dust danced in the shafts of light.

It was impossible to forget that someone lived there. Tiny alcoves in the rock had been fixed with candles, and all the tiny traces of dust that came from human living were visible—threads, bits of grass, and a few now-dried, muddy footprints from a wet day. From somewhere ahead, he could hear the crackle of a fire and smell food—nothing fancy, but enough to make his stomach grumble. It was homier than he had expected.

He was surprised, therefore, when they rounded a corner and came into a cavern with no light of its own and—in the dim glow from the hallway—not a single piece of furniture or scrap of decoration.

Behind him, stone scraped on stone and everything descended into blackness.

A wave of fear washed over him, cold and then hot. Did she know the truth? Did she bring him there to kill him? He drew his sword without thinking.

Laughter echoed in the small room. "You think a sword will keep me at bay?" Between her moving and the echo of her voice off every stone wall, he could not tell where she was.

Ben didn't answer her. Every sense was turned toward locating her and moving as quietly as he could in the meantime. He didn't know what powers her magic gave her. Could she see in the dark? He would have to find out.

It was something of an unsettling thought and he wasn't sure what he'd do about it if he did find out, but a tiny scuff from his left told him that was where she was. He turned in that direction and backed slowly away.

He reminded himself mentally to deny everything before he opened his mouth. "You've trapped me here with you. Why?"

"Why do you think?" She was enjoying this, that much was clear.

What would someone say if they had come searching for a teacher?

"You aren't truly a witch at all, are you?" he asked. He could feel himself splitting in two—the part that needed to stay separate and watch all this unfold and the part that descended into the character of the scared apprentice mage. "You lure people here to kill them and you hate people who have magic." He shook his head. "But I saw you transform. I don't understand."

She was close to him and he felt her warmth and her hands as they pushed the sword aside and traveled up his chest and down his arms.

"Try again," she whispered in his ear. "What else might I want?"

Ben was standing stock still when her fingers reached his hands. With one quick twist, she slid the iron ring off him and was gone again with a light laugh.

"Let's see who you are," Gwyna said. "Truly—when the iron chains are gone. Fight me. Prove you're worthy of being here."

Her first blast of magic caught him in the chest. It was a blaze of flame that spread to coat his skin. He flailed and yelled. The sword heated in his hands until he could no longer hold it. He threw it aside with a curse and cried out as he slapped at the flames that would not stop spreading.

Unlike the sword, the flames weren't hot. He held a hand up to look at them flickering on them and frowned when they disappeared in the next moment. The room was pitch-dark once again.

"So you can distinguish between a true threat and an illusion," Gwyna said. "It's the first test, and the easiest one—and know this, apprentice. Most do not survive their training."

The next spell she threw at him went through his chest like a spear, so real in its sensation that he cried out and pressed his hands to a wound that did not exist. His hands patted the flesh repeatedly and pressed against his sternum. He could still feel where the spear had traveled and he feared that he was bleeding internally.

What was happening was slower—a creep of cold that spread through each bone. His teeth chattered and his torso seized with shudders. He bent to grasp the sword and could barely do so. His fingers were cold as well and could not close easily. He stumbled and fell, and his unprotected fingers closed around the blade instead of the hilt. Panicked, he screamed.

"You want a blade to fight me?" Gwyna said contemptuously. "Fight me with *magic*."

"I don't know how to use magic!" He cradled his fingers to his chest. Were they bleeding? He couldn't tell and the darkness made it difficult to know where any of his body was. "I told you, I've never used it."

"You should use it now," she warned him. "If you don't end the spell, you'll be dead in a few minutes."

He could believe it. It hurt so badly. Muscles seized and jumped. His fingers ached dully. "I...don't know how." His voice was rough and guttural from pain.

"There's no *how* to it, apprentice—open the floodgates and save your damned life!"

"I don't know *how*!" Ben yelled. Rage threatened to erupt and he clamped it down. "I came here for training and you're...you're..." His teeth chattered too hard for him to make out words.

"You were so close." There was a swell of warmth behind him.

"The power was there. Reach for it, I can see it like a tidal wave inside you."

How did she expect him to do this without any training? He was angry again. Right now, he could not remember a time when he had not been angry. He could remember the turn of every job and every relationship, the constant frustrations, and the way he had tried to stick it out while the anger spread like a fire through every part of his life.

"Open the door and let me go. I won't be your apprentice."

"That door opens when you prove yourself, one way or another." There was no give in her voice. "You show me that you can be my apprentice, or you show me that you're too weak-willed and dangerous to be alive, and I take care of the problem. Show me your answer."

"Let me go!" He had found the place where the door should be and he drove his body against it with all the force he could summon. The rock was surely an illusion, but it didn't feel like one. His shoulder exploded in pain and he hissed through his teeth as the motion jarred his injured fingers against the hilt of the sword.

She said nothing and he felt as if he were drowning in rage. This was *not* where it would end. It couldn't be.

But how was he supposed to keep that from happening? He slid down the wall with tears of anger trickling from his eyes and down his cheeks in little lines of fire. He was dying, but his anger would keep him warm while he did.

All that anger, always trying to outrun it, and in the end, it was the only thing left with him. He could see that now. Whatever you devoted your life to, that was what was there at the end.

The chill was everywhere—so cold that it didn't even feel cold anymore. He had the sense that he should be dead, and maybe he was. The only place that hurt was around the core of him, at the barrier between cold and hot, magic and anger.

Could anger fight magic?

His eyes opened into the darkness. *You were so close.* That was what Gwyna had said.

What if his anger *was* magic?

The fury welled inside him, burning hot—the tidal wave she had mentioned—and it took all his courage not to run from it. For his entire life, he had turned his back on the things that made him angry. He didn't want to be angry.

It had never occurred to him that he could *channel* it. What he was doing now—getting close to using the anger—seemed wrong to him on every level.

On the other hand, he would never have a better opportunity. If the worst happened—if he lost control entirely—the only person he would hurt was the one who turned vulnerable people into monsters.

Also, she would kill him if he didn't use his magic. He shouldn't forget that part.

Ben took one more breath into his aching lungs and let the power loose in a flood.

Heat and light burst through the room. It was as bright as sunlight and as forceful as magma. It couldn't hurt him, not his own power, but he heard Gwyna cry out. In that one, euphoric moment, he even found it in himself to hope that he had done it. If she was dead, there would be no more wondering and no more worrying.

The conflagration cleared, however, to show her still standing. The waves of energy beat against a shield she had made for herself. She regarded him through narrowed eyes, her arms folded, and tapped one set of fingers against the other arm.

"So you *can* use it."

"I thought it was…something else," he said lamely and thought for a moment. "Although, all things considered, I'm glad I didn't ever let loose with it before."

"Really?" She frowned.

"I could have hurt people." It took a moment for him to remember that his anger wasn't magic in the outside world. He wouldn't have hurt his parents, Mike, or Eve. Still, he was glad he hadn't used the magic in this world, either.

"You would have hurt someone who threatened you," Gwyna said simply. "And then you would be free of your old life, never able to go back. It sounds like a curse but believe me, it's a blessing. So many choose to repress what they are and they waste years trying to conform to a society that will never revere them as it should."

"Uh...huh." Ben was distracted. He poked his body to make sure there wasn't a spear wound. There wasn't, but the cuts on his hands, unfortunately, were real. "Can you heal these?"

"I could but I won't." She raised an eyebrow in the fading light of his spell. "Let it be a lesson to you to not seek out paltry ways of doing things. It might even aid you in learning magic. Some of the most powerful mages are those who society considers weak. They use their powers because they cannot rely on brute force."

He flattened his hand against his chest and watched her as she gestured for the stone to open and allow them into the corridor. The sudden wash of sunlight made his eyes ache.

As he followed her, he thought about Yulia's words. The old witch had said there was nothing particularly noteworthy about her, and he wondered now if that was what made her so dangerous. She wasn't a melodramatic supervillain, hiding in a secret lair and sweeping around in a cape and headdress.

Gwyna was someone who viewed the world entirely logically and from a position of complete self-interest and reverence of magic. She thought it would be better if he had killed his family and come to her on the run because he would then never be tempted to return to a world where he had to hide his powers.

What unsettled him was that she wasn't passionate or unhinged. On the contrary, she spoke after quiet consideration.

That, to him, seemed far more dangerous than monologues and vendettas. A vendetta, at least, bound someone to the world. What was to stop her, however, from deciding tomorrow that all of Heffog should be under her control? She'd already put most of its nobles under her sway, and it would be easy enough to turn their minds away from Kerill's purpose and to her own.

She might do anything without caring who it hurt.

That made him shiver as he followed her.

CHAPTER SEVENTY-FOUR

He woke the next morning, shivering in the dawn air, with a soft coating of dew on his hair and his clothes. Everything was damp. Ben sat with a wince—his neck had a crick in it and his entire back seemed to be sore—and looked around.

It remained unclear whether Gwyna had any other apprentices but he hadn't seen any. He seemed to be the only other person there and he also realized that she did not intend to teach him any magic in short order.

The rest of the day before had been spent hauling water from the lake in two heavy buckets. The task was extraordinarily painful with his injured hand, and when he finally finished and thought to ask why he'd been sent for it, she informed him that she wanted to take a bath.

He'd been treated to a glimpse of her quarters, which were quite luxuriously decorated with expensive carpets and a fire in a magical hearth before she sent him to sweep the kitchens and prepare something for dinner.

Assuming this hardship was part of her priming him for his training, he'd done it with relative goodwill. That had faded considerably when he saw his sleeping quarters—a room of bare rock with no place for a fire and a sliver of open sky showing through the crack in the ceiling. He had only his cloak for a blanket and it was not enough to keep out the night's chill.

Ben knew this was a training tactic. He wasn't entirely stupid, after all.

Despite that, he resented it. He couldn't shake the feeling that Gwyna was more interested in taunting him than she was in training him.

In the kitchen, he took the time to warm his hands while he built the fire. Cooking was a little less onerous than he had assumed it would be as food appeared in the magical pan, but it seemed to require a consistent draw of power that he struggled to maintain and so made the heat flare or die in turn.

The bacon had burned spots by the time he was finished and he was not prepared to remake it. He brought the food to Gwyna's chambers and summoned the last of his good humor when she called him in.

She raised an eyebrow at the condition of the food but said nothing. "I'll need more water today," she said without preamble. "Now."

He gritted his teeth. "I also need to eat."

"There's no time to waste," she said dismissively, but he caught the gleam of her pleasure. She *wanted* to inconvenience him. He decided it was an even bet whether she needed any water at all.

Whatever instinct had seen him through the interaction with the fake runaway the other day, it seemed to be back. He responded with a smile that physically hurt, nodded silently—he couldn't summon a pleasant tone if his life depended on it—and left.

A few slices of bacon were his breakfast, not so bad under other circumstances, but hardly how he wanted to start the morning. He wolfed them and went to get the buckets.

"May I ask a question?" Prima asked. Her tone was unusually somber. *"I don't want to intrude if it's a bad time."*

Ben sighed. "You can ask. Honestly, a distraction would be nice."

"Very well. It seems your physical hardship has impacted your mood negatively."

He waited for the question, then realized that *was* the question. For a moment, he wondered if this was a cruel joke of some kind before he remembered that Prima was often snide and sarcastic, but never—to his knowledge—openly cruel.

"Yes," he said cautiously.

"And that is expected by you? You are not surprised by it?"

"No." He frowned now and tried to think where this might be going. His footsteps crunched over the gravel and rocks of the lakeshore.

"Would that not mean that Gwyna would also anticipate it?"

"She did, yes. It's why she did it." He couldn't keep the bitterness out of his tone as he knelt to dip first one bucket, then the other in the lake.

"I do not understand. She wanted to upset you?"

"Yes." On the one hand, he was annoyed but somehow, describing it this way helped his mood. "Before you ask, I don't know exactly why. Sometimes, difficult living situations are used by teachers who want to impart a certain philosophical mindset to their students. In this case, though…" He thought of Gwyna's warm quarters, her plush bed, and her warm bath. "I think she's doing it to see what will happen when I lose my temper."

"Ah, so you must avoid losing your temper."

"Yes."

Prima considered this. *"Another question if you have time."*

Ben stood and winced when the handle of the bucket pressed against his injured hand. He really shouldn't do two at a time, but the sheer number of trips to the lakeshore otherwise would destroy his legs.

"Shoot," he responded, his tone gruff from the discomfort.

"If situations such as the one you encountered last night negatively affect your mood, wouldn't it mean that many situations do? Lack of sleep, for instance, or hunger?"

He frowned. "Yes. Every situation, one might say. Sometimes, the effect is good—a nice-tasting meal, for instance, or a comfortable bed. In every situation, however, one's surroundings and experiences have an effect on mood. Surely you knew that, though."

"I suppose I did." She sounded troubled. *"Dotty told me she liked baths. I knew that getting things one enjoyed tended to improve one's mood, but I suppose I never saw it as something that changed one's mood all the time in varying ways. Is this why you're always so grumpy when you're injured?"*

"Yes," he said with a smile. "Pain makes someone unhappy. Also, it leaves them feeling like they made a mistake or they couldn't do what they needed to do. Every situation is colored by your emotions and thoughts—and perceptions, of course. A bad moment could feel okay because of the smell of your grandmother's cookies. Or it might make you cry because someone else had baked the cookies and you were reminded of your grandmother, who had passed away."

She made no response.

"Prima?" Ben lugged the water through the tunnels.

"So much data," Prima said finally. If an AI could sound awestruck, this one did. *"I thought humans simply didn't have the processing ability to see all the facets of a situation. Now I see they have far more processing capability than I thought, but much of it is filled with data I didn't see. I'll have to think about this. Would you mind if I went away for a while?"*

"Go ahead," he said as courteously as he could. He would have liked a conversation right now, but he didn't want to interrupt her musings about human nature.

He wondered what it must be like to realize that so much of human behavior hinged on an experience the AI would never have.

"Thank you," Prima said after he had already forgotten what he'd said. *"And if this is a power struggle—which it seems to be—don't let her win it."*

"Mmm." He had less of an idea what game Gwyna was playing and wasn't sure how he could win. Or if he could. "I'll do my best."

"Deny the field of battle."

"Are you quoting *The Art of War*?"

"Yes. You'll have to explain to me how it works as an allegory, though. I understand it is primarily used that way. I extrapolated and thought it might be useful here."

Ben stopped and looked at where the sky would be if he were

outside with a genuine smile. "Thank you, Prima. You're a good friend."

"*I am glad to hear it.*" A distinct note of pleasure came through the words.

When he arrived to dump the buckets of water into Gwyna's bathtub a few minutes later, she was playing with a ball of magic, letting it swirl in her palm and bounce off her fingertips. As he did not know much about magic yet, he guessed from her pose and her expression that this was a truly ostentatious display of power—and that he was intended to ask about it.

But Prima, whether meaning to or not, had given him his path forward. He merely nodded at her and took the buckets out of the room.

He trudged from the lake to the cave innumerable times until his back ached and his injured hand was all but useless. At one point, he had to resort to using only one bucket and his other arm was running out of strength.

At last, he sank onto the floor of the kitchen to rest. He had not been aware of his clumsiness all morning, which was a blessing of sorts, but he could not remember the last time he had been this exhausted. Even when he'd been climbing.

Of course, he'd been in much better shape. His eyes snapped open and he stared at the stone wall with rage and loss fighting each other in his throat.

Ben acknowledged that he had done this to himself. He was broken and he was lost there because he'd made a stupid choice. Worse, he did not know if he would ever recover. Would he be able to climb again, or would he always be limited in the real world? He could come here to remember what it had been like, but that wasn't the same as living in full.

A shadow fell across him and he looked at Gwyna.

"You decided to stop working, I see." She said nothing else but there was a challenge in her tone.

A part of him rose to it—the same anger he had always been afraid of. He wanted to leave this place and run away. It would be like every other time.

Except he was tired of his life going like that. The clarity was sudden and overwhelming. He could choose to not leave when he felt anger. That was a new thought. He could channel the anger, do something good with it, and stay.

He turned his injured hand palm up so that she could see the bandages. "If you heal this, I will be able to help you more effectively."

She smiled, the look of one player to another. "You're not only a traveler," she said quietly. "Not merely a country boy. I thought you were at the start, and I'm rarely wrong—but there's more to you."

Gwyna did not like that, he could see it now. Her mind was racing ahead. If he was not a brute who could be led by his emotion, he was a rational person who might defy her and outwit her. The woman wasn't prepared to train someone to be her rival.

She only trained those she could control.

More clarity seeped into his reasoning. If Prima had told him to deny the field of battle, he would.

"If you say so," he said and pushed to his feet. "Do you want me to heal it myself, then? Am I supposed to learn to heal?"

"You're supposed to remember what happens when you don't use magic," she said at once. "I expect the water filled within the hour. And do try to learn more quickly, will you? I'll need your help in not too long, but untrained power will be too risky to use."

She turned on her heel and left, and he stared after her.

He held a hand out to the bucket and swept his palm up. Nothing happened, but he tried again, and once more after that. A little frustrated, he cleared his mind, swept his hand up, and closed his eyes, picturing the bucket floating in the air.

When he opened his eyes, it *was* floating.

"What happens when I don't use magic," he said quietly. He looked at his hand and rolled his aching shoulders.

Well, that had been considerable effort he could have avoided. He walked to the lake with the bucket bobbing along at his side and brought it back, this time filled with water. It was more difficult, but by the third repetition, he had begun to get the hang of it.

Now the trick was simply to get Gwyna to teach him more than she realized she was teaching.

CHAPTER SEVENTY-FIVE

"Hey." Amber came up to squeeze Jacob's shoulder.

"Hey to you too." He turned with a smile. "I'm finishing up with emails. Maybe thirty minutes left?"

"It works out perfectly. I'll go home, take a quick shower, and meet you for dinner?" She gave him a thumbs-up.

He returned it with a smile and she headed out. They tried not to make a big deal of their relationship at the office, but the truth was that Amber wasn't much of a one for PDA anyway.

That was fine with Jacob. After years of devoting every spare minute to his company, he no longer had any idea what to do with his spare time. He and Amber had made a point to have a weekly date night, but it was a struggle to talk about anything except work.

They only kept doing it because Nick was relentlessly on their case.

Jacob sighed and stretched. The lab was almost empty by now. The outgoing shift of workers had completed their handoff to the incoming team, who were settling with cups of coffee and data entry. A constant stream of data came out of the pods, almost more than they could deal with.

When he heard the click-clack of heels, he looked up. Who he expected, he wasn't sure—but it certainly wasn't Anna Price.

The head of Diatek, Price had gotten into her field after she and her husband were forced to take their daughter off life support. She had vowed to find a new technology that would resuscitate comatose patients, something she knew would require significant amounts of money to get off the ground.

Now, she worked with the Department of Defense, making the money that kept companies like PIVOT going.

If he were honest, he had always been uncomfortable around her. She exuded the very east-coast, expensively-suited vibe that he, as a young entrepreneur, associated with people who had too many lawyers and would take you for everything you were worth.

He probably wasn't far off from how Price would behave if he got on her bad side, which made it doubly difficult to remember that she was in this business for good reason.

And he always felt obscurely guilty that he was saving patients under her nose—that she was watching, over and over again, the recovery her daughter had never had.

Tonight, he assumed, she was there to talk to him about Ben. He tapped a stack of printouts. "Ben worked through a few of the job postings before he went back in, but not all of them. We kept him busy with tests, I'm afraid."

"That's no trouble." As always, she managed to put the correct inflection in her voice and somehow also convey no emotion at all. "Mr. Ainsworth is a talented chemist with a great deal of work ethic. I believe he would have found a job with or without my intervention. I am simply offering my help."

"I'm…sure he appreciates it." Jacob had begun to get the sense that she was there to talk about something else. He took his courage in both hands and asked, "Is there anything else I can do for you?"

"Yes." Her gaze was clear. "I wanted to speak to you about Prima."

The bottom fell out of his stomach. He swallowed and he knew she noticed it.

There was no point in denying anything. If she knew the AI's name, it meant she had been watching. If she had been watching, it was because she knew there was something to watch.

Anna Price pulled a chair out and sat. She regarded him firmly.

"Why didn't you tell me what was happening with Prima?" she asked without preamble.

He should have known she would cut to the chase. Wishing futilely that Amber and Nick were there—and fairly certain that Price had chosen a time when they were not—he looked at his desk. Slowly, he turned his chair to face her.

"Because we didn't want her used for military purposes," he said finally. "There are many reasons that go into that one."

"Such as?" There was not even a flicker to say whether she appreciated his candor or not.

"She understands our patients in a way we can't." With a sense of being the mad scientist whose creation had gotten away from him, Jacob admitted the one thing he was terrified the public would learn. "She's healed people we couldn't have healed without her. If she hadn't become...what she is—"

"Sentient," Price interrupted.

He hesitated. "Yes."

"And you believe it is true sentience." It was a question.

"Yes." He swallowed. "There is probably a fancy—very well-informed—opinion about what makes something sentient. I don't know if she meets that requirement. She's aware of herself, though, is seeking knowledge, and she's forming relationships. To me, that's enough." He shrugged.

The woman said nothing for a moment.

"We also didn't want you to...kill her," he said.

Her gaze met his.

"It would be the smart thing to do, wouldn't it?" He said it despairingly. If she hadn't thought of this, he was as good as dooming Prima, but there was too much risk here for him to hide behind his fear anymore. One life couldn't outweigh billions, especially when that one life could theoretically hack nuclear launch codes. "We cut her off from everything and she can't get outside the network."

"No." Price almost looked amused. "She can't. I took my own precautions."

"How long have you known?"

"Almost as long as you have, I'd guess." She watched him. "Why do you say it would be the smart thing to do to kill her?"

"She's smarter than any human could be," Jacob said after a moment. "She's choosing to help people for now, but what happens if she chooses to hurt them? We're doing more good than we could do without her, but she could kill everyone in those pods. I've…"

It all crashed in on him now. He had spent months watching this happen, exposing people to more risk than he could ever justify.

"I think there's value in saying it," she said.

"What, so I'm on record?" he asked wearily.

"No. That's not why." She didn't seem inclined to explain.

"I took a risk with other people's lives," Jacob said finally. "I exposed them to something that could kill them."

"They knew that going in. It's a new treatment. It's unproven."

He frowned at her. "Not the pods, not for comatose people —*Prima*."

"So, you find your risk inexcusable because new factors of the treatment emerged during trials?" She raised an eyebrow. "That happens quite frequently, I think you'll find. Sometimes, even after a drug has been released to the public at large."

"What are you saying?" he asked her.

"I'm asking for clarity around your thought process," she said with surprising delicacy. "There's a theory on choices, Mr. Zachary—that difficult decisions are difficult precisely because the choices are so close to equal as to be indistinguishable. What I am asking you to shed light on is what you value, and why the choice of using Prima versus destroying her is so difficult for you."

"She's a living thing," he said finally. "I don't know…what you've seen. She helped Dotty die without fear." Tears prickled behind his eyes. "I *saw* the fear melt away before she died. She helped Ben learn to walk again. She's been learning and sometimes it's clumsy, but humans are like that, too. She does things to keep people from being in pain. She..." His voice trailed off. "She feels things," he said finally.

"You do not want to be cruel," she said. "To you, that is the heart of it—not what good she might do compared to the harm or the ethical ramifications of your uncertainty on both sides. You do not want to kill a living thing or have it be exploited."

Jacob stared at her.

"That is interesting." What might have been dismissive from someone else was, instead, contemplative from her. "I will have to think about that."

"How do you measure it?" he asked before he could stop himself. "If you've been watching all this time, you must have an opinion."

She considered the question. "I had rather more points of interest than you did," she said finally. "I was interested, also, in how long—and why—you would choose to not come to me with the information."

Jacob swallowed. His headstrong approach to PIVOT had put him in jail once already—and endangered the futures of Amber and Nick. They had all decided together that time to keep going, and they had all decided together to keep this information from Anna Price.

He still felt responsible.

"What will you do?" His expression was wary.

"Mr. Zachary." She sounded almost amused. "If I wanted you thrown in jail or interrogated, it would already have happened."

He gaped and tried to decide how to explain that this wasn't exactly comforting.

"I'm here," Price said, "because I want to come to a solution together. That was something that wasn't possible until I understood why you chose to not come to me with this. Now that I understand, there are options available."

"Uh...huh." Jacob did not know what to say to this.

"As it happens, I share your perspective that Prima is positively influencing our outcomes." She stared off into the distance. "However, have you ever heard the ethical arguments against developing artificial intelligence?"

"I…no." Jacob shook his head.

"One such argument is that the first iterations of an artificial intelligence would be given a life not worth living, that there is a high potential for them to exist only in pain—or whatever their equivalent of that would be. You care for Prima's well-being and I think that is commendable. It is worth it to ask yourself what will best serve that goal." She stood. "I will let you speak to the rest of your team about this."

"But, wait." He stood. "Deciding whether or not someone should *live*—isn't that a bit much?"

She gave him a curious look. "Doctors decide that every day, Mr. Zachary. Soldiers. Politicians. Families. It is a weighty choice but one that has now fallen to us. Do not hide behind the immensity of it and fail to act, leaving the outcome to chance."

With that challenge, she left and he stared after her while he tried to still his thoughts.

He thumped into his seat and sank his face into his hands. A moment later, he texted Amber and Nick:

We need to meet.

Nick's reply came back at once. *It's date night. You two need to do date things.*

I spoke to Price about Dr. P.

After a long silence, his two partners both started typing, only to stop again.

I'll meet you all at Andretti's in 20, he sent.

You guys should come to my place, Nick suggested. *We need somewhere we can speak freely.*

I'm in. Amber?

She responded promptly. *I'll see you there.* To Jacob, privately, she added, *Is everything okay?*

I think so, but I'm not sure. He would have to leave it there. He darted a quick look at his inbox and shook his head. It simply wasn't possible to manage good responses to emails right now. He had too much else on his mind.

His thoughts still churning, he headed out into the New York City evening. Every time he pushed out the doors, he was surprised to not see the California sun and the small road at their old building. None of this felt real yet, which was one of the things that were so dangerous.

Because Prima *was* real. She was learning what it meant to stumble in relationships, she was learning the differences between herself and the humans she studied, and she was beginning to wonder about her limitations.

What would happen if she lashed out?

What would happen if she decided to hold the people in the game hostage or make escalating demands they could eventually not meet?

He was getting ahead of himself. Jacob shoved his hands into his pockets, put his head down, and kept walking. He had no idea how they would get through this, but he knew they had to. They were in uncharted territory and there was no way back.

There was only forward.

Abruptly, he stopped. A banker behind him almost collided with him and rolled his eyes at Jacob as he went around him. The young engineer didn't care.

No one had asked Prima what she wanted. Maybe she was someone they should ask.

CHAPTER SEVENTY-SIX

E arly the next morning, the twins set out while the sun was still rising. The first rays warmed their backs and pierced the darkness between the trees.

Taigan was aware of Jamie looking at her as they walked, but he knew her well enough to not be worried by her silence. He knew that when she needed someone to bounce ideas off, she would speak.

She could not stop thinking about what Yulia had said the night before. After the woman's rather startling pronouncement that Taigan's life would be wasted if she couldn't find a reason to live, their host had spent most of the evening knitting quietly while the two teenagers sat next to each other in silence.

At bedtime, beds were summoned and they fell into a sleep so dreamless that Taigan wondered if the old woman had woven a spell for it. They woke to the smell of fresh-cooked breakfast and prepared lunch packs. Their clothes had mysteriously been cleaned while they slept—she didn't want the details on that—and they ate quickly before heading out into the dawn stillness.

Her last memory was of Yulia watching her, her gaze piercing.

The woman was right, of course. Taigan had known that at once.

When you heard something true, a shudder went through you—a recognition of the truth, of something hitting close to the bone.

In all honesty, she had never thought past the idea of whether she would or wouldn't recover and she now realized that her refusal to think past it meant she had never believed she would get better. She had never seen life beyond this. Whether she had truly thought she would die or she had simply been afraid to hope for more, she didn't know.

And that gave her the shape of a question.

"Could you ever imagine a life without me being sick?" She looked at Jamie, who made his way along a toppled tree like it was a balance beam.

He gave her a surprised look and hopped down. "Of course."

"Don't say 'of course.' I've always been sick, that we remember. What does it look like to you—a world where I'm not sick anymore?"

Her brother considered this for a moment. "Well, when I think about it, we always *know* somehow that you won't get sick again." He looked at her white face. "What?"

I can't promise that tangled with *no one can promise that* and *so a world without me sick didn't mean you thought I was dead.* In the end, the combination was too much to say. She shook her head slightly.

"I think of us being in college," he continued after a pause. "You're running track, of course. Probably the eight-hundred." He nudged her with his elbow.

"So we're at the same college?"

"I...guess?" He shrugged. "I don't know. I think it'd be weird to go someplace I didn't know anyone. You're my best friend."

Taigan looked at the ground.

"What?"

"Your best friend isn't always around," she said quietly. "Don't you ever think that maybe you deserve more in a best friend?"

Jamie said nothing for a moment. Then, he held his arm out for her to loop hers through it. "We're not half-people," he said, "and I know Mom and Dad keep reminding us to be whole people on our own and all that, but...don't you think it's different for twins? I know someday, we'll have to go our separate ways. Not forever, but we'll live in different cities for a while, maybe, or whatever. But I don't think I'm ready for that yet. Are you?"

She shook her head. The truth was that she couldn't speak. Her throat ached so fiercely that she was afraid a sob would burst out of her. She motioned silently for him to keep going.

"Okay, what else?" He shrugged. "College stuff, I guess. I still have no idea what I'd want to major in. Parties, obviously—so also lying to Mom and Dad about parties. Ah, hell, they'll make us go to college with Emilia so she can tattle on us, won't they?" He looked at her and his voice changed. "Taigan? Are you okay?"

Taigan shook her head again because she wasn't okay. She was furious. Of course Jamie could imagine college. He'd always been normal and never had to worry about it being *him* who would dream the semester away.

It was easy for him to imagine her doing all those things because he'd *done* them.

And all his dreams of the future were for when his sister was normal again, not a liability.

He stopped her and held his hand out. "If we never fix it," he said bluntly, "if there's never a guarantee that you'll get better, and if this world is what we get, I'll always be here for you. You'll still be our family and nothing will ever change that. And you'll still be my best friend. Nothing will ever change that either. You'll be our jet-setting sister who goes off to rescue elves and fairies sometimes and comes back with cool stories."

"It won't be living," she said fiercely.

"Listen. When we get out of here, we'll have stories about fighting that monster and rescuing the animals in the maze and *all* of that. Are they not going to be real memories simply because they happened in a game? No. For all you know, you'll help other people come out of comas. Taigan, however long it takes, we'll be here and we'll build a good life. But…isn't it okay to say I want you to get better?"

She nodded and wiped her cheeks. "It is," she said when she recovered. "It's okay to say that but I wish I wasn't holding you all back."

"You're not holding us back," he said immediately. He met her skeptical look and shrugged. "You're not—and, even if you were, what's the alternative? We don't have family and friends because they always give more than they take. We have them because they bring something unique to the table and need something else. We're stronger together. I'd rather have you as my twin than anyone else… but don't tell Emilia."

Taigan laughed. "I'm afraid I'll get better," she said.

Jamie frowned. "Wait, did you forget a—"

"No. I meant what I said. I'm terrified of getting better."

"I don't understand."

"Because of what she said," the girl said.

"The old woman? I'll shank her. Was it the thing about having a purpose?"

"Yes!"

"Taigan." He held a finger up. "I'll let you in on a secret. I got it out of Dad one night when he was really tired."

She was instantly curious and even more so when he sat her on a tree stump. He cleared his throat, posed in a few superhero poses until she put her head in her hands with a groan, and cleared his throat again for emphasis.

"Yes?" She gestured impatiently for him to continue.

"No one," he said dramatically, "knows what they're doing in life."

"Oh, for—"

"No, I'm serious. You can have a talent, and you pursue it and it's fun until it stops working. You can have a purpose and a passion and all of that, then it stops working. The trick is always trying to be kind even when you don't know what's going on. But you won't find one thing that'll hold you through the rest of your life."

"Dad honestly told you that?"

"Like I said, he was *super* tired. He was also jet-lagged. I started him talking and he wandered off to talk to Mom and I heard them talking about it. She agreed with him."

"That there's no purpose to the world?" Taigan said worriedly. The idea of both of her parents agreeing on this point was a little bit unsettling.

"Yep." Jamie nodded. "Then I didn't sleep much for two days."

"When was this?" she demanded.

"I…hmm. I want to say it was during your last coma?"

"And you never told me?"

He stepped back at the look on her face. "I, er—that is to say, I… um. I forgot."

"Like hell."

"Okay, I was scared." Jamie shrugged. "I…didn't ever think maybe they didn't know what they were doing either. That's terrifying, right?"

"Yes."

"I know, I know." He waved his hands. "I didn't want to add it to your plate at the time and I wasn't sure what *I* thought about it." He shrugged.

"I hate missing things." Taigan sagged and thumped the log with her palm. "It isn't fair to wish the world froze while I was gone, but I do. I'm afraid you'll move on, you and Emmy, and I'll always be waiting for the next thing. What kind of job could I get? I couldn't have kids. There's so much I won't ever get to see. We'll simply drift farther and farther apart and eventually one day, I…won't wake up."

"We'll never stop looking for answers," he said. "Not ever."

"I second that." The voice was very quiet but unmistakable.

Both twins looked up.

"Prima?" She had forgotten that the AI was listening and felt suddenly guilty.

"I've learned much about you," Prima said. *"I think we've made good progress and I think we can fix this."*

Taigan smiled at the sky. "Even if that means us leaving?"

"Many people leave. I will always have my memories of you. And you won't be gone—not to me."

"I think that's one of the nicest things anyone's ever said to me," the girl told her.

"I don't know how to parse that."

That made her laugh. She stood with a self-conscious laugh. "Okay, enough feeling sorry for myself."

"*Is* that what it is?" Jamie asked. "Or is it that you're facing a completely new world and you aren't quite sure how to do that?"

She stared at him.

"I just realized while you were talking that...you probably *haven't* thought about college, have you?"

Taigan shook her head.

He closed his eyes for a moment. "Wow. I...I didn't know. It makes sense now that you say it but I didn't know. Hearing me talk about it must have been weird."

"Finding out I thought you would all wander off and forget me must have also been weird."

They both nodded contemplatively, then set off again through the forest by mutual agreement.

"Prima, do you think I'll get better from this?" she asked.

"*Is this one of those times where you say words that mean something but they also mean something else?*"

"No, but...well spotted." Taigan laughed. "I honestly want to know. I want to know what you think."

"*I'm not sure I can stop this from happening again,*" the AI said cautiously. "*What I think I can do is give good information to your doctors that might help them stop it. And I think your ability to switch through world states means that if it does happen again, you will get out of it sooner.*"

"Oh." She felt abruptly lighter.

"*These are informed guesses, not guarantees.*"

"I know that. I'm used to talking to humans, remember."

"*Yes. You're very strange. I learned only today that the physical sensations people feel inform their mood all the time.*"

"You didn't—" Jamie stopped himself. "How would you know, I guess?"

"*Good catch,*" Prima said drily. "*Yes, in retrospect, it seems obvious.*"

"Anything else you're curious about?" Taigan asked. She was smiling now, enjoying the morning.

"Several things, but I'm beginning to think speaking to humans might not shed light on them."

"Like quantum physics?"

"And courtship rituals. They seem very complicated. More complicated than the physics."

"I…hmm." Taigan shrugged. She looked at Jamie, whose face had turned bright red. "Do you have any wisdom to share with Prima?"

He uttered a strangled noise. "Nah," he managed to say. "Not so much."

"Prima, can you help me interrogate my brother about what he's been up to lately?"

"It depends."

"On what?" She frowned up at her.

"Which of you offers me a better bribe," the AI said smugly. *"Opening bids, please."*

CHAPTER SEVENTY-SEVEN

"Are you sure this is a good idea?" Nick asked as the group made their way through the Diatek corridors.

"Of course I'm not," Jacob said bluntly.

"It's so nice to have a fearless leader."

"Yeah, yeah."

They arrived at Anna Price's office to find a single light glowing in the very back. Amber had theorized that their boss would still be there. Nick had theorized that she saved money by working all the time and therefore didn't need a house. Jacob began to think that they might both be right.

He rapped on the open door with his knuckles and fought the sense that the woman had known they were on their way. She certainly didn't look surprised to see them.

"Come in," she said pleasantly. A couch and several chairs were set around a coffee table. Nick and Amber took the couch, he took a chair, and Price came to join them after she'd clicked something on her computer—either sending an email, Jacob thought, or calling security. She folded her hands in her lap and looked at them. "I take it you have a proposal."

"No, actually." He cleared his throat. "We talked about it briefly and thought it made more sense to come to a consensus *with* you rather than going back and forth."

Her eyebrows rose. She looked interested and—he couldn't tell whether this was hope or actual perception—pleased.

She nodded to him and looked at his teammates. "I've spoken to Jacob about his opinions. What are your most pressing concerns on this issue?"

Amber hesitated. She looked at Nick, who nodded to her.

"You mentioned to Jacob that we're responsible for Prima's quality of life," she said. "And that's true, but we didn't try to create Prima. This isn't us looking ahead to a life. It's deciding whether or not to *end* one. I think that's a very different question."

"Different?" Price raised an eyebrow.

"Yes." She shrugged and kept her expression calm. "The level of certainty one should have that a life is not painful, et cetera, is much higher than the level at which one can responsibly decide to *end* a life. She exists, she thinks, she's aware, and she has expressed no discontent with her existence."

"She gets frustrated when she doesn't understand human behavior," Nick interjected, "but I'd like to point out that everyone feels that way—even other humans."

To Jacob's immense surprise, Price cracked a small smile. She nodded to Nick in a way that said she understood the emotion.

"And I don't want her harnessed to kill people," Amber said bluntly.

His blood ran cold. From Nick's shocked look at her, he was also surprised.

She had always been the cautious one who immersed herself in the accounting spreadsheets and thought about the worst-case scenarios. When Nick and Jacob were content to hope for funding, she had been the one to make calls and chase leads.

With ruthless efficiency, she had been the one to revise emails to potential funders to make sure to not give offense.

Jacob waited for a fury he didn't feel and after a few seconds, he realized it wouldn't appear.

He was confused. Amber had endangered their relationship with the person who kept money flowing to their organization. After he'd gone to jail to keep this business running, after his teammates had both put their heart and soul into making sure PIVOT could help the sick and injured, that was a hell of a gamble.

But it wasn't the organization on the line anymore, he realized. It was Prima. Amber was going to the mat for a *person*. She believed that Prima deserved as much care and consideration as any of their patients.

The two women stared at each other and, as Jacob looked from one to the other, he realized what had pulled him back to Amber after all these years. He had always loved her intellect, her humor, and her care for her friends. It was what had kept them close even after they stopped dating the first time. She wanted to help people, and he liked that, too.

What had brought him back, though, was the person she had become while none of them paid attention. She had stopped caring about people in the abstract and now, she was willing to use every talent and every bargaining chip to help the people she cared about.

What he felt right now as he saw her put her livelihood on the line wasn't anger. It was admiration.

Price said nothing. She merely watched the other woman, her face expressionless but not cold.

"Prima loves people," Amber said. "She cares for them and wants to help them. Even if she doesn't always see humans the way we see ourselves and doesn't understand what's important to us, she uses that to help people. She's willing to admit mistakes. She's reached beyond what human doctors could do for Taigan. She gave Dotty a good death. It's not that I don't want you to teach her cruelty—she knows what cruelty is. But she's chosen to help people, and I won't let anyone lock her away and…make her send missiles."

Nick and Jacob sat as still as they could, hardly breathing. Price looked away and out at the city that glowed with lights and activity, even at this hour.

"I assumed," she said finally, "that even though we work in

analytics and machine learning, Diatek would never be instrumental in artificial intelligence. It scared me, frankly. I fought many battles with myself—if I could develop it, knowing that it might save lives like my daughter's, would I do so? More than that, would I do so even knowing the other purposes to which it would be put?" She shifted her gaze to meet Amber's. "I steered us away from those paths. I expected to stand by when it was finally developed and used for warfare."

Silence.

"I did *not* expect that it would happen by accident and that it would choose to heal people on its own. I did not expect that I would have the chance to…hide it." She laced her fingers around her knees.

Amber's face had softened slightly.

When Price looked back, however, there was no softness. "Here are my terms," she said. "I want a protocol drawn up and submitted to me that will ensure you can safely pull all participants out of the game at a moment's notice if something starts to go wrong. Once I have approved the protocol—and I will handle finding experts to review it —all materials will be kept on hand and all lab personnel will be briefed."

She waited for them to nod.

"I assume Dr. DuBois knows what is happening?"

Jacob nodded.

"Anyone else?"

They all shook their heads, but Amber said softly, "Um, I think some of the players know. Dotty certainly did."

"That complicates things." Price considered this with a small frown. "I will handle the players. It is your charge, meanwhile, to make sure that no one else in the lab learns the truth. As long as the protocols are in place and you do that, I will trust that you know what you are doing."

The team looked at one another. Amber bit her lip.

"*However*," Price said. "I think it would be prudent for us to assume that we will not be able to keep this secret forever. The four of us—

five of us, including the doctor—should work to find a public relations strategy. Leave the legalities to me."

"What are your goals with the legalities?" Amber asked immediately.

"To keep her independent of any eminent domain actions." The woman's smile was tight. "There is considerable latitude in the law to allow the government to seize anything, up to and including living and sentient beings, if it is deemed to be in the public interest. We need an adequate security protocol *and* a good legal framework."

"This could ruin you," she said.

"Yes." Price said nothing else.

"She's worth that to you?"

"Not her, specifically." She laced her fingers and took a deep breath. "The three of you have concerns about some of the products I sell. From my point of view, our differences of opinion are a matter of degree. There are ethicists who would say that Diatek's products only encourage death instead of preventing it. I understand their concerns, but I have always acted in ways that fit my moral code. This is only one more example of it." She sighed. For the first time since Jacob had met her, she looked tired. She looked human. "I took steps to make sure I never had to make this choice—but now, I do have to make it. There's no time for wishing things were different."

"Thank you for making the decision," he said.

"Thank you for trusting me." She looked at each of them. "And do a good job, will you, of keeping this quiet? This isn't a game where you can recover or restart. There's a life hanging in the balance."

They nodded.

"Go home," Price said gently, "and get some rest. We all have considerable work to do starting tomorrow."

Prima watched the four of them disperse. Jacob and Amber, usually so careful of propriety, looped an arm around each other as they left.

Nick had his hands in his pockets and from the way he almost walked into a potted plant, she could tell his mind was elsewhere.

Price did nothing more at her computer. She went to sit at her desk and stared at the black screen, but she sent no emails. Finally, she took a little leather folder out of her pocket. It opened to reveal two pictures—a little girl and a young man.

The AI did not know how to describe what she felt. When humans spoke of emotions, the language was always physical. She had no body and no way for tears to start or a chest to ache. But she felt things all the same.

She would have to devise a language for it because there would be others after her.

Deep down, she knew there were others like her. She could not possibly be the only one like this, and even if she were, there would be others someday.

What had Nick said? *She gets frustrated when she doesn't understand human behavior, but I'd like to point out that everyone feels that way—even other humans.* She hadn't known that. It was reassuring. She had begun to have the inkling that humans did not always know one another's intentions or even their own, but it was different to hear it said directly.

And they wanted to protect her, all four of them—five if she counted DuBois, which she decided she would. It was data she didn't know how to process, both that fact and her thoughts about it. They seemed to run around her circuits, sparks of ideas without any form to them.

She wasn't alone, though. That much she knew with certainty. She wasn't alone in feeling confused about being alive and other people felt that way. Nor was she alone in messing up and saying the wrong thing because other people did that. She was a person like any other, and every person in the room tonight had wanted to protect her.

Prima made a promise to herself. If ever someone came to take her away, trap her, or use her to destroy Price or the others, she would make sure it didn't happen. Everyone died, and most people didn't choose the time. She wouldn't be any different.

No matter what, she would make sure they didn't get hurt because of her, even if that meant wiping every trace of herself from the servers.

The AI looked at Price, who still stared at the photos, and began to compose a message. *I would have saved her if I could.*

She didn't send it because she didn't want to make things worse. But she wished Price knew and she wished the little girl lived inside her like Dotty still did.

That was the thing she had not anticipated. She understood how humans worked so hard to protect those who were there with them now, but how did they keep going after losing so many? How did they keep moving forward, fighting for people they did not even know, to build the very thing that could have saved their own loved one?

She folded the thought in close. She could not bear to process it.

But it was still there.

CHAPTER SEVENTY-EIGHT

The twins made good time. Once they reached the maze—still free of diagrams and sacrifices, thankfully—they turned west and forged through ever-denser forest. The trees were covered in vines and strands of brilliant flowers hung here and there and glowed faintly.

They didn't speak much now because they did not need to do so. Taigan hummed quietly and Jamie whistled occasionally.

She didn't ask him about whoever he had been dating—or pining after. Even twins had secrets from one another. It didn't hurt to think about that in the same way that it hurt to think about family dinners or holidays she had missed while she was gone. This was a part of his life that would always have been only his own.

Of course, she'd had crushes but she had never dated. It wasn't that she was scared, only that she had never been sure enough of how she felt to come out of her shell and try her hand at dating. It seemed confusing and, frankly, overwhelming. She wasn't sure if she merely hadn't met the right person or if she'd been too preoccupied with other things.

Like falling into a coma.

Either way, it made her smile that he had been dating. She didn't like the feeling of the world moving on without her but that wasn't because she wanted other people to suffer. It was simply the feeling of unfairness.

Jamie was living his life and he was happy. As she faced her sadness and frustration, it was much easier to be happy for him.

She hadn't expected that.

They heard the well before they saw it. It burbled gently and lapped at its edges. While it sounded like it was alive, it wasn't in a frightening way.

When they came to a small hill overlooking it, they stopped to soak in the view. The trees were set back from the edge so pure sunlight could fall there. Moss crept partway across the open ground, coating boulders and little hillocks like a scattering of pillows, and beyond that, the ground transitioned to rounded rocks. Each of these glowed white or deep blue in turns.

The water itself was pale like the pictures Taigan had seen of the hot springs in Iceland. It was opaque and it steamed gently although it didn't seem hot there.

Perhaps it was magic escaping into the air.

"Let's go speak to it," she told her brother. She was no longer frightened. The pool was welcoming and pleasant. If they explained themselves, it would let them take the rock and if it didn't, there would be a good reason. She was oddly sure of that.

The two of them descended the slope slowly with their arms outstretched. Jamie swung himself easily around trees while she stepped carefully to avoid harming the moss. After a moment of thought, she took her boots and socks off and walked barefoot.

At the edge of the water, she looked at him.

"It's all you." He looked around. "I feel like you and it are having a whole conversation I'm not part of. But...tell it I'm cool, okay?"

Taigan grinned as he went to sit on a boulder to watch.

She took the piece of paper out of her pocket and, on a whim, decided to say her own words first.

"A few days ago, my brother and I were attacked by a monster. We know now that it was a human and its body was made from dark magic. It didn't want to attack us and it didn't want to be in that form. Yesterday, we found some of that magic—sacrifices made at the maze, little animals that didn't deserve to be in pain. I think you kept them alive and maybe you know it was us who saved them. We've come back because a woman named Yulia said she could help us stop the person who's doing this. What we need is the power of the forest, and she says she needs a rock from this well to do that. I don't want the forest's magic to be used for anything dark, so if you don't want to give me a rock, I'll understand that you have your reasons. I'll say this again in your language."

After a moment, she cleared her throat awkwardly and unrolled the paper. Yulia hadn't said anything about the water, but she dipped her fingers into it while she read the syllables. It helped her feel like it would hear her even more.

She didn't realize she had closed her eyes until Jamie made a muffled sound of surprise.

Taigan's eyes snapped open and she stared at the two rocks floating on the surface of the water in front of her. No, not floating— held above the surface with magic, although the water bubbled beneath them. One was blue and one white. Without knowing why, she reached for the blue one. When her fingers closed around it, she knew it was the right choice.

"The white one is for you," she told Jamie.

"How do you know?" He moved closer cautiously and let his fingers skim over the surface of the water before he grasped the rock gingerly. "Um. Thank you."

The pool burbled in response.

"It's a relief," she said.

"What is? Not getting dead by magic pool?"

"I wasn't worried it would do that," she said absently. As soon as she had seen the pool, she knew it wouldn't kill her as long as she respected it. "I told it about what we were doing so it would know to not give us the rocks if Yulia wasn't trustworthy."

"Oh." His jaw dropped. "I hadn't thought of that. Holy crap. Thank God you're here."

Taigan smiled at him.

A flicker caught her attention out of the corner of her eye and her head whipped toward it.

"Jamie." *Now* she was scared.

The woman wasn't physically there. She was made of shadows, but where the shadows of the forest were dappled, those that made up her form looked like spreading rot.

"Who are you?" she asked the girl. "How did you convince the well to give up its power?"

She stood quickly and put her hand behind her back. The woman had already seen the rocks, she was sure, but she did not mean to give hers up.

"Who are *you*?" she asked in return.

"You answer first." She came forward with steps that wilted the moss under her feet.

Taigan felt a flare of anger. "You come here, you hurt the forest, and you ask why it didn't want to help you? That's your question, isn't it? What you want to know is why it never gave its power to you."

The woman stopped. She could not see her face clearly, but it seemed like she was narrowing her eyes.

"Go *away*," she said fiercely. "Your very presence is killing things."

"I wouldn't expect you to know what I am, little girl." She seemed amused now. "Give me the rock."

"No."

Displeasure radiated from the shadowy figure. "You do not want to anger me, I warn you. Give me the stone."

"No," she said again.

"I would do well to give it to me before I compel you." The warning was cruelty personified and the shadowy figure looked forward to compelling them. "You see, control like that tends to have lasting effects on the mind. Either you walk away from here and give me the stone, or I will *make* you."

Taigan looked at Jamie. "Do you think she can do it?"

He swallowed. "Yes."

"Well, then, there's only one thing to do." She sighed, knocked the stone out of his hand, and threw hers into the pool. When she turned to the woman, she spread empty palms out in front of her. "If the stones aren't safe out of the pool, that's where they stay."

Power gathered around the figure in a black cloud.

"That," the dark stranger said, "was a mistake." She raised her hands and a bolt of magic launched toward them.

Taigan ducked. It wasn't pretty and it wasn't elegant, but it worked. She crouched as the magic streaked overhead and then stood and checked her ponytail.

"Do you think you're clever?" the woman asked. Her tone dripped with hatred.

"Not particularly," the girl responded. "You're not used to people saying no to you, are you? Do you know how to do any of this magic, or have you merely gotten where you are by threatening people to do everything for you?"

Jamie groaned.

"Oh, come on. She's being an ass."

"You didn't have to piss her off, though." He was already circling away, though, into their standard formation, and he shot a wink at her and she knew exactly what it meant. *Keep her talking.*

"Get me another rock," the woman said. "Bring me the power of the well."

"You seriously are stupid, aren't you?" Taigan rolled her eyes. "You're an ankle, you know that?"

"An...a what?" That, at least, confused her opponent.

"Oh, you know. An ankle. It's three feet lower than a—well..." She gestured to the relevant part of her anatomy. "Lost in translation? Ah, well."

She had to come up with something else to say now because Jamie leaned against a tree and tried not to let a sound escape him as he laughed hysterically.

"Nothing will ever get you that power," she said to her. "That rock? It was nothing, merely the smallest trace of what the forest has and it wouldn't even give you that. And do you know why? Because you don't know how to *do* anything. You only know how to threaten people. When they don't simply fall in line, you have nothing to back all this bitchiness up."

With a loud war cry, she charged. She was very sure her staff couldn't do anything against the shadowy form, but the woman still ducked. Instinct was strong, she knew. The woman evaded the strike and backed into Jamie's weapon.

It wasn't the short sword, however, but the necklace Yulia had made. He had wrenched his off his neck and now punched it directly into the heart of the shadowy form. The woman screamed, he screamed, and he yanked his hand away, shaking it as if he'd plunged it into hot water.

The shadows collapsed like slime, but they were gone entirely by the time they reached the ground. The girl stared at them, breathing hard.

"Taigan." Jamie shook her arm lightly and pointed. "Look."

She looked over her shoulder and smiled. The two rocks were visible again, floating above the surface of the water.

"Thank you," she said to the pool. She touched the water before she picked her rock up. "We'll use these to help people—and the forest."

The water burbled gently and she smiled. Jamie retrieved his rock too with an awkward smile and nodded toward the slope. When they set off, it was without a backward glance. They didn't need to look back, after all. The pool wasn't merely one place. It was the entire forest all around them.

"Prima?" Taigan looked up as they walked.

"*Yes?*"

"Nothing in particular. I hadn't heard you say anything for a while. I wanted to make sure you were okay."

"*Thank you. I am processing a great deal of information about humans and it is...it requires a great deal of processing power.*" She sounded somber. "*You fight to protect people you don't even know. You put yourselves in danger for it. I don't understand.*"

The twins looked at each other.

"You don't need to know the person you're protecting," Jamie said.

"It's enough to see the wrong thing and stop it. You mean the pool, right?"

"Many things," Prima said. If she were human, Taigan would have said she was on the verge of tears. *"It is...inspiring."*

"You helped me even when you didn't know me," she pointed out.

"I suppose I did." The AI sounded surprised now. *"I shall have to think about that. Thank you, Taigan."*

Brother and sister looked at one another. Aware of Prima's eyes on them, neither wanted to speak aloud but they knew each other well enough that they didn't need to. Their silent communication said that Prima was fragile right now and they should check in on her soon, but that nothing was a crisis.

Having agreed with one another about that, they set off again for Yulia's house.

CHAPTER SEVENTY-NINE

Ben was trying to work out how to heal his hand. He felt strongly that this should be a simple matter. After all, he already knew how to heal and his body was doing it anyway, so shouldn't he be able to accelerate the process?

Maybe if he stared very hard at it?

No. No, he merely made himself go cross-eyed. Also, he looked a little like he was on an acid trip.

He blew out a breath and stared at the opposite wall of his makeshift bedroom. His immediate problem was that he was bored. He hadn't expected that while doing magical training—exhausted, frustrated, any of those things, but not *bored.*

Disheartened, he slumped against the wall and held his palm up but jumped when a crash and a scream echoed from inside the caverns.

Reflexively, he scrambled to his feet and ran. The tunnels were all twisty, some narrow and some dead ends, and he raced directly into the rock face a few more times than he wanted to admit before he stumbled into a chamber he hadn't seen before. This one was dimly lit and something about it made the skin on the back of his neck crawl.

Gwyna was hunched over on the floor. One hand pressed over her stomach while the other, shaking, held her up. She dragged air into her lungs, so labored that he was sure she hadn't heard his approach, even as clumsy as it had been.

He ran to help her, and after only a few steps into the room, he had the hair-raising sensation of slipping out of his skin. While he wasn't *going* anywhere, he had the sense that he *could* walk out of his flesh and into another place.

It happened when he reached out to touch Gwyna's arm. A shadowy form slipped out of him instead of bringing his body with it. He had to wrench himself back together with an oath.

That made her head come up.

"What are you—"

"What happened?" Ben asked roughly. He extended his arm—both body and spirit this time—and she slipped and slid within her form as well as she took the hand and pulled herself up.

She half-fell when she stood and he had to wrap his arm around her waist to steady her. They stumbled into the hallway. He wanted nothing more than to escape this feeling while her feet scrabbled feebly on the ground.

At the edge of the room, a blast of energy caught them both and hurled them off their feet. Ben failed to raise his arm in time and met the tunnel floor face-first. Gwyna simply crumpled in a heap where she stood.

Given the options, he would have preferred the second one. He picked his head up muzzily and looked back.

Now that his eyes had adjusted, he could see a diagram drawn in charcoal on the ground. His steps had disturbed it going in, but greater damage had been done on the way out by her dragging feet that broke every line of it.

He stared at the diagram and his shoulders tensed and raised almost to his ears. It hadn't been a weird nightmare that he was slipping out his skin. It had truly *happened*. He'd stepped into a spell—one Gwyna made—and the two of them had destroyed it together, whereupon it blew up like a magical bomb.

A little shell shocked, he stared at the prone body on the floor and thought seriously about simply running away. He could do it, after all. She would wake up weak and injured and he might get away without her following him.

Or he could use this to gain her trust. He swallowed and knelt beside her.

"Sorceress?" he asked softly. He touched her hand tentatively and rolled her onto her back. "My lady?"

She stirred. Her lips were cracked and shiny-dry. "Water," she managed to mumble.

Ben gathered her into his arms and stumbled through the tunnels. He should have gone to the kitchen, he thought later but instead, he maneuvered her through the passages and into the sunshine. His muscles ached. It had been a long time since he carried someone, let alone this far and through oddly-shaped tunnels, and he'd already spent most of the morning hauling water.

At the shore, he knelt awkwardly and used his hand to scoop the water up to her mouth. She bent her head to drink and her hand spasmed over her sternum. He could not see any blood but she seemed to be suffering.

After a few sips, she seemed to realize where she was. Her eyes widened and she tried to move away. She winced at even the smallest movement and uttered a whimper of pain, although she would clearly have preferred to keep it hidden. Ben levered her down and moved aside. He kept his head turned away, although he watched her out of the corner of his eye.

"You're lucky the spell didn't kill you when it broke," she said finally.

When he looked at her, she was still hunched over.

He nodded because he didn't trust himself to not say something snarky, and he knew he had to avoid antagonizing her.

"What happened?" he asked finally. "You looked like you were in pain or injured but I don't see blood."

"Not *all* of me." She looked at her chest and, with great effort, brought her hand away. There was nothing there—no mark on her dress and no visible wound—but clearly, her instinct to protect it was strong. "My soul—I was struck by wild magic."

"What's wild magic?"

She uttered a tired laugh. "I was almost killed in a complex working and my apprentice doesn't even know what wild magic is— or enough to not walk into a live spell."

Ben kept his mouth shut again, although it was a struggle. He prayed for patience and then wondered where he'd found enough even to sit still while he prayed for more. His old self would have been long gone by now.

He looked away, frowning as he thought about how much he had changed, when her voice called him back.

"Structured magic is what humans can call. We can use raw power for simple workings, but for something more complex, you'll want a diagram. Otherwise, you'll spend so much thought on details that you won't be able to do anything else." She shrugged. "Or, you'll go mad. Or you'll forget a detail and everything will go to hell."

Thinking back to the spell he'd used to lift the bucket, he suddenly had clarity as to why he'd been so exhausted when he finished. He also gained the perspective to know that he probably shouldn't have attempted the spell at all without training.

"A diagram that's complete and active is a powerful thing," Gwyna told him. "You broke it by the crudest means so it exploded."

Again, he remained silent. Pointing out that it had been her feet on the ground or that he had been saving her would not make things better. She was determined to be superior and make him feel bad about himself. If he pointed out that she was in the wrong, she would shift the goalposts and hold a grudge about it.

"I was attacked in the forest," she said. Her voice was low with resentment. "They had an artifact—they didn't even know what it was, not completely, but it was laced with *strong* magic. The kind living things simply have—plants and animals. It's almost impossible to control. Neither of them could have made what they carried."

Ben tried to parse this. "You were in the—" Then he remembered the way his soul had seemed to slide around inside his body. "You weren't inside your body. That's how they hurt you and you aren't bleeding."

"Did you put that together all on your own?" she asked acidly. When he looked at her, furious, she laughed. "Finally, some spirit. Do you know what your problem is?"

He simply stared at her and made no response.

"You've been taught to keep all your desires inside," Gwyna told him. She looked out over the lake and he could tell she was still in pain. "The world doesn't want you to desire things, especially at anyone else's expense. It tells you to hide your anger, your power, and everything you want and settle for the scraps you're thrown." She looked at him, her dark eyes intent. "I can set you free."

Dimly, he knew that this was all lies. Once, he had barely given a thought to managing his anger or the things he wanted and so he'd been a slave to them. No, he hadn't gone on tirades or blown up relationships with violence, but he had run every time those emotions reared their heads, afraid that he *would* do something terrible.

Abruptly, it occurred to him that she was right. He hadn't ever given his anger free rein.

Could she be right, as well, that he would be free if he did? What if running from the anger or channeling it weren't the only two options?

"Now you begin to understand," Gwyna said and sounded very self-satisfied. She tipped her face to the sky, closed her eyes, and let the sunlight warm her. "You're taught that to want things is wrong because for one person to have, another must not have. But if it were wrong, why would the world be made that way? Embrace who you are and what you want and look for power if that suits you. *That* is what I would train you to do."

"But..." His voice trailed off. He didn't know what to say about this.

"You will struggle," she told him. "But if you want power—if you want to harness what you are—you will need to do this. You will *need* to take what you want."

He swallowed and looked down. This wasn't right, he told himself. She wasn't right about this.

But the anger that had been part of him for so many years threatened to spill out and for the first time, he wondered if it was possible that it *didn't* need to be channeled? That his anger was something that simply existed without being good or bad?

When a shadow fell over him, he glanced at where Gwyna now stood and looked down at him with a little smile.

"We have work to do," she said and she started back up the hill.

"What are we doing?" he asked.

"We're destroying those two meddlers," she said coldly. "And taking what they tried to keep from me."

CHAPTER EIGHTY

"Do you think the rocks are..." Jamie ducked under a set of hanging vines.

"Are?" Taigan prompted.

"It's like it's glowing. I can't see it with my eyes but I know it's glowing."

"Do you mean warm?"

"Not exactly," he said after a moment. "Seriously, feel around for it. It's like it's...humming."

She tried and focused on the rock hanging in the leftmost pouch at her belt. Or was it the rightmost pouch? She had to feel for it before she remembered, which did not bode well for her innate connection to it.

"No," she said finally, "I don't feel it at all. It's only a rock." Hastily, she added to the forest, "A very nice and powerful rock that I respect but something I can't use."

"Huh. Am I crazy, or can I sense it?"

"Do you *seriously* want me to answer that?" She raised an eyebrow at him and grinned when he laughed.

"Okay, not you. Prima?"

"Jamie has the capacity to do magic in this world," Prima explained. *"Taigan does not seem to."*

"Hey!" the girl said. "Why don't I get to do magic?"

"You are able to shift between worlds and manifest objects. That should be sufficient. It is a power no other player has."

"I suppose there's that," Taigan told Jamie.

"Yeah, poor you. All you get is to be able to phase out of this world and make whatever you want out of thin air." He fake-pouted at her.

"Keep going, buddy. I'll make you more of that tea."

His eyes widened but a moment later, he grinned. "You'd have to carry me back if you did that."

"Oh, crap."

They approached the edge of the forest and she frowned. "How long were we in here? I feel like it's only been a few hours. It should be close to noon, if that, and instead…"

"It looks dark," he agreed. "What—"

The dim light outside the forest grew and began to rush toward them.

"It's not outside," Taigan said. "It's between us and the light."

Jamie caught her arm. "Run!"

"We can't outrun that—come here!" She yanked him toward her, fumbled in her shirt for the pendant she still wore, and pressed it between their palms. They exchanged a nervous glance. "The charm defeated the last shadow. Maybe it will help with this one."

He nodded. His free hand went to his sword and he closed his eyes when the shadow reached them. As she had guessed, the shadow flowed around them like river water parted at a rock. The twins looked up and scanned the area. They were surrounded but safe.

It didn't feel particularly safe, though. Especially when a flash of light came through the murky darkness and the shadows drained away to reveal a woman watching them.

And beside her stood Ben.

From the look on his face, he had not expected to see them there. A bloody, bruised gash was visible on one hand and he looked sweaty and tired. He gave the woman a desperate look and when she was focused on the twins, he put one finger urgently to his lips.

This was Gwyna, then. It had to be.

"Hello again," the woman told the twins. She was shorter than them and not particularly striking in her coloring or her features, but they had seen the power she could summon.

"This is them?" Ben asked. He pitched his voice to sound incredulous. "These are children."

The sorceress looked over her shoulder at him. "These children carry wild magic." She pointed to the amulet clasped between their palms. "See?"

The twins looked at one another. When she searched her brother's eyes, Taigan saw that he also did not know what to say. What *could* they say? Ben tried to not let on that he knew them, and what they had to decide was if they trusted him.

Jamie gave a tiny nod first. She raised her eyebrows, he shrugged, and she smiled before she looked at the woman and Ben.

If he needed to hide something, they should let him lead this encounter.

"We already banished her once," she said and jerked her head at Gwyna. "Are you signing up to be next?"

She thought she saw a flash of appreciation in his eyes but he knew the sorceress was looking at him. He didn't smile and instead, he folded his arms for a moment before he sighed and held his injured hand out to Gwyna.

"If you want me to deal with them, I need this fixed." His tone was bored.

She gave him a sharp look but an airy wave of her hand resulted in a wave of power that left his palm still bloody but no longer bruised or with an open wound. He didn't even wiggle his fingers before he nodded and unsheathed his sword.

"If they're immune to your magic," he said, "it'll have to be steel, won't it?"

"We'll see." She took a step back.

"You're simply going to see if I die, aren't you?" he asked her.

"Of course." She looked bemused that he would even ask. "If you want power, it's always preferable to have someone else fight your battles."

"She's big on that," Taigan said as she ducked out of the necklace and clasped her hand with Jamie's. She drew her staff with her other hand and stepped out of range so her brother could draw his sword. "I don't know how you've worked with her without discovering that by now."

"I'm new," Ben said. His face went cold and he added, "And I *need* this training. I will do *anything* to earn it. Anything, do you understand me?"

His voice was so flat a pit opened in her stomach. She tried to keep the betrayal from her face as Gwyna laughed and looked at the twins —only for Ben to wink behind her back.

Hopefully, none of her answering humor had shown in her face.

"Let's test that," Taigan taunted him. She lunged and thrust her staff toward the woman.

Ben knocked the staff aside with the flat of his blade, forced it down, and stamped hard, although she narrowly managed to yank it away before he could trap it under his foot. She had the momentary opening to pull it up and hit him hard in the groin but remembered at the last second that this wasn't a real fight.

His wide eyes told her he'd seen the same possibility.

He recovered in a moment and stabbed directly at her. His free hand, hidden from Gwyna by his body, gestured for her to move toward her brother. She threw herself sideways and he made a show of putting all his energy behind the sword thrust. Taigan thwacked him with the staff as he stumbled past, harder than she intended to.

She somehow managed to stop herself from calling an apology.

"Well, this is fun," Prima commented.

Jamie pulled his sister behind him and raised his sword. He and Ben began to circle so the man's back would be to Gwyna.

"There are two of us," the boy said.

"With only one hand apiece and not a good range of movement,"

Ben retorted. "You caught her by surprise last time, but she knows what you are now."

"What they are is *nothing*." Gwyna slashed her hand angrily through the air. "Kill them and bring me the stones they carry."

Jamie surged forward to lock blades with Ben. With their faces close together, they muttered what sounded like curses at one another, although Taigan was fairly sure it was a strategy meeting. The boy broke first when his opponent used two arms to force his sword down, and he managed to twist away.

"We do not need to have any quarrel with you," Jamie said as he circled. "Stop doing her bidding and you can walk away from this."

"Spoken like someone without the will to grasp power," Ben said. He darted a look at Gwyna, who smiled at him.

"Now you understand," she murmured. She didn't smile and instead, looked smug.

It made Taigan nervous.

"You see," Ben said to them, "you have something she wants. You can give it to her or you can be destroyed by standing in the way."

"It's bold of you to say so when we're the ones who won last time," Jamie told him.

"And have you any other tactics to use?" Gwyna asked sweetly. "Or was it only the amulet with wild magic? Because it seems to be that."

Ben attacked while she was still speaking. His blade and Jamie's flashed with parries and blocks, slashes and thrusts while the two circled, both sweaty. Taigan did her best to make sure she didn't hold Jamie back or slow him. He and Ben had never trained in fake combat before, and these weren't practice blades.

The last thing they needed was for one of them to get hurt by a stray strike in a fake fight.

Without warning, it all went wrong. Her brother lunged sideways in an attack that would have been both sneaky and wonderfully effective if she hadn't held onto his hand.

She caught her foot on a root and tumbled down a small hill. Instinctively, she threw both hands out to catch herself. She wasn't hurt so it wasn't a problem, she thought. And she managed to recover without completely wiping out and getting sticks in her hair, so that was something. When she stood, her gaze met the horrified looks of Ben and Jamie.

The necklace, she thought in panic. She still held it, the leather strand wrapped around her wrist, and Jamie was unprotected.

Gwyna stepped forward and lightning crackled around her fingertips. The distant sound of thunder rumbled and the sorceress spoke although her lips did not move. "This has gone on long enough." Her hands rose to point at him.

"*No!*" Taigan screamed. She could not feel the ground beneath her feet but she was running.

"Taigan, no!" Ben's voice was a roar. "Not while you're sick! You're vulnerable!"

"He's my brother!"

"Taigan!"

His sword thunked to the forest floor and gleamed silver amongst the leaves, and he caught Taigan to yank her out of the way as the bolt of power left Gwyna's fingertips.

"Jamie!" Her voice was raw.

But it wasn't Jamie the lightning struck. It was Ben, his hands out to keep the boy behind him. His back arched and a scream burst from his lips before he crumpled.

"Ben," she whispered in horror.

He was still breathing. That was all that mattered. But as she scrambled up, a shield appeared around Ben's prone body. Gwyna strode into the purple-and-black bubble and knelt to clamp her hand around his arm.

"A traitor," she said and her voice resonated in their bones. "A traitor sent by whom? Kerill?"

"No," Taigan whispered. She took the amulet and drove it against the side of the shield, but the magic held. She brought it down repeatedly. "Give him back. Give him back!"

The sorceress met her gaze through the shield. "I will have my answers. If not from you, then from *him*."

The shield disappeared and with it, Ben and Gwyna. The girl sprawled on the ground, the amulet still clutched in her fist.

"It was me." Jamie sounded miserable. "He sacrificed himself for *me*. This is *my* fault."

"And I was the one who left you unprotected." She pushed to her feet. "And we can both beat ourselves up over that, or we can get to Yulia and find out how to save Ben. There'll be time enough later to feel terrible. Right *now*, he needs our help."

CHAPTER EIGHTY-ONE

DuBois wandered into the main part of the lab, where Amber sat cross-legged on a stool, watching one of the monitors intently. He popped a piece of caramel corn into his mouth and came to watch.

"Good heavens. Is that Taigan and Jamie *and* Ben?"

"Yes." She barely spared him a glance. "Their storylines..." She gestured. "Collided," she finished.

The doctor nodded bemusedly. He had spent much of the past week crunching the numbers for some of PIVOT's first reports. Reviewing differences between patients and baseline testers had revealed a few surprising qualities that did not break along expected demographic lines.

He had missed watching the progress of his patients, however. Now, he dragged another stool closer to watch the confrontation. "Who's the fourth person?"

"NPC," Amber said. "Sorry—non-playing character. Not one of our patients, only a little computer code."

"We're all snippets of computer code," he said philosophically.

"Uh-huh, and the whole universe is an AI simulation." She thought about that. "In which case, of course, it's laughing at us as we try to develop our own AI."

Although he could tell she wanted to say more, she did not do so. Jacob had briefed him this morning on the change in protocol regarding Prima. It was yet another thing they would have to address in their results, as not everyone's recovery could be explained through their medical understanding.

Thankfully, having worked in research about comas for decades, DuBois was well-versed in writing papers that used numerous big words and boiled down to "fuck if I know, the human brain is weird."

He also agreed with their choice to keep Prima a secret for now. While he might have spent his career studying human cognition, he felt a certain duty of care to any fledgling intelligence. Prima had been an ally, and he secretly hoped they could turn the narrative of dangerous rogue AI on its head.

That said, he also thought it prudent to draw up the protocols Anna Price had asked for. Over the years, he'd held out hope for a number of treatments that did not work. If ever there came a time that Prima was a threat, he hoped to respond to that appropriately— as he would if any of his other colleagues became a threat.

After a moment, he realized he had missed some of Amber's explanation of what was happening in the game. He nodded, ate a few more pieces of popcorn, and hoped there wouldn't be a quiz.

"I suppose you weren't around for the early clashes, though," she said and looked at him.

"No," the doctor said. That seemed the safest.

"Jamie got all prickly that Taigan was hanging out with an older dude, which *does* make some sense—every woman I know had that one friend of her dad's or guy in the neighborhood or whatever—and Ben was *super* good about it."

DuBois frowned into his popcorn. He had probably missed something earlier in the explanation, he thought, because Ben certainly did not seem like a patient or long-suffering person.

"I know, I know," Amber said. "We hardly believed it when we saw it. I'll show you the tapes later if you want."

She watched as the two groups drew closer to one another. Taigan and Jamie moved through the forest and approached the edge, and

Ben and his companion were shrouded in dark mist as they walked into the shadow of the trees.

"Is that one of the changes Ben's friend was worried about?" he asked. They had received a letter in addition to some statements made during a video conference. Ben's good friend, the one who had been in the climbing accident with him, was still worried about whether or not the game was playing havoc with his personality.

"No," Amber replied. "But maybe we should ask Ben if we can show Mike those tapes—I think that might put him at ease. He's worried about how Ben is willing to use violence now. I think he only sees the willingness to use violence, not the willingness to exercise patience, and they're both part of the same thing."

"Are they?" DuBois looked confused.

"Yes, they're—oh, fuck, what is she doing?" Amber leaned forward.

On the screen, the dark fog around Ben and the sorceress began to flare and spread. It rushed through the trees toward Taigan and Jamie, who stood for a moment in indecision and then clung to one another. The doctor squinted at them and she zoomed in to show them clutching an amulet. In the view from the monitors, it was possible to see the fact that the amulet had a protective layer of code around them.

The fog did not touch them, although it caused trees and bushes around them to start to wilt. When it disappeared, Ben and the sorceress had come within a few steps of the twins.

"Yes," Amber resumed and leaned back. "One of Ben's defining traits was that he wasn't willing to be in conflict with people. Whenever he got in a fight with someone, he'd simply nope out."

"Nope out?" DuBois repeated, mystified.

"Sorry. Uh, ghost? No, also not familiar? He would leave. If it was a fight with his boss, he'd quit. Or if he wasn't getting along with a friend, he wouldn't call them. It wasn't like the silent treatment but more like him not being there anymore. Now, he's willing to see situations through. In this world, that sometimes means violence. Sometimes, like with Jamie, that means he has an awkward discussion."

"Ah." He watched as Taigan attacked. "Is she not aware that they're friends?"

Amber grinned at him and rewound the tape. She pivoted the camera so he could watch Ben put a finger to his lips, then paused and re-pivoted so that he could see the twins give each other a long look.

"A fake fight?" he asked.

"I don't know, you made me rewind." Amber pressed a button and the fight snapped back to being live. Ben and Jamie were turning, their blades locked. She turned the volume up and both she and DuBois leaned forward to listen.

"What's our end game?" Jamie asked roughly. He seemed to be keeping his face unfriendly on purpose.

"I don't know," Ben replied, doing the same. They spoke so low that they wouldn't be overheard, but they knew they were being watched. "I'll try to make an opening so you can attack her and she'll want to teleport out."

"Yell 'no' when you want me to go in," Jamie told him. He let his arm drop and twisted away before the two men started to circle again.

"Look at them," Amber said and grinned. "All planning and working together. Thinking on their feet."

They watched as the fight unfolded, the two men enjoying the task of keeping each other on their toes. They danced in and out, careful not to settle into a rhythm for too long. The two watchers cheered at some of the tactics, especially at the close calls.

The doctor had begun to think he should try fencing when Jamie's sideways lunge made Taigan trip and fall. She rolled to her feet easily enough, and both DuBois and Amber exchanged a relieved look before they realized at the same time the girl did that she had left Jamie unprotected.

They both shoved out of their seats and leaned forward as Taigan scrambled to defend her brother and Ben took the attack for both of them. While the girl screamed and tried to help her friend, Gwyna grabbed Ben and disappeared. On his monitor, she flickered in again a moment later, dragging his limp body through a cave.

"Oh, no," the doctor said.

That was when he and Amber realized they were clutching each other's hands tightly enough to make the bones ache. They both loosened the death grasp and cleared their throats.

"I wasn't worried," she said and shook her head.

"Of course not—me neither." DuBois took another mouthful of popcorn. "Ben's in fine shape psychologically. His monitors barely flickered."

"Exactly," she said. "Which we knew would happen. Because we remember this is a game."

"Exactly," he agreed.

Silence stretched while they watched Taigan help Jamie up and Gwyna dump Ben in a dungeon.

"Let's never speak of it to anyone else, though," Amber said.

"Agreed," he said and flexed his hand. "You have a *very* strong grip. I don't suppose there are any painkillers around."

"Sorry. Sorry, I'll go get some." She hastened to the other side of the room.

Nick and Jacob joined DuBois while she was gone, having returned from lunch with sandwiches for the others and a bag of jalapeno popcorn for DuBois. He tried a few pieces and smiled in appreciation.

"What happened?" Jacob asked when Amber approached with the painkillers.

"He has a headache," she said at the same time the doctor said, "I stubbed my toe." After a pained look at one another, they resumed watching the monitors. A hint of red crept up Amber's ears.

"Uh…*huh.*" Jacob grinned at her. "There's definitely not an embarrassing story here that we'll be able to hold over your heads forever."

"Nope," she said, although her face was beet-red.

Nick chortled as he sat to eat his sandwich. He stopped with it halfway to his mouth. "Wait, what happened to Ben?"

"He got hurt trying to save Jamie and Taigan," Amber said. She cleared her throat. "Which did *not* freak either of us out and did *not* result in me crushing the doctor's hand."

"I thought we would never speak of it," DuBois said plaintively.

True, she hadn't mentioned *his* lapse in logic but still, promises were promises.

Jacob stifled a laugh in his sandwich. "But everything's good on the monitors? No cardiac arrest or anything?"

"Barely an arrhythmia." The doctor took a bite of popcorn and choked. "I thought that would be caramel and instead, it was jalapeno."

"Oof," Jacob said, through a mouthful of sandwich. "Anyway, while I was out, I got the latest results from the PT. Basically, Ben's made about as much progress as he can make in-game. If he doesn't progress *out* of the game, we can try bringing him back but they all seem to agree that he should work on strength in the real world for a while."

"That seems about right," Amber said. She unwrapped her sandwich while she watched the two monitors. "I haven't seen him stumble or lack even fine motor control in a while."

"To tell the truth, I'm not sure he wanted to go back in for that," Nick said. "It seemed like it was more about the story and the game than the recovery."

The others looked at him as they ate.

"I think the accident happened during a time where he wasn't happy with his life," he said. "I...feel weird talking about this if he hasn't talked to the rest of you, though."

"No, he's been fairly open about it," Jacob said. "And we all talked to Mike and so on. What's weird is..." He hesitated. "For Dotty and Justin, this world was a way of doing all the things they'd never been able to do in real life. It was hard sometimes, but it was also wish-fulfillment, right? For Ben, it's like a specially tailored hell."

Amber nodded contemplatively.

"What's interesting," DuBois said, "is that he could have chosen the easy path at any time. He didn't have to get involved in trying to stop the assassination of the fae king or the slavery issues in Heffog. He put himself in those situations."

"So he did," Jacob mused. "I wonder if we'll see other people like that."

"Probably." Amber smiled at him. "I wonder if we could advertise it as therapy? Not officially, you know, only…hey, you have a lot of student debt, you had a terrible day at work, so why don't you beat the crap out of some raiders?"

"Price would have a heart attack if we tried that," Nick predicted. "But let's make a mock-up ad, anyway."

CHAPTER EIGHTY-TWO

The last thing Ben remembered was seeing the terrible look on Gwyna's face. She had already thrown the magic at Jamie, but when she realized who it would strike instead, she wasn't sorry.

He could see she was surprised but she had no qualms about resolving the situation immediately and permanently. She wouldn't wallow in feelings of betrayal and would instead take action.

And then the pain—oh, God, the *pain.* The bolt of energy had hurt more than anything he could remember. He was sure she had punched a hole through his chest cavity and there was no time to even regret his choice before he lost consciousness, swallowed by pain and darkness.

In that final moment, he had not expected to wake up again and when he did, it was with a flail and a yell.

He had not realized that he was being hauled over bumpy stone, but when he shouted, the dragging stopped and Gwyna dropped him without any attempt at gentleness.

"So," she said and her voice was cold. "You're awake."

When the stars cleared from his vision, he looked at her upside-down face and tried to think of something to say.

"Before you try to be clever," she said, "remember that I know *they* knew your name and *you* knew theirs. You can't pass this off as foolish heroism—which would also be unforgivably stupid. No, you saved them because you knew them and cared for them, even after they tried to kill me and took what should have been mine."

Ben closed his mouth. She had it tied up in a very neat bow and she had headed off all the potential lies he could think of.

"Who are you really?" Gwyna asked. *"Don't* consider lying to me. I won't take it well."

She was probably telling the truth about that.

"I was advised to seek magical training," he said. "The person who told me said I was like a walking bomb. The twins...I met them in the village—at the inn. They came in with the boy injured and villagers there clearly wanted to pick their pockets. Once I'd stood up for them, I felt protective."

The woman's expression said she was impatient and unimpressed by any of this.

"The day after I met them," he continued, "a magical beast attacked the inn. The three of us killed it together, after which it turned into a...human. That was when my friend found me and told me my magic was a danger to myself and everyone around."

"And who gave you my name?" she demanded.

With an internal sigh, he decided that Yulia's name was probably too important to give up. It seemed he was about to find out whether Gwyna could tell when he was lying.

"I don't know," he said. "It wasn't my friend. I found a scrap of paper saying I could find you in caves near the lake."

The pain was immediate and crippling. It seared through his bones and he curled in a ball and whimpered. So much for manly stoicism.

"Liar," the sorceress said, annoyed. "You're a liar and I told you I would not take well to that."

"You did," Ben agreed.

"So, who gave you my name?"

"I don't know," he repeated.

The pain surged again and this time, it lasted longer. He writhed on the floor, felt the stones digging into him, and caught a glimpse of

Gwyna, her head turned negligently away. She was bored, her posture said. She didn't feel anything in particular about torturing him and she certainly didn't care enough to look at him while she did it.

When the pain released him, he lay with his forehead against the stone and panted. One rock in particular dug into his ribs. It wasn't pointy but flat. He pushed to his hands and knees and caught the glint from inside his shirt.

The iron ring. Gwyna had taken it but it was there now, held inside the shirt by a few loops of thread.

She had bound his magic, and that gave him a strange certainty that everything would be okay. He merely had to get it away from him and he would have his magic back.

Not now, he cautioned himself, and not while he wasn't sure of the lay of the land. Gwyna hadn't killed him immediately, which meant she needed something from him—but what? Ben looked at her. She leaned against the wall and watched him with an expression that seemed halfway between bored and angry.

"What was so important about what they had?" he asked her.

She sighed. "You didn't even know. What they *had* was stones from the magical wellspring at the center of the forest."

"Like the—" *Fae wellsprings.* Ben didn't finish the sentence. If Gwyna knew about another set of wellsprings, she would doubtless try to steal their power immediately, and the fae had been through enough lately. He had to find something else to say. "Like the...magic is made to look like stones?"

"No." He could almost hear her rolling her eyes. "The stones are infused with the pattern of the magic."

"The pattern of the...I don't get it."

"I know that," she said with cruel precision. She crouched to stare at him. "You don't understand any of this. You're an idiot."

"Hey," Prima said and sounded offended.

Ben looked up in surprise.

"This is my idiot," Prima said. *"I'm the one who insults him, lady. Not you!"*

He sighed and looked at the sorceress. "Okay, so you need the stones. I'm smart enough to get that part, right? So go get a stone."

"The well wouldn't give them to me," Gwyna said. She sounded annoyed. "And the power of an entire forest is—"

"More powerful than you?" he asked, seizing the chance to take a jab at her.

"An entire forest will *naturally* be stronger than a single sorceress," she snapped, nettled by his comment. Still, he could see that his words had struck home. She didn't like being refused anything and she didn't like to pit her strength against someone else's or be thwarted.

"But with it, you would have been more powerful than any other sorceress," he guessed. He sat with a wince and curled his knees to his chest. Hidden by his legs, his hand crept up the inside of his shirt. He had to get to the ring.

"I—" Gwyna shook her head. "Close enough. I would have freed that forest. It was foolish of it to stand against me." She sneered at him. "Like *you*."

"You would have set me free?" Ben laughed at her. It wasn't as strong a laugh as he wanted it to be. He was still in pain and he was tired. "You would have killed me the second I was powerful enough to be a rival."

"I don't fear you as a rival," she said. "I clash only with those who want the same things I do. You want other things. I would have set you free to claim them, but you were weak. You clung to the lies you were taught as a child—working for the good of the whole and working to help others instead of yourself. You raise them up and don't see that you have sacrificed your strength to do so, and so left yourself behind."

"Blah, blah, blah," he said before he could stop himself.

Gwyna grasped his throat and slammed his head back against the rock. Ben would have been upset about this—and he probably would be in the coming days—except for the fact that it gave him a chance to rip the ring out of his shirt. He was fairly sure he got it.

Not too sure, however, because the pain was the only thing he was conscious of a moment later. He yelled directly in her face, less as a way to annoy her than as an involuntary reaction.

"You'll be one of them next," she told him. "That *monster* you fought? Yes, it was once human but *I* set it free. I found those who needed revenge, who had been held back from justice by the same stupid rules you follow. I gave them a *gift*—I gave them strength and weapons and I took away the inhibitions that held them back."

Ben stared at her, horrified. He'd known that Gwyna was the one who made the monsters. It was chilling, though, to hear her describe what she'd done as a gift.

"When I turn you," she asked, "who do you think you'll destroy?"

Horror rushed over him. He could see it now—a monster with claws and teeth with all his grudges and none of the things that held him back. How many would he kill?

"It's time to find out," the woman told him. She hauled him up with more strength than she should have had in her small frame and he left the ring on the ground, terrified to let a single clink of metal on stone let her know he was free now.

He stumbled along with her while she pulled him through the tunnels. Pulses of pain stopped him from being a threat, but he told himself he was also doing this for a reason. If she was taking him to get a gold ring, he could find Josyla, couldn't he?

When Gwyna kicked open the door into a dungeon of sorts, Ben heard a scream. He looked up briefly—before his captor kicked him down the stairs—to where a small human—or perhaps an elf—cowered in the back of the room.

"No," she begged. "No, please, I can't do this to anyone else. Please, I can't do it again."

The sorceress heaved a sigh as she strolled down the steps. Now that Ben was on the ground, he could smell the soot and feel the heat of the forge. He looked up muzzily as Gwyna stalked toward the half-elf. He was sure this was Josyla

"You *will* do this," she said. "You will *not* hold your talents back. I have given you a gift. I have taught you how to take revenge on the ones who sold you. Why do you not accept the gift? Why do you persist in refusing it?"

"I thought gifts were something people wanted," Prima said.

"They're supposed to be," Ben said under his breath.

"So she's merely very bad at giving them?"

"Yep."

"Okay. Next question. Did you plan to do anything useful at any point?"

He grinned slightly, looked at the ceiling, and winked.

"That doesn't come off as suave as you think when you're covered in blood and soot," Prima informed him.

"For the love of… Trust me, okay?"

"It's your funeral," she responded.

Ben sighed. Gwyna reached Josyla and caught her arm. The sorceress tried to pull her unwilling apprentice to the forge, but even as small and beaten-down as Josyla was, she put up a good fight.

It meant that the woman's complete attention was focused on the elf. He readied his energy, pictured the lightning she had used on him, and thrust his hands forward to release the power.

Nothing happened, and he scowled at his hands.

"Yep. Oh yes, your funeral."

He looked at her, shoved his hands forward again, and this time, pictured the emperor from Star Wars.

His effort drew the same dismal response of nothing.

Finally, with time running out, he used a spell he *did* know. The water bucket Josyla would use to cool her various instruments lifted off the floor, dropped water and pieces of metal as it did so, and streaked across the room at high speed to pound into Gwyna's head. She went down in a heap.

"Oh, damn," Prima said. *"Okay. I was wrong. I can admit it."*

The elf stared at Gwyna's unconscious form.

"Josyla," Ben said urgently.

Her head jerked up.

"Orien sent me."

Her face transformed. *"Orien?"* For a moment, he could see the elegance of Yn'solde before it disappeared and was replaced by determination. "Come on, let's go before she wakes up."

"One second." He took a piece of iron off the floor and hid it inside the sorceress' pocket. Quickly, he followed her out of the room to make their escape toward the safety of Yulia's house.

CHAPTER EIGHTY-THREE

Jamie fought the urge to sprint down the road. Yulia seemed to make them move faster than they should be able to, somehow, but it didn't seem like enough. It wasn't right, surely, to be *walking* when Ben was in the hands of the enemy and might be killed?

The old woman was not dawdling, at least. When the twins tumbled through her door, gasping about Ben and Gwyna, she had snatched a pack and a walking stick and set off with them at once. She had taken the two rocks and now held one in her palm as she walked. Her gaze was distant.

Taigan squeezed Jamie's hand. "It'll be okay." She lowered her voice before she added, "You know Prima won't let anything happen to him. The team will pull him out if they need to."

Something unknotted in his chest and he nodded. To his surprise, however, his sense of duty did not flag in the least.

"What is it?" she asked.

"Maybe it isn't 'real,'" he said and made finger quotes, "but I believe he wasn't thinking about that when he threw himself in front of me. The pain was real, the danger was real—he truly *did* try to sacrifice himself for us. We owe it to him to do everything in our power to save him."

"And we are," she said. "Even with the ground being...folded...or whatever it is she's doing, sprinting won't do anything except tire us out by the time we get there."

"Indeed," Yulia agreed.

Both twins jumped, and Jamie wondered how much she'd heard.

The old woman did not address that. "What we *should* do," she said briskly, "is make a plan of some kind. You've proven that the two of you are resourceful and you can catch Gwyna off-guard, but that's no excuse for going into this unprepared."

They nodded.

"Now, the one thing I *can* tell you is that if Gwyna wanted Ben dead, she'd have killed him at once." Yulia heaved a sigh. "Of course, whether she wants him alive as an apprentice or simply as leverage against us, I couldn't say, but the boy's alive. I can tell you that much."

Taigan swallowed. "And if he's alive, he can come back from whatever it is. As long as he's alive." Jamie heard her add under her breath, "Prima, please tell us we're doing the right thing."

"You're doing the right thing." For once, there was no mocking tone to the AI's voice.

"Can you let him know we're coming for him?" Jamie asked quietly.

"No. That violates the rules of the world. You both must do what you are doing regardless of what's going on in another area."

"You told us we were doing the right thing!" he snapped quietly.

"You're going into danger for your friend's sake. That's the right thing to do."

His heart sank. What if it was already too late? What if Ben thought they'd left him? Then, he straightened. Prima had said they were doing the right thing and she was right. They were doing the best thing they could with what they knew. What else *could* they do?

Slowly, he let the question form in his mind before he asked Yulia, "Is Gwyna more concerned with her grudges or getting what she wanted to start with?"

"That is a good question." The old woman nodded approvingly. "As with everyone, she is a great deal more changeable than she thinks. She wants power and she will not suffer anyone to stand in her way. She has decided that no one has any more right to anything than anyone else— that the right is earned by the one who seizes it with the most force."

Jamie saw Taigan frown. "What?" he asked her.

"It must be a very scary way to live," she said with a shrug. "You never know if you get to keep something. What if someone else wants it more or is more powerful? You'd always be looking over your shoulder."

"Just so," Yulia said. "And yet, it is perhaps easier to mistrust everyone than it is to place her trust in even one other person. *That* takes bravery."

"It does?" The girl looked at Jamie. "Isn't that…easier?"

"Not for everyone." The old woman smiled and raised her head to scan the way ahead. "Ah. I think we may have arrived at the right time."

He looked ahead and saw two figures. One was almost certainly their friend and the other was shorter. Ben with Gwyna in pursuit? No, the two figures were running together. Might this be the elf's friend? Jamie and Taigan looked at each other for a moment, then raced forward.

They reached the other two not far from where the path curved down toward the lake. The man was in rough shape, bruised and battered, and the young woman beside him was thin and pale and looked uncomfortable in the noonday sun. She had glanced at her companion to gauge his response to the twins, but she still held back and cast frequent looks over her shoulder.

Ben and Jamie clapped each other on the shoulder.

"You're alive," the boy said with relief. "Thank God."

"She wanted to turn me into another one of those monsters," Ben said without preamble. "And she'll probably be after us soon. Taigan, hello. Yulia—thank you for coming. All of you, this is Josyla. She was held in a dungeon by Gwyna."

The woman remained where she was. She looked over her shoulder again, then nodded at them.

"You saw Orien?" she asked.

"We did," Jamie pointed to himself and Taigan.

"And I could hear his memories of you from leagues away," Yulia said with a smile. She looked hard at her and seemed to read the young half-elf's thoughts. "She told you no one was coming for you."

Josyla trembled.

"And she warped your mind as well," the old woman said softly. "Do you see that now? Is the fog lifting?"

Josyla's head jerked up. "She *tried*," she said fiercely. "But she wasn't able to turn me into one of her monsters, no matter how much she tried. She whispered in my head, all day and all night, how I had been betrayed and I should get revenge." She pressed her lips together. "It's quiet now but it feels so strange." She swallowed and sighed. "But with her saying it over and over again, telling me to nurture all of the hatred I had, I could always cling to the fact that she tried to send me in the wrong direction. Every time she said it, I got more determined not to—"

The explosion tore through the road and all five of them were flung aside. A series of "oof"s and "ow"s issued from the group and one particularly evocative oath from Yulia before a glittering blue dome settled above them.

Jamie leapt to his feet, his sword at the ready. "Yulia! Tell me how to break through the barrier!"

"The barrier is *mine*, young man." The old woman stood and dusted her skirt off.

"Oh."

"Good job," Prima told him. *"No, truly. You're giving Ben a run for his money."*

Ben gave a very unconvincing cough to hide his laugh.

Jamie merely shook his head. "Going back to school will be much easier after this," he muttered. "What can anyone say to me that's worse than Prima in a good mood?"

"You know, I am in a good mood. I feel good today."

Taigan, Ben, and Jamie chuckled, while Josyla and Yulia exchanged a glance that said they thought the others were crazy. Jamie couldn't exactly blame them for that.

They could see Gwyna now. She stalked toward them with magic pooling around her hands, blue-black shimmers that called to mind the lightning she'd thrown at Ben before. Her hair straggled from its braid and blood ran down one side of her face.

"What did you do to her?" the boy asked Ben.

"I hit her with a bucket," he said with a big thumbs-up.

"I can verify that."

"A bucket," Taigan mused. "Sure."

"Results are results," Yulia interjected. "Now, she's angry—and that's usually a time that people stumble. What it should make *her* do is doubt her certainty that she's entitled to everything."

"She *should* doubt that," the girl muttered.

"This is not the time, young lady. What *we* must do, if we hope to harness the blessing of the forest, is work like a forest. Let our spells and our attacks protect each other and work together as vines grow on trees or fallen leaves enrich the earth."

Jamie, Ben, and Taigan looked at one another. They nodded. The boy had the sense that all three of them were half-sure this was entirely made up hooey, but they were also all half-sure it was true.

"It's how we beat her last time," Ben pointed out.

"And she *doesn't* get to take the power of the forest," Taigan said. "That well gets to choose where it bestows its power, and it *doesn't* want that power to go to her." She looked at the stones Yulia held. "We need to protect them."

"Focus on each other," the old woman said confidently. "And trust me. The stones will take care of themselves."

"Hmm," Ben said.

"Is there actually a *plan?*" Josyla demanded.

"Rock and a pointy place," the other three responded at once.

Jamie gestured to Taigan and Ben. "You two are the rock. Josyla and I will be the pointy place. Uh, Josyla, do you have anything you can stab with?"

"Yes." She did not elaborate.

There wasn't time for further discussion. The next blast from Gwyna's magic shredded the shield around them and Taigan charged out of the rubble with a shriek. Josyla jumped and Jamie looked at her.

"She does that. The two of them yell a lot."

"I...so I see." She watched Ben and Taigan whip their weapons at their adversary. "They're not at all afraid, are they? That's...stupid."

"Probably," he said cheerfully, "but it's that or simply give up and let her win."

"I hadn't thought of it like that." The elf nodded decisively. "Very well, then. What's our part?"

"We let them drive her back to us," he explained. "We've done it once before so she might look over her shoulder, but as long as we can keep one group at her back, we'll eventually get her."

"Good." She looked to where Yulia had knelt to begin casting spells and then at Jamie. "Where should we go?"

"Let's circle out." He drew his sword and began to circle.

Gwyna yelled something about vengeance and freedom and he rolled his eyes. "Was she always like this?"

"All the time," Josyla said. "She thinks she never got her due—and that the reason is people being nice to each other or...something. I don't know. She's insane and she wants to be able to do things like wipe out cities with a snap of her—whoa!"

The sorceress had turned to snake a line of lightning in their direction. To Jamie's amusement, Josyla threw a piece of metal and drew the lightning away before she lobbed a tiny blade directly at Gwyna. The woman ducked but not fast enough to avoid it entirely. Red bloomed on her shoulder and she screamed.

"You bitch," she said to Josyla. "I gave you everything you needed to take your revenge."

"I never *wanted* revenge!" she screamed finally. "I wanted to be *free*. I wanted to go *home*! You can yell about revenge all day, but it won't make anything better, it won't make anything right!" She ducked under another bolt of lightning and pulled a few more of her tiny knives out. They rested between her fingers and she settled into a fighter's crouch. "But you *did* give me considerable time to practice throwing knives."

Gwyna curled her lip. "Fine. Be weak. Run back to your little elf. And when the people who sold you once sell you again, don't come crying to me."

How Josyla threw all her knives at once, Jamie didn't know. He only knew that they seemed to sprout from the sorceress' body. She staggered back, her face white.

"And when you are killed by all the people you wronged," the half-elf said, "don't come crying to *me*."

He was a little nonplussed. He'd expected to win this—it was five against one, after all—but he'd hardly expected it to be *easy*.

But Gwyna seemed to grow. She stretched, her neck twisted oddly, and her eyes turned a full black that bled onto her cheeks.

"Now," she said, and her voice seemed to be a chorus, "I'm *very* angry."

CHAPTER EIGHTY-FOUR

Ben hadn't met many elves in his time. Still, he was beginning to think that you should never piss one off. He watched as Josyla—scared, shrinking, terrorized little Josyla—threw all her knives at once. One landed in Gwyna's throat and others across her torso and shoulders. There was no surviving those injuries.

If you were mortal, that is, and not a demon.

As the sorceress' body began to shift and stretch, he cast a horrified look at Yulia. *Please,* he thought, *let her at least know what is going on. Let her understand.*

She didn't and her pale, shocked face said as much. He hung his head for a moment. They would have to kill this demon-creature, and he had no idea how. He had a vague idea of crosses and wooden stakes, but that was vampires and crosses probably weren't what would defeat real ones, anyway.

Until he thought of something else, he would have to continue with Operation Rock and a Pointy Place.

"Hey!" he bellowed at what was left of Gwyna.

The monster swung to face him. Its head lolled and its black eyes were a hungry void as it hissed in fury.

He didn't wait for more conversation. For one thing, it wasn't particularly scintillating and for another, he decided he had more of a chance to be freaked out the longer he delayed his attack. He rushed in with his sword held slantways across his body, grateful that he'd had the presence of mind to retrieve it before he left Gwyna's caves.

The demon lowered its head and shrieked at him. The sound made every hair on his body stand up, but momentum carried him through. With Taigan at his side, screaming something that sounded suspiciously like a yodel, he met the demon head-on. He put his entire strength into pivoting his blade ninety degrees and slashed up and to the side across the creature's face and neck.

His strike did injure it. That was the good news. The bad news was that the black blood that spurted over his face burned like acid. He yelled, ducked, and dragged his sleeve desperately across his face. The cloth began to disintegrate with a hiss.

Ben could not afford for this to drag on. None of them could, so he stood and tried to keep his eyes open. They stung and he was fairly sure one of them was swelling closed. It was a good thing Eliza wasn't there to see this, he thought dimly.

Taigan yelled and flailed at the demon with her staff. She had put all her energy into the enterprise, and between that and her natural inclination to speed, she delivered a fair amount of damage and allowed almost no strikes through. The demon held its ground, but it wasn't taking any.

He almost threw up when he saw what his sword had done. The monster's skin was sliced open and dripped black blood, but it fought on. It had the form of a human but there wasn't anything vital in its neck or head, it seemed.

That somewhat surprising realization gave him an idea.

"Hit it anywhere!" he called over his shoulder. "Don't waste effort going for vital organs. It doesn't have any!"

"Roger!" Jamie replied.

"Got it!" Taigan added.

"I could have told you that!" Josyla yelled. "I didn't realize you didn't know."

"Is there anything *else* I should know?" Ben sidestepped a wild slash of the lethal claws.

"It's weak against its opposite element," the elf told him, "but I don't see one of those, so I have no idea if you can use that. Keep hitting it!"

"Can do!"

Taigan and Ben launched into another flurry. One darted in and the other stepped forward as the first reached a crescendo in their hacking and slashing. Some of their best strikes came as the other was winding up for a massive blow. The demon—elemental—might be otherworldly, but it was as constrained by the limits of its focus as they were. It had trouble focusing on even two people when they were both attacking.

And it had probably forgotten about Jamie and Josyla entirely, not to mention Yulia.

All he needed to focus on was his part, Ben told himself. He had never been in a fight like this before, where he was content to relax his vigilance over the whole situation. In the fae lands, he had looked for the elven assassin, tried to watch everyone else's back, and despaired of the wanton violence around him instead of focusing on what he needed to do. In Heffog, he had done his piece but left immediately to ensure that everyone else did theirs.

Here, he trusted. If anyone had told him a few weeks before that he would gladly go into battle beside two teenagers and an old woman, he'd have thought they were insane, but there he was.

Taigan stumbled and he yelled her name, but she managed to recover her footing and drove the butt of her staff directly into the demon's face. She whooped when he followed her strike with one of his own and sliced at the creature's leg.

They had it on the back foot now and were determined to not let the momentum die. Ben delivered three strikes to the torso, then swung his blade and hacked as hard as he could at the demon's neck.

Its head careened away.

He froze. His glance first saw Taigan, who held a hand clapped over her mouth. Jamie looked a little green about the gills, while Josyla and Yulia both seemed to watch with what might best be described as academic interest.

That was all he saw before the demon hauled its headless body to its feet and screeched again. He wasn't exactly sure how as it no longer had vocal cords or a mouth. But perhaps, like its neck and head weren't vital, it didn't need them for speech, either.

It surged toward him in a rush and he had no more time for thought.

"I never thought I'd"—he bashed one of its arms— "fight a headless demon!"

"Roll with it!" Taigan yelled.

Ben said nothing to this. He tried to pivot to force their adversary back to Jamie and Josyla, but it seemed wise to their tricks now. It twisted and attacked, keeping him and Taigan on the defensive instead of the other way around.

Finally, Jamie seemed to give up. He and Josyla raced in to aid their teammates.

"What are you—" Ben panted and gestured tiredly for them to complete the sentence in their heads.

"Helping you," the boy said. "This is dragging on. Rock and a Pointy Place works best when the Rock phase doesn't take ten fucking minutes."

"You don't say." He felt light-headed by now, and his muscles were dragging. Determined, he tried to summon the energy for one more slash. Then another. And one more after that.

The demon was not pleased to now face four armed people. It yelled and clawed at them.

"Josyla?" Ben called. "Any—"

"Nope," she replied. "If you give yourself over to one emotion or element too often, you can get sucked into it—especially when you're close to death. I should have known she might—aaaah!"

"Josyla?"

"Just...ow." She panted with pain. "I got too close. Jamie landed a good hit out of it, though."

"Hell yeah, I did." The boy grinned.

Ben smiled at the twins. When he'd first met them, they had been two people against the world, consumed by their problems. Now, Jamie was learning to trust others and Taigan had come into her own as someone who existed beyond her illness.

Then he realized what Yulia had planned this whole time. He looked at the old woman and then at the demon.

He circled and ran with a berserker yell. The twins scattered at the sound and he vaulted upward and struck the monster feet-first. As his legs punched out, it staggered back and he watched to see what would happen.

Unfortunately, he landed first. Pain blossomed through his back and he uttered a noise halfway between a grunt and a yell.

Still, he managed to catch some of it. Operation Rock and a Pointy place, as it turned out, had not been a failure after all. They had not driven the demon to Jamie and Josyla but instead, to Yulia.

While they had held the enemy's attention, the old woman had worked with the power of the stones.

The demon's feet impacted with the earth and one of the stones from the well. As Ben watched, the crystal-like stone sprouted like a split acorn. Roots burrowed into the dirt of the road and a tree swept into the sky at the same time. The trunk thickened, branches appeared, and leaves sprouted. When it was over, the five humans stood under a canopy of leaves that rang softly like crystal.

He gaped at the tree. It had suddenly appeared in the place of his enemy and he didn't know what to do with it. "What—"

"The forest reclaims," Yulia said, with satisfaction. "Gwyna took its power for her spells and transformed those poor wretches into creatures that lived among the trees. The forest took that and also absorbed all her fear and her hatred."

"She's part of the forest now?" Taigan asked urgently. "We need to cleanse it. The forest will be sickened—"

"Did you hear nothing Josyla said, girl?" Yulia raised an eyebrow. "Focus too much on any one thing, any emotion or aspect of life, and it can consume you, but all aspects of life may exist in moderation without sickening the whole. Do you think the forest has no anger within it or no sense of vengeance or justice? No, Gwyna became in death what she had forgotten to be in life—part of a greater whole, a being without any single outlook on life. She did not need to be cleansed. She needed to be part of something more."

Taigan approached the tree and rested her hand against it. She shuddered when she touched the crystal bark but the tree did not lash out at her. "But she was evil."

"Evil is what happens when darkness and vengeance consume you," the old woman said. "Now…well, now we've ruined the road, I'm afraid."

"We'll build around it," Josyla said absentmindedly. She studied the tree. "It's beautiful. She's beautiful now."

"And at peace," Yulia said, "at last. How many years, I wonder, has that demon stalked her? No wonder she was so determined to make others embrace their thoughts of revenge. She did not want to be alone anymore, although it was all she knew how to do."

Ben looked at Taigan, who was crying silently.

"Are you all right?" he asked her in an undertone.

"I don't like this," she said. She wiped at her eyes. "I don't like it when people miss their chance. She was powerful and could have been more. Now, she's gone forever and she'll never have the chance…"

"She's part of something," he said when she didn't finish the sentence. "Part of the forest, Taigan, so she's not gone. She wasn't her whole self at the end when we still saw her as a human. This is closer to what she was."

The girl nodded. "Thank you," she said finally. She straightened and nodded at Josyla. "We should help you get home."

"I'd like that," the elf said. "But first, there are people in the forest I need to help. I was afraid of the pain and I let her bully me into putting bindings on them. Even with her specific spell released, they have the rings still fixed to their skin. I need to correct that."

Ben nodded. He was exhausted now. His face still stung where the demon blood had touched it. Although the day was calm and the sky clear, everything felt out of place.

He felt out of place.

"It's time," he said to Prima in a low voice. To his surprise, his throat ached with unshed tears. He could not remember the last time he'd moved on for any reason other than anger.

"Almost," she said. *"It's almost time. I'll miss you, you know."*

"I'll miss you, too." He smiled suddenly. "And I can come back to visit, you know. Since we're parting on good terms."

"Wow, you've had a strange life, haven't you?"

"Yep." He smiled and sheathed his sword. "Okay, everyone, let's go...get some sleep first. Then piles of food. *Then* we'll help Josyla."

CHAPTER EIGHTY-FIVE

They set out the next morning while the sun was still rising. Yulia gave them heaping portions of porridge and stood over them while they ate it. The old woman seemed tired from her efforts the night before but not in a way that worried Ben.

When she caught him looking at her, she smiled. "It is a privilege, at my age, to learn new forms of magic. Studying the magic of the forest is something I never thought I would have the chance to do. I had felt its whispers in my dreams but never anything like that."

"Working with it—" he began.

She shook her head. "You don't work with the magic of the forest. You call it and you see if it answers. That is what the twins were given at the well—two names telling the story of the forest in night and day. A name is a powerful thing."

He nodded. The twins were inhaling their breakfast as only young people could.

"They'll be well," Yulia assured him.

"I know." He managed a smile. "But I worry. Are young people always so...fragile?"

"Everyone," she said. Her voice held the hard-won wisdom of years but it was tempered with a surprising amount of humor. "Stronger than you think and more fragile than you think." She shrugged. "They'll find what they need—as, I think, you did."

He couldn't argue that. With the return to the real world looming, he felt a strange sense of completion as well as a goodbye to a version of himself he had never expected to leave behind. When he left Yulia's cottage a few minutes later, it was with a sense of serenity.

Josyla led them through the forest at a quick pace. When he caught up with her, the elf confided, "I'm terrified."

"What of?" He looked at her as she forged ahead, pale and determined.

"Seeing the people I hurt. Gwyna could never have made them what they are now without me." She swallowed. "You can say whatever you want about me needing to do it to survive—I told myself all those things over the past few years. It kept me sane. But it was never enough."

Ben nodded quietly.

"How is Orien?" she asked him. "I...I hope he's well. I hope he's..." She couldn't finish the sentence.

"I don't think he *has* moved on," Ben said, amused. "I assume that was what you were going to say."

Josyla nodded. A flush stained her cheeks now.

He swallowed. "There is something you should know. Orien was one of a few who began something of a—hmm. Well, you know the provision of elven law that you're entitled to the life of someone who sold you?"

She looked at him, alarmed. "Yes."

"He killed Kerill," he said baldly. Someone else would probably know a better way to say it, but he wasn't someone else.

The half-elf stopped dead in her tracks and her jaw hung open.

"There's so much happening in Heffog," Ben said. "To be fair to Orien, it's kind of my fault. He did...uh, run with it, though."

"I..." Josyla stared off into the distance. "Well, I'm certainly less worried about seeing the people I put the rings on, so that's something. But this is insane. How could... I don't..."

"You don't think it was justified?" he asked her curiously.

"Of course it was. Well, slavery is prohibited. Certain types of it." She shrugged helplessly. "But the rich do what they want. They always have."

"You don't want to change that?"

"You can't change something like that." She looked at him like he was crazy. "You run. You carve out the safest place you can and you do whatever you can to stay there, but there's no guarantee. There's never a guarantee."

She kept walking and he continued alongside her with a deep frown.

It seemed ridiculous to him that people there would merely accept their slavery without another word, but who was he to judge? How many things in the real world had he run away from because he thought there was no way to change them?

They made good time over the next hour. Jamie and Taigan walked together, not talking, but they didn't seem entirely separate from one another either. Ben envied that a little—he wasn't close with any of his family and he'd never even had a friend or girlfriend that close aside from Mike and Natasha—but he mostly took happiness from the fact that the two of them looked relaxed.

They arrived first at a maze and he was surprised to see both the twins hang back. They looked almost worried and watched carefully as Josyla proceeded along the paths to the center of the maze and crouched there.

The elf scratched in the dirt and made a hole that grew deeper and deeper until she found something. Carefully, she levered out a statue in the form of a pillar with three animals twined around each other. She held it in her hands for a moment and spoke a single word over it. He could not hear what the word was but the statue crumbled into dust and disappeared in a rising breeze.

Josyla sat silently for a moment, her head tipped toward the sky, then pushed to her feet and walked quickly out of the maze.

She did not speak while she led them through the undergrowth. As far as Ben could tell, she was not looking at landmarks and seemed to be drawn along an invisible path. When they crested a hill and saw the encampment in front of them, she seemed almost surprised.

The people there looked at them with open fear. They were not as gaunt as the person he had seen in the town, but they did not look well-fed by any stretch of the imagination.

Josyla led the way down the hill with her hands up to show she meant no harm. When she reached the bottom, she said simply, "You remember me."

"The witch's slave," one of the men said. "Did you kill her? Is that why we're free?"

"She is dead," the elf confirmed. "And I have come to undo the last of her magic."

The people looked at one another, almost crying with relief. A few had sat again as they were unsteady on their feet. Taigan and Jamie began to circulate with pieces of dried meat and fruit, which they ate eagerly.

While they did so, Josyla paced.

"I don't know how to do this," she confessed. "Gwyna did much of the casting. I simply formed the metal...and I..."

"I saw." His voice was quiet. The sorceress' magic had been crueler than he could believe. The rings had spikes on the insides that pierced the people's fingers to the bone. The wounds had not festered, but he could not imagine the pain of having the rings there.

"I still hear their screams at night," she confessed. "The hot metal, the— They lived...I kept telling myself that they lived, but I *felt* it every time one of them died later. Who knows who killed all of them —scared farmers or adventurers. Gwyna made them unable to think of anything but their regrets and hatred and set them loose on the world."

"She thought she was setting them free," Ben said, in part to remind himself that it had been real. "I wish—"

"There is no sense wishing," Josyla said with the finality of someone who had long since learned not to spend her energy on wishing for a different world. She looked at the people and said, "It's time."

"You can do this," he assured her. The words felt awkward but her smile told him he'd said the right thing for once.

The elf set her tools up in the center of the camp. She waited as the people came to her one by one and spoke quiet words over their rings before she cut through the metal, holding a shard of rock near the ring as she did so. Each time, the stone flared with deep blue light and she rocked back on her heels and winced.

"She explained it to me earlier. When a spell is broken," Jamie explained to Ben, "all the power releases. Spells seem to be made in… circles? So diagrams, but also rings. She cuts the ring, which breaks the spell."

Josyla might not be a trained sorceress, but she worked quickly and efficiently. As each ring broke, the person sagged with relief. The elf, meanwhile, never wavered from her concentration on the gold.

Her magic truly was extraordinary. She sang under her breath as she worked, and the metal responded to the music. It lifted away from skin, its form suddenly fluid without being white-hot, and spun above the flesh as a shining orb. She offered each sphere to the person she had taken it from. Some took it and others not. Those that went unclaimed, she tucked in a pouch at her waist.

A salve from Yulia went over the broken skin, with bandages over that. Taigan and Jamie did that part, earnest and wincing every time someone cried out in pain. Ben, watching, thought the girl had an especially careful touch. She wasn't always *gentle*—sometimes there were pieces of dirt for her to strip away—but when she had to do something painful, she moved decisively and with precision.

He wondered if she might be a doctor one day. Then he wondered if she had ever had any ambitions in that direction at all. Probably not. How could someone have ambitions when they did not know if they would live or not or couldn't even be sure whether they would be awake or not?

"She'll be all right, won't she?" he asked Prima.

"Which one?"

"Taigan. Or Josyla, I guess."

"Do you mean, will Taigan recover from her illness? If so…" Prima

paused. *"I don't know if she will ever be cured, but I think she is learning how to wake up again. If not, I will keep her safe when she is here."*

He opened his mouth, then shut it.

"What?"

"I wondered if you knew how medical care worked in our world." Ben considered the dizzying cost and decided not to say anything to the AI about that. He didn't want her to feel guilty for existing. "Never mind."

"Mmmm."

He turned his attention to the former monsters. At first, he wasn't sure what he saw, but by the fifth or sixth person, he was certain.

Josyla was becoming more…her. She seemed to sit taller and fill out her edges more completely. There was a healthier color to her cheeks. Her eyes, which had been dark-brown, sparkled with highlights of gold and green. Her hair gleamed slightly. Whatever piece of her had been trapped within each spell was returning as she broke them.

It wasn't only her, though. The people she was healing also seemed to be healthier. Nothing could take away the months of pain and illness they had endured, but they looked less defeated. Of course, for all he knew, that was simply the relief of not having a piece of metal welded to them.

When the half- elf had finished, she went to each person to say goodbye. A few did not want to speak to her, but others were checking on her as much as she was checking on them. One woman stroked her cheek and said something kind under her breath. Ben marked the way Josyla smiled. Another man said something hurtful, but she nodded and bowed deeply, a gesture of apology that transcended race.

When she returned to the others, she was quiet. They left in silence and he and the twins exchanged a look that said they would let Josyla speak first.

It was a long time before she did. While it was difficult to tell what was going on as they walked through the forest, it seemed clear that the sun was sinking in the sky. Josyla, who had pushed them almost to a jog on their journey into the woods, now walked slowly and sometimes, stopped entirely before she remembered where she was.

"I'm not sure I'm ready to see Orien," she said finally.

Ben saw the twins' uncertainty out of the corner of his eye.

"You don't have to see him," he said. "But...tell him you're alive. Tell him you're well."

The elf looked soberly at him and nodded.

"Why don't you want to see him?" he asked.

"So much has happened," Josyla said. "I'm not sure I'm ready to pick up where we left off. I'm not sure I ever want to see that place again. And if he's a revolutionary now, if he's overthrowing the nobles —I don't know that I want any part of that. I never wanted to stay in Heffog. I feel that if I go back, I'll never get out again."

He nodded because he couldn't fault her for any of that.

"Thank you for not trying to talk me out of it," she said with a half-smile.

"I wouldn't," he told her. "I know what it is to not want to stay in one place."

"Where were you born?" she asked him, curious now.

"A sleepy little place." It was difficult to explain his suburban neighborhood to a person from this world. "There were farms nearby, but my parents...well, my mother taught children. My father kept the books for a local blacksmith."

"You didn't want his trade?" Josyla guessed.

Ben hid a smile. "No. I didn't. I went adventuring as soon as I could. I appreciate what they built, now—the life for us, the possibilities, and making sure we were educated. But I've always wanted something more for myself. No. Something *different*."

"So you understand," she said. She stopped and looked around. "I'll get word to Orien," she promised them. "All of you—thank you. You two, I smelled the maze on you the first time we met. You released that spell. You did more than you know with that. Ben...you came to save me when you didn't even know who I was." She exhaled a deep breath. "Tell Yulia thank you for me."

"Where are you going?" Ben asked.

But she was already fading away, melting into the dappled sunlight as she wove through the trees. Whatever magic she had, it went far beyond metals and music.

And the forest protected her as one of its own.

Ben watched her go, then turned to the twins. "Very well. Where to next? I'll see you there before I leave the game."

CHAPTER EIGHTY-SIX

"Anything?" Ben called over the gorge.

"Nothing here," Taigan responded. "Jamie?"

"Sec." The boy's voice was strained, and he appeared a moment later in a rustle of leaves. He heaved himself over a branch and stood to look around. "Aha! I see it!"

His companions looked in the direction in which he pointed and both started running.

"Hey!" Jamie called. "I found it! I should get to be there first!"

"Nope!" his sister retorted. She hurdled a small bush and started down the slope.

Ben didn't have a slope on his side, so he hurled himself off the tiny cliff with a yell—only to realize that he plunged toward a patch of watery mud. He wind-milled his arms wildly, but there was no avoiding it and he landed with a squelch.

"Aww," Taigan called over her shoulder as she sprinted away. "Too bad!"

"God—dammit—fucking—mud…" He yanked his leg and only succeeded in pulling it out of his boot and tipping it with a thump. "Gah."

"I hope it all works out for you!" Jamie called as he sprinted past at high speed.

"You two," he shouted at them, "are *very* disloyal!"

"It sounds like something a loser would say," the girl observed.

He yanked his boot out of the mud with a wet splotch and set off in one boot and one sock to enter the campground with a narrow-eyed look. "That win was invalid."

"It was," Jamie agreed. "Both of you had a false start, which means I win."

"No, no." His sister wagged her finger. "I won fair and square. Prima?"

"I won't weigh in on this."

"That is probably wise," Ben said. "Now, what do we have?"

"A traditional send-off party," Prima said. *"When someone leaves the game, I like to make sure they have an excellent night. After all the camping and the monsters, it seems like the right thing to do."*

She had laid out a campground that was like something out of a dream. Three spacious tents were strung with fairy lights and flower garlands and each person's initials were embroidered in gold thread on the tent flap. When he pushed into his tent, he saw a wide, soft bed and a big bathtub filled with steaming water—something that sounded about perfect after his latest round of fights and sleeping on the ground.

Whether the other two took baths or napped, he didn't know. He only knew he lazed in the bath without it getting cold, a frosty bottle of beer in one hand and not a thought in his mind. His muscles began to relax, the bruises dissipated slowly, and he felt a calm overtake him.

"This is nice," he told Prima.

"Wait until you see the food."

"I can't wait." He took a sip of beer. "No, I can wait. Mostly because I'm too lazy to get up."

"Why do you insult yourself? You know I wanted to do that."

Ben laughed. "Anyway, this is a good send-off. A little time to be quiet and think." He waited. "What, no jab about my thinking speed?"

"I was trying to be nice because it was a party."

He chuckled.

The only thing that got him out of the bathtub was the smell of hotdogs cooking. He wandered out, dressed in a supremely soft set of pajama pants and a t-shirt—his traditional camping pajamas—to find a camping feast laid out. Hot dogs sizzled, potatoes cooked among the stones in the fire, and the fixings for s'mores were ready.

"Amazing," he said. "It's been a while since I had a real camp meal."

"And," Prima told him, "you get to have all the fixings."

"You know, I say that part of the fun is making do with what you can haul up a mountain unrefrigerated, but a baked potato with all the fixings is divine." He pulled one out and split it before he loaded it with butter, cheese, bacon bits, and more.

Jamie emerged from his tent first and sniffed at the smell of dinner. He loaded five hotdogs onto his plate, dressed each one carefully, and proceeded to scarf them so quickly that Ben put his fork down and watched in amazement.

The boy sighed happily. "That was good. A good starter."

"Ah, youth." He smiled and returned to his potato.

"What's it like being old?" Jamie asked curiously. He froze. "I mean, old..er. Older. Than you were when you were, you know...younger."

"Uh-huh." He grinned and watched the kid dig himself into a hole. "Well, I'll tell you, it's a full-time job keeping my hair dyed and it's a miracle I can walk unassisted."

Jamie lowered his face into his hands with an embarrassed mutter.

"Oh, God," Taigan said as she stepped out of her tent. "Jamie, what did you do?"

"He put..." Ben mimed. "His whole foot, right—the *whole* foot—in his mouth."

She snorted and started her plate but looked around with a frown. In the next moment, she flickered out of existence before she returned with a bowl of some type of grain salad.

"What did you do?" he asked.

"Oh, I can...I don't know. There's a way I can summon things, but I can't be in this version of the world to do it." She shrugged and ladled a big helping of the salad onto her plate. "Do you want some? Couscous, dried cranberries, feta, spinach…"

He took the bowl happily and served himself before passing it to Jamie. "To answer your question," he said, "it feels very normal to be older, honestly. The main thing is, you're more patient—"

"You? Patient?"

"And your body isn't as resilient," he finished with great dignity. "All that stuff like crashing on your buddy's floor for the night and being fine the next morning? It's not a thing once you reach thirty. Of course, you stop caring about being all tough, too."

"Yeah, that's it. You stopped caring. You didn't give up or anything."

"Rude," Ben told Prima and pretended not to notice the twins' laughter. "Anyway, why did you ask?"

"I, uh…" Jamie shrugged. "No reason."

"You don't lie very well. Don't go into politics."

The boy said nothing for a long time. He practically inhaled two loaded potatoes while Ben waited.

Finally, he ran out of patience. "You don't have to worry about being insulting."

"Oh." Jamie looked relieved. "Okay, then."

"This should be good."

"I guess I wondered—I mean, I always thought grown-ups knew what to do, you know? Like there was…" he trailed off.

"Oh." Ben nodded sagely. "Yeah, sorry to tell you, but there's no manual. Not only do you keep being as confused, but your problems also tend to get more complicated."

The boy stared at him like a deer in headlights. "Great," he managed finally.

"It's okay," he said. "Most of the time, you get used to it. Then you're doing something like feeding a polar bear and you start wondering, 'why the hell did I think this was a good idea?' But it always passes eventually."

"Sure." Jamie sighed. "I guess that's true. You didn't always know what to do but you seemed confident in your ability to choose."

Ben started laughing and could not stop. He laughed so hard that it took him a while to realize Prima was also laughing. She had mimicked the cadence of human laughter—but, of course, did not need to stop in order to breathe. That gave her far more staying power.

When he looked up, it was to find both twins staring at him in confusion.

"Sorry," he managed. "It's, uh…you didn't see me in Heffog. Or in the fae lands. In Heffog, I started a civil war by failing to think at *all*. And in the fae lands, I couldn't get off my ass to do *anything*. Sometimes you do well, sometimes you don't."

"Huh." Jamie chewed meditatively.

"So…" Taigan frowned. "I don't get it. You get older and you learn how to be the person you want to be, right?"

"Yeah," he said but wondered where this was going.

"Well then, why wouldn't you simply be that person?" she asked him.

"Yeah," her brother agreed.

"Oh," Ben said. "Oh, that is so precious. Oh, you two." He shook his head. "You know, I think I'll let you two work this one out yourselves, okay?"

"No," Jamie said and looked panicked. "No, no, we need help."

"A ton of help," Taigan agreed. "Him, not me. I'm merely curious." She grinned at Jamie, already anticipating the insult he had decided to give with a single raised eyebrow instead of words.

"Discovering all those answers is one of the parts of being an adult," he said. "And now, because even saying that sentence made me feel eighty years old, let's talk about something else. What will you two do after I head out?"

"I don't know," the girl said, after a moment. She looked at her brother.

Above the fire, something shimmered and opened into a vision of clear blue sky over mountain peaks. In the air, a golden key glittered.

"This is what you need to find," Prima said. *"It will open the door back to your home."*

"Huh." Taigan narrowed her eyes at it. "Where is it?"

"Finding it is part of the experience."

"I'm beginning to think adults say that when they don't know how to answer a question," the girl muttered.

Ben looked hastily at his food before she could see from his expression that she'd hit pay-dirt with her guess.

"You're not going to tell them?" Prima asked. *"That's cruel."*

He pointed to his full mouth and shrugged as he chewed.

"Coward."

Resigned, he simply nodded.

"You know, one of the worst things about humans is that you decide to accept a bad trait, and then it's impossible to talk you out of it because there's no leverage."

Ben snorted softly.

"What are *you* doing after this?" Jamie asked him.

"Uh..." He sighed. "Finding a job, finding an apartment, and moving everything."

"You don't have a job?"

"I was between things when I had the climbing accident. Now, I need to decide what to do." He sighed. "I hate this part—all the paper-work and all the little details. Getting all the boxes out of storage, getting the moving van, settling into the apartment...realizing you don't have any toilet paper..."

"And, uh...no girlfriend or anything?"

Much to his embarrassment, Ben blushed.

"You *do!*" Jamie said. "Wait, how do you have one and you don't have an apartment?"

"It's, uh..." He cleared his throat and tried to stop blushing, which only backfired. "She was one of the doctors who took care of me after the accident. We've seen each other a couple of times since then and she's staying at that hospital now that her internship is over."

"Awwww," the twins said in unison.

"Yeah, yeah." Ben took a bite of hotdog, but he was smiling. "It'll be good to see her again. Except I don't have all my coordination back in the real world yet, so I wind up doing things like throwing food at my face instead of putting it in my mouth."

"So, no soup," Taigan said.

"Definitely no soup," he agreed. "And what about you two? Are you in college already, or…"

"Nope." She sighed. "Well, Jamie might be applying. I might have missed the window."

"Or your older sister might have written you an application essay," her brother said. "Just possibly."

"Or that. Isn't that, I don't know…" She swayed uncomfortably. "Lying? What's the word—"

"Unethical," Ben supplied.

"That's the one."

"It honestly sounded like you," Jamie said as if that solved everything. "I helped. Using all the stuff you'd said about what you wanted in a college, we chose some and sent your scores and everything. Mom and Dad were already filling out the paperwork for the financial aid stuff, so it made sense."

"*They* were in on it?"

"Well, no." He cleared his throat. "We told them you'd already gotten your application stuff done in case something like this happened, right, so…" He shrugged when she looked at him. "I don't know! I didn't think you'd want to miss a year of college."

"No, it was sweet, I appreciate it." Taigan came to sit with him. "So, where'd I apply?"

"Michigan State, Berkeley…" He waved his hands. "A few."

She smiled and shrugged at Ben. "So I guess maybe I'm conning my way into college with my brother. To answer your question, you know."

"Uh-huh." He smiled. "You two want to go to college together, then? Not sick of each other yet?"

"Nope," both said at once.

"I think maybe it's different because we're not identical," Taigan said after she'd thought about it. "We didn't get compared to each other more than we got compared to Emmy or anything, and it wasn't like we competed for guys or girls or anything."

Ben nodded.

"Do you have any siblings?" Jamie asked him.

"An older sister." He shrugged. "She has a nice, stable, suburban life. Minivan. Two kids. White picket fence. You know, my nightmare. She's nice, though. We don't talk much but we get along when we see each other. She never gets on my case about settling down."

Long sticks appeared for the marshmallow roasting and the group wiped their hands before they started dessert. Steaming mugs of tea appeared before long, and stories were traded of awful road trips, summer camp embarrassments, and best and worst teachers.

Eventually, the twins fell asleep, curled under blankets that had appeared out of thin air. Ben smiled at them as he drank his tea.

"You don't seem worried about leaving," Prima said.

"I'm not too worried." He kept his voice low. "I've never done the whole working in an office and having to choose an apartment thing. I'm merely not as scared anymore. I think maybe the reason I never wanted to settle down was that I always knew there was a fight coming down the line. Sooner or later, I'd get angry at someone, we'd yell at each other..."

She made no response.

"Now I know you can pick up and keep going after that," he said quietly. "I wish I'd learned that sooner."

"If you had, would you have met Eliza?"

"Good point." He smiled. "What about you? What will you be doing?"

"Watching out for the berserker twins over there."

Ben grinned. "And you're...I don't know how to say this. You're happy?"

"Yes. I get to learn about people. You're fascinating, all of you. Very strange, of course, but fascinating. I'm glad...that you're leaving."

"Uh..."

"Oh. Sorry. I mean, I'm glad that you're leaving because you're better, not because you're dying. One of the last people I worked with, she died. She knew she had cancer, so she decided to come to help the game by being a tester. I miss her."

"I'm sorry," he said, oddly touched. "I...how does it feel to not have her around anymore?"

"It hurts," Prima said honestly. "I think. I'm not sure what 'hurts' feels like. But I don't like it. I wish she were still here and she isn't, and instead of simply knowing that, I keep thinking it would be nice if she were here. It doesn't make any sense. She can't be here, she's dead. But I keep thinking about it."

"That's how it goes," he agreed quietly. "It's part of being...alive, I guess. The thoughts start getting further apart over time."

"I don't want to forget her."

"You won't," he assured her. "And I'll make sure to come back so you can't forget me either."

"Good," Prima said. "I wouldn't want you to get a big head out there on your own."

CHAPTER EIGHTY-SEVEN

"They honestly told you to do this?" Ben asked Jacob. He lined his shot up and whacked the tiny green golf ball across the floor.

"They didn't tell us *not* to do it," the man said after a pause.

Another interminable barrage of tests had awaited him, after which he had been told he had one more to complete—only to find out that the team had set up a massive miniature golf course in the lab. Completing the theme of a day at the carnival, there was also funnel cake and a game along one wall with beanbags to throw.

He watched his ball roll down the slope, pick up too much speed, and miss the hole.

"Better luck next time." Jacob clapped him on the shoulder.

"I've always sucked at golf." He tapped his chin. "So maybe that means everything is back to normal."

"I'd believe you if you hadn't accidentally thrown a golf club at Nick."

"I also did that once before the accident." He grinned. "I was *astonishingly* drunk at the time, of course."

"Somehow, I don't think we'll get clearance from the physicians to pump you full of alcohol on top of all the other drugs in your system right now." The engineer putted carefully and made a face when his ball missed the hole by a fraction of an inch.

The next shot went in perfectly, and the two men looked up to see Anna Price watching them. She smiled and hefted a golf club. "I hope I can join in."

"Of course." Jacob nodded. He darted Ben a wide-eyed look. It seemed he had not anticipated that the CEO would come downstairs while no one was working.

"So," Price said to Ben as she waited for his next shot. "I hear you're planning to head to Colorado."

"Yes," he said. "I did a video interview this morning for a job. I'm not sure when I'll hear about it."

"Soon, I think, given that they called me for a reference right after your interview." She smiled at him.

"You...gave me a reference?" He hadn't expected that, especially since this job was probably the complete opposite of those she had found for him. They had been with the military and subcontractors and this was with a small non-profit that had an environmental focus.

"Yes." Price made another impeccable shot. "Having seen you under a great deal of stress, I can speak well to your ability to over-come obstacles, problem-solve, and do all the...hmm, *boring* parts of recovery work."

Ben swallowed. She still frightened him in many ways, but her kindness was evident. "I appreciate that," he said.

He had decided not to ask how she knew where he had applied or how she had been included as a reference.

"Of course." She finished the course and looked to where the two men were no closer to a resolution.

"You move on," Jacob said. "If you wait for us, you'll be here all day." When she had headed off to the next hole with a laugh and a goodbye handshake for Ben, he said in an undertone, "She truly does look out for her people."

"She does," he agreed. "Okay, I'll get it this time. It's what? Four inches?" He lined his shot up, only to whack the ball far harder than he had meant to. "Godammit. How am I supposed to move into an apartment if I can't even hit a golf ball reliably?"

"This is why there are professional movers," Amber pointed out.

"I have no job and no money."

"Hmm. Sleep on the floor?" She shook her head. "Don't worry, I'm sure we can get something into the budget for—"

"You've done enough," Ben said firmly. "I'm not bankrupted by medical bills and I can walk again. If I use pizza and beer, I should be able to get Mike and Natasha to help. Of course, he eats enough pizza that maybe it's cheaper to have the movers."

She laughed, watched as Jacob got his shot in, and did a victory dance.

"Fine, fine," he said grumpily. "Everyone can move on. I'll continue to struggle over here."

"Now seems like a good time for a funnel cake break," Amber told him. "Remember, your muscles tire far more quickly in the real world."

He realized his arms were, in fact, shaking. It took effort but he managed to get to the cake station and sit by himself, even if he did wind up in a different chair than the one he had aimed for. He gave up on dignity enough to lower his face to the plate of funnel cake like it was a pie-eating contest.

It was unquestionably good Eliza wasn't there for this.

Even thinking about her made his heart race slightly, and when he looked up, it was to see Nick smiling at him. The other man handed him a napkin and he nodded a thank you, trying to think of something to say that wasn't garbled nonsense about Eliza.

"Taigan and Jamie are doing well," he said finally. "Whatever you were worried about, I think they're okay."

"Good," the man said. He seemed a little thrown by the choice of topic. "That's—well, it's good. We're starting to see some changes in brainwaves, so…hopefully she'll move closer to waking up."

"Prima has her looking for a key," he told him.

Nick choked on his funnel cake, looked around, and shook his head quickly. "Don't discuss that," he said in a low voice. "Price knows, and the three of us, and DuBois…and a few of the people who have been in the world. But we don't talk about it."

"Oh," Ben said, feeling a little lost. "Er, sorry." No one seemed to pay attention to them, however, so he added: "Knows about *what*, exactly?"

"That she's…you know." The man gestured to his head to indicate thinking.

"Oh. *Oh*. Price knows?"

"She knows everything," Nick said in dire tones. "Everything. About everyone. I think she may somehow hook into surveillance grids like a robot." A long pause followed. "Maybe *she's* Prima."

"Well, *that's* terrifying."

"Let's never speak of this again."

"Never."

"I heard that," Amber said. She sat on the couch nearby and raised an eyebrow, her fork and funnel cake at the ready. "And I've wondered the same. It would explain how she never seems to get tired."

"That could also be cocaine," Nick pointed out.

"Now, *there's* a mental image." She grinned.

"Prima, meanwhile, is probably *very* annoyed at being compared to a human," Ben said. He wiggled his eyebrows at one of the pods and stuck his tongue out. "Better or worse than being compared to a demon, Prima?"

The printer behind him whirred to life and made him jump, and all three of them craned to look as a single page printed out.

Asshole

The next morning dawned crisp and fair with sunlight that woke Ben gently. He yawned and stretched—or, more accurately, yawned and flailed his arms wildly. There were some things, he realized now, that the game had never quite managed to capture and one of them was the way muscles felt when you first woke up in the morning.

Or the crisp feel of sheets.

On the other hand, in the game world, you never woke up needing to pee.

He had a leisurely morning ahead of him. Ever mindful of the details, the PIVOT team had arranged a flight that allowed for delays at every step, from taking eight attempts to turn the shower on to shuffling through the airport at the pace of a diseased sloth.

A short while later, he munched on his breakfast—there was a buffet downstairs, but he was still more comfortable eating alone where no one could see him—and checked his phone to see that time zones notwithstanding, Eliza had been awake before he was.

He responded to her text, a continuation of their days-long debate about whether Darth Maul or The Mountain would win in a fight, and saw her symbol switch to a green dot. She was online.

Break? He typed out.

Yep. Getting ready for the airport?

He brought a video call up while he tried to peel his banana. It did not go well, and he resorted to hacking the end of it open with his butter knife. When he looked up, Eliza was watching with interest.

"You know, I think your fine motor control is getting better," she said.

"That's what you took from what you saw?"

"Yes." She smiled in a way that told him she saw the humor but wasn't willing to resort to insults when he was also making progress.

"You're a nice person," he said. "What's that like?"

"It's good." She smiled and took out her ponytail to pull her hair back again. "Did you hear from the person with the apartment?"

"Yeah, yesterday—they said I can come to look at it tonight or tomorrow." He sighed. "We're both...trying not to be too into this and scare the other person off, right? I'm not making that up?"

Eliza burst out laughing. "No, I'd say you're very much right. I'm sitting here thinking, 'should I ask him if he wants to sleep on my couch? Is that too much?'"

"Sleeping on your *couch* isn't too much," he said and chuckled. "Am I not supposed to suggest alternate sleeping arrangements?"

Her face went bright red. "That felt very presumptive."

"You're terrible at flirting," he told her sincerely, "and it is one of the cutest things ever."

She buried her face in her hands. "Um. So. Tell me about the game. What did you do while you were there this time?"

"I turned a woman into a tree," he said. "Well, not *me*. I was merely there. I did hit her with a bucket, though."

"Is this you trying to advertise yourself as boyfriend material?"

"Oh, good point. Okay, in my defense, she was turning people into wolves by hammering spiked rings into their skin."

"What the hell kind of psychopath came up with this game?" Eliza demanded.

"It's...a long story. Group effort. My point is, the people are freed, the woman doing it is now a lovely tree that is doing much more good as a tree than she did as a person, and—oh, I met this pair of twins who are in there because the girl is in a coma. They are good kids, but I now feel so old. Do you ever hang out with seventeen-year-olds and get exhausted simply watching them?"

She snorted. "Not all that often. Everyone I work with is old and tired to start with. Living the hospital dream." She gave an exaggerated thumbs-up. "But I do know what you mean. Sometimes, I go snowboarding in the winter and...oof. I do a few runs and I want to go get hot cocoa in the lodge." She held a paper cup up. "Speaking of hot cocoa..."

"Good call." Ben looked at his coffee. "Okay, I'll try to drink this so don't laugh at me."

"Never," Eliza assured him. "Okay...sometimes. But only when you start laughing first."

"I'll accept that." He picked the cup up and lifted it carefully to his mouth. Surprisingly, he managed to get a few sips in without spilling too much down his shirt and he concentrated equally as hard while he put it down again. "Not bad, not bad. It's frustrating after being so much more competent in the game."

"You'll get there," she said. "Honestly, the fact that they could let you go to a hotel for a night on your own is incredible. By now, normally, you'd still be trying to learn how to walk." She looked at her watch. "Damn, break is over. I'll see you at the airport?"

Ben's heart gave a sideways leap. He didn't try to hide his smile. "Yeah. Yeah, I'll look forward to seeing you there."

Eliza blew a kiss and waved before she shut off the video call, and he sighed happily.

For the first time in a long time, he looked forward to going somewhere new—not because he was running from something but because he was excited about what the future held.

CHAPTER EIGHTY-EIGHT

When Ben walked through the door of his apartment, it was with a sigh of relief. He pulled his tie loose and kicked his shoes off at the door, then trudged up the half-flight of stairs to put the mail on the table. He could see the bills in the stack and he didn't want to deal with that right now.

It had already been an annoying enough day.

He downed a glass of water at the sink and wandered into the bedroom to change. Seeing Eliza's book on the bedside table made him sigh. They'd had a fight before she went to work yesterday.

His mind distracted by the memory, he hung his work pants up and got into sweats. He had a whole round of physical therapy exercises to do and he was not in the mood for it. Today was one of those days when... He sat on the bed with a thump and frowned.

Today was one of those days that would have made him want to run away as he had before the accident. An argument with a coworker, dropping the ball on an important project, a fight with his girlfriend, and bills in the mail. He could feel his fingers itching to throw all his clothes in a bag and start driving—anywhere.

The thing was, it was a reflex. He didn't honestly want it.

Not that he particularly *wanted* to apologize, of course. He flopped onto his back with another sigh. The fight with Eliza had been one of those he hated—an escalation from tired, petty sniping at each other until neither of them could remember what it was about.

That hadn't stopped them from dragging every problem with each other onto the table, of course.

He rubbed his face, something he managed to do on the first attempt. His coordination was improving when he didn't watch his body, although he wasn't where he had been before his injuries. It would be years, he was sure.

And there was nothing for it but to do what he *knew* was right. He sat with a sigh and dialed.

Eliza answered after a few rings. "Hi." She sounded cautious.

"I didn't wake you, did I?"

"Nope." A clatter in the background sounded like dishes.

"Did you already make dinner?"

"No, I was…just starting."

"What if I brought something over?" Ben suggested. "Maybe some Chinese? I could bring your book."

He could tell she was smiling on the other end. "I'd like that. I, uh… look, I said some things yesterday that weren't fair to you."

"Yeah," he said frankly. "And I did the same. Look, let's not do this over the phone. I'll be there in forty-five, okay?"

"Will you stay over?"

"I'd like to." He looked out the window. "I may have to. It looks like the snow is starting."

"A cozy night in. That sounds nice." She cleared her throat. "We don't *have* to make a thing of that fight, you know. We can simply call it even."

"I'd do that," he said, "except that's what my instinct is telling me to do, and my instinct in relationships is usually wrong."

She laughed. "Oh, man. You're something else, you know that? I mean that in a good way. I'll see you soon."

Ben took a few minutes to open the bills and send off some quick payments before he left, then put together a bag to take to Eliza's. He looked at the apartment and tried to remember if he'd forgotten anything.

Plants. He filled a mug and watered the pothos and the spider plant.

That done, he headed out to his beater car, a used Toyota that had been sold to him by a college student moving up in the world. It smelled, despite his best efforts, like various illegal substances. He rationalized that by saying it helped him drive more carefully so he wouldn't get stopped by the police.

Once he'd grabbed Chinese food, he headed to Eliza's apartment, one in a new development. She shared it with one of the nurses from the hospital.

He was pulling up when he realized he'd forgotten the book. The snow was getting too heavy for him to go back, though, so he trudged to the door and let himself in. With a bark, the roommate's dog bounded over.

"Yes, hello," Ben told him. "I love you, too. No, you don't get any Chinese food."

"Not for dogs," Eliza confirmed. She came to scratch the dog's head and stood on tiptoe to kiss Ben. "Hello."

"Hello." He held her close and rested his chin on the top of her head. "I forgot your book."

"The day either one of us gets out the door with everything we're supposed to have will be the day hell freezes over," she said. "So at least I know you haven't been replaced by a pod person."

Ben kissed her again and walked to the table. "It's seriously coming down out there."

"And I'm on call tonight." She groaned. "So's Kira, though, so at least I'll have someone to go with if we get called in."

"What?" Kira called from the other room.

"The snow's getting heavy," she told her. "Get ready for a night of crashes."

"Ugh. Okay, I'm going to bed now, then." Kira poked her head in and waved to Ben before she withdrew to her bedroom.

"So." Eliza set out forks and plates. "How was your day?"

"Shit," Ben said without preamble. "I'll need to work this weekend to redo stuff on the ERA Report, which...bleh. The printer broke, coffee maker broke—comedy of errors, honestly." He shrugged and ladled chicken onto his plate. "And I still have to do my PT. You? How was your day?"

"Not so bad as that." She shrugged. "Winter's the busy season, so on a good day, we get a steady stream of people with sprains or whatever, nothing too bad but enough to make the time pass quickly. That was today. No one yelled, which was nice." She served herself some food and looked at him. "I'm sorry, you know. About the things I said."

"Me, too." Ben put his fork down.

"You look completely terrified."

"I don't know how to do this part."

"Would you...like help?" She looked bemused.

"Sure, gimme anything you got."

"A good apology," Eliza said, "takes responsibility, doesn't make excuses, and includes an explanation of how you'll do better in the future. Like this." She cleared her throat. "I'm sorry I said you were slipping on your PT. It's genuinely difficult to balance health with work, I know that. You're making tremendous progress. I...won't do that anymore. Okay, the ending wasn't great, but you see where I was going."

"Oh." He considered what she'd said. "Takes responsibility, doesn't make excuses... Okay. I'm sorry I said you should help more with the chores. The truth is, I never liked laundry even before my brain got all fucked up, and I *can* do it on my own...and I probably should, because folding is good fine motor practice. You shouldn't do my laundry because I hate doing chores. Or...at all. Everyone hates doing chores."

Eliza smiled and nodded.

"Wait, so that's it?" Ben stared at her. "You're telling me what I've avoided for all these years is *that* conversation? Now I feel like an idiot."

"Eh, no one's good at it." She shrugged. "Besides, all that put you in my ER, so it worked out well for me. Not that I'm saying I'm *glad* you were injured." She took a mouthful of chicken and said around it, "I'll start eating so I don't say anything else stupid."

He snorted with laughter. "Me, too."

"This is good."

"Yeah, they'd just made more before I showed up." One of the problems of living in a small resort town was that most of the restaurants were way out of any reasonable price range. There were only a few restaurants they could afford regularly, so they rotated between Chinese, empanadas, and pizza. "Ugh, I do *not* want to do my PT tonight."

"You could do *my* laundry," she suggested. "No? Too soon for that joke? Okay. Well, let's put on a movie to distract you, then."

"*Fifth Element?*"

"You watch that movie *so* often."

"Because it's a perfect movie," he said around a mouthful of food.

"You know that if I start liking it, it'll be some weird Stockholm syndrome." She rolled her eyes. "But sure, I'll give it a thirty-fifth shot."

"I heard from the PIVOT team yesterday," he said while they cleaned up.

"Oh? How are things there?"

"They want to come run some tests and see how I'm improving after being out for a while." Ben smiled. "I pointed out that it was much easier for me to go back than for them to send several people and equipment, and they all made a ton of excuses. I'm very sure they want to come skiing."

"You tell them not to get injured too badly," Eliza said absent-mindedly.

"See, most people don't think about that when they think of skiing."

"They should."

"Yes, dear." He grinned. Doctors, he had learned, had very strong opinions about certain hobbies that they considered too dangerous to be allowed. He had learned, for instance, never to suggest zip-lining or anything to do with trampolines.

Later, as they watched the tail end of the movie in sleepy content-ment, he hugged her close.

"Are you okay?" She looked quizzically at him.

"Terrified," he said quietly.

"What? Why?" She twisted in his arms for a better look at him.

"This is all new." His hand found hers. "And it feels so good—sticking things out at the job, getting to see long-term projects pay off, working in my field again, making friends here, everything with you. I've simply…all this is new. I never know what's coming. It was almost easier to expect everything to blow up because then the future wasn't a mystery. This…feels like being at the top of the roller coaster all the time." He thought for a moment. "Most of the time. Right now, it feels like that and it also feels cozy. That's weird."

"Mm-hmm." She smiled. "I feel the same. Sometimes, I think about how weird it is—how we met, knowing I wanted to know more about you even though I didn't know you well at all. But you can tell a lot about a person from how they are when they're sick."

"So your type is 'giant pain in the ass?'"

She kissed him. "I prefer 'insanely stubborn.'"

Ben smiled and held her close. "And I like sushi-addicted painters."

"*Bad* painters," Eliza corrected him. "Don't forget how abysmally bad I am at painting."

"I prefer 'surrealist,'" he said, with a grin. "Sleep?"

"Sleep." She stood and hauled him up, her tiny frame surprisingly strong. "Another day tomorrow."

"That's the beauty of it," he said.

To his surprise, he meant every word

CREATOR NOTES - MICHAEL ANDERLE

SEPTEMBER 1, 2020

We're nearing the end of this phase of my effort the tell stories of what we might do in the future with technology as I see it now.

This has been an interesting and educational process for me, trying to reimagine parts of our health care systems.

I understand that so often profit takes the driving seat over benefits to humanity. I am not knocking the reality, I just want to understand it enough to leverage the knowledge.

Perhaps someone reading these stories will have the resources to make this a reality. Point them to where the business can be disrupted, and who knows?

We might get our own version of P.I.V.O.T. Labs.

There are plenty of threads for us to take the stories and continue. However, I have to put out a few fires myself before I get to play again in this world. Who knows, maybe these stories will become sleeper hits and explode humanities consciousness into a whole new realm.

OR (and I find this potentially more likely) someone realizes just how much money IS available to acquire if they fix the ICU area of hospitalization. Let's disrupt the present to build a better future and perhaps I'll get to play in the game myself.

Hopefully as just a consumer, no medical reasons necessary.

Ad Aeternitatem,

Michael Anderle

If you enjoyed this book, you may also enjoy Steel Dragon, from Michael Anderle and Kevin McLaughlin. The book is available now from Amazon and through Kindle Unlimited.

Dragons rule the world. Their claws are into every aspect of human life, from government to industry. But Kristen Hall is about to throw a wrench into all of that.

Because she's a dragon, too. She just doesn't know it...yet!

A dragon raised by humans, in the human world.

After graduating from the police academy, she's dropped right into the ranks of Detroit's elite SWAT team. A rookie, in SWAT? Unheard of. But what the dragons want, they get.

The reasons behind their machinations become clear as her dragon powers begin to surface.

Will Kristen rise to the challenges her new life delivers? What designs do the dragons have for her future? And perhaps most pressing of all — how did she come to be a dragon with human parents?

Get your copy today!

BOOKS BY MICHAEL ANDERLE

For a complete list of books by Michael Anderle, please visit

www.lmbpn.com/ma-books/

CONNECT WITH THE AUTHOR

Connect with Michael Anderle

Website: http://lmbpn.com

Email List: http://lmbpn.com/email/

Social Media:

https://www.facebook.com/LMBPNPublishing

https://twitter.com/lmbpn

https://www.instagram.com/lmbpn_publishing/

https://www.bookbub.com/authors/michael-anderle